FORTUNA AT THE RUDDER,
OR
THE CURIOUS ADVENTURES OF
GAIUS OBSEQUENS DOLO
TRIBUNE ON THE RHINE

BY

ERIK HILDINGER

To my wife, Elizabeth, for her unstinting support on this book
and for so many other things.

Published by Catchall Books
2024

ISBN: 979-8990695900

CONTENTS

A BRIEF NOTE TO THE READER

* * *

Gaius Obsequens Dolo's story begins when the Western Roman Empire was old, though it still had about a hundred years left to go. It was not the Empire of Augustus or Trajan; it had changed greatly, and these changes are reflected in Gaius's story—they are the armature on which it is built. Corruption, always endemic in the army, had spread and become institutionalized in the Empire as the result of rule by soldier-emperors, and the government bureaucracy had grown in size by an order of magnitude. To a reader unaware of these developments, this Late Antique world might seem unfamiliar.

Latin Words and Names

Latin plurals of the third declension look odd to the English reader, so they've been pluralized as though they were English. Thus, *mansio* has been pluralized to *mansios* instead of the correct *mansiones*, and *optio* appears in the plural as *optios*, not *optiones*. My apologies to readers who know Latin—these plurals will look illiterate to them. Plurals from other declensions have been generally kept in their Latin forms when they would be familiar to the average reader.

Roman names generally appear in their Latin forms unless they are better known in their English versions, thus *Gratian* and *Valentinian*, not *Gratianus* and *Valentinianus*. The Alamanni (or Alemanni) were a German tribe whose name, in Gaius's story, is given as the Alamans.

Money

By the time of this story, coins such as the *denarius* and *sestertius* had been replaced by other coins, such as (in order of increasing value) the *nummus*, *follis* and *solidus*.

The Late Roman Army

Readers interested in the late Roman army, which differed sharply from that of earlier days, should look at the afterword, though it's not necessary to read it in order to understand Gaius's story.

1

ROME, 382 AD: GAIUS OBSEQUENS DOLO LOOKS FORWARD TO A PLEASANT FUTURE

* * *

Gaius Obsequens Dolo ducked through the entrance to the tavern, mulling over all of the wonderful possibilities that had opened to him since his father had died. His death back in Narbo had been unexpected and, of course, unfortunate, but it had to be admitted that Gaius's horizons had been marvelously broadened upon his receipt of the news in Rome.

He was a young man in no way particularly striking: of average height, brown-haired, grey-eyed and with regular features. His waved at his companion to follow him, another young man, but darker, taller, somewhat leaner and more simply dressed. He did not have three names; he was a slave. The tavern regulars sat in a torpor in dark corners and no longer remarked that Gaius let his slave eat at the table with him—they'd seen it often enough. Gaius and his slave took a table by the window because they preferred the heat and dust wafting in from the street to the fug of the tavern's interior. The small round table had been diligently carved with misspelled names and inventive ungrammatical obscenities, artfully set off by brown rings from the bottoms of innumerable damp wine jugs. Gaius snapped his fingers with a confident supe-riority and called out, "Two plates of lentils, each with a sausage. And bread and wine!" Then he leaned back against the table and gazed out across the street at the huge walls and varied structures of Trajan's Market, which marched along the street on either side for fifty yards and spilled down the face of the Quirinal Hill to the complex of Imperial forums below. He nodded admiringly. "Do you know what's in there, Faustinus?"

"Actually, yes," the slave replied with the patience born of answering those who don't listen. He rested his elbows on the table and waited again for Gaius's explanation. The landlord dropped off a jug of wine and two cups—a brief and welcome distraction. Faustinus poured, sat back, and answered the question in a vain hope to close the topic. "Functionaries, Master Gaius. Functionaries are in there."

"The building is filled of functionaries, Faustinus." Gaius absently took a sip of wine and pointed unnecessarily across the street. "A few merchants, yes, but it's mostly bureaucrats! The great motor of the empire! That's what they are. They sit in there with their tablets and clicking abacuses noting down transactions, recording figures, writing memoranda, and considering petitions. They even act on some of them now and again. You know, helping relatives and clients, that sort of thing. Of course, they have clerks to do the menial work."

Faustinus rested his head on his hand and glanced out the window. "Transcription. The actual calculations, I suppose. Showing unwanted petitioners the door. That would be most of the petitioners, I imagine."

"Exactly. That's if they're let into the building to begin with. Keep the petitioners at a safe distance, and the functionaries can concen-trate on the more important aspects of their administration."

"Taking cuts from transactions. Accepting *beneficia*.[1] Or is the term *sportula*?[2]"

"The exact term's unimportant—it's the practice that counts."

---

[1] Bribes.

[2] "Bait," thus a bribe. The reader probably suspects a certain pervasive practice.

Gaius shook his head admiringly. "What a life!"

"I'm sure the sportulae help."

Gaius turned back to the table. "Indeed they do. They're what make the world go round! And there's nothing wrong them if they're not too large. Quite the opposite, in fact. It's the law."

"*Moderatio in omnia*," Faustinus said.

"Quite right. One twenty-fourth, I think, is usual on most transactions."

"On top of the tip for access in the first place."

"You can see why their life is so attractive. Status, respect, money, no risks run."

"Unless you reach the top. You encounter real dangers at the top of the ladder."

"Well, yes, of course. At the top of the ladder." Gaius was looking for the landlord to see when the food might come.

"The Emperor Valens, for example," Faustinus paused for emphasis. He enjoyed discomfiting his master when he could get away with it. "A master of the world, and yet quite dead now."

"He made the mistake of leading his troops himself." Gaius spotted the landlord and waved at to hurry him up. "It was an elementary error."

"But he wasn't the only one to die. They say the whole eastern Field Army went down with him at Adrianople."

"But that's the trick." Gaius drummed the table top absently with his fingers. He shifted his position. "First, stay out of the military. And second, just get comfortable—toward the middle of the bureaucracy—and stay there." He noticed his cup was empty and slid it over to Faustinus. "You see," he continued, "We've got the Emperor Gratian up in Milan where he's no trouble to anyone here in Rome…"

"Except perhaps to the Great Men," Faustinus said. He was thinking of the aristocrats like the Petronii, the Syagrii and so on, men with fabulous fortunes made by three hundred years of careful wealthy marriages and commercial opportunities open to those in the stratosphere of politics. It was a wonder they didn't quite own the whole Empire.

"I'm not so sure even about them—the Great Men seem to persist no matter what happens to the emperors." Gaius reflected on this a moment. "And then there's Theodosius sitting on his throne in Constantinople, too far away to matter at all.[3]" He gave a little flick of his hand and took a sip of wine. "And besides, he's busy chasing those Goths that killed Valens. They're still romping through the Balkans, I hear."

"The Goths…" Faustinus said ruminatively. Although six years had passed since the battle—and it had been far to the east—the thought of it made him uneasy. What did it mean that such a terrible thing could happen to a man as great as an emperor? He looked up to see Gaius shrug carelessly.

"The odds are he'll just settle the Goths on abandoned land somewhere and enroll them in the army."

"You don't ever feel as though things are, well, creaking, Master?" Faustinus enjoyed troubling Gaius from time to time with vague questions that suggested somber answers. On the other hand, the creaking of the Roman World as it settled into the mud—that's how Faustinus saw things—disturbed him too. More than it did his master. He thought about things more.

"Creaking? What things?" Gaius asked, blithe at first. Then the import of what Faustinus had just said struck him and he misinterpreted it. His looked up apprehensively at the grimy beams of the low ceiling.

"No, Master. Not the building."

"Oh, I see! You're speaking in the abstract." He smiled. "No, I'm not worried at all." He warmed to the prospect of contradicting Faustinus. "Quite the contrary, in fact. You see, our glorious, eternal Empire creaks along comfortably, the skids greased by overtaxation, compulsory labor, serfdom, military bravado and administrative corruption. The world has come a long way—the rough-and-tumble world of the Greeks, for all its art and philosophy, couldn't hope to offer what the Empire offers to men of limited talent and middling ambition."

Faustinus looked at him sardonically. "In view of your explanation, I see why you aren't uneasy."

---

[3] Theodosius was emperor of the Eastern half of the Roman Empire, which had been officially divided by this time for ease of administration. Perhaps the next footnote will be more amusing.

Gaius looked at him, surprised. "Of course I'm not uneasy. Worry is for men who look too far into things. That's your problem, Faustinus." He put his cup down. "Look at it this way: the Alamans and Franks are lurking harmlessly across the Rhine, and that military commander from, where? Spain?" He paused to think. "Count Maximus, that's his name.[4] He's driven the Picts and Scots north of the Wall of Hadrian. There may even be garrisons there still. And since my father's unfortunate death I'm in rather a good position to enjoy a comfortable life entirely on my own terms and far away from any distasteful squabbles over the Imperial frontiers."

Faustinus asked, "And Master Arcadius? What about him?" He was thinking of Gaius's brother. He enjoyed watching his master's frown.

"Well, Arcadius, yes. Of course, I've considered him." His face clouded for a moment.

"I'm just musing, of course, but with your inheritance, you could certainly afford to free me." Faustinus judged that Gaius had drunk enough wine to take the suggestion with equanimity.

"Well, yes, I could." He tempted Faustinus with the phrase but then went on: "But let's not get ahead of ourselves." He leaned over the table. "Listen. If your father hadn't had to sell you as a baby to pay his taxes, you'd just be out in Gaul somewhere chopping up a field with a hoe and praying for sunset."

"That's what you say," Faustinus answered tartly. They had grown up together as boys, and those years gave him license to speak impudently from time to time.

"That's just what I do say." He lifted his hands in a question. "Who isn't a slave, when you come down to it?" Faustinus began to answer, but Gaius rolled over him. "Almost everyone. Actual slaves, of course, but the peasants too—they're tied to the land and sold with it. Common soldiers doing hitches of a quarter century. Everyone truckling to some sort of superior or patron. Why, until my father died, even I was a slave."

"You know, Master, that had entirely escaped me until now."

---

[4] The Latin title is *Comes*. "Count" sounds odd to modern ears when used in a Roman context, but there's not much to be done about it.

Faustinus gave him the look he was accustomed to do when Gaius uttered a fatuity and, as usual, Gaius failed to notice it.

"In a manner of speaking, of course. Father controlled all of our holdings and made the big decisions for Arcadius and me. Remember, he even decided I should marry Livilla."

"I suppose he thought it in your interest to, ah, narrow your horizons."

"Who knows what he was thinking? When it came to his plans, he kept me in the dark much of the time."

"Imagine that."

"So, only now am I free to act in accordance with my desires and judgment."

Faustinus blinked slowly at this, holding his tongue. Gaius went on: "What it comes down to is this: you don't appreciate your good luck." The corners of Faustinus's mouth went down slightly. Gaius went on with his usual innocent insensitivity: "We can't all be *honestiores* [5]. The world just doesn't work that way. So, instead of grumbling, consider your luck. You find yourself in Rome doing a little light work for, if I may say so myself, a very indulgent master." He indicated himself as though Faustinus didn't know whom he was talking about and then handed his cup over for another inch of wine.

Faustinus poured and changed the subject. "When do we go back to Narbo?[6]"

Gaius waggled his head a moment, a sort of yes-and-no gesture as though he didn't know his own mind. "We may go soon; we may not. Hard to say at this point. After all, my future's just opened up, and I need to consider it carefully. Father's plan to have me trained as an advocate for the law-courts back home never compared favorably to the life of a bureaucrat here in Rome." He shook his head as he thought about the contrast. "Consider the beauty of bureaucracy—its safety, security and unmatched scope for lucrative inactivity."

Faustinus said dryly, "It does seem the sort of life that lacks a

---

[5] The higher class of citizen. They had more rights under the law than *humiliores*, the lower class. And there were even further subtle subdivisions of Roman society.

[6] Now Narbonne in southern France. The passage of time has evidently nasalized the last syllable.

certain…" he paused to think. "A certain snap and dash."

Gaius went on, oblivious. "So, the choice is mine. With father gone, Arcadius and I will share the estates by halves. He's already at the new estate near Milan—Father sent him there last year. I can't think why: it's smaller and he doesn't know anyone in the area. Odd, really, when you think of it." Gaius shrugged. "But at least he never comes to Rome—that's some consolation. In any case, when the business is all settled I'm sure to get the old estate outside of Narbo." He looked down and swirled his wine, which turned in a claret ring at the bottom of his cup. "You know, I could sell the estate, take the cash and buy a middling position in the Imperial bureaucracy—move into a comfortable town house here in Rome—there's a nice one on the Oppian Hill I've had my eye on—and settle down to a pleasant life of short hours, routine, beneficia and trading favors. Holidays at the theater. Sitting in the peristyle with a plate of delicacies and listening to the mobs attacking each other over fine points of religious doctrine in the little forum at the foot of the hill. That sort of thing."

"I see you have it all planned out."

"Perhaps." He waved his hand airily. "On the other hand, I could to go back to Narbo and do as I please when I get there—forget the law courts and just plunge into the mediocre social whirl of the province. I'll marry Livilla and lobby her cousins in the government for an exemption from property taxes. That sort of thing. Big fish in a little pond, you see. Even easier than bureaucracy. Maybe it's best to be a provincial aristocrat. Ah, here are the plates."

They both ate in silence, Gaius looking out the window now and again with great longing at the Market. He nodded toward the government buildings, ready with some fatuous remark about the value of corruption, but his attention was drawn to the landlord, who stood in the broad open doorway ineffectually trying to shoo away a weedy, ragged boy of about sixteen who kept ducking and weaving about the heavy old man, squinting into the dim interior of the tavern. Seeing Gaius's face, the boy called out: "Noble Obsequens Dolo! A message!" Despite his obvious poverty and low station, he spoke confidently and held his ground against the landlord. The other denizens of the tavern turned to watch the little drama with the usual Mediterranean interest in other people's business.

"Let him in." Gaius waved at the tavern keeper, who turned aside but said, "He goes out after the message—he's too scruffy by half."

"Even for this place?" He waved the boy over. "What is it, Mus?"

The boy bowed, straightened like a soldier, and glanced about, confident even under a dozen gazes. "There's a messenger with a letter for you." He pointed in the direction of the Subura. "You weren't there, but I told him I could find you."

"Good fellow," Gaius said. Mus eyed the plate of food longingly. Gaius pushed it over to him. "Here—finish it." Mus sat down and began to eat ravenously.

"Who sent the letter?" Faustinus asked, always practical.

"A sailor." Mus looked up between mouthfuls. "He's got a funny walk—I bet he's had a broken leg at some time. But he's big in the arms. Strong. He talks a bit odd too. Do they all talk that way in The Province?[7] He says he's from there. Marseilles, I think."

"Never mind the sailor. Who sent the letter?" Faustinus asked.

The boy smiled at them both. "Begging your pardons—he only told me that it comes from a lady."

Gaius looked knowingly at Faustinus. "It's from Livilla. It must be."

Faustinus nodded. He pushed his half-empty plate over to Mus.

"She's probably getting a bit impatient with our long engagement," Gaius said.

"No doubt." Faustinus took a sip of wine and sat back. "And you?"

"Me? Well, not really. Of course, I have the advantage of a philosophical temperament—as you know—so the delay of a couple of years is as nothing."

"After all, you've been occupied in your rhetorical and legal studies."
"Indeed."

"And the theater, the taverns, the races, that house at the edge of the Subura run by Domitia Lupanaria—"

---

[7] Officially *Gallia Narbonensis*, commonly called *"Provincia,"* or The Province, by the Romans. Roughly modern Provence in the south of France. Of course there were many other provinces.

"We can leave aside the more tiresome details, Faustinus."

"But the details convey snap and dash."

"I'll tell you when snap and dash are called for." He watched Mus take a last bite and then stood up. "Landlord!" he called.

The man counted up the dinner on his fingers and said, "Twelve *nummi*.[8]" He put out his broad, greasy hand.

"Pay him," Gaius told Faustinus and followed Mus out the door. Faustinus counted out the coins and hurried up the street and found Mus walking proudly in front of Gaius, threading among the passers-by, officiously waving away strolling hawkers and leading the way down the street, whose narrow sidewalk was blocked here and there by vegetable sellers sitting on rush mats calling out the attractions of their sweltering produce.

"Livilla's not a bad sort, really," Gaius said as Faustinus caught up with him. He was thinking about the letter. "Not bad looking, all things considered, though her teeth are large. As I'm sure you've noticed."

"Is that so important, as long as she has them all?"

"Good point. Still—and I shouldn't remark on this—when she laughs they do give her a bit of a horsey cast."

"I don't recall seeing her laugh a great deal." Faustinus pushed an aggressive beggar away.

"She does laugh now and again. Usually at me. So, in a way it's a consolation to notice them. They remind me of a horse we have on the estate." He mused in satisfaction for a few moments. "A bay with a white blaze."

"But she has other qualities, of course. Quite apart from her dentition."

"Yes." Gaius said vaguely. He seemed to have lost interest in the subject.

"And they must spring right to mind, those qualities." Faustinus assumed a false, enthusiastic tone in order to provoke Gaius into thinking about her more than he quite evidently wished to.

"True. The most important, of course, is her dowry. It's a rather a good one. It helps you look past the teeth. And she's some very distant relation of the Syagrii, so I always reckoned there'd be some help

---

[8] A tiny late Roman coin that hardly anybody talks about. Have you ever heard of it?

there when I had to begin my law career. I looked with real distaste at being a provincial advocate, as you know, but I expected, with her help, to start near the top and then finish early." He clasped his hands behind his back as he walked. "But now, with the inheritance, I can just skip all of that."

"That will be some compensation, anyway."

Gaius turned to him. "An inheritance can never compensate for the loss of a father," he said priggishly.

"I meant for the large teeth. Especially if she passes them on to your children."

Gaius slowed, disconcerted by the image of buck-toothed children. Mus pointed ahead. "Noble Gaius Obsequens, there he is. By the *insula*.⁹" The street had narrowed appreciably and was lined on either side with four and five story apartment buildings, the ground floors crowded with little shops giving out onto the street. Thirty yards ahead a stocky tanned man in a broad hat leaned back patiently against the building, arms crossed and one foot back up against the wall. A satchel was slung across his chest and his hand rested on it to discourage passing thieves from expressing any interest in it.

Mus strode ahead importantly and called out: "Master Aurelius, I have brought Master Gaius Obsequens!" The man stepped away from the wall, gave a slight nod and assessed Gaius for a long moment without speaking.

"Well, Aurelius? I understand you have a letter for me." Gaius put his hands on his hips and put one foot forward in quite a noble attitude. The sailor was obviously quite unmoved. He regarded him silently for another moment and then glanced casually over his shoulder down the street, where the paving stopped and gave way to beaten earth.

"I've never been to this part of the Subura," he said. "Aren't most of the whores down that way?" He pointed north with his thumb.

"As my master tells everyone, this is only the very edge of the Subura." Faustinus glanced at Gaius. "It's quite a different thing, the edge."

"What? No whores?"

---

⁹*Insula* means "island," hence, in Latin, an apartment building—often of four or five stories.

"Around here they're courtesans," Gaius replied defensively.

"You see?" Faustinus said, slyly watching Gaius out of the corner of his eye. "It's quite different around here. Somehow." Gaius glared at him.

The sailor grunted. He reached into a purse on his belt and took out a nummus. "Here's for your trouble, boy." Mus ducked a little bow, and backed away, rubbing the coin on his tunic and admiring the sheen of it.

"The letter?" Gaius pressed.

"Gaius Obsequens Dolo?" The sailor drawled the full name; he was absolutely not to be hurried.

"Of course. Yes."

"And your father's name?"

"Marcius Obsequens Lutatianus."

The sailor nodded and turned to the slave. "And you?"

"Faustinus." The sailor nodded again, half satisfied. He looked back at Gaius.

"Show me your ring." He pointed to Gaius's left hand.

Exasperated, Gaius made a fist and displayed his signet ring under the sailor's nose. The sailor squinted at it closely, comparing it to some description in his memory and finally nodded.

"The letter!" Gaius put out his hand.

"I'll need a reply," the sailor said, making no effort to hand it over.

Gaius sighed theatrically.

"So he can be paid on his return, Master. And to prove receipt," Faustinus said. Aurelius nodded at Faustinus's explanation and then rummaged in his satchel and brought out a folded packet of vellum.

"All right, all right. Wait here." Gaius nodded to Faustinus to take the letter, and the sailor resumed his position against the wall. The two young men went to a doorway between two shops, climbed the steep switchback brick stairs to the third story, where Gaius stepped back on the landing to let Faustinus at the door. The slave took an iron key from his belt, turned the heavy lock, and followed him into the apartment, closing the door and shooting the bolt.

Gaius took the letter from Faustinus and made out Livilla Marciana's signet impressed on the seal: a tiny cupid holding a laurel wreath above his head, the letters L and M on either side. Faustinus was already sitting at a table preparing to take dictation. "Tablet? Or papyrus?" he asked.

"For Livilla, papyrus, I think. As my fiancée and all that, you know. We don't want to let the side down." He turned the folded packed over in his hands, dropped it unopened on the table, and opened the shutters of the window that led onto the balcony.

Faustinus lifted the lid of an ornate box, took out a small sheet of papyrus and began to sharpen a reed pen with a small knife. He looked up inquiringly until Gaius got the message and began to dictate: "From Gaius Obsequens Dolo F. M. Obsequentis Lutatiani to Livilla Marciana…" He scowled and snapped his fingers. "What on earth is her father's full name? He's got about six. Rather pretentious for a provincial, even of his standing. You'd think three or four would be enough for him." He stepped out onto the balcony, folded his arms and glanced about vaguely for something interesting to look at.

Faustinus called after him: "Titus Livianus Marcianinus Victorinus Rufianus." He used some of these to complete Livilla's name in the customary form. He pointed to the unopened letter with the pen. "Do you have any interest in reading her letter first? In the event that you'd like to address a few of Livilla's points."

"What?" Gaius turned back to him. He had been leaning over the balcony rail looking down at the waiting sailor below. Mus was chattering at him. He seemed excited about something.

"Not with that great lout waiting down there. It's really just a receipt, after all."

Faustinus shrugged, dipped the pen again, and suggested a start to the letter: "'I am well, I hope you are well. Greetings from Rome?'"

Gaius waved his hand airily. "Right. The usual. Thank her for the letter and then write something to the effect that I'm counting the days until we can be together again. Oh—and I look forward with great eagerness to a life of profound happiness for both of us. And so on and so on."

"How much 'so on and so on?' Three lines or four?"

Gaius turned back from the balcony rail. "What do you suppose they're talking about down there?"

Faustinus ignored the question. "How much 'so on and so on?'" he repeated. "Will three lines do?"

"Three should be enough. Just make it clear that her letter brightened my day as only the sun itself might do. Can you do that in three?" He walked over and glanced down at the sheet.

"I think so," Faustinus said, then added puckishly, "How about following 'the sun' with 'a train of myriad flashing stars?'" Faustinus looked down at the page so that Gaius couldn't see his expression. "It would show that you've been paying attention to Enthymemus. Or," and here he looked up at Gaius, "that someone has, anyway."

"Oh, all right. But that's the limit. And no flowery valediction." When Faustinus had finished and folded the letter into a packet, Gaius sealed it with his ring and told him to take the letter down to the sailor. Faustinus took it up but made no move to leave the room.

"How much do you want to pay for delivering the reply?"

"Livilla will pay him at the other end for receipt. If I pay him now, by the time he's finished he'll have been paid three times."

Faustinus shrugged indifferently.

"All right. Give him a *follis*[10]." He looked back into the apartment. "And who's knocking at the door?"

"The sailor's come for the reply." Faustinus opened the door to him and handed the man the letter and the follis, which he stared at closely, as though he suspected a counterfeit. Gaius found extremely insulting to one in his social position, but there it was—the man already had the coin, there was nothing to be done.

"One thing more," the sailor said.

"Yes?" Gaius let the man hear the irritation in his voice, but only mild irritation because, after all, he was a gentleman and subtlety counted.

"That boy, Mus."

"What about him?"

"Says he's an orphan."

"Well?"

"No family?"

---

[10] Another late Roman coin you've probably never heard of.

"That's why he's called an orphan," Gaius said tartly. He was still irritated that the sailor had examined the coin. The sailor, completely indifferent, nodded placidly.

Faustinus added some color to Gaius what had said. "The landlord lets Mus sleep under the roof tiles of the attic in return for sweeping out the stairs and doing the odd job."

The sailor grunted as he stood in the doorway, but he made no move to leave.

"What's your interest in him?" Gaius asked.

"The boy wants to go to sea, and we could use another hand. Do you recommend him?"

Gaius was taken by surprise. The sailor regarded him placidly. "The boy says you're his patron."

"His patron?"

"That's quite true," Faustinus interposed, enjoying the imposition on Gaius, who glanced at him in surprise. But then Gaius thought about it. Well, he had gotten the boy the odd job, and Mus had run his errands from time to time, and he saw that the boy never went a whole day without a meal.

"Well, yes, I am his patron." He couldn't make the claim seem very grand, though, given Mus's low status. Still the sailor had posed the question as though it were up to Gaius to decide whether Mus should go to sea, and he owed the man (and Mus) his answer. He hesitated a moment, thinking what a life at sea would mean for the boy. Well, whatever its dangers, it would be a better life than he had in Rome. If he wanted that life, then let him grasp it with both hands and let him do what he could with it. "Would I recommend Mus? I would, yes. If he wants to go."

The sailor nodded. "He does. And so you permit him to join us?"

"Yes, I do."

"We'll be coasting west toward The Province and Spain, but we mean to head to Britain." It suddenly came to Gaius that he would never see Mus again. He felt an odd pang when he thought of it, but he only said, "And may he have the very best of luck." It was Mus's life—let him live it as he would.

"Do you want him to dismiss him yourself? He's in the street." The sailor pointed down the staircase. Gaius shook his head, surprised at his own hesitation, at his reluctance to formally say goodbye. It pained him to think that he'd seen the last of the boy, but there was nothing, really, to be done about it. The sailor nodded and went down the staircase.

Faustinus closed the door after him and turned to Gaius. "I think the change will be good for him. He has no future sleeping under the tiles and running errands for pittances."

Gaius nodded and, on impulse, stepped out onto the balcony and waited until the sailor stepped out to join Mus on the street. The two of them spoke earnestly for a few moments, and the boy nodded vigorously. Gaius shouted down. "Mus! Look up here!"

"Yes, Master Dolo!" he called back up. His face beamed with excitement.

"So, you're off to be sailor?"

The boy nodded enthusiastically. "I'm off straightaway to The Province! And then Spain, and then…" He turned back to the sailor to hear something. "And then to Britain. I'll see the whole world!"

"And this is what you want?" The thought of going to Britain appalled Gaius.

"Oh, yes!"

"Wait a moment." He told Faustinus to give him a pair of coins, heavy silver ones, from the days when they were purer. He leaned over the rail. "Catch." He dropped them one at a time to the boy, who snatched them from the air and marveled at them: he'd never seen coins so large or fine. Gaius looked at the sailor. "You'll watch out for him?"

"He won't need watching—I can tell he's a quick one." He put on his wide hat and the two of them walked off.

"That's the last we'll see of him," Faustinus said. He had joined Gaius on the balcony. "Britain. It seems like the end of the world."

Gaius nodded. "It is."

"The letter?"

"What? Oh." He felt a sudden indifference to it. No doubt it was freighted with polite fixed formulas and puffed up with a vapid account of life in the estates outside of Narbo: tedious narratives of who attended whose tiresome dinner, second hand accounts of vacuous conversations involving people he didn't know, reports of the weather—perhaps the story of how some young aristocrat had managed to wangle his way out of local government, or the expenses of it, anyway. He picked up the letter, glanced at it incuriously and gave it to Faustinus. "Here. You read it to me." He lay down on a couch with his eyes closed. He heard the snap as Faustinus broke the seal.

"How long is it?" Gaius rested his forearm over his closed eyes.

"Not long."

"Good, but why the funny tone?"

"It's on palimpsest, Master. Not clean vellum."

"Odd. Perhaps she's taken a turn toward frugality." Would that be a good thing or bad? Hard to say. "Well, go ahead." He flapped a hand.

Faustinus glanced at him, hesitated, and began to read: " 'From Livilla Marciana F. T. Liviani Marcianini Victorini Rufiani to Gaius…' "

"Yes, yes." He lifted his hand in impatience. "Get past the boilerplate, and skip the weather, the results of the town elections, who's in charge of repairing the main street, that sort of thing."

Faustinus hesitated, then glanced down the single page, and read: "'You can imagine my distress at your situation, a distress greater even than your own distress, if that were possible as—"

"Wait a moment," Gaius interrupted, opening his eyes. He found the repetition of the word "distress," well, distressing. "What do you suppose she's getting at?"

"We could try finishing the letter."

"Yes, go ahead."

"'…a distress even greater than your own distress, if that were possible, as I had dreamed, no less often than you have done, of the day when our lives would form a graceful and happy conjunction to be envied by all who learned of it and emulated by all to whom fortune afforded a similar opportunity. But you, who have experience of the world, you whose tutor is Rome Herself, Great Mistress of the World, you who live where, daily, Fortuna with her Hand upon the

Rudder steers some to greatness and trips others as they fare along the highway of life, you have surely been granted the perspective to see that, faultless as you are, I can no longer accept the prospect of a marriage with you.'"

Gaius sat up and put out his hand for the letter. "Wait a moment! Let me see that!" He took the letter from Faustinus. "Tripping people with a rudder?" He scanned it quickly. "That's a mixed metaphor! And I think there's a fault in the syntax—after those three relative clauses the subject shouldn't be repeated."

"I think the larger point here is that she's jilting you, Master."

"Well, yes," Gaius conceded. "There is that. And her valediction is just as clumsy as the rest of the letter."

"Since she's jilting you, you can take comfort in not being subjected to more letters littered with—what's the term Enthememus used?—asyntaxis. That will be a relief, given your refined literary sensibilities."

"Don't try to cheer me. Her connection to the Syagrii would have been extremely helpful, and in my heart I'd already forgiven her those large teeth." He sighed, shrugged, and tossed the letter aside. "Well, there are other quite marriageable prospects back home."

"Of course. Many," Faustinus assented politely as he sought for unsuitable examples. "Might I suggest Clausia Secundina?"

Gaius, looked at him narrowly, suspecting his motive, but decided—wrongly—that there was a chance Faustinus might be in earnest. "Clausia Secundina? Quite beautiful really—everyone says so. Statuesque, you know. But, of course, disconcertingly imposing. Tall and a bit wide in the shoulders. One of her forebears was a commander of some sort in the army on the Rhine eighty years ago—they still talk about him. I can't think why anyone gets involved in the military when bureaucracy offers such opportunities. Anyway, you can see why I suspect there's a German back in the family somewhere—probably one of those Batavians who were always so thrilled to join the army. I'd lay odds she could swim the Rhine and swarm up the bank with a knife in her teeth."

"Any other views about Clausia's teeth? Aside from swimming with a knife them?"

"Oh, fine. Just fine. All part of her strapping health, really." He got up from the couch, drifted to the door leading onto the balcony, and looked out pensively. "One thing, though."

"Yes, master?" Faustinus did not smile at Gaius's discomfiture this time. He was thinking back to the letter.

"I mean, quite apart from her imposing figure, I don't know whether her family's got the connections to get me that property tax exemption." When he did not hear a reply, he looked back at Faustinus, who had taken up Livilla's letter and was scanning it with a frown. "Well, what is it?"

"Master, it's this: Livilla refers to your situation. What is your situation?"

II

THE IMPERIAL GOVERNMENT
TAKES AN INTEREST IN GAIUS

* * *

Gaius mused over Faustinus's question: what was his situation? It was a troubling question, though what bothered him more immediately was his fatuous response to Livilla's letter. "I wish I hadn't sent that asinine reply. I suppose it's too late to call it back. Do you have any idea how you'd find the fellow's ship? I can't recall his name."

"Aurelius." Faustinus helped out. He was amused to compare his competence with that of his master. "His name is Aurelius."

"Of course, I recall it now." Faustinus looked at him doubtfully.

"There are always hundreds of vessels in the city." Faustinus said. He dreaded the idea of a trudge up and down the banks of the Tiber in the blazing sun calling out for the sailor.

"Well, yes…" Gaius sat on the couch and rested his chin on his hand. "Still…"

The chance that his master would dispatch him to the docks inspired him: "Livilla's familiar with your wit. She'll take your reply as a subtle and amusing satire of social forms." He didn't believe a word of it, but thought Gaius might.

Gaius nodded. "You really think she'll take it that way? I mean, irony, the sardonic touch, a certain shallow suavity—all that sort of thing. They're more your style."

Faustinus bowed ever so slightly.

"I'm more the bluff, forthright type."

"Indeed." Faustinus had long since given up marveling at how little self-knowledge Gaius showed.

"You are right to wonder about my situation, though." Gaius lay back on the couch and clasped his hands behind his head. He studied the ceiling intently as though he might find a clue to his situation hidden among the beams. "Her remark is a bit unsettling. Still, as a philosophically-minded man, I can accept whatever the world might toss my way—" He flicked his hand in a casual gesture.

"Fortuna with her hand on the rudder, tripping people on the road of life?"

Gaius again flinched at the faulty metaphor. "Still, the uncertainty is a little unsettling."

Someone was calling out in the street below, and Gaius sent Faustinus out to the balcony to see what was happening.

"Who's making that racket?" Gaius called after him.

"It's a public slave," Faustinus called back over his shoulder. "He's looking for someone." Faustinus turned back to the street and shouted down. "Whom do you want?" Gaius heard an indistinct reply, and then Faustinus said, "Up here. Third floor, left-hand door." As he stepped back into the room Faustinus said, "He's looking for you."

"A public slave? Looking for me?" He sat up.

"He's well dressed. For a slave, that is. I'd guess he's from one of the Imperial Offices."

"Ah," Gaius said but stopped, unable to find anything further to say. His enthusiasm for the Imperial bureaucracy waned sharply now that it seemed interested in him. Faustinus opened the door to a sharp knock, and the slave stepped in without invitation. "Gaius Obsequens Dolo?" His tone entirely lacked servility. Faustinus swept his arm back toward Gaius; the slave advanced on him and held out a letter marked with the Imperial seal. He bowed just the slightest bit as form demanded, but without even a hint of subservience. "I give you this summons from the office of His Splendor, Flavius Afranius Syagrius, Consul, Praetorian Prefect of Italy and Prefect of the City."

Gaius stood and took the letter. He looked at it apprehensively. "A summons?" **The Prefect Syagrius was the second man in the Empire,** he thought to himself. "What has he to do with me?" he asked the slave impulsively, forgetting that a man of his position shouldn't reveal any unease to someone so far beneath him socially.

The public slave smiled irritatingly at the misstep. "How could I guess, Master? Any more than you?" He grinned impertinently. "Perhaps one of his minions will clarify his interest in you, Master. You will understand that His Splendor the Prefect will be too occupied to concern himself with you in person." He seemed to enjoy saying this. He turned and left, his footsteps fading away down the stairwell. Faustinus closed the door behind him.

"Impertinent bastard!" Gaius said as he slid his thumb under the seal and flapped the message open. The letter and read.

> Flavius Clementianus, Second Notary of the Roman Office
> of the Prefect of Italy, invites Gaius Obsequens Dolo to attend
> him at the tenth hour today at his offices in the Trajan Market.
> A display of this letter and its seal is requisite for admission.
> Use the west entrance.

Gaius set the letter on the table and sat down at it, drumming his fingers. Faustinus watched him for a few moments in silence and then said, "Don't be too uneasy, Master. After all, it was not an arrest. He didn't bring soldiers." He picked up the letter and read it himself. He was uneasy too but only said, "I'll get your good clothes out."

"Yours too, Faustinus. You're coming along."

* * *

The two men set out for Trajan's Market in the late afternoon. Gaius wore a deep blue dalmatic embroidered with silver thread. A well-pressed white tunic showed carefully below. Faustinus had polished Gaius's dark-blue shoes until they glimmered. Wearing his best had moderately elevated Gaius's mood—he felt only a mild uncertainty about his situation, and the deference of the people in the narrow, crowded streets was encouraging too: they stepped back against the walls, often bowing, as Faustinus cleared the way, followed by Gaius in his finest. Perhaps they mistook him for a *clarissimus*, a senator of the lowest rank (but still a senator!), who had inexplicably gone out without his litter and entourage. Best to show deference. Gaius condescended to nod at a few of the better sort as he went down the sloping street toward the Trajan Market.

The street levelled as it approached the park along the back of the Market, and the two of them stopped to glance at the gnomon of a sundial standing out from a wall. Its shadow fell at the edge of the mark for the tenth hour.

"This way." Gaius headed toward a doorway where a squad of soldiers lounged in their pillbox hats, gaudy tunics and military belts. He straightened his back and strode grandly past them toward the doorway.

"Hold it! Stop there! Right there!" Two soldiers casually drifted into the doorway to block it and rested their hands on their hilts. A third stood to the side with his hands in loose fists and watched him with close-set threatening eyes. Gaius stopped and looked about. "Yes?" He raised his eyebrows in what he reckoned was an imperious manner.

A fourth soldier stepped up. "Your business—" he paused and then added with a practiced sneer, "Master?" He was obviously the officer of the squad: his tunic was finer, and he slapped a polished truncheon lightly into his palm. He looked Gaius up and down contemptuously.

"And what is that to you, officer?" Gaius asked, his back now fully up.

"What it is to me is you don't go in if you can't show why it is you ought to." He glanced to his men, who laughed with practiced obedience. The man spoke a poor, vernacular Latin with a strong Gaulish accent.

"He's a dandy, Captain," one of the guards in the doorway said in some outlandish accent, perhaps Illyrian. "I say we let him in. Just to show the clerks inside what real style is." More laughter. Gaius flushed at the taunts.

"Shut up," the captain said quietly, but without rancor. It

was automatic.

"I am Gaius Obsequens Dolo."

"Surely you have been told to expect him?" Faustinus stepped up to support his master.

"Of course we have! We've been waiting all day for His Splendor here!" He spoke in a crude mocking tone. And then he added, suddenly and sharply, "Be quiet, slave." He pushed Faustinus back a step with the tip of his baton, but kept his eyes on Gaius, who stepped quickly between them, forcing the soldier to step back in turn. "Don't touch him again!" Gaius said sharply. The soldier looked him up and down with quiet menace but said nothing. Gaius went on: "The Notary Flavius Clementianus requests that I attend him shortly." He looked the soldier over with theatrical contempt. "It's clear from the looks of you, soldier, that you have nothing like enough position to keep the notary waiting." He tried to sneer; it wasn't one of his usual expressions, but he was pretty confident that he'd pulled it off. "Show him the letter, Faustinus."

The captain opened it and frowned. Gaius was delighted to put the worst construction on this, and said in Gaulish (as though the man's Latin were too poor for conversation): "Don't strain over the hard words. My slave here will help you with them."

The Illyrian soldier, who didn't speak Gaulish, cocked his head, puzzled, but the others, who were Gallic, snickered. The captain bristled and turned savagely on them. "Quiet!" They all stood instantly at attention but bit their lips ostentatiously, pretending to suppress laughter. The captain glowered ferociously, slapped the letter against Faustinus's chest, nodded at the entrance and turned away.

Gaius and Faustinus passed between the soldiers and into the great softly echoing hall. Once inside they found themselves at the edge of the Empire of Administration, and Gaius sighed like a buffeted voyager who has finally reached shore. He stood reverently taking it all in, the floor carpeted in mosaic, the high arched walls daubed with frescoes, the halls suffused with a warm soft light from windows through whose screens he caught happy flashes of the blue Italian sky. All about them clerks sauntered, drifting in and out of offices. The murmur of calm voices, blended as it was with the stately tread of unhurried bureaucratic feet, implied a steady activity, splendidly lacking any sense of urgency. Gaius was suffused with sudden calm. "Welcome back to civilization, Faustinus. Put the soldiers out of your mind." The slave glanced down the long hallway punctuated into the distance by doorways.

"Now we have to find Clementianus's room." Faustinus said. His practicality struck Gaius as unseemly, as not showing sufficient reverence for the establishment.

"Don't hurry me. Just let me stroll a bit and take in this splendid atmosphere. We must have a little time yet." He ambled down the great hall, entranced by the magnificence of the administrative atmosphere. "Such masterly inaction!" He marveled as he strolled along, stepping aside now and then for low-level functionaries padding along on unhurried errands. He glanced into the rooms he passed and saw administrators at worktables dictating notes to each other or shifting the beads on abacuses and calling out totals to be entered on large sheets of vellum. Moderately important men, or even just those who had attained only a comfortable mediocrity, sat listening as their secretaries droned petitions aloud to them. Some nodded as they listened; some opened their eyes from time to time to glance out a window.

Gaius stopped halfway down the great hallway and turned slowly to take it all in, at which point Faustinus, impatient with the delay, stopped an errant secretary. "The office of Flavius Clementianus?"

The man pointed toward the end of the hall. "The big room on the right. At the end." He floated off and disappeared down a stairway to the level below. Gaius shook off his reverie. "A splendid place, this." He stepped quickly to catch up to Faustinus, who, determined to get them to the Second Notary's office, had set off without him. "And wonderfully calming," Gaius said as he caught up. "Though I must confess I still feel a tinge of unease at Clementianus's 'invitation.'"

The door of the Second Notary's office was surrounded by frescoes of great cities, each overtopped by a tablet and stylus, and the lintel was surmounted by winged victories holding laurel wreaths, the whole ensemble a blatant suggestion that Office Work had led to Empire.

A pair of wooden benches flanked the door, and half a dozen men of modest station sat on them, radiating a resigned but not quite hopeless patience. They looked up incuriously at Gaius and Faustinus as they spoke to the Head Clerk, who had stepped out at their approach and glanced cursorily at their summons. As he handed it back, he looked meaningfully at the petitioners waiting on the benches, turned back to Gaius and waited with a bland expression. Faustinus, ready for this, handed the man a coin. He made it disappear with the skill of a conjurer and waved them right in.

In the outer office two young civil servants read memoranda aloud to a pair of clerks who rewrote them into fair copies to be filed in duplicate in a record room where they would probably languish unread for a century.[11] The Head Clerk showed the way past the droning dictators to an internal doorway leading to a second, bigger office. He pulled aside the heavy curtain that secluded it, murmured an introduction, and left them to the attentions of the Second Notary of the Prefect The Illustrious Flavius Syagrius. Faustinus retreated to a corner where he stood motionless and obscure next to a statue on a plinth. In the darkness of the corner it was hard to tell which was which. Gaius envied him his effacement; a suspicion—faint at first—that things weren't going to go altogether well for him had begun to seep into the back of his mind, like damp creeping at the foot of a wall. He approached the notary's table, his face, he hoped, a blend in equal measure of confidence and noble humility.

The Second Notary Flavius Clementianus rose from behind his desk, a stout sixtyish man, balding and florid, his face full of a complacent self-importance. Gaius noted the man's fine clothes—the spotlessly white tunic decorated at the shoulders with finely-embroidered purple roundels, the military belt (an obligatory sign of the imperial civil service), made of particularly fine leather and finished with a buckle decorated with the chips of different colored gems that winked even in the muted light of the office. When he waved Gaius to sit on one of the chairs across from his table, several rings glinted

---

[11] After which they could be used (with the text scraped off) for the end papers of account books.

on his fingers.

"Thank you, Your Excellence," Gaius said, but waited diplomatically until the other had sat before he took his seat. Clementianus regarded him for several moments, his hands clasped and elbows resting on his marble-topped worktable. "Well, young man, first I must say that you are very fortunate. Very fortunate."

Gaius said nothing but nodded politely, relaxed now that he'd been assured of good things to come. He wondered what happy turn of events the Notary would reveal to him. Clearly Livilla had written in ignorance about his "situation"—silly woman. Really, it was bad form to allude murkily to illusory misfortunes, to provoke worry where none was called for. Should he bother to straighten her out when they met next? No. He was a better man, more noble than that. The engagement was off, and she was the loser the by it. That would be enough of a lesson to her, Gaius thought—more than enough—as she watched him go down the road of life, climbing from height to height. He frowned to himself at the mixed metaphor and then realized that the Notary was talking to him.

"His Splendor the Prefect Flavius Syagrius has taken a personal interest in your case."

"My case?" He didn't like that expression. His earlier unease resumed its percolation through his thoughts, despite the Notary's earlier assurance that he was somehow fortunate. Fortunate and case? An incongruous pairing of words.

"The case of a provincial aristocrat such as yourself, from one of the Gallic Provinces..." He frowned in thought a moment. "Help me here—which one?"

"I'm from Narbo. So, Narbonensis Prima."

"Yes, of course. So many provinces now, don't you know? Not like in the old days." He put a hand to his chin, reflecting.

"Yes, so many, Your Excellence."

"On the other hand, it's indisputable that the subdivision—and hence multiplication—of the provinces, has been a gift to administration. No small thing, that. A hundred governors, a hundred staffs— that sort of thing. A hundred high provincial military commanders, each with a staff." Clementianus called himself back from his bureaucratic reverie. "It's so easy to drift off the point. Now, where were we?"

Gaius couldn't really say, so he mutely watched the notary and smiled at him in guarded encouragement. It was difficult to smile, though; the word "case" still haunted him.

"Ah, yes. I recall it now. It is this: your situation would more usually be dealt with by the Office of the Prefect of Gaul…" He came to a halt as he shuffled a pair of documents on his worktable.

"And what is my situation—exactly?" He did his best to hide his curiosity—it was so unsophisticated to show it.

"I'm getting there." He put up a hand. "Your father," he hesitated. "Help me here."

"Marcius Obsequens Lutatianus."

"Ah yes. You're quite right." He seemed pleased that Gaius agreed with him about who his father was. He went on: "Your family are clients of Flavius Syagrius?"

"Yes, we are. It goes back a couple of centuries at least. But of course, Flavius Syagrius is a *spectabilis*[12]. So, of course, we don't trouble him with trifles." By this Gaius meant that he had never seen the man himself, and his father had done so only once.

Clementianus nodded. "Of course not." He picked up a sheet of papyrus and glanced down at it. "Clients of Syagrius. And there is some property near Milan. So, Italy. That's another connection with Syagrius, but this time in his capacity as Prefect of Italy." He put the sheet down and looked at Gaius. "I'm just trying to make the connection, you understand."

Gaius did not understand at all. What had the second estate in Italy to do with anything? For that matter, what had his family's clientage to the Syagrii have to do with the over-subtle subdivisions of the Imperial bureaucracy?

"I take it this why you asked to see me, Excellence. To clarify these relationships. And, of course, I'm quite pleased to do that."

Clementianus nodded. "Relationships are important, you see. Critical really. Orders and actions must go through the proper channels

---

[12] The highest level of Roman senator and noble.

or else there's nothing but muddles. Muddles day in and day out as the result of competing jurisdictions and competencies." He looked as though he was about to shudder at this appalling prospect.

"The proper channels. Yes." This seemed a safe thing to say to the pompous old fool. He squirmed in his chair and fought an impulse to look over his shoulder at the doorway.

"Of course, there must always be exceptions. As in this case."

Why did he keep circling back to this damned *case* business? Gaius decided then and there he would forgo any good fortune Clementianus meant to confer, if he would just drop this case business and excuse him, but curiosity drove him like a goad. He grasped the nettle. "And what is my case?"

"Your case? Oh, yes. It's the loss of your family's estate outside of Narbo."

Gaius sat stupefied for several moments and then shook his head, unsure that he had heard correctly. "Loss of the estate?" He turned abruptly in his chair and look at Faustinus. The slave stood stone-faced but with his eyes very wide in surprise. Yes, Gaius had heard correctly.

The Notary casually heaped on more distress. "And the moveable property too. The crops. And the tenants, of course. All gone." He said it as though he appreciated the neatness, the totality of the event.

Gaius sat up straight, suddenly hot and faintly sick to his stomach. "Loss of…" He couldn't finish the sentence.

"Merely through operation of law, Dolo. Nothing more than that." Clementianus said it as though it were a consolation. "I've invited you here to sign a document relinquishing any claims to your family estate and property. It's a matter of proper form and relieves us at this end from executing other documents through a second office to achieve the same end. I'm sure you appreciate the opportunity to do the Administration this courtesy."

III

GAIUS SUDDENLY DISCOVERS THAT HE IS A ROMAN MILITARY OFFICER

* * *

"I'm to sign away the estate? But why?"

"Oh, that. I'm sorry that I overlooked that detail. It's a matter of taxes." He tapped the bottom of the papyrus with his finger to show Gaius where to sign. "It's purely a formality," he said with the graceful obtuseness of the career functionary. He rotated the sheet and thrust it across the desk. "You may use my pen." He made it seem an honor.

"Father didn't pay his taxes? Surely not!" Gaius had felt hot a moment before, but now he was cold; this was all part of a world suddenly become confusing.

"No, no. You misunderstand the situation entirely," the Notary said in a smooth tone. "His Sacred Majesty is planning a special expedition in Numidia to support the southern border."

"Expedition?" Gaius couldn't follow this either.

"A Numidian expedition. Doubtless just a few raids against nomad chiefs south of the frontier." He shrugged. "But even so his Sacred Majesty needs to muster a few extra horsemen. He might need, say, three thousand. And so, to get them, he'll have to raise about three thousand seven hundred (officially, you see) to take account of the commander's skim, and then there are the administrative costs of the expedition. It all adds up." He leaned over the desk and tapped the place where Gaius was to sign with his pen.

Gaius looked at him dumbly, shaking his head.

"Oh, don't look so concerned, young man, a little demonstration of the whip hand is all those nomads require. They're really just bandits, when you come down to it."

"The tax. I don't see…" He began and then stopped.

"Honestior Dolo, your father was one of the *duumviri*[13] last year in that provincial city of yours and as you know, your father, as a duumvir, had to collect the year's imperial taxes and make up any shortfall."

"He didn't want the position—the other aristocrats maneuvered him into it. He'd served just two years before. They maneuvered him into. He told me."

"Ah, local politics," Clementianus said philosophically. "Quite rewarding, I'm sure, for those who come out on top."

It struck Gaius at that moment that those other aristocrats—the Ardeati and Nebulosi—must have known what was coming: they were cannier than his father had been, richer and better connected.

The Notary went on blandly. "So, really, it's the tax for the Numidian campaign that's caused this. It's the law: the shortfall must be made up, and the estate in outside of Narbo just does it, according to the imperial assessor. So, I will call in a pair of witnesses, you sign this, and your father's obligation—your obligation now—is entirely expunged." He smiled cheerfully at the thought of an afternoon's work accomplished.

"What about my brother Arcadius, Your Excellency?"

"Don't worry about him," the Undersecretary said soothingly. "He's is still in possession of the estate outside of Milan."

Gaius looked up suddenly. "But surely he must share it with me now? Under the circumstances?"

---

[13] One of two leaders of a provincial town or city council. This obligatory duty fell upon local landholders who met a wealth-requirement. They had various duties, among which was collecting imperial taxes and making good any shortfalls, from their own funds if necessary.

"A good question, but one for the lawyers, I'm afraid." Clementianus assumed a sympathetic smile. "Your father seems to have realized—rather late, unfortunately—the difficulty entailed by the military tax, and he passed the Italian estate quietly through the hands of a friend, who then deeded it to your brother. I would guess that a gift made free and clear to your brother by way of a third party is likely to stand—as a practical matter anyway, quite apart from any legalities."

"And the good fortune you mentioned earlier?" Gaius grasped at this last straw.

"Oh, yes, that. It's this: His Splendor Flavius Syagrius has determined to erase your misfortune in a display of that fabled generosity and attention to the duties that he owes to his clients—however modest—such as you."

Gaius looked at the Notary without quite seeing him. His expression resembled that of a stunned boxer who has discovered he's no longer in the ring. The Notary displayed another document. Gaius blinked his eyes at it. The Prefect has given me another estate?"

The Notary chuckled. "Of course not. This is something altogether different."

Gaius fell back in his chair wondering listlessly what that could be.

"As you see, this bears the official seal of the Prefectural Chancery of Italy."

Gaius stared hopelessly across the table at the tight brown uncial script.

The Notary, holding the document toward him, pointed at it with his other hand. "Young man, this is nothing less than a commission in His Sacred Majesty's Army."

Gaius at bolt upright in alarm, the gang of soldiers at the doorway flashing through his mind: their bravado, their crudity, their drum-shaped caps.

Clementianus laid the document on the table before him. "Gaius Obsequens, I sense that you hesitate to accept this generosity. Now, we all understand that change can be difficult, but this opportunity comes through the good offices of His Splendor the Prefect Syagrius as recompense for your father's lack of foresight—and your resultant, ah, situation. Such gifts do not come often." The Notary took the tone he might have used with a recalcitrant child. "In fact, this is a pure gift—Syagrius's action in obtaining this commission means that you are excused from the customary *suffragium*[14]. Just think: you don't have to pay anyone anything in order to take your commission." He leaned back and folded his hands over his stomach. "A most enviable situation, don't you agree?"

Gaius, shaken by the ghastly prospect of military service, couldn't muster any better response than: "But I'm a trained rhetor. I've practically completed my studies." An idea was coming to Gaius. It bubbled up suddenly, as all of his good ideas did, and he grasped it with both hands.

"Of course, I thank the Prefect for his generosity—thank him a thousand times, in fact! Who could ask for a more thoughtful patron?" He stopped here to gather his thoughts now that he'd expressed enough formulaic gratitude. "But useful as a soldier is to the Empire, let me assure you (and the Prefect, of course) that my services would be much more valuable in the Imperial bureaucracy." The thought of administration inspired him. "Nothing grand, of course." He fanned a growing confidence in the fragile foundations of his claim. "Clerk to one of the jurists here in Rome—that sort of thing. Reading and answering petitions with the correct level and tone. And according to the law, so far as it can be determined in these days of constant edicts. My tutor Enthymemus calls me his most promising student," he lied.

But the lie was unimportant, for the Notary was already frowning. "Enthymemus?" His face held the expression of a man trying, after years, to recall the details of a half-forgotten story. He shook his head. "I can't say I've heard of him."

Gaius closed his eyes in frustration. Enthymemus was a bit of a duffer, but Gaius's father had understood that study with any tutor in Rome would have given his son enough cachet—and perhaps even skill—to rise in the courts about Narbo, and the old geezer's fees were quite reasonable. But he could tell from the Notary's expression that he was less than impressed with Gaius's training.

---

[14] Price paid to the government by an official in exchange for his position.

He looked away for a moment, thinking hard about his finances. He had a few dozen folles in ready money, and a *solidus*[15] hidden behind a tile in his apartment. That was the limit of his fortune now that the estate was gone. He could live in Rome another three months, perhaps even a year or two if he sold Faustinus and lived frugally, but he was ashamed that the thought had even flashed through his mind, and he dismissed it. A commission in the army, appalling as it was, offered opportunities though. What the Notary had said about the Numidian campaign and the commander's skim suggested possibilities. And surely his brother Arcadius would be willing to share the rents of the new estate with him?

"Let me ask…" Gaius hoped for the best and continued. "This commission is in the Field Army, of course?" There was this much to hope for: a post in one of the larger provincial cities, a decent house to live in and some pastimes while he looked for a way out of the army.

Clementianus shook his head. "Your commission is in Border Army, young man. And think what scope it offers for an adventurous life!" He tapped the document in vicarious enthusiasm. "You have been made a tribune and have been given sole command of a fort. Quite a position to start from." He drew his finger over part of the page and read out, "'Castellinum Ripae'[16]. You'll command a detachment of cavalry, the Second Pannonian Horse, and some foot soldiers. Let's see here. Ah, yes, a cohort called the *Milites Feroces*[17]." The Notary held the document up like a signboard and pointed to the bottom, "And you can see here the signature of his Splendor the Emperor Gratian himself. A Master of the World has touched this very document." He put it down and reverently and touched the dark-purple signature with a fingertip.

Gaius pulled a handkerchief from his sleeve and wiped his forehead. "Castellinum Ripae? So, it's on a river, I take it. But where?"

"Germania Superior. A bracing climate—Doubtless the fort has a beautiful view of the Rhine."

---

[15] The *solidus* was a late Roman coin. There were seventy-two to a pound of gold.

[16] Latin for "Little Fort on the Riverbank." Not very inventive, is it?

[17] "Ferocious Soldiers." The late Roman army had a penchant for vivid troop names.

IV

GAIUS'S BROTHER
ARCADIUS IS PLEASED TO LEARN
OF HIS NEW CAREER

* * *

Tribune Gaius Obsequens Dolo found himself rather uneasily the highest ranking member of a military column moving along the highway north from Rome along the Via Flaminia toward Milan, stopping every night at a *mansio*[18] to rest and change mules. The Imperial mules, shuttling back and forth for years between the same two or three mansios, knew their way to the very step and, utterly indifferent to their riders, plodded comfortably along at their own pace. All of Gaius's attempts to direct them were futile as they carried him ineluctably north, indifferent and determined as anything he'd ever encountered. Like bureaucracy perhaps. Still, for the sake of appearance, he held the reins in one hand and, from time to time, rested his other on his hip in a jaunty attitude meant to suggest negligent and yet complete control of his mount. No matter: the rest of the company paid no more attention to his riding than did the mules.

---

[18] Post station for the Imperial couriers.

The column was led, in actual fact, by an experienced *optio*[19], but out of deference to Gaius's official position as senior in command, he was encouraged to ride at the head of the column, Faustinus beside him. He sat more easily in the saddle than his master, as though he had had some experience that way. The slave's formerly hidden talent was just some native gift, really, and this irritated Gaius all the more. He settled himself in a way that chafed his buttocks in new places and pulled back the reins experimentally. The mule ignored him. Two light wagons drawn by teams of mules trundled along the road behind him, headed, like Gaius, ineluctably north, their wheels traveling in the channels grooved into the road over the centuries. The determined mules and the half-directed wagons seemed to Gaius, who had a literary education and a great deal of time on his hands now to reflect on it, like some cheap literary technique of which he was the victim.

The first wagon was loaded with Gaius's personal property: two chests of clothing, a chest of law books and Milesian tales[20], and the furniture from the apartment. It had been hard to get the second wagon: he was entitled to the use of one, and he had had pay off a supply officer with a hundred folles to rent the second one. Still, it seemed to him a bargain (if rather a close one) because he'd not had to abandon the furnishings of his apartment. His finances were low now, but he consoled himself that his expenses were covered until he reached his post, and then who knew what opportunities he'd find there? His helmet and armor reposed in another chest tied down at the back of the second wagon, and his oval shield, its bright design hidden beneath a canvas cover, was wedged on its edgewise in the middle of things. The wagons thumped irritatingly at irregular intervals as they passed over high road stones, and one of them, despite repeated greasing, cheeped steadily, mile after mile.

After several days riding in the late summer sun, they crossed a gray stone bridge over the Po, and the column was joined by thirty

---

[19] A military officer above a common soldier, but below a centurion and well below a tribune.

[20] Adventure stories often involving princes, maidens, pirates, magic and so on, all in vague Hellenistic settings, the popular literature of the time. Gaius's adventures would be quite different than those he read about.

young men, dusty and utterly dispirited—the sons of tenants who had been turned out by landlords as conscripts for the army as part of the military tax. They trudged behind the last wagon under the care of half a dozen cavalrymen who watched sharply to prevent desertions. Gaius learned from the optio that they would be parceled out to serve in units somewhere along the Moselle. *Twenty-five years*, Gaius thought. ***Well, it might have been worse for them: they might have been sent to Britain.***

Gaius turned his mind to other things. He took a chance and leaned a bit out of his saddle as though he were confident of his seat and told Faustinus to ask the optio how much farther it was to the little town of Ad Duodecem, then he straightened up and adjusted his broad round traveling hat to keep the sun from his eyes. Undignified, this; between the big hat and the mule, he felt like a yokel on a jaunt. Faustinus turned easily in the saddle to study the road behind and then tipped his own hat back to glance for a moment at the sun. "About two or three more miles, Master." He nodded at the road ahead. When we top that rise we should see it."

Why didn't he just ask the optio as he'd been told? Gaius considered rebuking him, but he always felt uncomfortable when he did it; he should have started when they were boys—it was too late now. So he merely casually dropped this: "I'll call a halt there for a couple of hours." Faustus turned to him questioningly, and Gaius continued: "I need to pop over to our new Italian estate—the one Arcadius is running—and establish a few things for while I'm away on the border."

"I see," Faustinus said. He noted silently that it was "our new Italian" estate, not simply "Arcadius's estate." He pondered what Gaius implied by this.

"I understand the property starts about a mile from the highway as it passes through Ad Duodecem—the villa can't be much further beyond it."

"Very good, Master."

The two of them rode on, Gaius considering where he would be financially in about three years with this military pay (and the results of any opportunities for peculation) all supplemented by some healthy fraction of the income from the estate. Half. Half would be reasonable. Half the net, not half the gross. No need to overreach.

The village of Ad Duodecem was twelve miles from somewhere (opinions differed about where). Two smaller roads leading to estates in the countryside crossed the highway there, creating several narrow intersections harboring a pair of taverns, a small bakery, and a cheap hostelry with immensely thick walls and no windows on the ground floor. Its massive front door stood open, tended by a rough doorman, one of the largest men Gaius had ever seen. Twenty small houses made up the rest of the settlement.

"So, this is your brother's neighborhood," Faustinus said, looking straight ahead as they entered the town. He kept any judgment out of his voice.

"The estate is everything, Faustinus," Gaius countered defensively. He nodded to his right. "That stand of trees. It's past there. No more than a mile. That's how Father said you could tell." He reined in his mule, which was willing to oblige him so long as he was stopping. "Halt!" Gaius ordered, raising his hand as he'd seen the optio do, and sat with as much stability and dignity in the saddle as he could. The column came to a halt, the cavalrymen turning to look at him in surprise. The optio rode slowly up to him and narrowed his eyes, surprised at seeing Gaius assert any authority. He asked, "Well?" And then added "Your Excellence?" It sounded like a an afterthought. He was a tough little man with a three-day beard and a scar on his cheek and was quite evidently civil to Gaius only under the habit of military discipline and the knowledge that Gaius was an officer. An inept and utterly inexperienced officer, but an officer just the same and in a position to make trouble for him.

"We will halt here for two hours." The optio widened his eyes in surprise. "Two hours," Gaius repeated, looking over the column. The optio leaned over from his saddle. "And why, if I may ask Your Excellence? Begging for your indulgence, I might remind the Tribune that the standing orders are to keep on to the next mansio."

"There's yet time, Optio. I have business with my brother, the Excellent Arcadius Obsequentius Macro, whose fabulous estate lies just beyond there." Faustinus looked away and raised his eyebrows at "fabulous." Gaius looked as haughtily as he could at the optio. "It's hardly wise to keep great men waiting, is it?" The optio regarded him sourly but didn't object. Gaius saw he'd gained his point, so he added: "Order two of the men to accompany me."

The optio stared in the direction of the estate and then shrugged, deciding that it might—just, might—be unwise to thwart this callow tribune. "The men might use a rest," he said, as though it were concession, but he stared pointedly at one of the taverns as he said it.

"Ah," Gaius said. "Quite right. Give each man a drink." He urged his mule toward the byway, at first doubtful that it would obey, but the mule, faintly attracted by the unaccustomed novelty of the route, condescended to veer onto the narrow way and amble along, Faustinus and the two troopers following. Gaius turned to his slave. "Here. Take this straw hat." He pulled out his little military cap, looked at it with distaste and put it on. "Appearances, you know."

"I must say, Master, that it does lend you a bit of dash."

Gaius grandly ignored him and, the reins in his left hand, his right fist on his hip and elbow out, rode off toward the estate with what panache he could muster after half a day in the saddle. When they reached the villa, Gaius dismounted, told Faustinus and the troopers to wait for him, and stepped through the gate with his cap set jauntily forward.

* * *

"Not a bad estate we've got here," Gaius said, easing himself with a creak into a wicker chair next to that of his brother in the peristyle of the villa. Arcadius Obsequentius Macro, a few years older than Gaius, was a large, soft young man with thinning hair and a chilly expression.

"Father described this place to me once, but not in detail."

"You might have let me know you were coming." Arcadius looked at him accusingly.

"No, it's not a bad estate at all, though I'd hoped for something a bit larger. A few more peasants, another flock or two of sheep, another stand or two of timber. That sort of thing. Still, the tenant village is quite a tidy little place, and Father did pretty well in bequeathing us—" Arcadius flinched at the pronoun—"an estate this pleasant in view of the loss of the old family estate outside of Narbo." Gaius took sip of wine. "How are the rents, by the way?"

It was on the tip of Arcadius's tongue to say that the rents weren't any of Gaius's business, no, not at all, but he controlled himself and sat back, determined to disabuse his little brother when the conversation took a more opportune turn. Instead, he shifted off the point. "Your uniform's nicely cut, all things considered." He leaned forward and looked his brother up and down and then pointed to his shoulder. "That roundel might be a truer red—less brownish; it would have been a bit nicer. But the embroidery's quite fine, actually. The stitchery."

"Roman work. From the city. You can still get good work there." Gaius brushed the roundel ostentatiously and glanced about trying to finish his assessment of the estate. From the quality and appointments of the villa, it should be worth nearly a thousand solidi. That depended on the acreage, of course—it had been hard to gauge the extent of it from the road. The floor mosaics were quite fine, and the wall frescoes cleanly executed and in quiet good taste. Really, it looked promising, the more you thought about it. Not in the league of the old Narbo property, but promising, really. Gaius contrasted Arcadius's situation with his own during those last few days in Rome, when he struggled to survive on his last few folles while waiting for the bureaucracy to issue him his equipment and travel money. (He'd finally expedited the process by giving a government clerk a twelfth of his first pay-installment in return for having the pay issued at all.) Arcadius brought him back to the present.

"I see you're already wearing trousers. Rather barbaric touch I've always thought, though I suppose they'll help you fit into your new surroundings. And you've got one of those little round hats." He pointed at it sitting on the table, a little maroon drum. "It reminds me of a shallow flower pot, but in felt." He smiled nastily, recalling how, even in childhood, Gaius had been careful of his dress.

"All part of the military kit, you know," his brother said defensively. "You wear it under a helmet to improve the fit." He frowned at it.

"But you're not wearing a helmet. And I must say that your boots are a little hard on the floor. The hobnails." Arcadius scowled at Gaius's feet.

"Think of your floor as a sacrifice for the Empire. An uncharitable brother might suggest that it's the only one you're likely to make." Gaius settled back in his chair, taking care as he did it to scrape the soles of his boots, as though casually, across the tiles.

Arcadius flinched but managed a sour smile and kept his sharp little eyes on Gaius's face. "Of course, of course—it's nothing when you come to think of it." He picked up a stemmed wine glass and took a sip. "And you're in for, what, twenty-five years? I think that's usual." He rolled the wine over his tongue and closed his eyes, tasting it. His expression lightened as he considered the length of his brother's service.

Gaius, drawn away from renewed mental calculations about the value of the estate, looked over at him. "What?"

Arcadius favored him with a vague, enraptured expression. "Twenty-five years. Your stint in the army." He sat back, savoring the situation. "That should give you a lot of time, scope, really, to exercise your talents—whatever they might be exactly." He looked up from under the colonnade in which they sat and stared at the northern sky, enjoying the prospect of Gaius's absence. He took another sip of wine. "Yes, think what you'll accomplish in a quarter century—even up there. A wild province must present a wide ambit for ingenuity. You'll build a little house, marry the daughter of some local magnate—they must have them even along the border itself—start a family, try to introduce some modern farming methods when you're not busy drilling the men or drudging in your headquarters or trudging through some German forest. I'll lend you my copy of Columella! And you'll try hard to teach the children proper Latin. That sort of thing." He glanced at Gaius and looked down at his feet with a smile and shook his head. "And feel free to visit when you can—the passes should be open during much of the year, though I suppose that's when the bandits operate. Still. . ." He shrugged at the uncompleted thought. He seemed quite cheerful suddenly.

"I think I can spare you the visits, Arcadius. I'll take my interest in this estate in the form of half of the rents." His brother blinked at him.

"Half the rents." Arcadius repeated mildly.

"Half, Brother. That's more than fair."

Arcadius laced his fingers over his belly and watched Gaius with a mildly sardonic expression. Gaius went on obliviously. "Half the rents, Brother. From the looks of the place, that should leave you with quite a comfortable income—" he pointed at Arcadius for emphasis—"and you'll have the use of the property itself. The house, local society, proximity to the court in Milan—not that you're going to rub shoulders with His Serenity—still, even the fringes of the Court enrich an area. So, half the rents. It could hardly be more fair. Net, that is, not gross. And unless there is some reason not too, I'll trust you to determine that." He smiled winningly at him.

"Half, you say? And for twenty-five years?" Arcadius shook his head and clucked his tongue softly.

"Oh, it won't come to that. You're thinking of the common soldiers: it's twenty-five years for them. But I'm a tribune: '*Hoc officium honor est*,' as it says on my commission. My office is an 'honor.'"

Arcadius looked uneasy. "An honor…" His voice trailed off.

"So, you see, I serve at the pleasure of the Emperor. At a guess… " Gaius fiddled with his wine glass and said casually, "At a guess, I'd say I'll be done with this soldiering business in two or three years."

Arcadius narrowed his eyes. "Oh yes?" He tried to look casual. "And then what?" Still, his unease was quite evident to his little brother.

"Why, I expect I'll come back here. We can decide how to share the estate then." Gaius smiled at him in feigned innocence. Really, it was amusing to discomfit Arcadius. More entertaining, even, than when he gotten the upper hand over him in childhood. It hadn't happened often enough, he mused. "Halves or something. I'm sure we can work it out. I wouldn't insist on actually living here—don't worry about that. It will be like old times, but without Father to keep us apart. Perhaps we'll just renegotiate the rents."

Arcadius picked up his glass, swirled the wine and, looking into it as though casually, said, "I'm afraid, Little Brother, that you very much mistake your position."

* * *

"If I may remark, Master," Faustinus said, as they rode back toward Ad Duodecem, "you seem quite subdued. Apparently the reunion with your brother was less than satisfactory."

Gaius reached out for his broad traveling hat and pushed it violently onto his head. "He means to keep the whole estate for himself, the grasping bastard. All of it!"

"Ah."

Gaius turned toward him in a fury. "You might say something more supportive."

"I'm working on it. But remember: I've known you both since childhood."

Gaius harumphed.

Faustinus, unflustered, turned to flattery: "You must certainly have the beginnings of a plan."

"Of course I have a plan." Gaius rode on in silence for a while trying to come up with a plan. He pulled ahead of Faustinus and then, sudden as a spark jumping from the hearth, a plan came to him. He reined in the mule and, as Faustinus came up alongside, he said: "Litigation! I'll sue him for my half."

"Of course, Master. And the basis for your claim? In view of your father's arrangements, which seem to give Arcadius the estate free and clear?"

Gaius was looking away across the late summer fields but didn't see them—he was casting his mind back to Enthymemus's lectures on property law, wishing he'd paid better attention. "What? A basis? I don't need a basis. I have disorder on my side."

"I don't follow you."

"I admit my subtlety can be a bit much sometimes." He smiled in a self-congratulatory way. "The law's in utter disorder these days: decrees, Imperial laws, local laws, customs, rescripts, constitutions, Imperial directives, advisory opinions, the views of the great jurisconsults. It's all one twisted skein that's beyond anyone's skill to unravel. And then there's the question of whether any particular law is valid. That just adds to the general confusion. Well, is the law from a Good

Emperor? Then yes. A Bad Emperor? Then no. If you can tell which is which." Gaius was warming to his topic. "So, the validity of my claim hardly comes into the question. In fact, this welter of conflicting laws is, from our standpoint, the magnificently incoherent and deliquescing fruit of, what?—close to four hundred years—of Imperial legislation, decrees and ad hoc local decisions."

"I begin to see your point, Master." He didn't sound particularly enthusiastic.

Gaius turned to look at Faustinus. "Of course you do. Now that I've explained it, it's simple: there's so much law now that there's hardly any law at all, really."

"A lesser legal mind than yours might find this paradox disconcerting."

"A lesser legal mind, yes." Gaius looked ahead, and his eyes took on a dreamy look. "But for someone of my scholarship?" He smiled as he considered his scholarship. "As the law recedes like a tide, one just trudges, squelching about to one's ankles in the exposed muck, gathering up long hidden, if rather dripping and sometimes noisome, opportunities."

"Quite a figure of speech."

"Thank you. It's all part of my training."

"Yes, I was there." They rode on a few moments in silence as Faustinus hid his dubious expression by adjusting the set of his wide straw hat against the lowering sun. "So, you're confident of success, Master?"

"Yes, I am. If I get my half—even a third—then fine. If not, the process is the punishment."

"So," Faustinus looked at him sardonically, "it's a win-win situation. Like tossing a two-headed coin."

"Very apt." Gaius looked around the village as they came back to it. "A two-headed coin. Yes." He glanced over at the soldiers who were now leaning up against the tavern wall hoisting cups. The landlord stepped out, wiped his hands on his apron, and grinned alarmingly at him. Gaius knew, somehow, that he had just spent a great deal of what little money he had.

V

GAIUS FILES A LAWSUIT
AND HEADS TO UPPER GERMANY

* * *

After their arrival at the mansio in Milan, Gaius spent half a day drafting the complaint in his lawsuit against his brother. "Here, Faustinus. You take this to Aulianus Crastinus. As it'll soon be midday, I expect you'll find him at the courts in the Imperial Forum. He'll remember me from the last year he was studying with Enthymemus before he came up here to make his way." Faustinus took the document, now rolled and carefully sealed, and looked at it doubtfully. Gaius said, "The complaint's all drawn up. All Crastinus needs to do is file it."

"As I recall, you didn't care much for him."

"Nobody does. He's a nasty little bugger and just starting out, so he's doubtless ruled entirely by his worst instincts; he's perfect for this case because he'll be cunning, vicious, and cheap." He handed Faustinus his last solidus. "This is for expenses. Now take the complaint and don't dawdle."

After Faustinus's return, he and Gaius passed two more days in the Imperial mansio. Their door let out onto a covered loggia that looked down into a large square courtyard through which a diverting parade of messengers, soldiers, and wagons passed from first light until evening every day. The thirty recruits who had marched at the tail of their column spent those nights locked into a barrack across the courtyard to discourage them from drifting away. On the morning of the third day, the column set out once again, lengthened by a dozen more cavalry, fifty light infantry, six more wagons and three glum low-level secretaries jostling in the back of a wagon on their way to Augusta Treverorum.[21]

Three days later the column had entered a new country, rolling, rising, climbing, cooler. The land sloped all about in broad plains or in abrupt grassy flanks climbing the sides of narrow valleys. The road no longer surged forward regardless of obstacles; it had to negotiate with the landscape, and so it curved along the low areas as it passed north through the Alps. A new optio had taken charge of the column in Milan. He was leaner and more serious than his predecessor, and his manner was an indication that his stretch of the highway was more unsettled, more dangerous than that further south. He scanned the country more constantly than had the first optio, but his attention was less, not more, reassuring to Gaius.

"Surely bandits can't be a threat to us," he said to the optio, hiding his unease behind a studied carelessness.

The optio answered, but kept his gaze on the steep slopes to the right where, here and there, foot tracks led up to settlements and farmsteads hidden among trees or behind outcrops. "Not if we watch." He turned to Gaius and looked at him appraisingly. "No service before this, Tribune?" Gaius shook his head. There was no use in trying to hide his inexperience. "Well," the optio said, leaning forward in his saddle and glancing up to the slopes on his left, "Watch."

"Watch?"

"Watch and be seen to watch, Tribune. You'll likely be left alone." Then he nodded to his right and pointed ostentatiously at a distant figure leaning on staff, or perhaps a spear, far up a slope near the margins of a wood into which he could step back and instantly disappear. "He sees that I've seen him. He sees that we're alert."

"Surely bandits wouldn't attack an armed party this large?"

---

[21] Trier, the provincial capital of the Gallic Provinces.

The optio shrugged. *"Bagaudae*[22]? Sometimes they come a hundred at a time."

"I've never grasped why the Emperor doesn't put an end to them."

Faustinus spoke quietly from behind them: "It's said they have protectors in the provinces, that the Emperor's writ doesn't have the force this far north that you might expect."

"Just pay attention, Tribune. Keep watch and let them see you do it—that puts them off."

"Anything else?"

"A show of force now and then. Always a good thing." The optio tapped his forehead in a salute, turned his horse abruptly and went to the tail of the column to see about things there.

In the evening they came to a walled mansio hard on the edge of the road in a flattish area otherwise surrounded by ground that sloped ambitiously up to mountains whose tops gleamed in mottled white and blue, now shifting to orange as the sun fell. The commander of the mansio, a lean, wiry man about sixty, signaled from the parapet over the gate at the optio, who waved casually back at him. This done, the optio shouted in a startlingly loud voice, "Up front! Boar's head!" The light infantry jogged to the gate, spread themselves into a loose blunt triangle and faced out, the optio on his horse in their midst. The infantry set their shields on edge before them and casually hefted their spears, finding the balance points. They stood confidently: none bothered to put on a helmet, but they swiveled their heads slowly, scanning the slopes all about for movement. The optio glanced at them, satisfied, and nodded to the commander on the wall. The massive wooden gates swung back, grinding on their hinges, and the column went in, horsemen first, then wagons, recruits, light infantry and, finally, the optio with a single, backward glance. The gates ground shut, and the bar dropped into place with a heavy thump.

Gaius's mule came to a halt placidly in the courtyard of the mansio which, unlike those in Italy, was quite plainly a fort. Roughly square, it held a barracks along one wall, lines of stables along two others,

---

[22] Peasant insurrectionists

and a granary and *praetorium*[23] along the fourth on either side of the gate. A half-dozen archers looked out onto the countryside from the parapet.

"Not a very attractive place, this," Gaius remarked, getting off his mule and handing the reins to Faustinus. "Such high walls. It's off-putting."

"Raetia's always been a rough country." Faustinus said, turning their mules over to an ostler. "Perhaps Upper Germany's more placid." His tone skirted the edge of neutrality, but on the whole he sounded sardonic.

"There's been no campaigns up there in a good ten years or so," someone said.

"No campaigns?" Gaius turned around. A powerful young cavalryman in a very fine tunic stood openly assessing him—and clearly with disdain. His soldier's hat was tipped forward aggressively, and he wore a heavy gold ring on either hand. He was clearly an officer, a tribune like Gaius, but above him: a tribune of the Field Army.

"In Germania. No campaigns worth the name in years. With a bit of luck you might see a skirmish or two." His tone was irritating, and he was taller than Gaius, which was irritating too. "Fortunately for you, it's almost as peaceable as the old days. You'd better hope it goes on that way." He poked a finger into Gaius's chest. "Just do your best to slow any rascals that cross the border, and don't get in our way if there's real war." He slapped Gaius on the shoulder with impudent familiarity, turned his back, and sauntered away toward the refectory, where a sinewy young slattern leaned casually in the doorway, one large rough hand against the jamb. She gave him an inviting smile, and he hooked his thumbs into his belt as he approached her and swaggered. Gaius opened his mouth to say something sharp, but he couldn't at the moment think of anything to say, sharp or otherwise. He turned to find Faustinus looking at him with a studied placidity.

"Who the hell does he think he is?"

Faustinus nodded across the courtyard at a wagon with

---

[23] Commander's headquarters.

EQ PRO IUN

daubed on the side. "An officer of the ***Equites Promoti Iuniores***.[24] It looks like a troop of them's headed south."

Gaius and Faustinus watched the man disappear after the woman into the dark of the doorway.

"Probus Martialis," said someone behind them. Gaius turned to find the fort commander—the *praepositus*[25]—at his elbow. "He's been here two days." The old man rubbed the stubble on his cheeks as he measured Gaius up and down. "Thinks a lot of himself. Got a few of his men with him and they do too. You might decide to keep away from him. It shouldn't be hard—he leaves tomorrow for Milan to be accepted in the Protectors[26]. He's going to 'adore the purple,'" as they say." He turned his head and spat. Gaius regarded the lean old officer, searching for something judicious to say, but the old fellow abruptly changed the subject. "I want to show you the country."

"I've seen a good bit of it already."

"It matters where you stand when you see it. It changes things." He headed to the stairway up the wall, gesturing to Gaius to follow him. When they had reached the parapet, the old man said, "Up here you get rather a long view." He crossed his arms and leaned casually, his back against a merlon.

"True enough. And yet I could see the mountains from the road." Gaius kept his tone light and inoffensive. He was flattered that the old officer had taken an interest in him. The praepositus smiled vaguely and then glanced for an instant over his shoulder to the slopes rising to the west. He looked back at Gaius with a question in his face.

Gaius said, "Well?"

"Look, my young friend. Take your time. Look hard."

Gaius hooked his thumbs into his belt in what he judged was the

---

[24] As the name indicates, a cavalry troop. Don't be fooled by the "junior"—it only means they were enrolled after another unit of the same name.

[25] A common, and often imprecise, term for the commander of many different sorts of units.

[26] Special troops under the direct command of the Master of the Infantry (the highest military commander). They often undertook special duties.

proper military attitude and went to gaze out at the countryside. The sun was lowering, half hidden behind a peak, and the shadows of the mountains, unbelievably long, splashed down toward the road. Quite a sight really—not like anything near Narbo. Not like anything in Rome. But what was there to say, really? What was this old officer? Some sort of misplaced provincial esthete? A crank who wrangled strangers into experiencing the natural beauty of the landscape? Trapped as he was on the guard walk, Gaius felt obliged to rummage in his mind for something aptly bucolic, perhaps some poetic phrase. Yes, that must be it. Upon reflection it seemed clear the old fellow was inviting him to join in some pathetic, rural appreciation of nature. Ridiculous, really. He decided it was only polite to join the old codger in his enthusiasm. He thought a moment and then declaimed: "As the poet says, '***Montes qui supersunt nobis nubibusque sub fulgente luna***[27] and something something something...' And, well—" He flapped his hand. "I'm sure you recall the rest," he said, with counterfeit flattery.

"Can't say I do," the old commander cast a quick glance over the wall. "Not very good, is it? Just speaking as an old soldier, you understand." He looked up a moment in thought, sucking his teeth. "One of the minor poets you don't hear of up here, I expect."

Gaius smarted under the criticism: he'd made the verse up himself right on the spot. And though it really wasn't very good, who was this old rustic to judge? When he talked he couldn't even keep his accusatives straight from his datives and his ablatives had disappeared entirely. In fact, when you came to think of it, the Latin had been growing worse the farther he got from Italy.

The old man said frankly, "Tribune, you seem an odd one to be in the army."

Gaius, still embarrassed at his failed poetics, looked down the guard walk to make sure there was no one in earshot and then said, "Of course, that wasn't the poet's best effort," and before the praepositus could agree, he went on. "I'll confess that I'm not very experienced." Gaius knew he wasn't going to gull the old soldier. "Let's just

---

[27] "The mountains that stand above us and clouds, but beneath the shining moon." Gaius never went back to the poem.

say that my enthusiasm for military service is, at present, my greatest asset." He was pretty certain the old praepositus couldn't tell that there wasn't much of that. "As for military science, I expect to pick that quickly enough." He gave the old soldier a smile in which he tried to blend intelligence with the appearance of eagerness.

"No choice, young man. No choice. So you must. And quickly." The old man turned to look over the wall at the wooded slope and took up his earlier topic. "I'd say there are thirty of them. Not more than thirty, though." Gaius looked at him questioningly. The commander came alongside and pointed at the shadow-laden lower slopes that swept from the west of the road up the mountainside. "Look along my arm, young friend. Squint—it'll make things clearer." He did as he was told and found the spot at which the officer was pointing: a band of pines on the wooded slope a half a mile away, now in shadows that deepened as they watched.

"Do you see them?"

Gaius put his hands on the wall and leaned out, narrowing his eyes. "I see some movement. Some flickers of brown. No—tan. Among the trees." He turned back. "Men?" But he knew the answer even as he asked it. "Bandits, you mean."

"You need to learn to see—to notice these things a glance."

"What are they doing there?"

"They're staying off the road while they're in view of the mansio." The old man leaned out over the wall and pointed north. "Look up there, to where that spur hides the road. That's where they'll get back on it."

"Shouldn't we do something?"

"The gate's barred." He turned and leaned back against the wall. "And they can't climb a wall this high. I'll put another few men on the wall walk in case someone gets ambitious."

"But shouldn't we alert someone?" He gestured vaguely toward the south.

The officer chuckled. "Alert someone. Yes. Perhaps I'll call on the Master of the Cavalry for Gaul[28] and ask him to lend us some troops." He shook his head, amused. "But you see, son," the old man's familiarity warmed Gaius, "I'm the only power hereabouts: twenty soldiers, eighteen slaves—men, women and boys—and any soldiers who might happen to be passing through." He looked over his shoulder at the darkening mountainside. "More than enough to hold this place. But enough to go out adventuring?" He smiled and shook his head. "Where's your post?"

"It's on the Rhine in Upper Germany, a fort called Castellinum Ripae. I understand it's north of Argentovaria."

"Wherever that is, you'll be the only power thereabouts. Never forget that. So, look after yourself." He turned toward the stairway. "You'll have supper with me."

"And Probus Martialis?"

The commander shrugged, a small gesture, but full of expression. "I don't like him. Not at all. He can eat with his men." As he descended the stairs, Gaius heard him mutter to himself. "*Nobis nubibusque.*" He chuckled quietly and shook his head, as at a little sad story.

The next morning Gaius was awakened by the familiar chirruping of a poorly greased axle, but very faint, very distant. He climbed to the wall before breakfast to stretch his legs, and glanced up and down road. Half a mile in the distance Probus Martialis's column headed south toward Milan: twenty horsemen and three wagons, the last, its cheeping call fading in the distance, was one of Gaius's. He spun around and looked down into the court: his furniture was stacked neatly in a pile in the corner where the refectory wall met the stables. He turned back to the road and watched the column and his wagon fade into the distance.

---

[28] The *Magister Equitum per Gallias,* despite his name, was the supreme the commander of all troops, horse and foot, in the Gallic provinces. Upper and Lower Germany were two of these provinces.

VI

ARCADIUS RANKLES AT BEING SUED; TRIBUNE DOLO ARRIVES AT HIS COMMAND

* * *

Arcadius Obsequentius Macro stumped back and forth within the narrow limits of his villa's office, his agitation growing as he ranted at his advocate, Themistius Silvanus. He threw up his hands theatrically, and his dalmatic slipped back and settled over his paunch. He looked mildly ridiculous, which recompensed Silvanus in a small way for the trouble of listening to his maunderings as he sat impassively across the green marble table watching Arcadius's shuttle back and forth. He'd seen this sort of thing before. He waited patiently, a small thin man with graying dark hair.

"How can he do it? What right does he have to contest our father's will? And ask for half the estate?"

Silvanus said nothing, simply waited for him to calm down.

"It's a simple question!"

The advocate watched him without expression.

"Well? Isn't it? Unjust! Father had an absolute right to dispose of his property as he wished! If he wanted to exclude Gaius, then that was his right." He'd been looking up, speaking at the ceiling as it were. Now he stopped and turned on the advocate. "And why not?

He's the younger son—he never applied himself to anything. He was always a bloody trial to me when we were growing up." He shook a soft fist. "All I'm asking for is justice."

Silvanus nodded vaguely. "Sit down, Arcadius Macro. Try to calm yourself."

"How can I calm myself?" He seized the parchment roll on which the complaint was written and swatted the table in a clumsy flourish. "This time Gaius has outdone himself."

Clients who wanted justice, who delighted in chasing an abstraction like a hound a hare, were difficult to handle. As a rule, Silvanus preferred to see a matter settled. Even though a victory in court was best and a loss not necessarily so bad (a loss could pay well if the case dragged on, and the publicity was helpful), a settlement could be lucrative enough and easy into the bargain. So many things to consider, for example what the allegations were and who the judge was.

"Sit down. Please. It will go more easily." The advocate put his hand out for the scroll and waited until Arcadius had seated himself. "I must read the complaint. It may well be baseless," he said to soothe this client. He unrolled the document, scanned it with narrowed eyes.

"What are you looking for?"

"The judge's name." Silvanus looked up, thinking.

"Well? What about him?"

"Not to put too fine a point on it, let me just say that, though you are an esteemed (here he smoothly exaggerated) honestior, all the same this judge's social position is, of course, markedly higher than yours—his brother was a provincial governor years ago. He's married into an important family and so on."

"Well?" Arcadius asked.

Silvanus looked at him and took the tone he might have with a dullard. "This means, Excellent Arcadius Macro, that he cannot be," he took a moment to choose his words, "he cannot be immediately urged into issuing a favorable verdict." He hesitated. "Unless, of course, you have a particularly powerful patron."

Arcadius frowned and then smiled slowly; he was suffused with a warm confidence. "Flavius Syagrius! The Prefect. He is my patron."

Silvanus blinked and then blandly disappointed his client. "It follows, of course, that he's your brother's patron too. We must take that as a draw."

Arcadius leaned forward in his chair and tapped the table for emphasis. "But I'm richer than Gaius. I've got that on him."

Silvanus nodded. "That will help. You say he's just been posted to the frontier? It's reasonable to suppose that he can't yet have built up sufficient savings to meet the expense of prosecuting the case as vigorously as he might like." Silvanus was thinking about what he knew of the army, of peculation and officers selling favors to soldiers. "In other words, he's unlikely to outbid you when questions of law arise."

"I see." Arcadius's tone dripped with cynicism.

Silvanus was a seasoned lawyer; the cynicism rolled off him like water from a duck's back. "Still, for some time at least, we must litigate the case on its merits." He rolled up the document and tied it closed. "One thing though: We need to make the customary gift. But," he added encouragingly, "this judge is not too expensive—as judges go."

* * *

The road led north atop bluffs, the Rhine flowing just below to the east. Graceful slopes, for the most part wooded, climbed dark green to the west. The sun was just hinting that it would set behind a line of gray clouds when Gaius's column, his remaining wagon piled high with everything he owned (and creaking alarmingly with the strain) approached Castellinum Ripae. The light infantry and recruits had been left behind in Argentovaria to be distributed to provincial posts along the Moselle. Only the cavalry remained and the three glum secretaries jouncing about in a wagon at the rear. Two miles ahead the forest had been cut down halfway up the ridge, and the gentle slope below was under cultivation. It was the first farming Gaius had seen after twenty miles of unremitting woodlands and empty slopes. He pointed ahead with a calculated carelessness meant to suggest confidence and said to the optio, "Castellinum Ripae. Just ahead." He hoped he was right.

The optio agreed that he was.

Inspired by his lucky guess, Gaius continued. "A tight unit, I should think. Situated up here as it is facing off against the barbaricum."

"Well, as to that..." The optio's reply faded away.

"They're all tough as nails, no doubt. Yes, tried and true." The cliché bothered Gaius, but it would do until he could find a better one.

The optio just nodded and smoothed out his face. Then he coughed softly and added, "As good as any border soldiers in the province." He tapped his mount with his heels and moved to the head of the column, avoiding further conversation.

"It's a good thing you bought a horse back in Argentovaria. To cut the right figure before these crack troops," Faustinus said riding up alongside.

Gaius didn't care for his supercilious tone, but the jade turned her head and tried to close her great yellow teeth on right toe, so he concentrated on tugging ineffectually at the reins. His horsemanship had improved during the journey, but this mare tested its modest limits. He glanced with barely hidden envy at Faustinus's mule and then straightened in the saddle and peered ahead, distracted by the fields coming into clearer view. He nodded ahead. "This looks promising, Faustinus. Very promising. There must be a good a hundred acres under cultivation and another hundred of grazing. What do you suppose the skim is? A twelfth? Say, thirty solidi a year? That'll more than pay for gifts for the judge in the lawsuit."

"What about the attorney? What about Crastinus?"

Gaius waved dismissively. "Don't worry about him. It'll be the judge who's more expensive." Two dozen brown cattle browsed in the grass over a broad sunny slope ahead. He began totting up figures in his head. "A hundred acres, twenty-four cattle. And that's just what we can see from here. There must be swine too and vines on the slopes down to the river." He smiled at Faustinus in his enthusiasm and looked up, thinking. "A twelfth of all that..."

"I think, Master, that you may be overestimating."

Gaius turned and looked at him sharply. "Be quiet a moment; I'm adding up sums in my head."

"Your pardon, Master." Faustinus knew that fractions were extremely difficult for him.

Distracted, Gaius gave up on the arithmetic. "So, you think I overestimate? Well, I'm an optimist. Call it a fault if you like, but I suspect we can exact a little in passage tax along the river too. These ideas just flash into my mind: I begin to think I might have some unsuspected talent for the military life."

"Undoubtedly, Master. But if I understand the custom, a commander's skim is from his soldiers' pay, and these villagers and farmers—not soldiers." He paused for emphasis. "And besides, it's likely that many of them pay their rents in kind to the garrison. Their goodwill may well be worth more to us than whatever you could extort."

Gaius prickled. "Why do you have to spoil things when you see I'm enjoying myself?" He rode on for a few moments and then sighed. "I suppose I'll have to concede your point. Still, there's the usual skim from the soldiers' pay; the exact figure depends upon the size of the garrison. And then there's dockage and passage tax along the river. I see definite possibilities there." He nodded to himself, and his voice took on a more hopeful tone.

After another half-hour they came upon the outskirts of the village. It had grown up within the slumping ramparts of an old legionary camp set up a couple of centuries before when the legions were still big. The optio dispatched one of the riders to announce Gaius's arrival, and then he headed off with the rest of the troop, leaving Gaius, Faustinus, and the leaning wagon behind. This last was now driven by an old peasant they'd found wandering down the road a mile back.

Gaius and Faustinus sat their mounts as they looked about and took in their new surroundings. A paved way led from the highway and cut through the slumping bank that had been one of the ramparts of the old legionary camp. Sheep grazed along the top of it, cropping the grass to a low green velvet. Through the opening in the bank, they could see the houses of the village huddled along the street. "This must have been the old Porta Sinistra," Gaius said, showing Faustinus that he knew a thing or two about military history.

The cavalryman sent to announce Gaius's arrival trotted briskly out from the village and shouted as he passed, "You've been announced." He flung a negligent salute, turned north on the road, kicked his horse into a canter and was gone after the rest of the column. As he vanished, it struck Gaius suddenly, and with great force, that he was on his own, sent to do an unfamiliar job in a strange country. He suffered several moments' unease before his usual baseless self-confidence returned, after which he said to Faustinus, "Look at that wagon, piled up like that. It's practically tipping over. And that rustic with the reins. He really lends a touch, doesn't he? We look like we're fleeing an invasion."

"At least they've left it too us—and the mules to draw it."

Gaius gave him a withering expression. "Only for a week until the optio takes the whole equipage back when he returns south." He handed Faustinus his straw hat and pulled his military cap from his belt and settled it on his head. "Go find my sword. It's a bloody nuisance the way it slaps into things every time you turn around, but I've got to look martial when the command is handed over. What's the commander's name again?"

"I really don't know." Faustinus slid off his mule. "I suppose you might have asked the optio." Before Gaius could scold him for his implicit criticism, Faustinus was at the leaning wagon, lifting out the tailboard. "You have two swords, Master. Which do you want?"

"I do? I didn't realize that. Well, whichever one looks more impressive."

A few moments later Gaius, wrapped in his commander's cloak, the more impressive of his swords at his side, rode down the road into the village. Faustinus followed close behind and then the creaking wagon, teetering hard to the left like a drunkard in a strong wind. The rampart they had passed through was one of four, each about two hundred yards on a side, that made a great squarish enclosure. Here and there sections of masonry remained, but most of it had been stripped away over the years for building.

The village within amounted to about a hundred habitations— houses and hovels—straggling along the street or fading back from it along narrow alleys. Most were of timber and daub; a few of the more impressive were built on footings of stone taken from the old ramparts. A small church stood away to the north, an old pagan temple to the south. A patchwork of fenced gardens sprawled toward the north and west, and a piggery had been established up against the western bank, its smell wafting gently over the settlement.

A handful of cows wandered complacently up the street toward them, followed by a small boy who swatted listlessly at them with a switch to keep them moving. Roosters distributed widely throughout the village crowed with a strident regularity. A crowd of all ages gathered along the way, bowing as Gaius's diminutive entourage plodded down it toward the heart of the village: a half dozen ramshackle buildings and a half-timbered tavern at the edge of a small forum. A lanky woman of about twenty-five stood among the crowed. Her hair was bound up in a cloth and she wore a stained apron over her shift. She watched him with narrowed eyes and held the hand of a little girl who stared up at him, wide-eyed and solemn as he rode off, trailed by Faustinus, the alarmingly tilting wagon, and a handful of villagers gawking at a respectful distance.

The far side of the little forum had been kept clear up to the end of the former legionary camp where, nestled in what had been its northeastern corner, stood a stone fort, the home of the Second Pannonian Horse and of the Milites Feroces. The fort was a grim square of gray stone with walls of forty feet topped with battlements standing out like square teeth against the gray afternoon sky. The main gate was fitted with heavy wooden portals, now drawn back, and behind them a raised portcullis were just visible in the shadows of the gateway. Gaius frowned at the fort. Wasn't it a shade small? How did it house a cavalry troop and an infantry cohort? Maybe it went back further than it looked, some odd provincial trick of perspective. Anything might happen up here.

"Three years in this place," Faustinus said. The gray clouds were hurrying in from the west, threatening rain.

Gaius clucked his tongue. "A bit drab." He nodded and then pointed with his thumb back over his shoulder to the village and the cultivated slopes beyond it. "But let's not forget the scope this situation offers for profitable activity. Of course the garrison will be a bit understrength—they always are—but even at, say, eight hundred men, the skim should be considerable."

"Then perhaps you would consider freeing me? Cost is hardly a consideration now that you're so well set-up." Faustinus wasn't particularly hopeful, but it never hurt to press the question. At some point, in a thoughtless fit of magnanimity, his master might just do it. You never could tell.

"Cost is always a consideration, Faustinus." A vague suspicion about the size of the garrison had begun to unsettle him. He firmly turned his thoughts away. "Tell that rustic to hold the wagon out here until he's called for."

"Certainly. There must be no dilution of the grandeur of your entry."

Gaius had no chance to censure him for his sarcasm, for in the next moment they were in the shadowed gateway and passing out into the courtyard of the fort, where the men stood quietly in ranks to receive him, big oval shields and spears grounded. A dozen others peered down from the walkways atop the walls.

"It seems a few men are missing," Faustinus murmured.

Gaius silently counted the first row of men: twenty-two across. They stood about seven or eight deep. Shouldn't there have been eight hundred men at the fort? Well, at a good least seven hundred, even if there'd been a few losses and lackluster recruiting? He began to feel some serious misgivings about his command. His rough multiplication came to less than two hundred men. He thought for a moment, idiotically, that there might be a second troop somewhere, that several hundred men were off on some expedition that somehow and—incredibly—no one had mentioned to him on the way to fort. Even the commander seemed to be missing. Gaius scanned the courtyard and the entrance to the praetorium but saw no sign of him.

As he sat his horse, wondering quite how, precisely, he was to accept the command of the garrison, a rough-hewn centurion of about forty-five shambled up to him with the rocking gait of an old injury. He doffed his cap. "Welcome, Master Gaius Obsequens Dolo, Long Awaited Tribune of our noble soldiers. Vellianus Arverno here,

Head Centurion, overjoyed—as indeed we all are—to greet Your Nobility." He turned to the soldiers and waved his arm; they gave a dozen cheers, ragged at first, and then passably enthusiastic at the end. Gaius nodded affably at the soldiers, put his hand out and took from Faustinus the wooden diptych laced with a scarlet cord that set out his commission.

"Centurion Arverno, where is your tribune?" He sat up in the saddle as tall as he could and grandly held up the diptych. "You see here His Serenity's Imperial Commission, which custom requires that I present as the command is exchanged." Gaius assumed a censorious expression. "My dignity requires that your commander receive me. I may say that I am not pleased with the snub."

"Indeed not, your," Arverno seemed to think about this for a moment, and then bowed—a short bob, really—to show respect. "Quite right, Your Exactitude. You are of course quite right. A snub. Yes, quite the right word, Your Clarity. How, indeed? How could Your Pomposity not be otherwise than snubbed? Or is it otherwise?" The old officer looked away and tried to think though his syntax, but couldn't do it. In the end he fobbed the task of construing his statement back onto his new commander: "Of course, Your Sublimity can appreciate and understand what I am trying to say."

"Despite my natural sublimity—and thank you for remarking on it—I don't follow you at all. For the well-being of your listeners, I insist that you abandon any further attempt at rhetoric and leave that skill to those who have been trained to employ it. Rhetoric in the wrong hands is dangerous, and your discourse is certainly an object lesson in that regard."

The centurion bobbed again. "Very good! I thank Your Magnificence for the instruction."

"Now, send for your tribune."

"Much as I would like to oblige Your Magnificence, I simply cannot."

"Indeed? Why not?" Gaius tried to sound irritated, but he felt a certain relief. Now he wouldn't have to face some hardened veteran of the German frontier, crewcut and battle-scarred, with leathery fists, the muscles of an ox and a short temper.

The centurion smiled happily. "Because, Your Greatness, our former commander handed the command to me two weeks ago, and left the business of the fort under my care until Your Splendor's arrival."

"Really? That's extraordinary." It certainly seemed rather a breach of military discipline though, as a novice, he could not be quite sure. He asked, "Who is this fellow? What's his name?"

"Probus Martialis."

"Probus Martialis?" Gaius looked up in thought; he'd heard the name before. Faustinus whispered at him. "The Tribune of the Equites Promoti Iuniores."

"The bastard who stole my wagon!" Gaius was confused. "But he's in the Field Army."

"He stole your wagon?" Arverno said. He rubbed his chin thinking deeply about this interesting development.

"You find this in character for Martialis, Centurion?" Faustinus asked.

"Quite so…" He hesitated and then pressed on: "Quite so, your Helpfulness." It was clear he was unsure of Faustinus's station and couldn't tell how splendid a form of address to use.

Meanwhile Faustinus glanced over the assembled soldiers. Their eyes were fixed on the new arrivals, their heads turned ever so slightly to catch the odd word here and there. Faustinus saw his chance and seized it. "I am Tribune Dolo's Domestic[29]. You may address me that way." Gaius started sharply at Faustinus's arrogated promotion, but then caught himself. He'd sort this out later when he wasn't in front of the common soldiers. If he could.

"Domestic?" The centurion's tone suggested he sought a name.

"Faustinus Aquitanius," Faustinus said, giving himself a last name too. Gaius gaped at him. It was time for the slave to stop enlarging himself, but he'd stolen such a march on him that he was helpless for the moment. Arverno nodded and took up the earlier thread.

"Martialis got himself promoted, Domestic." The centurion stepped close, looked at both Gaius and Faustinus, and dropped his voice. "I expect that's why you're here to take command, Your Excellence. All

---

[29] Personal assistant. Aide-de-camp. Faustinus has just given himself a promotion of sorts.

the same, I might say it surprised us all—his promotion came rather sudden and unexpected. Not that we weren't glad to see the back of him, if you'll excuse me for saying it, Your Splendors."

Gaius frowned at being lumped together socially with Faustinus.

"Well, don't concern yourself with the mysteries of administration, Centurion." Gaius grew rather lofty. "Leave it to those who, like me, are trained to it. Instead, turn your attention solely to military duties: guarding the fort, commandeering supplies, patrolling the roads hereabouts, collecting rents, scaring Germans, exacting taxes, charging customs duties. Those sorts of things."

"Of course, Your Lugubriousness." He bowed, and then, as an afterthought, he pulled a letter from his belt.

"And don't call me that again," Gaius warned.

"Certainly not, Your Punctiliousness." He flourished the letter. "What I do have, Your Magnificence, as you might say, in recrudesence—"

"In recompense," Faustinus corrected him. "Though I don't think that's quite what you mean either, now that I think it through."

Gaius gritted his teeth. "Yes, yes. What is it?" Between Faustinus's self-promotion and the old centurion's ramblings, he was growing peevish.

"A letter from His Magnificence, The Consul of the West and Prefect of Italy."

"From Flavius Syagrius?" This was startling. "What about?"

"Men who tower like that, they don't write to men like me, and so I certainly don't know, Your Effulgence." He held the letter up for Gaius to take. "And I don't read so well either."

"The Consul Syagrius is the Tribune's patron," Faustinus told him, much louder than necessary. He looked out of the corner of his eye to make sure the men in the front rank had heard. Good—he might as well reinforce Gaius's stock before the troops. He turned to Gaius. "You certainly receive interesting correspondence these days, Master."

"Centurion," Gaius said casually, as though imperial correspondence were an everyday occurrence, "hand the letter to the Domestic here. I'll read it later." Gaius swung out of the saddle, pleased that a month on mule and horseback had taught him to do it with passable skill, and he ascended the tribunal to give the men the set speech he had memorized from a form-book some weeks before just for this occasion. The sky was now completely overcast and a steady rain began. Which paragraphs could he leave out of his harangue? In the near distance, just beyond the gate, he heard the squealing sound of overstrained wood, a great dull thump, and the indignant honking of two angry mules. The wagon had just tipped over. He sighed, drew himself very straight, cocked his hat at a jaunty angle, and stepped forward to give his first address to the sodden troops.

VII

GAIUS RECEIVES UNSETTLING NEWS

***

Gaius relaxed in a chair, his feet on a stool, and gazed about the shabby little sitting-room of his personal suite in the praetorium. The rain continued: water dripped from the eaves overhanging the high row of windows and splashed noisily outside. A weak light filtered into the room and gave everything a pallid cast. Quite different from Italy, he mused. He pulled his cloak a little more closely around him. Faustinus sat turned halfway away from a small table and leaned casually back on one elbow. "Perhaps you might like to know what the Prefect Syagrius has written to you?" The letter lay unopened on the table.

"His continuing interest in my situation is rather puzzling."

"It does seem difficult to explain." Faustinus paused a moment for emphasis and then went on wryly: "Moving in the rarefied air of the Imperial Circle as he does. That he deigns to shift his scrutiny from the supernal heights of Empire, scene of countless imperial transactions of the highest significance, toward the rude banks of the Rhine where a half-forgotten but plucky officer toils to lead—by his martial example—his troop of rustic but doughty soldiers in the maintenance of the frontier and—"

"That's dreadful, Faustinus. Really dreadful. I wish you hadn't amused yourself during Enthymemus's lectures by paying close attention to them. You should have followed my example and let your mind wander. And I really wish you wouldn't indulge yourself in a parody of what I remind you is *our* present situation."

Faustinus ignored the reprimand. "Your father was Syagrius's client, but I don't believe he ever spoke to him directly."

"He did actually. Once. He told me he attended Syagrius's Morning Salutation at that ornate townhouse of his in Narbo. The one dripping in marble and silk. Can they drip? I suppose not."

"Despite the figure of speech, I know what you mean."

Gaius glared at him a for a second. "In any case, you get the picture. It must have been twenty years ago, though."

"Did Syagrius do him the high honor of actually speaking to him?"

"If I recall, my father told me that Syagrius said something to the effect of 'How pleasant to see you. How are things in the countryside?' Or maybe it was 'How are the sheep doing this summer?' The Great Men seem to favor a sort of gentleman-farmer image when they aren't at court climbing over each other for position." He leaned his head on the back of the chair and looked up at the beams of the ceiling. "Go ahead. Read me the letter."

Faustinus broke the seal, took a few seconds to scan the page and then began.

"From Flavius Afranius Syagrius, Spectabilis, Consul, Prefect of the City of Rome and Praetorian Prefect of Italy, to Gaius Obsequens Dolo, Filius Marcii Obsequentis Lutatiani, Tribunus Equitatae Secondae Pannoniorum et Militum Ferocum, Greetings."

"Yes, yes. You can skip the front matter."

"I think you should savor every word—one doesn't receive a letter from the Second Man of the Empire every day," He read the introduction over again and went on:

"Congratulations on your position in the ever-victorious army of His Serenity and Splendor the Emperor Gratian. His Serenity joins me in reposing complete confidence in your vigilance with regard to enemies of any sort and in your complete loyalty to Himself. As a client of mine, who owes much—if not indeed the largest part—of his current good fortune to my patronage, you are of course aware that your prospects for the continuation of that good fortune are bound up in the proper exercise of your abilities and in the zeal with which you carry out your duties. Those duties, it pleases me to remind you, may well require a certain attention directed not merely toward the petty German kings across the Rhine, but also to any interesting developments within your province or those bordering it. You will understand that the interests of the Empire may depend upon your duties as client to myself, which interests require your diligence in the execution of the duties necessary to secure them. Please receive my wishes for your continuing health and good fortune."

Gaius sat up. "Any more to it?"

"No."

"It reads rather oddly, doesn't it? Apart from the stilted language. High marks for that. Still, it's understood that I'm to carry out my duties. Within reason, that is—like everyone else. So why send the letter?"

Faustinus stared at the letter. "Perhaps the point of it is to clarify your duties."

"My duties are soldiering, of course. Whatever the precise meaning of the term."

"That's part of it, Master. That's part of it. But don't you think this implies something more?" Faustinus tapped the letter meaningfully with the back of his hand.

Gaius looked out at the rain and then turned back, a little fretful. "Maybe."

"Clearly, the Prefect Syagrius wants you to act as his personal agent as much as anything else."

Gaius shrugged. "It's a reasonable construction. But what can I do up here? Really, what is there to do in these parts apart from scratching out a living and watching the Alamans?" He couldn't think of an answer right away, so it wasn't worth puzzling over. He settled more comfortably on the couch. Faustinus, though, folded the letter back into a packet and gazed at it thoughtfully.

* * *

The rain had stopped by the next morning, but Gaius stayed indoors. He had some important questions to settle, in particular the exact number of soldiers in the garrison and the state and extent of the finances of his command. They held much more interest for him than the drill being conducted in the courtyard. Shouted commands floated in under the eaves, followed by tramping, clunking (apparently of shields against each other) and a stream of colorful invective. All of this was repeated from time to time. Clearly the martial side of things was taking care of itself without Gaius's interference; this left him free to concentrate on what mattered.

The office of the praetorium was a dusty little room lighted by a high row of small barred windows and a pair of lamps suspended on chains from the ceiling beams. A mosaic of white and black pebbles in simple interlocking squares made up the floor, and a pair of battered wooden cupboards held stacks of tablets of accounts and half a dozen ledgers listing the totals of various things: foodstuffs, money, clothing, arms. A crude bust of the Emperor Decius on a square pillar lurked in the shadows of a corner and stared stonily at him like a ghost from the last century. Or maybe it was of Claudius II, or even someone else—no one knew anymore, but it conferred a faint and faded imperial authority upon the room. Several lines of graffiti decorated one wall: over the years semiliterate soldiers had practiced their misspellings before committing them to the official records.

He looked up from the ledger that summarized the unit's accounts, settled himself more comfortably in his chair and asked, "Why Aquitanius? Why did you choose that name for yourself?"

"I think I was born in Aquitania. I seem to remember hearing someone say so when I was small. Ceio the bailiff maybe—I don't quite recall." Faustinus cast his mind back, trying to recover the memory. He was a little boy standing in a sunlit garden minding a smaller boy who squatted and drew figures with a stick in the gravel walkway of a garden: the little boy was his charge, Gaius. Ceio was speaking quietly in the background to someone else, perhaps behind a box hedge, about Aquitania. The memory was like a dream: inexplicably clear on one point and blurred on all else.

"It seems likely," Gaius said. "Anyway, you're stuck with the name now. Doubtless, the garrison's taken it up by now."

Faustinus smiled to himself. This was just what he wanted. There was no way Gaius could undo it.

"I'm not sure you needed a last name." Gaius persisted and put his finger on a figure in the ledger to keep his place. "It's not as though you're free. It might lead to confusion—your having two names."

"Of course if I were free, no one could make that mistake." Faustinus opened one of the cupboards, looked among the books, and took one out.

"What mistake?" Gaius glanced over at him.

"The mistake of thinking I'm free. Because I would be."

Gaius glanced at the ledger on the table in front of him and scowled at a misspelling. "Let's not bring that up now. As with any new situation, there are many things to deal with, and we don't need anything to distract us."

"It was just an impulse," Faustinus said. And that was true, though he was glad to have succumbed to it.

Gaius shrugged. "Well, let it go." He looked up at the roof, listening as the rain began again—autumn was creeping in.

"Why '*kalendae*' with a C?" Why '*inceptum*' with a k?" Gaius mused, looking down at the ledger. "The spelling in this ledger is atrocious." He shoved it aside.

"Perhaps the clerk didn't have your advantages—assiduous study under a trained rhetor such as Enthymemus."

"That's pretty evident. If they keep up with this sort of thing, they'll be speaking their own language up here."

Faustinus brought over the ledger he had taken from the cupboard and set it in front of his master. "Here's the muster roll, on these pages." He ran a finger quickly down the columns of names and looked at the total at the bottom of the second page: CCLII. "Two hundred and fifty-two. It's not the eight hundred you'd hoped for, but it's a good deal more than I'd have guessed from what we saw yesterday."

Gaius still looked glum. "But even this figure..." He hesitated a moment. "It's only about a quarter as many as I'd expect for two units." He rubbed his temples. "Am I losing my mind? How many men in a cavalry troop?"

"Something under five hundred. Four hundred and fifty, I think. At least officially."

"So, what should it come to really? Three hundred and sixty, say, what with lax recruitment, retirements and the occasional loss here and there?"

Faustinus shrugged. "You're the soldier, Master, but that number seems about right."

"And the same for an infantry cohort."

"Officially."

"So, three hundred and sixty again." Gaius slid the beads in their slot on the abacus by his elbow. "That comes to seven hundred and ten."

"Seven hundred and twenty," Faustinus corrected him.

"I wasn't quite done," Gaius said crossly. He slid another bead to correct the error. "So where are the missing men? We're more than four hundred short."

"More than four hundred and fifty."

"Stop correcting me. It's vexing."

"I'm only helping." Faustinus knew the expression always vexed Gaius.

Gaius, distracted by the problem of the troop numbers, let the remark go. "I was uneasy when I saw the size of the fort, and I could see how few men were turned out when we arrived yesterday, but I assumed quite a number must be off on some maneuver. Or repairing a road. Or building a wall somewhere. You know—whatever it is they do when they're not actually fighting. Which is most of the time, really. And yet, that can't be right: the muster roll shows we've only a fraction of the soldiers we should have." Gaius rubbed his finger over the number at the bottom of the page, as though it might get bigger—but the number stayed the same. "This is all rather unsettling."

Faustinus looked at him with facetious concern. "Half the unit lost on the second day without even a battle to blame it on. I wonder how the Duke[30] will take it? Perhaps you'll find a way to blame it on the Alamans."

"This is no time be a wag, Faustinus. You talk airily about your freedom, but here I am faced with the strong possibility that the chance to puff up my income has been reduced by what?—two thirds?" He pointed at the slave for emphasis. "You're not getting freed any time soon if things continue this way." He stared down at the ledger disconsolately and then said, "Call in that old centurion— what's his name?"

"Arverno." Faustinus went off after him. Gaius sat staring fixedly at the unit's numbers until Faustinus returned with the centurion, who hobbled in shaking the rain from his rough brown cloak. Gaius looked up from the ledger and spoke straight to the point: "A question for you, Centurion: where are the other men of the garrison?"

Arverno looked at him, puzzled. "What other men?

"Look here. This muster roll shows only two hundred and fifty-two men in the fort." He tapped the ledger with his finger.

Averno looked mildly surprised. "Well, Your Exactitude, that seems an odd number, to be sure." He rubbed his chin.

"Yes, it is rather an odd number," Gaius replied.

"Not strictly speaking, of course. It can be divided into two equal parts."

Gaius closed his eyes while he gathered his patience. "Keep to the point. The question is this: why does this muster roll indicate that the unit has only two hundred and fifty-two men?"

"As to that, I really couldn't say, Your Excellence."

"And why not? You're the senior centurion." He clasped his hands on the table and looked as commanding as possible.

"I haven't ever seen the books. Not up close, you know. I've seen them lying about, of course. But not the pages of them, you see. I'm more of a field officer, you might say. Ordering the boys about, collecting the odd tax, seeing to it when the Alamans trade on this side of

---

[30] The Latin is *Dux*, a word for military commander. "Duke" sounds rather odd in a Roman context but, as there's no good alternative, the reader will see it again. The title was often given to the commander of border troops in various provinces.

the river they pay customs duties." He lapsed a moment into reverie and added: "I had to boss a gang of the boys to repair the masonry around the west gate. You can see what's the new stonework—it's a bit lighter. I'm rather proud of that."

"Yes, yes."

"But, I've never done any clerking." He pointed to the ledger. "So I can't tell Your Exactitude why the book doesn't agree with what's what."

"You're veering off the point again." Gaius closed his eyes and sighed. "Let me put it directly: why are there only two hundred and fifty-two men here in the fort?"

Arverno frowned at the question. "But, Your Magnificence, there aren't."

"There aren't what?"

"The two hundred and fifty-two. That number's not right."

"That's a relief."

"Happy to oblige, Your Excellence." He straightened up, full of pride. "To be exact, as I'm sure that Your Precision would wish me to be, I must say that the number stands at two hundred and two."

"Two hundred and two!" Gaius gawped at him, trying to make sense of the number. It kept getting smaller, like a ship sailing away. He said in a small voice, "But that's fifty less than the muster roll."

Arverno squinted in thought, started counting on his fingers and then nodded. "I believe your subtraction is correct, Your Magnificence."

Faustinus smiled wryly and observed, "The more we look into the garrison, the more it dwindles. Perhaps we should stop our investigation while we still have enough soldiers to man the walls."

Gaius felt as though he were standing on some crumbling bluff, helplessly watching as the ground slipped away beneath his feet. He took control of himself and said, "This is no time for levity, Faustinus."

"Cynicism, actually. It's more sophisticated. Remember your Enthymemus." There was no sense in missing this chance to recall to his master the hours during which he'd waited at the back of the classroom and listened to the old rhetor's rambling and detailed instruction—and paid attention.

"Well, whatever it was exactly, we don't need it now. Remember you're stuck up here with me and in quite the same difficult position." He turned to the officer. "Let's get back to the numbers." He rubbed his eyes as though he were waking from a bad dream.

"Yes, two hundred and two is quite right the right number. That's to say, apart from two dozen calos[31], the blacksmith, the baker, the cook, the grooms and the cobbler. As far as the soldiers, there are one hundred and eighty-six of them. And then sixteen officers. Not counting yourself, that is. And, of course, we officers are as ready as any of the common soldiers to face the foe. *Ferociores sumus gregaribus*[32], as the poet says."

"What poet?" Faustinus asked. He leaned against the wall with his arms crossed, smiling to himself.

"I can't really say, Domestic Aquitanius, now that you ask."

"And neither am I," Gaius added. "So let's put aside the poetics and answer the question."

"And that was, Your Inquisitiveness? If Your Excellence would be so kind as to remind me?"

"Where is the other half of the unit?" He thumped his clasped hands on the table desk to emphasize the question.

"They're nowhere, Your Splendor. Or, that's to say, they're all here."

Gaius rubbed his face with his hands and looked over at Faustinus beseechingly.

"I believe the Centurion means that two hundred and two is, in fact, the total number of the garrison." It was just the answer Gaius had feared.

"Yes, Domestic Aquitanius. Now, it's true enough that eight of the men are on duty at the moment three miles down the road at the watchtower where they can keep an eye along the road to Argentoratum[33] and down on a reach of the Rhine. There's a split in the road there; one branch goes off west somewhere. First, towards Tullum. After that..." he shrugged. "I can't say where it goes. A long way, I'd guess. Maybe

---

[31] *Calo*: Camp servant

[32] "We're as ferocious as common soldiers." Hardly worth a footnote, is it?

[33] Now Strasbourg.

to Lutetia?" He looked at Gaius as though he might know.

"Thank you for your interesting geographical speculation."

Faustinus said, "What the Noble Tribune wants to know, is why the soldiers here don't number about seven hundred."

"Seven hundred?" The old soldier was startled by the question. "Why so many?"

"A troop of cavalry should come up to about five hundred, and so should a cohort of foot soldiers. That's a thousand. Discount that number for losses and lax recruitment, and you should still have seven hundred. Maybe more."

Light dawned on the centurion. "As Your Excellencies will know, no unit in the army is up to strength. Circumstances—well, they get right in the way. Take a cavalry troop—our Pannonians for example."

"It would seem an apt example." Gaius crossed his arms across his chest and sat back, working to be patient.

"If the wing had even four hundred men or so these days, well, I'd consider that about full strength, whatever the army says is an official troop size."

"Four hundred then. But why only about a hundred now?"

"Oh, that!" Arverno chuckled. "That's nothing for Your Amplitude to concern himself about, if I may be so bold as to suggest what it is that Your Amplitude should worry about. My apologies, Excellence, if I go too far."

"Keep going," Faustinus interposed. "Where are the rest of the men?"

"It all has to do with His Serenity Valentinian's campaign. The one against the Alamans some years ago." The old centurion pointed over his back with his thumb as though the past lay somewhere behind him.

"Wait. What?" He had to think a moment to see what Arverno was getting at. "So, they were lost in the campaign?"

"In a manner of speaking, yes."

"It seems rather a lot," Faustinus said.

"That's right." Gaius agreed. "Half the men lost? And it was a successful campaign." It was appalling to think of—what had he gotten himself into by accepting a military commission? He braced himself and asked, "How were they lost?"

"Two hundred of our Pannonians were joined to Valentinian's Field Army as what they call *pseudocomitatenses*[34]. Funny name that, isn't it? But that's what they call them." Arverno shook his head as he thought of it.

"Well? What happened to them?"

"They were joined to some other troops up at Moguntiacum[35]. You see, there was talk that some Alamans would cross the Rhine up that way, but they never did. The rest of our men, they were left here to hold this fort."

"Now we're getting somewhere. Good. So, where are these others now? The ones sent to Moguntiacum?"

"They're still there." He nodded to the north. "A hundred and eighty miles that way, I guess it is. They're called the Equites Moguntiacenses now."

Gaius finally grasped the situation: they had been stationed there for fifteen years and they weren't coming back.

"It happens to a lot of units, Your Magnanimousness. Take the Cuneus Gallicanorum, for example. They're over at the fort near Noviomagus, but they only number about sixty. Where the rest of the unit got sent to, who knows? Word is that some are in Britain and some in Egypt."

"An enthralling geographical conjecture." Gaius was desperately trying to recalculate the loss on his projected income. "And our foot troops? The Feroces?"

"A detachment of them was brought in, oh, about ten years ago. There must be some others somewhere else, but we've got eighty of them." Arverno smiled proudly.

"Well, that's splendid."

"Thank you, Your Effulgence. And, if I may say something, our numbers may be an advantage quite soon."

"Oh yes? Believe me, I'm eager to learn how having so few men could be of any advantage." Gaius's cynical tone was wasted on the centurion.

---

[34] Border Troops drafted into the Field Army. It is a funny name—half Greek, half Latin.
[35] Now Mainz.

Arverno looked around to make sure the office door was closed, took a step forward and spoke quietly. "Merobauda tells me—in confidence so the men don't worry—that there's a problem with our supplies."

"A problem? What problem?" Gaius could not see how a problem could be an advantage and, what was more, he found the name distracting. "Merobauda—it seems a suspiciously Alaman name."

Arverno nodded. "Indeed it is! Not suspicious, of course, but Alaman. It's a nickname, Your Excellence. To keep her straight from the other two Cornelias in the village. Three Cornelias in the village, well, Your Excellence can see how that can be a challenge to anyone coming into the middle of a conversation."

Gaius watched Arverno in silence, impressed with the man's uncanny talent for veering from the point of a conversation. Arverno plodded on. "Her father was Aulus Cornelius Merobaudes. And so we just naturally call her Merobauda after him."

"Merobaudes?" Gaius involuntarily repeating the name.

Arverno looked at him in surprise, "As I'm sure your Excellence recalls, Merobaudes is the chief military commander of His Serenity the Emperor Gratian." He seemed confused by the apparent question.

"Don't be obtuse! Not that Merobaudes, you—" Gaius contained himself with an effort. "This other Merobaudes. This woman's father. That one!"

The light dawned on the centurion. "That one, yes. Well, he enlisted young, saved his pay, and set up as the landlord of the tavern by the forum when he got mustered out. And now his daughter keeps it."

"And she's the one telling us we have a problem? This woman who keeps a tavern?" He put his hand up to stop Arverno from answering. "Just tell me what she says this problem is."

"Well, Your Excellence, it's just that we don't have enough supplies to make it until next spring. Merobauda—she's a pretty direct speaker, you might say—she says we'll be boiling our boots for soup come March."

"How would this Merobauda woman even come to know this?"

Arverno spread his hands. "Of course Your Magnificence has only been here a day, and so you wouldn't know Cornelia Merobauda is the fort's *actuarius*.[36] Actuaria, really." He looked back and forth between the two men.

"You mean that this woman keeps the garrison's records," Faustinus said, grasping the point while Gaius sat trying to take in this latest bit of startling news. His afternoon had taken on a dreamlike quality. Some aspects of it were entirely ordinary, while others were quite otherwise, but somehow treated as commonplace.

"Is that even legal?" Gaius finally managed to ask with a touch of indignation. "I mean, mustn't the garrison's bookkeeper be in the army?"

"Well, now," Arverno said, trying to help. "As to that, I couldn't say. But we do have a number of women here in the fort, as Your Perspicaciousness may have noticed." He counted off on his fingers. "My wife, another six wives of other officers. The cook's wife. And the blacksmith's, and baker's, and carpenter's of course. A good three dozen of the common soldiers have wives too, though we don't let more than about half of them actually live in the fort. It's just a matter of discipline."

Gaius, by dint of great effort, called his attention back to the important question. "Do you mean to say that this Merobauda woman is let into the books because she's a soldier's daughter? Is that what I'm to understand?"

"Well, Your Eminence is quite right about her being a soldier's daughter. And she was a soldier's wife too, but she was widowed about two years ago. You see, Your Effulgence, her husband—he was one of the optios—he was returning from a visit to a cousin..." He nodded toward the east.

"Across the Rhine?" Gaius asked. "You mean to say, he was visiting the Alamans?"

"Well, yes." Arverno looked surprised at the question and then added: "Not all of them, of course. Just a cousin. Or maybe two of them. I don't recall the particulars."

---

[36] As used here, a bookkeeper. Arverno is doing his best to find the proper ending for the word.

"Just a cousin. That's a relief, I'm sure." Faustinus smiled sardonically at Gaius.

"His name was Rutuolf, by the way."

"Yes, yes," Gaius said wearily. "What about this Rutuolf?"

"Your Excellence, he was struck by lightning."

"What?" Gaius felt a bit stunned himself.

"In the dark on the way back to the river. Struck by lightning. It's a rare thing, Your Magnificence."

"Thank you for the reassurance."

"Perhaps there's a a good deal more lightning on the other side of the Rhine than over here," Faustinus suggested. Before Gaius could address his facetiousness, Arverno plowed on: Coincidentally, he was riding a horse when it happened."

Gaius simply stared at the officer, unable to work out the significance of this equine detail.

"And yet the horse was untouched." Arverno went, marveling at the thought of it. "Apart from being startled, of course. But that's to be expected." The centurion shook his head wonderingly. "The horse used to be called 'Foggy' because he's a gray, but now the Alamans call him 'Lucky.' Perhaps Your Excellence would care to see him? We could take you across the river to visit the cousin. They're very proud of Lucky." Arverno, inexplicably, seemed to share in their pride.

"I think we can spare His Excellence that," Faustinus said, heading off further talk about freak weather and horses.

Gaius plodded on, trying to grasp the situation. "Do you meant that this Merobauda woman's tenuous relationship to the army is why she's let into all of our private affairs?" He leaned forward for the answer. Who could say what her intrusions might have resulted in, and what effect they might have on Gaius's plans? He pressed the centurion further: "Quite apart from noting and inventorying the supplies, has she had any hand in reckoning the finances—the soldiers' pay and the Emperor's bi-annual gifts to them? Has she had anything to do with those?" Gaius kept his voice bland, but it was an effort.

"Oh, yes! None better than her, Your Effulgence! You should see how she can add and subtract, Your Honor. It's a thing to see. And multiply and divide. No one's ever seen anything like it!"

The centurion's inexplicable enthusiasm for Merobauda's arithmetic was just another utterly perplexing feature of their exchange, and he couldn't think quite how to reply, so he took up a stylus and fiddled with it.

"And now, if Your Magnificence has no more need of me," Arverno said, "I should give the password for the evening and set the watch." He nodded at a window that framed a dimming sky. Gaius nodded and waved him away—he'd had enough of the disconcerting interview. The old soldier turned back as he reached the doorway and pulled up the hood of his cloak. "The boiled boots, Your Excellence. By March." He smiled with childlike trust at Gaius. "Of course, Your Competence, now that you're here, there's nothing for us to worry about." He beamed, bowed and went out.

Faustinus leaned against the wall with his arms crossed and watched Gaius with a wry smile. "Arverno's confident you have a solution." He waited a few moments more. "You do, of course, have one?"

Gaius flapped a hand negligently at the question. "Oh, I'll come up with something."

"What are a few missing tons of food, after all?"

Gaius sat back in his chair. "You fail to focus on the most important aspects of the situation."

"Oh, yes?"

"The important questions are these: What has this Merobauda woman been up to? Has it cost us anything? If so, how much?" Faustinus looked at him dubiously. He was thinking of the shortfall of supplies.

They heard grinding of the gates closing for the night, and the clacking of the dogs on the gears as the portcullis was lowered.

"We'll talk to her tomorrow," Gaius said.

VIII

SOMETHING IRREGULAR
IS GOING ON

* * *

During a break in the spring rain Gaius took a tour of the wall for a glance at his surroundings. He and Faustinus stood on the guard-walk atop the eastern wall of the fort, which overlooked a steep bluff down to the Rhine, where a narrow island covered in green brush seemed to navigate like a galley down the middle of the reach, the water foaming gently past its southern end. Tall grass and bullrushes bordered the far bank, which rose more gently than that on the Roman side. A dirt road—really, just a wide path beaten by centuries of feet and wagon wheels—climbed the bank to disappear into trees crowding down to the river. The road led into the canton of the local Alamans and their settlement a few miles away. Now, what was their king's name? He'd ask Faustinus; he paid attention to details.

Below them in the courtyard officers shouted, men trotted about on errands, and the guard changed. The main gate creaked open and the portcullis rumbled like distant thunder as it was drawn up. A dozen men climbed the stairs to different points on the walls, and the dozen on the last watch went down to their breakfast. Another four relieved the guards on the towers and scanned the country, each with a crossbow resting against the wall. Gaius made a point of looking and nodding sagely in all directions as though he'd seen this sort of thing countless times before and that it was all done to his satisfaction. That done, he rested his hands on the wall and looked down its face to the bluff below. A small gate at the foot of the wall gave onto the top of the bluff, down which a stout timber stair led to the fort's dock, to which three skiffs were tied. At the top of the stairs a crane leaned out over the bluff ready to hoist loads. As Gaius gazed downriver to the north a freight barge came upriver, drawn by a pair of mules ambling along the tow-path. A man walked along leading them on a line, while another sat in the stern of the barge, his hand on the steering oar.

"She's full of barrels," Gaius observed as she went slowly past. "Wine or beer. Or flour."

"She's probably headed with supplies to Argentovaria."

That made Gaius think. "Hmm."

Faustinus cleared his throat quietly and asked, with unaccustomed diffidence, "Master Gaius, now that I'm officially your Domestic, I'll naturally be called upon to carry out any number of duties for you."

"Of course you will." Gaius continued to look over the parapet at the little barge as she went by. "Pretty much as you do now. Only with a surname. That should make your work more pleasant."

Faustinus ignored the inanity. "That's just it. The surname suggests that I am a free man—and this might help in any number of situations…"

"Perhaps." Gaius answered absently. He leaned out over the parapet to get a better view of the barge. "I suppose we could interrupt the river traffic a bit. To collect some tolls, you know. What do you think of that?"

"From boats supplying the army camps? Like that one?" Faustinus was peeved at Gaius's inattention, and his voice showed it. Gaius turned in mild perplexity at his tone.

"I think I'm missing something here," he admitted.

Faustinus took a deep breath and plunged ahead. "It's this: if the mere misapprehension of my freedom is helpful to you, consider how much more of an advantage you would gain by actually freeing me."

The approach was clever; Gaius had to admit that. He looked vaguely into the distance just as though her were giving Faustinus's remark careful thought. "A rather canny argument. It has that neat and vaguely specious quality one so admires in Enthymemus's rhetorical instruction. But then, you were at his lectures too."

"I didn't sleep during them, if that's what you mean."

Gaius looked narrowly at Faustinus but decided not to press the question of who it was, exactly, he implied had been sleeping. Instead he decided upon an economic defense. "I told you not to hound me about your freedom, when you can see that my prospective income has been so severely reduced." He gave Faustinus a severe expression. "We only have two hundred and two men in the garrison."

"There is something odd going on, Master."

"Something odder than that?"

Faustinus brought up a theory he had been mulling over the evening before as he reflected on the disparities between the ledger, the muster roll and the centurion's statements. "Is the question really how many men are serving here, or how many men are on the muster roll or whatever they call it?"

"The 'return,' I think they call it. What officers send to Milan to establish the official numbers of their units. But what are you getting at?"

"When we looked at the muster roll it showed two hundred and fifty-two men in the garrison. But we know that's fifty too many."

"It's probably the fault of that woman with the Germanic nickname. The one who can't spell properly."

"Are you sure?"

"Of course I'm sure. She spells *'inceptum'* with a **K. *'Inkeptum.'*** It jumps right off the page. Who knows what else she's capable of?"

"Forget the spelling, Master. The question is: why doesn't the muster roll agree with the number of soldiers actually here? Why does it show fifty more soldiers than we have?"

Gaius looked up and down the wall-walk to be sure there was no one in earshot and then asked Faustinus what he thought. "Well, you tell me. Why doesn't it?"

"Because there must be another ledger, a second one."

"But why?" Gaius asked. "It's enough trouble to keep one ledger. Imagine how tedious bookkeeping is. Why double the work?"

"Because a second, but accurate, ledger would help the commander keep track of the actual expenses and pay of the garrison."

Gaius considered this for a few moments. "A second ledger. Different from the one we saw yesterday?"

"Exactly. So, two sets." Faustinus mustered all of his patience. "A true ledger with the real numbers of the cohort and a false one that says the garrison is fifty men larger than it is."

"I take it that you're positing something quite different from the usual government ineptitude." He reflected on this possibility. "Do you think that's likely?" He took off his military cap and let the fresh breeze from the west ruffle his hair. All the thinking had warmed him up.

"Yes, Master, I do."

Gaius shook his head doubtfully. "Where the government is concerned, ineptitude explains everything."

"Consider this, Master: the numbers in the official ledger don't agree with the number of men. Why bother to keep inaccurate records?"

"All right. Why?"

"For some purpose other than actually keeping track of the men and supplies."

Gaius caught a glimmer of where he was going. Faustinus went on: "If the government sent supplies and the Emperor's twice-yearly gift for an extra fifty soldiers—soldiers who aren't really there—all of that would go to the commander, wouldn't it? He could keep the money and sell the extra supplies for even more cash, and that would go to him too."

On hearing this, Gaius felt suddenly warmed as by the sun on a summer morning, and he grew hopeful about his situation. More hopeful anyway. He tried to recall when the emperor's birthday was and when he'd taken the throne; those were the dates when the donatives— the Emperor's gifts—were sent out. "I see your point. If you're right, this could help a great deal." Faustinus saw Gaius look up as he tried to calculate in his head. He said, "Don't try to work it out, Master."

"You're right. I'll use the abacus when we get back to the office."

"No, Master. I've only pointed this situation out to protect you, not to encourage you to continue the practice. I suggest," and here he assumed a factitiously humble tone that he hoped might convince his master, "that you stop the practice of collecting supplies and money for any phantom soldiers before the practice comes to light."

"Stop trying to be my keeper. That was your task twenty years ago. Why can't you keep up with the times?"

"Old habits are hard to break."

"I'll say." He clucked his tongue at Faustinus and then turned his mind to more important things. He rubbed his chin and concentrated on his multiplication tables. "Even though the unit is far under strength, the supplies and donatives for fifty 'phantom' soldiers would give me the income that I'd expect from the skim on a garrison of…" He arithmetic failed him. "Of what?"

Faustinus watched him coldly and said nothing. Gaius snapped his fingers impatiently. "Come on! Help me here!"

Faustinus continued silent for a few more moments and then relented. "It should be equivalent to the official skim on a garrison of about four hundred and fifty men."

Gaius beamed at him. "Really?" He looked about him exuberantly. "I have to say, Faustinus, your theory looks promising, quite promising. If your guess about the ledger is correct, then all we have to do is continue on along the trail blazed for us by that bastard Tribune Probus Martialis: collect the pay and donatives of the phantom soldiers, sell their supplies, and squirrel everything away. Seems simple enough."

"But, Master, that's extremely dangerous. I only revealed my suspicions in order to warn you."

"I don't want to hear any more defeatist talk." Gaius put up his hand. "If Martialis has been squeezing out a little extra pay from the army, he can't be the only one. Do really think a lout like him would have thought this up on his own? Really, Faustinus. Sometimes you surprise me with your dangerous innocence."

"So, I take it that there's no point in cautioning you not to continue this practice?"

"There's risk with any grand enterprise, Faustinus." He crossed his arms and stood his tallest, leaning back the littlest bit in what he took as a heroic pose. He'd seen a great many statues in Rome.

"So, the answer is 'no'."

"Quite right. The answer is 'no'." He clapped Faustinus on the shoulder. The slave gritted his teeth. Gaius settled his cap at a jaunty angle. "We'll be safe enough. The ways of the Imperial Administration, at every level, seem rather—what? Hopelessly intricate, I think is the way to put it. Imagine: layer upon layer of law and bureaucracy, each woven of strands at odds with the others, some seemingly cooperating and yet all at cross-purposes like a badly woven rug: thin here and there, lumpy in most places and fraying at the edges."

Faustinus winced at the simile, but kept to his point. "So, your plan is to rely on government inefficiency to escape detection." It was not a question.

"Bluntly, yes."

Gaius turned and leaned back against the wall, his face up to the mild sunshine. "The immediate question though, is how do we confirm our theory?"

"*Our* theory?" Faustinus let that go. "Cornelia Merobauda may be a help."

IX

TRIBUNE DOLO MEETS
THE LOVE OF HIS LIFE.

* * *

A young woman swept boldly past Faustinus and into the praetorium office towing a small blond girl-child with one hand and brandishing in the other a pair of wooden tablets tied up and bound with a seal. She released the child and pointed, without looking, at a battered chair in a corner. "Sit there and be quiet." The little girl trotted over to it, clambered onto the seat and sat swinging her legs a few inches above the floor. She looked solemnly over at Gaius, who sat at the worktable trying to work up some interest in the day's duty roster. He looked up, disconcerted at the woman's boldness and obvious familiarity with the surroundings. He seemed to think he might have seen her before, but he couldn't imagine where.

"Here," she said. "These are for you." He took the tablets without comment and glanced at them. His lawyer Crastinus's name was printed across the top: doubtless news of his lawsuit against Arcadius. Well, that would be worth looking at, though he'd first have to dismiss this young woman.

Faustinus closed the door and announced: "Master, let me present Cornelia Merobauda." Gaius put the tablets aside and looked up at her. Now he could see that she was the woman he'd seen standing before the tavern in the village when he had arrived: about twenty-five, tall and thin, her dark blonde hair drawn back snugly and tied in a knot with a black ribbon. She wore a long, unbleached tunic over a longer light gray shift. Her little brown shoes shone faintly of oil. She was dressed in the provincial style, but very neatly. That was some concession, at least, to his authority and importance.

He hesitated to speak. He had intended to overawe her before questioning her closely about burrowing through the garrison's secrets; she had to be deeply involved in them, but he opened his mouth and then closed it like a fish. He searched for some way to start, but Merobauda beat him to the punch. "Well?" she asked. Her tone implied that he was keeping her waiting. Gaius was nonplussed. What did she expect of him? Finally he laid a hand on the tablets she'd brought him. "How did you come by these?".

"Those? I ran into Arverno in the portico bringing them in. He talks too much. If you haven't noticed that, you will. I knew if he got here ahead of me, I'd wait half the morning to see you. So I brought them myself."

"I see."

"You're welcome." She sat down without being asked. She gave Gaius the impression that he was sitting on the wrong side of the table.

Gaius pushed the tablets a little further away to indicate that they had moved beyond that subject. He needed to take things in hand before she asserted herself further, but he couldn't think quite how to do it. He glanced at the little girl, who continued to stare at him as though fascinated. He pulled at the sleeves of his tunic and sat up straight in his chair. He fidgeted with a stylus as he tried to think how to start. Gaius had meant to subject this Merobauda woman to a harsh interrogation, but her confidence defeated him. Finally he said, more mildly than he had intended, "I understand that you keep the books of the garrison."

"That's right." She looked boldly at him. He sensed that she was sizing him up.

"Perhaps you can tell us why?"

"What's there to explain? There can't be any problem with the books."

Gaius and Faustinus looked in surprise at each other, impressed with her bravado. Faustinus smiled faintly; Gaius did not.

"There can't be any problem with them because I don't make mistakes."

Gaius was staggered by her assertion but managed to say, "An interesting claim, to be sure. But we'll put that aside for the moment. Tell me, how do you come to be doing the bookkeeping? Arverno says you took it over from your late husband."

"I did it for him while he was alive too."

"Then how long have you kept the books?" Gaius's distress at the situation was growing.

Merobauda crossed her arms and looked up to her left for an instant. "Three years. I started in the early spring a little over three years ago."

"But why?" Gaius asked.

"Rutuolf—he was my husband—was sloppy with figures. The books were in a mess, and the tribune—Martialis—said he'd break him to a common soldier, and we'd lose the extra pay. Rutuolf was a pay-and-a-half soldier—you know: for the extra work, for the bookkeeping."

"What I would like to know is how you, as the wife of a soldier, were able to learn the job."

She shrugged. "There's nothing to it really. Just columns of numbers and totals."

"So, you can read and write?"

"Of course!" She gave him a haughty look, folded her arms and crossed her legs to show, by her casual attitude, her contempt for his surprise. She glanced at Faustinus and nodded her head at one of the cupboards against the wall. "Look in there on the top shelf. You'll find an abacus. Faustinus rummaged in the cupboard and brought it out. He offered it to her, but she kept her arms crossed and shook her head. "Give it to the Excellent Tribune." There was a hint of amusement in the way she said 'Excellent', as though she were flattering a child. Gaius shifted uncomfortably: he didn't like her tone. And he didn't like arithmetic either. Faustinus set the abacus down before him.

"Now, Cornelia Merobauda, I think we're drifting off the point here." Gaius looked down at the abacus with a mixture of unease and distaste. It reminded him of his lessons as a boy on the estate in Narbo.

"Twelve," she said.

"Twelve? Twelve what?"

"Just twelve. And nine. And sixteen."

"Twelve and nine and sixteen what"

"Just add them up. They come to thirty-seven."

"They do?"

"Just add them." Her tone was sharpish. "And while you're at it, add two-hundred and eight to it and take away thirty-two. That comes to two hundred and thirteen."

Gaius gently pushed the counters about, and after a while he said, "No. It comes to two hundred and nine." He grinned at Faustinus, proud to have bested the young woman. She snorted. "No, it doesn't. You're as bad as Rutuolf! Do it again." She pointed at the abacus.

Gaius, rather overwhelmed by her, worked at it again and then nodded sheepishly.

"Now, subtract eleven, and then nineteen, and then add eighty-eight. After that, tell me how many times sixteen goes into all that."

"Just give us the answer," Gaius said, pushing the abacus away.

"It goes in almost sixteen times, but not quite. So, fifteen times and the remainder is eleven sixteenths."

Gaius stared at Faustinus, who was smiling at her virtuosity. Faustinus asked her, "What is nineteen thirteen times?"

She waved her hand at him for asking something so simple. "Two hundred and forty-seven."

"And nine-and-a-half goes into that how many times?" he asked, watching her closely.

"Twenty-six times. Exactly. You can't trip me, you know. No one can." She smiled, softening for the first time as she looked at Faustinus. He smiled back and said, "You can't make mistakes of arithmetic, can you?"

She shook her head. "No. The answers just come to me. It's a gift." She looked back at Gaius. "Now, Tribune, why did you call me in?

The books are up to date. And," she added rather tartly, "correct in every detail."

"Can we leave soon, Mama?" The girl spoke for the first time.

"Yes, soon, darling." She smiled at the girl.

Gaius, nettled at Merobauda's confidence, opened the ledger and turned it about so that she could read it. Here, at least, there was something with which to take her down a peg or two. "These, then, are your entries?"

"Of course." She didn't bother to even glance at the page; she kept her eyes on his face.

"Ah. That explains things," he said with petty self-satisfaction. He put on a superior expression.

"What things?" Merobauda sat forward an inch, a hint of suspicion in her voice.

"Oh, this, for instance. And this and this." Gaius pointed among the entries. Merobauda pulled the ledger to her side of the table and scanned the text, four tightly written columns in dark brown ink; from left to right were words or names and then figures, then words and names and then figures again. All done in a very neat hand. After a few moments she shrugged and sat back. "Well?"

"It has to do with the entry for June when our last load of grain was received and entered."

"Anyone can see that. It's right here," Cornelia Merobauda said, pointing to a line in the ledger. It read *"frumentum per kopias reseptum."*

"Yes. But you see, this *S* should be a *C*, not an *S*. "

Merobauda's eyebrows went down, but she didn't say anything.

"And, what's more, the *K* should also be a *C*." He said this with less force: he could tell from her expression that his assertions had no effect on her confidence.

She looked at him witheringly. "So, you're telling me both the *S* and *K* should be the same letter. You're saying they should both be *C*." She smiled craftily at him, as though she were leading him into a trap. "Why should the *S* be a *C* ?"

"Because *C* sometimes sounds like *S* ."

"Sometimes."

"Well, yes," he conceded. "Except, of course, when it's hard *C*." He made a hard sound: "Kuh."

"So, just like *K*."

"Well, yes," he conceded further. "Sometimes."

"So this *K* should be *C* because *C* can sound like *K*. But only sometimes."

"That's right." He could see the trap closing.

"But *S* is always *S*. And *K* is always *K*."

"You could put it that way."

"Then *S* and *K* are all you need." The trap was sprung.

"It's just not what people do. And this is an official document." He was irritated with Faustinus, who was clearly enjoying the byplay.

"People do all sorts of stupid things," she said. Her tone implied he might just be one of those people.

Gaius thought a moment and tried a final maneuver. "Look, in Italy *C* is sometimes like *CH*. They say 'chuh' there for it. Well, sometimes. And that's different. So…" He couldn't really think how this helped him, now that he reflected on it.

Merobauda gave him a superior and indulgent smile. "What's that to us? We don't have that sound. And, besides, we're not in Italy."

He threw up his hands. "So, not only are you a human calculator, you're a provincial spelling reformer. Do you have any talents I'm missing? Apart from brewing, that is?" She loftily ignored these last comments.

"Are we finished, Tribune?"

"Not quite. Through a clever process of deduction, I…" and here he threw a quick glance at Faustinus, who kept a bland face, though robbed of the credit due him, "I have deduced that there are two ledgers. One, as it were, is the 'official' ledger, and the other is the true ledger by which the everyday business of the garrison is tracked." He beamed; he couldn't hold back his pride.

Merobauda smiled superciliously. "That must have been the work of twenty minutes once you'd counted the troops and seen the totals in the book." She pointed across the table. "Why is that ledger even out?

You should have the other set out instead in case there's an inspection. That ledger—" she pointed at it—"should be back in its place."

"So, you know about the two ledgers! And where this one goes."

"Of course. I set them up and I take care of them both." She pointed again. "You really should put that one back."

"Where should it go?" Faustinus asked.

"In the bedroom, where it belongs."

"Whose bedroom?" Gaius asked.

"Yours now, I suppose. It used to be Martialis's." She nodded in the direction of Gaius's sleeping quarters.

"What? You've been in that bedroom? With Martialis?"

"It was strictly business."

"That's what I'm afraid of," Gaius said.

"Not that kind of business." Her tone was very sharp. "The chest where he—you—keep your clothes. The one on the east wall. It has a false bottom. Evidently you haven't noticed it."

He shook his head.

"Well," she said, "let's go and get the other ledger. I'll show you how to tell them apart."

X

FAUSTINUS AND MEROBAUDA
HAVE A LITTLE TALK.

* * *

Merobauda's tavern was the rambling building of timber and daub at the edge of the forum, its interior lighted by a half-dozen little windows distributed irregularly in the longer walls. A kitchen smoked at one end behind a counter made of a roughly planed baulk of timber darkened by decades of spills and greasy smoke. The tavern was floored with bricks salvaged from some forgotten old building. Most bore the stamp of a long-gone Eighth Legion that had held the earlier camp, a legion broken up and redistributed through the provinces by the vagaries of administration and civil war. The atmosphere was dark, warm, and pervaded by the heavy sweet-sour smell of stale beer. The odor of boiled lentils and sausage mingled in the fug. It was late morning and the place was empty.

Merobauda watched from behind the counter as Faustinus stepped into her tavern. He glanced about the place, at the uneven walls, the bare rafters above, the shadowed corners, the shaft of sunlight spilling in from the far window. A row of greasy sausages hung—out of reach of the customers—over the brick stove. It was no worse than one of the better places in the Subura. He took a seat at a table near a wall. *What's he here for?* Merobauda asked herself, narrowed her eyes for an instant, and then, practical as ever, said to the old woman who helped her, "I'll take care of him." She took up a jug of beer and a cup, went over to his table and set them down. Now he would have to talk to her.

He nodded his thanks, though he didn't reach for the jug. He seemed suspicious of it. She shrugged and poured some beer into his cup. It was a challenge. He took a tiny sip of beer and smiled weakly.

"You like it, then?" His reaction amused her.

"It's the best I've ever had," he said truthfully.

"You've never had any before."

"I'm sure it's excellent."

"It is. Everyone agrees. Even you." She gave him wry smile— unexpected, but a smile.

Faustinus smiled back. She was a sharp one, all right. He toyed with his cup but didn't bring it his lips. "I'm not here for refreshment," he said. "The Tribune sent me."

"Did he, now?" She sat down across from him without being asked. "What for?"

"To tell you he wants you to continue to keep the garrison's accounts."

"What with his views about spelling, that's generous of him." She seemed amused at the squabble over spelling. Faustinus thought, *She's rather handsome when she doesn't frown.*

"It's a good decision on the Tribune's part." She leaned forward conspiratorially. "He wouldn't get the right answer half the time if what he did on the abacus is any indication."

"I suppose that's true enough, Cornelia Merobauda. Still, I wouldn't push him too far."

She waved a hand at him. "Push? That's nothing."

"He has his pride."

"Dolo. Dolo's his name."

"His cognomen. Yes."

She thought a moment. "A dolo's a trick."

"Well, yes. It can mean that. In Latin, anyway."

"He comes from Italy, doesn't he? Actually from Rome. That's unusual."

"He was studying there. He's actually from Narbo. We both are. The estate's there." He pushed his cup aside. "Do you have any wine?"

"An estate? So, he's rich? That explains why he's a tribune without any experience in the army. I should have figured that out for myself." She shook her head slightly embarrassed at missing the inference. Then she answered Faustinus's question. "We have some white wine. It's sweet. Not very good, frankly. The best gets sent down the river to Argentoratum." She called in a language Faustinus did not understand—Alaman doubtless—across the empty room to the old woman at the counter and turned back to him. "Tell me about the estate," she said, with feigned casualness.

"The important thing to know is that it's gone." The old woman stepped up with his cup of wine, trailed by the little girl Merobauda had taken to the praetorium the day before.

Faustinus took a sip of the wine.

"Well?" Merobauda asked, stroking the child's head.

"Not so bad." He'd had worse, but not by much.

"Better than beer, anyway?"

He smiled without saying anything.

"How did he lose the estate?" She seemed not so much disappointed as curious. She took the child into her lap. "Is the Tribune a gambler?"

Faustinus shook his head. "He'll take chances now and then, that's true. But not for sport." He hesitated a moment. "No, the estate was seized to pay for a sudden military tax." He looked away as though the thought pained him. "His father was in charge of collecting it just before he died—he was a duumvir that year. There was a big shortfall."

"He didn't see it coming?"

"I think he did, but he couldn't do much. He was maneuvered into taking the fall by the other nobles. The government sold the estate to one of them make up the difference. The Nebulosi have it now."

"They're powerful. They have an estate hereabouts too." She nodded to the west. "A few miles over that way." She sent the child off. "Is there any other property?" Her directness startled to Faustinus, but it was guileless, he could tell.

"His brother has an estate outside of Milan, but it's his." No sense in mentioning the lawsuit. "The Tribune has only his commission."

She changed the subject abruptly. "You miss your home, do you?" She surprised him by asking about his feelings.

"Actually, yes. And I'm sorry for the Tribune." He looked down a moment, embarrassed at discussing his feelings with this unsentimental young woman. "You know I'm his slave, but I was attached to him when we were boys—to mind him, you see. And keep him out of trouble. He was about five, and I wasn't much older—eight."

"Did you keep him out of trouble?"

"Oh, sometimes. And sometimes I had to share it. I think I may be true now."

"That's why you're advising me not to vex him, like about the spelling and the arithmetic?"

"I suppose so." He smiled at her. "I'd like to say that it's because, if you keep it up, he'll throw you out of the job and give it to some unfortunate like me." He looked down and at his cup of wine. "And you'd lose those half-rations you get paid for doing the bookkeeping." He shook his head. "But, in the end, somehow—and I don't really know why—I think it's that I don't like to see him humiliated."

"So you worry about his feelings? Well, he's going to have to toughen up if he's going to run the fort. You should have seen how Martialis encouraged the officers to beat the men for the slightest things."

Faustinus sat back. "I don't expect much of that. I just hope he can find some other way to handle them."

A large figure darkened the open doorway for a moment and then lumbered in. A blocky man with astoundingly powerful shoulders and arms and a dull expression on his face stepped into the tavern and waved a greeting to Merobauda. Faustinus noticed a truncheon hanging from his belt. The fellow trundled over to a stool in a far corner, sat down, crossed his arms, and fell asleep.

Faustinus gave Merobauda a quizzical look.

"Parvinus." She leaned across the table and spoke quietly. "He's got a limp and they say he's too dull for the army. But he's loyal, strong, and fearless and, limp or not, they can't get away from him in here. I feed him, and he sits there in case I need him. He's very good at keeping order. For the most part, he does it just by napping where the customers can see him."

Faustinus sipped his wine and glanced at the huge man cloaked in the shadows of the corner.

"I give him a big bowl of lentil stew and sausage twice a day. And beer, of course."

Faustinus nodded and sipped his wine.

"It's mostly charity: there isn't much trouble here. But it gives him something to do." She grew reflective. "I can tell it's important to him to have job, something useful to do."

Faustinus glanced around. "So this is a quiet place?"

"For the most part, though we did come near to having a little trouble about a month ago. A handful of officers from the Field Army passed through. At first they dickered over the bill, and I thought things would turn nasty, but Parvinus got to his feet, and a few of the locals backed him up." She looked away for a moment in thought. "It was odd, though."

"What was odd?"

"There were half a dozen of them: three tribunes and three *ducenarii*[37] from a cavalry troop headed north."

"What was odd?" he repeated.

"It was odd they didn't stay at the fort—or even stop there. They could have eaten and had their horses tended there for nothing. And they had swords—they could have done pretty much whatever they wanted here. But suddenly they seemed to want to disappear. You know, like when you say something awkward and everybody looks at you. You just want to shrink away and be forgotten. They could have stood off Parvinus and villagers, but they just paid up and slipped off on their horses into the night."

She sat back and returned to the earlier topic. "So, anyway, tell me: if the tribune isn't rich, how did he get his commission? I know they don't come cheap: Martialis complained about what they cost."

"His father, through his patron Afranius Syagrius, got him a place

---

[37] *Ducenarius,* a subordinate cavalry officer.

in the army since his brother got the other estate."

Merobauda's eyebrows went up in surprise. "Syagrius? He owns a third of Gaul, or so they say. And who knows what in Italy and Spain?" She glanced toward the tavern door beyond which the fort perched in the distance over the river. "What's a little border tribune to him?" Faustinus grimaced at her casual frankness.

"As I said, a client. Saving him from penury adds to Syagrius's glory, I suppose. Though I admit that Gaius seems rather small fry to him."

"Syagrius is a courtier of the Emperor." She rested her chin in her hand. "Imagine rubbing shoulders with the Emperor." She looked into the middle distance. "Pretty splendid, I suppose. All that marble and gold leaf and fancy clothes."

"And all of the obsequy," Faustinus added.

"What's that?"

"A fancy word. It means 'fawning.' When you meet the emperor, it's called 'adoring the purple.'"

She looked contemptuous at the expression. "I suppose they have to keep things high-toned at court."

"Let me ask you a question about one of your own expressions. What about about boiling boots?"

"She looked at him quizzically and then grasped the allusion. "So, you've found out. Arverno must have told you." She looked up and away, doing a quick calculation. "Say, two hundred and fifty people—a hundred and eight-six soldiers, sixteen officers. Their wives get rations too. And then there's you and the Tribune. Some of the officers get one-and-a-half rations, some two. The Tribune gets five. We'll estimate the extra for the officers and wives: a little over thirty should cover it. That comes out to two hundred and sixteen rations a day."

"You could round that to two hundred and fifteen. To make the calculations easier."

"I don't need to." She looked crossly at him and then softened. "You'll run short by about March the second. The next regular shipment comes in the middle of April. That's about forty-five days shortfall at two pounds of food a day. So, that's nine and eighteen twenty-fifths tons of food that you're short of. That's a rough figure, of course. I had to guess a couple of numbers, but the arithmetic is perfect."

"Of course."

"So, it's a very close to that figure." She looked at him very seriously. "You need to come up with those supplies, or you'll have a mutiny in the spring. Well, maybe not a mutiny, not if you're lucky."

"You don't need to illustrate the danger." He frowned. "But what happened to the supplies? Were they never received?"

"Oh, they were received. What I didn't realize for a while was that any had gone missing. I took an inventory of the stores last week and saw right away that Martialis must have sold them."

"But where?"

"Probably across the river or to a barge passing by. The supplies didn't go through the village, or I'd have known."

"But the soldiers? They'd have done the loading."

"They do what they're told. And how would they know it was wrong? Maybe they were told they were loading supplies for the Second Legion upriver at Argentovaria." She shrugged. "It must have been something like that." She folded her arms. "It's obvious what he was up to—getting money to buy his place in Field Army, but it shouldn't have cost that much."

Faustinus thought a moment and said, "It happens that we met him at a mansio in Raetia on our way here. He was headed south to Milan. How does that make sense?"

"The Emperor's down there." Merobauda looked thoughtful. "Some officers of the Field Army are taken into the Protectors[38]. I see it now. His plan was to get a commission as a tribune in the Field Army and then get into the Protectors. He's on his way to Court to jump up another step! It's clear enough: whatever he's got left over from buying his way into the Field Army he's going to slip to someone at court and then—" she tapped the table sharply—"he's a Protector. That accounts for why he sold so many supplies."

"And the men go hungry in the spring."

"You'd better not let them go hungry." She looked sternly at

---

[38] A select group of soldiers directly under the *Magister Peditum*, who formed a sort of staff and sometimes carried out missions as agents of the Imperial Court.

Faustinus. "You've got to look after the men—it's obvious and it's the right thing to do. But there's this too: the Tribune's not a provincial magnate—not any more. But he is a Tribune, and if he keeps out of trouble—and that means looking after the men—he can settle down pretty comfortably in ten or twenty years. At least the way we look at it out here. I wouldn't like to see him stumble over this business."

Faustinus said nothing to that. Merobauda went back to the topic at hand. "I was going to tell the new commander about the shortage, but Arverno beat me to it. So now, Domestic Aquitanius, what's the tribune going to do about it?" She leaned forward. "You want to keep him out of trouble, so here's what you **_don't do:_** don't let him squeeze the village. The garrison gets half of its supplies from us as it is, and half of the men have family here."

"The tribune has something up his sleeve; he's been hinting to me, but he's too coy to tell me." Faustinus stood up.

"I get the impression he tells you everything."

"Generally he does, but not this time. That's why I'm worried." The room suddenly darkened: the windows had all gone vague and gray with overcast. He could hear rain start on the tiles over his head. He looked up for an instant.

"Fall's here. Winter's coming," she said. "It's time to do something."

XI

GAIUS SOLVES A PROBLEM

* * *

Gaius was at the table in his sitting room in the praetorium. Like the rest of his quarters, it was simply fitted out: a heavy table, three sturdy chairs and a blocky couch fitted with cushions lumpy with horsehair. The floor repeated the mosaic of the office down the hall; three windows were set high in the wall for privacy and covered with screens of light wooden slats in the Roman style, as though to block Italian sunshine. The floor was warm and there was a hint of smoke: he had ordered a pair of calos to light the hypocaust. One wall was decorated with a simple fresco of deep red, umber, yellow and black rectangles, the other three were covered in dingy whitewash.

Gaius faced his dinner. Not so bad, perhaps, but not much to enjoy: two hard-boiled eggs, some salad made from pallid, late cabbage and dandelion greens, soup with millet and a few indeterminate chunks of meat bobbing in it, and bread from coarse flour. He waved a chunk of it at Faustinus, who lounged on a chair nearby—now that he was the Domestic he no longer waited on Gaius at the table. Faustinus shifted comfortably. "Well?" he asked.

"This bread is spread with butter, not oil."

"We knew things would be difficult up here."

Gaius murmured suspiciously, eyeing the bread. He sniffed at it. Faustinus said, "I visited Merobauda yesterday."

"Oh, yes?" Gaius took a nibble of the bread and rolled the buttered morsel suspiciously on his tongue. "And why was that?"

"Because you sent me to tell her she should keep on taking with the garrison's ledgers."

"Oh, yes. Of course." Butter, he reflected, didn't taste so bad. "How did she take it?" he asked incuriously. He tasted the buttered bread again.

Faustinus ignored the question. "I thought she might have an idea of what was going on here with the supplies since she keeps the accounts."

"And?"

"She does have an idea about it."

"Well, of course she does. That woman strikes me as altogether too sharp. And she's forceful. Kind of like Boudicca, now I come to think of it. Only thinner. Though I'm not sure she's against us."

"So, I take it you'd consider any advice she might have?" Faustinus folded his arms, sat back, and looked at Gaius. Gaius did exactly the same to him. For a moment there was no sound but the errant creak of a chair. After a few moments, Gaius gave in. "All right. Tell me what she said."

Faustinus told him, emphasizing Merobauda's admonition that they should not despoil the villagers for supplies. He watched uneasily as Gaius began to smile.

"She has nothing to worry about. I've worked out a brilliant solution. You wouldn't have expected any less of me, would you?"

"I suppose not."

"I sense your—what's the word?"

"Dubiety." Faustinus had learned a good deal from Enthymemus.

"Yes, I suppose that's it. But you're wrong to be dubious about my plan. You'll soon see it's a masterpiece of simplicity and elegance."

Gaius sat forward at the faint sharp sound of a whistle. Moments later Arverno rapped on the door, entered and announced, "Your Magnificence, the sentinel on wall reports a barge coming upriver."

"Thirty men in the courtyard, Centurion. I want them there now!" Arverno bowed and hurried off.

"Come along, Faustinus. I'm about to solve the supply problem. Oh, and bring some writing tablets and a stylus."

* * *

Gaius and Faustinus stood on the dock of the riverbank below the fort. Arverno and a dozen soldiers stood at a respectful distance, and on the bluff above them a knot of soldiers began to lower a block and tackle from the crane above.

"Now, Master, you might tell me what this is all about."

Gaius turned back from watching the tackle descend. "I couldn't resist keeping this from you; you've been so superior lately.

"Have I?"

"More than just lately, come to think of it." Gaius smiled. "So, it amused me to solve the supply problem by myself and spring it on you as a surprise."

"I see."

"There you go. You sound dubious again." Gaius looked hurt.

"Not at all, Master. I'm looking forward to your solution."

It as Gaius's turn to look dubious, but managed to say, "Much better! Now, I ordered the men on the wall to signal the next time they saw a supply barge heading upriver towards us. I reckon she'll be here within the hour."

"And then?"

"I'll stop her and we'll resupply the fort."

Faustinus looked at him critically. "Your simple and elegant plan, then, is to seize the cargo of a passing barge."

"You make it sound so predatory," Gaius said. They looked at each other in silence a moment.

"But we are going to seize the cargo?" Faustinus pressed.

"Of course not. We're not *just* going to seize the cargo. My solution, as you see, has the elegance of absolute simplicity, but only with regard to gathering in supplies. When it comes to the—" he hesitated, searching for a word, "—the legalities—when it comes to them, then things will get extremely complicated." He looked as though he enjoyed the idea.

"I'm not surprised."

"You see, that's the brilliant part of the plan—"

"I don's suppose you're using the word 'brilliant' lightly? As a fetching rhetorical exaggeration?"

"You know me better than that."

Faustinus admitted that he did.

"You see, the complications will work in our favor. So, the more of them the better."

"I'll have to see that for myself." Faustinus looked at him earnestly. "Please think about the repercussions." But he knew that it was too late; Gaius's enthusiasm for his scheme had fully blossomed, and nothing Faustinus could say was going to squelch it. In his exhilaration Gaius coined an aphorism: *"Quis non audet, non meretur."*[39]

"Shouldn't that second verb be subjunctive?'"

"We won't worry about that right now. We'll put the grammar aside and focus on the task at hand." He walked to edge of the dock and glanced downriver. "Ah! Here she comes."

Faustinus joined him. "You asked me to bring writing materials." He indicated the wax tablets. "But I don't see what my role is in all of this. I mean apart from being seized and handed over to the government and then sold to strangers to do menial work. That will be after your arrest, trial and conviction for misappropriation of property, of course."

"Trust me. You don't know the half of my plan. And stop caviling—you're taking the joy out of this whole affair."

The barge approached, pulled slowly against the current by a pair of mules trudging along the tow-path. She drew enough water to suggest a largish cargo. At Gaius's nod, a pair of soldiers stopped the mules and another pair caught the mooring lines tossed up to them. She was made fast and it was time for business. Gaius sauntered over to the barge to show his mastery of the situation—no hurrying for him. Faustinus, masking his uneasiness with an expressionless face, followed at his elbow. The captain, a big man with a mane of wild

---

[39] Amazingly, Gaius anticipates Napoleon by more than fourteen hundred years: *"Qui ne risque rien, ne gagne rien."*

hair and a weather-beaten face, stood at the gunwale looking up at Gaius and the crowd of soldiers and waited silently to be spoken to. "Welcome to Castellinum Ripae," Gaius said. The captain nodded wordlessly. Gaius glanced at the open hold loaded with barrels, sacks, boxes and crates. He asked the captain's name and told Faustinus to write it down. "You have a manifest, of course. You will hand that over to my Domestic."

The captain said, "Begging your pardon, Noble Tribune, but what's this about? We carry supplies to Argentovaria, to the legion there—" he pointed upriver, "and so there should be no toll." He looked confused.

"Quite right. There will be no toll. Now, let's see the manifest."

"Hello, Mus," Faustinus said, casually. Gaius started and looked around him in surprise and realized that it was Mus who had been leading the mules along the towpath. He had grown an inch since their last meeting, and the sun had lightened his brown hair.

"Hello, Faustinus!" Mus waved in his enthusiasm for his old acquaintances. "And hello—" But Gaius held up his hand for silence. "Mus! Hush! I have business to attend to." The boy looked hurt at the rebuff, and the captain looked over at him curiously. Then he shrugged and headed aft to his little cabin for the manifest. Gaius signaled to Mus, who left the mules in charge of a soldier. As he drew him away he said, "Now, don't ever speak my name to the captain or the crew." Mus looked at him, puzzled, but nodded. "That's a good fellow. It's all army business—you wouldn't understand. But you can help me with your silence. In fact, I'm counting on it, Mus. I must depend on you in this." He gave the young man a meaningful look and watched him till he nodded. The captain returned with pair of tablets and clambered onto the dock. He handed them to Faustinus but kept his eyes on Gaius, curious at the business with Mus. It was no use hiding their acquaintance, so Gaius said heartily, "Tell me, Mus, how you come to be here on the Rhine."

"Well," he hesitated a moment to avoid saying Gaius's name. "Your Excellence, when we reached Marseilles, the voyage to Britain fell through. Our wares—the ones intended for Londinium—were snapped up on the spot, and Aurelius heard of a new opportunity in Carthage. But I'm still for seeing Britain. And so, Your Nobility, I took jobs working the tow-boats and little freighters along the canals eastward out of Narbonensis to see a bit of the world and get onto the Rhine. It's like a highway, the Rhine. Now I'm here, I'll get up to Britain someday…" he hesitated, about to name Gaius, then finished "…Noble Tribune."

"I can't imagine why, Mus. What's there up there anyway? Gloomy weather and a wall at the edge of the world. Still, everyone should have an ambition." He clapped him on the back in valediction and turned to face the captain. He said casually, "Mus here is a client of mine." Then he looked seriously at the captain for effect and said: "As for myself, well, I count His Splendor Afranius Syagrius as my patron. So, see that you look after my little client here." The captain regarded Gaius with a mixture of surprise and awe, and then at Mus, reappraising him.

"Now, Domestic, what have we in the hold?"

Faustinus studied the manifest for a short while. "Fifteen tons of wheat, moderately coarse, in sacks. Six tons of flour in one hundred and twenty barrels. Ninety flitches, smoked, each at about eighty pounds. Baskets of dried apples—two hundred pounds. Thirty tunics of undyed wool. Twenty-five cloaks in the Gallic style—."

"Hooded, that means," Arverno explained, to bring himself into the conversation.

"Twenty-five cloaks in the Gallic style of brown wool stuff," Faustinus finished and looked up.

"And all accounted for, Your Excellence. All of it is," the captain said defensively.

"I'm sure it is, Captain. I'm sure it is." He feigned scanning the tablet Faustinus held out for him.

"Now, if all this is about a toll," the captain went on. "If it's about a toll, though I'm assured by the supply officer and by yourself there's no toll be assessed…" He coughed softly into his fist. "Still, I'm sure something could be arranged to recognize the honor and importance of Your Splendor's position." He looked meaningfully at Gaius. "Of course," the captain went on, "I keep no ready cash, um…" here he shrugged gently, a man caught helplessly in difficult position. "Well, that's to say I don't have none of what you might see as a sportula fit for your station. Not right here aboard, you understand. But I'm sure something could be arranged down at Argentovaria, and when we pass back here in, say, five days…" The unstated details of the bribe hung in the air for a few seconds. "And so, Noble Tribune, now that we've got our little, ah, understanding, we'll shove off, now." He took a step toward the boat.

"Stay!" Gaius said. He looked loftily at the soldiers on the dock. "I am jealous of my honor." He hesitated for effect. "Jealous indeed. Bribes simply do not come into this situation." Faustinus drew his mouth into a tight line and looked at his shoes.

"What, then…" The captain began. He stopped and scratched his head, unable to think what the situation called for.

"This is simply a military requisition," Gaius said, and the captain opened his mouth in surprise. Gaius nodded. "Simply that." He turned to Arverno. "Begin unloading. Start with the barrels of flour and the sacks of grain. The ship's men will help." Arverno nodded, and went off shouting at the men.

At first, it seemed that the captain would have to be restrained, but a pair of soldiers sidled up to him with bland expressions and hands resting casually on their sword hilts. He waved his hands in agitation. "What happens when I get to Argentovaria? What do I tell them there?"

"That's up to you, of course, but I'll give you a receipt for it all. Just present it there. All quite proper and legal." Faustinus grimaced a bit at this last.

The captain was still uneasy. "But what about the tribune of the Second Legion? Are you taking it all? What will he do for supplies?"

"I really don't know, but it hardly concerns you, does it?" The captain looked doubtful at Gaius's offhand reply.

"And no, we're not taking all of your cargo. Just nine and half tons. Well, ten tons. To give us a little leeway, as you nautical fellows are inclined to say." The captain seemed inclined to say something quite different. Soldiers and boatmen were now rolling barrels up a gang-plank onto the dock. Faustinus had one set on end and improvised a desk on the barrelhead. He began noting in neat columns what was taken from the freighter. The tackle descended from the crane on the height above and ,in a short while, barrels were swinging up the face of the bluff to the platform by the river gate and rolled into the fort. And then came sacks of grain and half of the flitches.

Gaius pointed to the last of the soldiers still in hold of the boat. "Bring a basket of the dried apples. I can see that they may be useful." He was thinking ahead to winter, when they would be particularly welcome. "You'd enjoy some stewed apples now and then, wouldn't you, Domestic?" Faustinus looked at him gravely. "Why not? We're in deep enough that a dessert or two won't tell against us, Tribune."

"I welcome your realistic view of things." He beamed at him.

"Noble Tribune. I believe that the commander down the river will be unhappy to find so much taken," the captain said with irritating persistence.

"What? A mere ten tons? That wouldn't be very broadminded of him, would it?" Gaius considered for a moment and waved the captain over.

"Look here, Captain. I grant you that this could get a bit awkward for you. I concede nothing more. But you'll have your receipt. I shall sign it to show that you acted according to a military order. Apart from some possible—I say possible—unpleasantness when you reach the Second Legion—and that's only if their tribune is unreasonable—there shouldn't be anything more to it."

The captain just stood there looking very glum.

"So, in view of the possibility of some small unpleasantness, here is what we do." He looked at Faustinus next to him by the upturned barrel, stylus in hand. "How many barrels of flour have we requisitioned?" Faustinus glanced down. "Fifteen." Gaius said, "Domestic, mark down sixteen on the receipt. A barrel of flour is worth what, up here?" He looked at the captain.

"About thirty folles."

"That should do nicely as a sportula for you to help you weather any unpleasantness downriver. Submit the receipt to the supply officer and keep the money for the—shall we say, 'extra' barrel of flour—for yourself."

The captain seemed somewhat mollified at the suggestion, but asked "How about two barrels?"

"That seems a bit grasping." Faustinus looked at him censoriously.

Gaius felt expansive. "Oh, put down two, Domestic. What's the difference between one phantom barrel or two to the Empire?"

For the first time, the captain smiled faintly.

Faustinus indicated where Gaius's name and signature went on the tablet. Gaius gave it the merest glance and said, "You fill in the name, Domestic—you have such a good hand, and then I'll put my signature to it." As Faustinus bent to do it, Gaius laid a hand on his arm. "Now, spell it carefully." Faustinus looked up at him, puzzled. "I can spell it."

"Very good. Then do so: Probus Martialis."

XII

FLAVIUS SYAGRIUS AND THE EMPEROR HAVE A TALK AND GAIUS IS SENT ON AN UNEXPECTED TRIP

* * *

His Serenity the Emperor Flavius Gratian stood in the high loggia of his palace and stared moodily north into the night sky. The roofs of Milan spread out below, the edges of a few of the grander houses dimly sketched in the moonlight filtering past the scant clouds above, faint lines and angles standing out yellow where lamplight slipped past a shutter. The shadows of pillars slipped over him as he moved restlessly in the gloom.

Years of campaigns had lent the Emperor the aspect of an older man, but his movements were lithe: he was twenty-three. Staring into the distance, he tried to imagine an island eight hundred miles away. He rested his hands on the stone railing and spoke quietly out into the night—it was almost a murmur—as though thinking out loud. Behind him, deeper in the loggia and almost lost in the shadows, a spare man in stood in silk robes that glimmered in what little light strayed from windows of the palace. The Consul and Prefect Flavius Afranius Syagrius stood listening.

The Emperor said, "There are rumors of trouble in Britain. About the Count[40], Magnus Maximus." He stared into the night as though by sheer effort he might see even just a sliver of the island, some brief sight of that country, as happens for an instant when a flash of lightning at night shows a tree, a hill or a house very distinct—bleached of all color, but sharp in its outlines.

Gratian turned to Syagrius. "But they may be exaggerated." His tone was moody, unsure.

"Rumors arise in all of the provinces. But nothing comes of the greater number of them," Syagrius said.

"But the greater number isn't all of them, and what comes, comes." He beckoned to Syagrius. "And there has been a portent."

"A portent." The other man kept his voice flat and glanced at the guards lurking here and there as he approached the Emperor with a slow deliberate step.

"Olybrius mentioned it in a dispatch."

"The Duke of Upper Germany," Syagrius said, who seemed to keep most of the Imperial administration in his head.

The Emperor nodded.

"Portents tend to ambiguity, Your Serenity. Think how seldom—if ever—their meaning is evident until events have made them clear."

The Emperor seemed not to hear. "It was a comet, evidently. Over Britain. Low on the horizon. We couldn't see it here in Italy."

"Perhaps it doesn't concern us, then," Syagrius said. He trusted more in plans than signs.

"Perhaps not. But Olybrius saw it, and so Maximus must have seen it too. And the commander of the British shore forts. But no mention of it from any of them."

"Of course, it is best not to be complacent, Your Serenity." Syagrius spoke deliberately and refrained from gestures—the Alan guards, whose Latin was too poor to follow the conversation beyond its broad outlines, watched him closely with practiced, menacing expressions. A sudden step, a sudden turn, a raised hand could bring them over,

---

[40] In Latin, *Comes*, which means "companion." Again, the term *Count*, which derives from it, seems a bit jarring but, as with *Duke*, there's not much to be done about it. *Comes*, or *Count*, was often a high military command, usually in the Field Army.

eager to display a violent loyalty.

"Exactly." The Emperor looked at the ground and began to pace. Syagrius joined him. "But the difficulty is to know things. What the true situation is in Britain; what the true situation is in any province, really."

Syagrius nodded sympathetically as he walked beside him, awaiting his chance. He had prepared for it already.

A dozen steps and the Emperor stopped and said, "You're a canny old fellow, Syagrius."

"Thank you, Your Serenity."

"The sort who could offer some useful advice."

"It would be an honor if I could do so." And Syagrius thought he could. And help himself too, so he said, "Of course, it depends upon the trouble. But as for information, there are ways to ferret out what is happening in Britain." Syagrius's face reflected calm competence. "Still, we might ask ourselves what threat there could really be."

The Emperor shook his head. "Britain has spawned too many usurpers." He started walking again, Syagrius keeping pace.

"If Count Maximus dares to overstep his authority—"

"Attempts to usurp, Syagrius. Let's say it plainly."

Syagrius stepped closer—but carefully. He could feel the eyes of the guards on him. "Revolt is a difficult exercise, not something to be attempted alone."

"He'd hardly be alone. The Field Army of Britain would keep him company."

Syagrius raised his eyebrows. "But would that be enough?"

The Emperor pursed his mouth. "Perhaps not."

"Certainly not," Syagrius said soothingly. "Should he proclaim himself Emperor in Britain, what then? He's no more than a rebel on an island at the world's rim."

Gratian looked over at him. "It's a mere step over to Gaul. They've all done it: Albinus, Carausius, Allectus."

"Of course Your Serenity is correct: it has been done. But all the same, to do so he must land troops and he must ship horses and supplies to Gaul. For that he needs a harbor, perhaps two. And he must land unopposed. And once in the Gallic provinces, he must depend upon the nobles for supplies and money."

"With an army he might well expect supplies and money." The Emperor sounded bitter, as though the revolt had already taken place. He stood brooding. "You're from the Gallic provinces." His voice was vaguely accusing. "How do you judge the attitude of the great men there?"

"Oh, all quite loyal, I'm sure." Syagrius smiled encouragingly. The Emperor looked at him, dubious. Syagrius continued. "Quite apart from any views they may have about Maximus's merits, the provincial nobility would hardly support him if they expected him to face the Gallic Field army and, later, your Palatine Army combined with it."

Gratian nodded. "It would be a dangerous alliance for them." He looked Syagrius in the eye. "A very dangerous alliance."

"You can see that the chance of revolt is remote."

"Still, I don't trust him. The rumors—they're indistinct, but persistent." He looked out into the sky, as though another comet might flare across the night.

"But in view of the situation, what need have you to trust him?" They had come to the end of the portico. Gratian swung around and started back. Syagrius, though in his sixties, kept right alongside.

The Emperor continued. "I have half a mind to recall him."

Syagrius said nothing to this.

"Yes, I could recall him. A charge of some sort could be found." He flapped a hand to show how trivial it would be to find one. "Then a trial and exile. Or death? On the other hand, the rumors may be baseless. And he's competent. He shored up the defenses in the north under very difficult circumstances, and if I exile or execute him, commanders in other provinces may distrust me." He stopped pacing and rubbed his face with both hands. He looked suddenly very, very tired.

"Your Serenity needs a little information, that's all."

Gratian narrowed his eyes. "A little?"

"Not a great deal, really, it seems to me. May I suggest something? Something quite simple. After all, it's elaboration that multiplies difficulties."

The Emperor began to pace again. Syagrius looked away for a few moments, as though he needed time to gather his thoughts, and then he said, "A letter to Magnus Maximus may be all that is needed." The Emperor looked questioningly at him. Syagrius went on: "Not from you, Your Serenity, not from you. But from someone who would be well placed to help him if he should indeed be contemplating to overstep. A letter from someone whose important interests would be directly affected if Maximus were to revolt. Someone who, if there were a rebellion against Your Serenity, might be compelled to support that rebellion, regrettable as it might be to do so. Such a letter would, of course, be laced with a hint or two about a possible openness to such regrettable cooperation. All in the interest of protecting estates and clients in the Gallic provinces. Allusions to duty, honor and the good of the Empire might be added. A sort of burnishing of the hints…"

"To make the lure more attractive."

"Exactly, Your Serenity."

The Emperor stopped abruptly in his tracks. One of the Alan guards took a step toward them, his hand on his hilt, but the Emperor waved him away. "A noble with great holdings in Gaul," he mused.

"Quite, Your Serenity."

"One of the Petronii perhaps. Or…"

"One of them might do admirably." Syagrius paused, pretending to think. "Or perhaps a Gallic noble who is even better placed to help him."

"Because of his position in the Imperial Court." Gratian looked at him steadily.

Syagrius shrugged and put on the expression of one offering to undertake an unpleasant task. Gratian watched the Prefect silently for another moment. "You, of course." Syagrius inclined his head to suggest a bow. "I don't like it. No. You posing as a traitor."

Syagrius spread out his hands, as though helpless. "And yet the answer to such a letter might tell Your Serenity a great deal. It might well put Your Serenity's mind at ease."

"It might. I grant you that, but I don't like it, even though you would only play the traitor to gull Maximus." The tone with which he had said "play" was ambiguous, something not lost on Syagrius. "Still, it might be the best that can be done." He looked around vaguely. "You'll show me the letter before it is sent."

"Of course, Your Serenity." Syagrius had it worked out in his mind already—he had it verbatim. Not written down yet—that would be foolish. But it would be done by the next morning. Yes, he had thought it all out ahead. He had even decided which client to use as an intermediary. That minor tribune on the Rhine. The one he had looked after, the one whose father had been ruined by taxes. He would do very well. Syagrius bowed and slipped into the shadows.

* * *

"I see you've been reading the post," Gaius said as he entered the praetorium office. Faustinus, sitting at the worktable, looked up but didn't rise.

"I had to. The despatch rider delivered them this morning, but you weren't here to receive them," he said pointedly.

Gaius shrugged indifferently. "You have to expect this sort of responsibility now that you're my domestic."

Faustinus sat back as Gaius took the visitors' chair. "Anything interesting?" He pointed to the stack of tablets.

Faustinus nodded. "I signed a receipt for these. In your absence, of course, I had to."

"Of course." He smiled amiably.

"Because you were off somewhere…"

"Now, don't press, Faustinus. Remember your place: you're not free yet."

"All the same …" he pressed.

"Oh, all right. I'll tell you: I rode out to that villa west of here that the Merobauda woman told you about. It's a holding of the Nebulosi—lots of tenants in two dependent villages. Every one of them a client of theirs." He smiled at Faustinus. You needn't have worried about me—I took Rufinus. You know, the second centurion—the one who scowls all the time. And a dozen horsemen."

"What for?" Faustinus didn't like the sound of all this.

"To announce my plan to hold an assize court for the district at the end of the month."

Faustinus's eyebrows came down as he watched Gaius warily. "You plan to sit as a judge over their disputes? Is that it?"

"That's what I announced to Marcius Nebulosus. He's a cousin of that bastard who maneuvered my father into ruin. I explained to him that I looked forward with special relish to any disputes his clients had with him over their leaseholds, and that I would listen with a particularly sympathetic ear to any of them who reckoned that their rents were too high."

Faustinus said, with a patient hopelessness, "But you don't have any jurisdiction. Only the governor has jurisdiction over provincial courts."

Gaius waved carelessly. "Don't be so pedantic. This wouldn't be a provincial court. It would be my court."

Faustinus flinched and shut his eyes a moment. "With respect, Master, the point is that, in law, you have no jurisdiction."

"I don't see why not. Local nobles hold their own courts all the time. You know that. It's customary and tolerated."

"True," Faustinus conceded. "But the government winks at it because, for the most part, the litigants are the nobles' clients. These people aren't your clients—they're the Nebulosi's clients."

"What does that matter? After all, I've got the whole garrison behind me. That's more than Marcius Nebulosus can raise. You should have seen his face when he heard my plan."

"After which he threatened to report you to the governor? That's just a guess, but I'm pretty confident."

"As you should be. Of course he did. I have to say he's a game fellow and full of bluster. The boys offered to get rough with him, but I squelched that. There was no need for violence."

"I sense there's more to this story."

"Let me finish." Gaius slid his chair forward and folded his hands on the table. "Lots of piffle about jurisdiction and so on. He argued along the same lines as you."

"Was he any more successful than I've been?"

"He was a great deal more successful, Faustinus. He has recourse to something that, for all your cleverness, you lack."

"And that is?"

"Money." Gaius took a large pouch from his belt and displayed it.

"So, he paid you off. He paid you not to hold an assize court."

"You're quite right. Of course, I feel sorry for his peasants: I might have done many of them a good turn, what with my innate sense of justice and my training from Enthymemus." He plopped the pouch on the table. Faustinus took it up and hefted it experimentally.

"Twenty-five solidi. And of course there's always next year's assizes."

Faustinus looked at him critically. "If I were brutally honest, I'd say that this whole thing was mere extortion…"

"Your manners are too good for that. If it helps you, think of it instead as a gift from the Nebulosi. A small recompense for what they did to us."

"I'll shift my ground from mere morality to expedience. You might want to curb this sort of activity."

"Why?" He looked at the slave with the innocence of a child. Faustinus found it so provoking that he was almost happy to hand a certain tablet across the table to him. "This letter is from the Governor."

"The Governor? Well, now, that's rather flattering." Gaius turned it over in his hand and glanced at the seal.

"And here's another. This one's from the Duke."

Gaius looked across at the table at it. "I'll peruse them later but, for the moment, just give me their drift."

"The drift is that you're in trouble."

"Let me guess: complaints about the requisition last week."

Faustinus nodded. He slid the purse full of coins over to his side of the table and out of Gaius's reach. He looked pained, but Faustinus was unmoved. He said, "Now that you've extorted this money, we might as well use it for the judge's sportula[41] in the case against your brother."

Gaius looked longingly at the money but then shrugged. "What's the official freight for a judge's sportula? In Milan? I'm sure it's published somewhere."

---

[41] In case the reader has forgotten, a bribe. In this case, the customary gift to the judge.

"Five solidi should do it."

"It seems a bit high."

"Another for the clerk," Faustinus went on.

Gaius grunted unhappily.

"And another to hire and pay the expenses of a dispatch rider to take the money to Milan." Faustinus paused for emphasis and then added, "And then something for your lawyer Crastinus. To keep him enthused."

"So, what's the total? Eight solidi?"

"It depends a bit on how much enthusiasm you want to buy from Crastinus's. Nine, I'd say."

Gaius pursed his mouth. "Nobody ever said that justice comes cheap. That still leaves sixteen solidi."

Faustinus rested his hand back on the purse. "You need to save the rest for the inevitable costs as the case drags on."

"I suppose you're right." He brightened a bit and smiled puckishly. "Now, what's this about trouble with the Governor and the Duke?" He gave the Faustinus the disturbing impression that he relished these difficulties.

"The thrust of the letters is that the tribune of the legion in Argentovaria has complained of the "requisition," as you call it. And so the Governor and the Duke of Upper Germany say you've overstepped your authority."

"Let me correct that for you, Faustinus: Probus Martialis has overstepped his authority."

Faustinus rose from the table, turned to the window, and took a deep breath of fresh air. When he had gathered himself, he turned back to Gaius. "Surely you don't plan to pin your hopes on that single forgery?"

"Of course not—Do you think I'm a fool?" He looked hurt. "I'm depending on the institutional ineptitude of the Imperial bureaucracy as well. Fraud joined with bureaucracy—it's an unbeatable combination."

"Really, Master…"

"I sense a certain lack of enthusiasm."

"If you'll pardon a metaphor, it seems to me that you're preparing to march into a swamp."

"A vivid image, but you've got it backward. I intend to lead other people into a swamp. A metaphorical swamp." He smiled with a splendid self-assurance. "It's here that you'll see the brilliance of my defense to the requisition. I could see at the time that you thought I was overreaching. Now you'll see how the complications arising from my little maneuver are going to be our strongest bulwark." He pointed to the empty chair. "Sit down and I'll clarify things for you." Faustinus resigned himself and sat down. Gaius stood up and paced slowly as he gathered his thoughts.

"The first thing to keep straight, Faustinus, is what we call in the law, "concurrent jurisdiction.""

"When two different courts may each assert jurisdiction over the same matter."

"Exactly. You recall your Enthymemus. Tiresome as he was, his instruction had its value. Thus, many legal matters could, in theory, be handled by the Governor, the Duke, the Vicarius[42] of the Gallic Provinces, or even the Emperor himself." He raised a finger pedantically in unconscious imitation of his old instructor.

"And your point?"

"It's quite simple. We'll respond to these complaints by dragging in any administrator who might, conceivably, have any right to be involved. What are the chances that they'll all decide against me? Against Probus Martialis, that is? And if any one of them decides in my favor (or, well, Martialis's that is), then we use that decision to exculpate ourselves."

"But they'll object to all being brought in together." Faustinus kept his tone reasonable, though he wondered why he bothered.

"Not if we don't tell them. You see, we respond to the Duke, and then reply to the Governor independently. We respond to the Governor and reply to the Duke without mentioning the Governor. And we complain to the Vicarius while we're at it."

"Complain about what? Anything in particular, or do you have some fiction up your sleeve that you haven't told me about?"

---

[42] An imperial official in charge of several provinces, each with its own governor.

"Oh, lack of supplies. That would frame the requisition issue when it comes up. It gives our position context."

"Context. I see."

"But we don't tell any of the parties that the other parties are involved."

Faustinus sighed.

"I see you appreciate the strategy. We enhance our approach by using different arguments with each authority. First, of course, we say that it was Martialis who did it. It might take them half a year to find out from Milan when he was last in command here. With another, we say that we had intelligence that suggested that we were about to suffer a raid from some errant Germans and we needed extra supplies for a counter-raid. We can ask Merobauda for a likely tribal name—some obscure group to the northwest that no one's sure about. To another official, perhaps the Vicarius, we assert that we were justifiably taking supplies to make up for what had been given out to support another unit."

"What other unit?"

"The Second Legion. We'll say the original missing supplies were sent down to Argentovaria to them. They're the ones complaining. This will make them look ungrateful. It will take years for the authorities to work the whole thing out."

"But after it's all disentangled, you'll still lose."

"Why on earth do you think that? What are the chances three different bureaucracies will come to the same decision? And if there is a positive decision from any of them, we'll use it to stymie the others. And delay alone should be enough even without a decision. A lot can happen in a couple of years. With any luck, we'll be out of here to some place civilized where it doesn't rain half the time. And by the way," he said glancing over at the purse on the table, "send a little money along to the clerks in the various offices—I'm sure we can buy a good deal of delay—more time for things to be forgotten or, you know, for documents to get lost." He looked regretful. "I hate to spend more of that money, but it's in a good cause." He sat back, crossed his legs comfortably and said, "Let's start that first reply."

The voices of two men and a woman grew louder as they approached the office. Gaius looked questioningly at Faustinus, who shrugged. "It sounds like Arverno and Merobauda."

"I wonder who's the third."

The thunderous rapping of a baton on the door raised Gaius two inches from his seat. "Let them in," Gaius said, recovering his dignity as quickly as he could.

Faustinus opened the door and Arverno stood, back straight in his best attitude of attention. An Imperial courier daubed in sweat and dust slouched with fatigue next to him and, just behind, Merobauda stood with a remarkably cross expression.

"Your Excellence…" Arverno began in a splendid round tone intended, no doubt, to impress the Imperial courier.

Merobauda cut him off: "I was coming down the hall to do the books, and I told these men to just give me the letters because I was going to see you anyway, but they insisted on coming themselves." The courier, irritated, glanced over his shoulder and said something sharp to her in a language that Gaius couldn't understand, doubtless Alaman or some other German dialect. She replied in the same language—tartly apparently—because he flinched as though she'd slapped him. Arverno intervened and announced the obvious—that the object of Merobauda's disdain was an imperial courier. "And with a letter from the Consul and Prefect of Italy, His Magnificence Flavius Afranius Syagrius, Spectabilis and Companion of…"

"Yes, yes," Gaius said. "Just put a bung in your barrel of honorifics." He waved everyone in. Arverno and the messenger competed to pass through the door first and were briefly held back by the jambs, but after some subtle maneuvering they made it through, with Merobauda behind them before she could be excluded. The formalities were handled quickly, the messenger left, and Gaius found himself with two letters, one to him, and one—oddly—to Count Magnus Maximus, Commander of the Field Army of the British Provinces. Gaius laid them next to each other on his desk.

"Well?" Merobauda asked.

"Well what?" Gaius replied.

"Why is the Consul Syagrius writing to you?" She looked at him with a mixture of curiosity and respect. "Are you someone very important?" Her childlike candor took him aback.

"The Tribune certainly agrees with that view," Faustinus interposed.

Before Gaius could reprimand his slave, Merobauda pressed on with the directness that he was learning to expect from her. "Let's find out what the Consul says." She faced him across the worktable.

"It's a letter to me. Do you get into everything, Merobauda?" Still, he was weakening. This young woman seemed to exert a subtle power over him. Well, he would just resist it.

"It's a good thing I do, if you ask me."

Arverno smiled at her in a fatherly way, and Faustinus transmuted a laugh into a brief cough.

Gaius sighed and then broke open the seal on the letter to himself and scanned it briefly. Merobauda put her hands on the table and leaned toward him, standing on her toes as she tried to glimpse the text.

Gaius stood up suddenly in distress; a chill went through him. He reread the letter closely, turning his back on everyone, and then looked up from it and gazed distractedly at the wall. Faustinus sensed his master's uneasiness and glanced over at Merobauda, who was about to prod Gaius about the letter again, so he shook his head to warn her off. Arverno, meanwhile, beamed, happy at his entirely tangential relationship to the affairs of the Great Men of the Empire. Here was something to tell his wife about at supper.

After several moments of silence, Gaius felt that he must say something. He turned around. "A minor affair of state." He gestured with his left hand with an entirely unconvincing carelessness.

The three of them watched him in polite silence, all with raised eyebrows. When the silence had grown unbearable, for Gaius at least, he announced, " I see from this that I'll have to make a junket over to Britain." He kept his voice level, but he was deeply jarred by the prospect of a sea voyage in autumn to that chilly corner of the world.

XIII

GAIUS SAILS TO BRITAIN

* * *

The little ship groaned as though alive—her flexing strakes and timbers screeched as she heeled in the gray-green sea, climbed the waves and slid into the troughs, where she wallowed briefly before undertaking the same alarming career again. The squeals of the timbers seemed an inarticulate warning to Gaius, who clung nervously the stern rail and leaned out to starboard (but not too far) as he searched ahead for land. He had forgotten to make some sort of offering to a deity before he'd left; in the rush and complications of the trip he'd lost sight of his wan paganism.

"Ha! A gale this, just as forecast! But it'll kick us to Britain by evening!" the captain said, a broad grin hiding somewhere in his thick red beard. Incredibly, he kept on his feet on the rocking deck without so much as a handhold; by contrast Gaius's set his feet a yard apart and held the rail, his knuckles white. The sail was clewed about to catch the wind on a broad reach, but cold salt spray struck him in the face despite its protection. He pulled the hood of his cloak down and watched the crests and troughs of the waves shift about as they competed to spring her timbers. The sea surged about, more menacing than anything he'd ever seen, and with each roll it seemed the vessel would have to come apart. He tried to prepare himself to go to the bottom but couldn't quite think how to do it.

"You're no sailor, I must say!" the captain laughed. Gaius was too frightened by his circumstances to object to the man's rude familiarity. He turned to him (still holding the rail) and said, "I'm surprised anyone is." The captain found this extremely amusing—he laughed boomingly and interrupted himself to glance at the set of the sail and shout at the steersmen.

"It's a bit rough out here, I grant you that, my friend." He gave Gaius a cheerful smile.

"I really can't share your morbid enthusiasm," Gaius shouted through the wind. "Though I suppose that's why you were the only captain who dared to cross this morning."

"True. But then nothing frightens me, Tribune." He looked up at the sky, apparently reflecting on this curious fact. Gaius decided the man was more than a little mad. "No, nothing frightens me," he repeated with satisfaction. The ship climbed a wave and pitched down into a trough. A sudden gust of wind snapped the sail, which cracked like thunder, and the stays squealed under the sudden stress. Gaius looked around in terror, quite undecided which threat to concentrate on.

"Well," the captain said, "I reckon that did no harm!" Gaius was appalled at the captain's exhilaration.

"I'm baffled how you could find a crew for this passage." Gaius braced himself against the slap of an incoming wave.

"Oh, as to that—well, I'm known as a lucky captain. Lucky indeed." Gaius couldn't see the man's luck persisting if he kept tempting it.

"What's that noise?" Gaius took a chance and pointed forward with one hand. "That odd humming?" He had to shout to be heard. The captain answered without a glance at the bows. "The forestay. It's the breeze makes it hum. In a gale, that is. If you're headed just so."

"The forestay—it won't snap?" The little ship wallowed in a trough and Gaius snatched at the rail with both hands.

"Likely not, my friend. Likely not." The captain glanced over the port rail as he called back an old memory. "Quite a thing, my friend, when a forestay does snap in a strong wind, though. And I've seen it happen, oh yes! Just a lad I was, and we were coasting off Vectis[43] in a gale near as strong as this very one, the forestay humming and singing like an entertainer just like now, but not so persistent, and then, sudden as anything, it frayed about the middle and burst apart." He shook his head and grinned as though he approved. The deck rocked with a sudden violence, but he kept his feet with the grace of an acrobat as Gaius was thrown against the rail. He glanced down at the two soldiers he'd brought as attendants. They sat huddled in the waist of the ship near the mast, their hoods drawn against the weather. He hoped they were as terrified as he.

"And?" Gaius asked, against his better judgment.

"Oh, the mast rocked a good bit in the step before she come down. And, after that, the sail half hung over the gunwale and dragged in the sea."

Gaius looked up at the sail in terror. Here was something new to worry about.

"She'll hold, she'll hold," the captain said, following Gaius's glance. He sounded mildly amused. "Quite likely anyway."

Gaius, shifted his gaze to the sky, which was filled with high gray clouds racing east and south back to the coast which he deeply regretted having ever left, no matter that Syagrius had ordered it. Meanwhile, the crazed captain continued enthusiastically with his alarming reminiscences, savoring the dangers he'd passed through. "Of course, what with the wind as it was and the sail half in the sea, it didn't take long at all for the boat to heel over. No, indeed. She's lying on the bottom somewhat south of Vectis. I'd say about three miles from here. And some of the crew with her too. I think of that whenever it happens I'm sailing over where they must lie."

Gaius shuddered.

"Three of us clung to a floating chest and, what with the wind doing a bit of a shift, we made it to shore the next day. Now that's what I call a bit of luck!"

Gaius turned away and reflected on his will. He had made it

---

[43] The Isle of Wight.

just before he left, and it seemed to him, on the whole, a rather pitiful document. Faustinus would be freed by its terms, and he'd left him everything he had: twenty-two solidi and all of his effects and furniture. For who else was there, really, to look after? The will provided for a modest tombstone because, after all, why spend the money? Who would look at it in Upper Germany? He could see it now, crudely carved and roughly painted, greening with moss in the German weather. Faustinus would see to it that the Latin was correct, though. He knew that it pained Gaius to see solecisms on tombstones, to imagine that the last words about a dead man transmitted grammatical mistakes down the ages.

And all of this danger and self-pity was Syagrius's fault. Why couldn't an imperial courier have delivered the letter to Magnus Maximus? Why the insistence that he deliver it himself and, what was more, deliver it directly to him in person? Why expose him, a military tribune, to such inconvenience and danger? And if he survived the voyage, then there was the crossing back to the continent. More danger. Probably more self-pity too, come to think of it. A particularly angry wave struck broadside, and even the captain staggered from the buffet. "Aha!" he shouted. "A confused sea!" He seemed, if possible, even more exhilarated by this development. Gaius looked at him fearfully, and he went on: "We're approaching the estuary, my friend. We'd see land in an hour or two if it weren't for the mist. Let us hope it rises and we can see a bit further—let me tell you, it's quite a task to keep off the rocks by guesswork alone. I'll never forget when the bottom tore out of vessel I was crewing on as a lad…" He screwed up his eyes, counting. "Must have been thirty years ago." He shrugged. "Still, I made it ashore." Gaius couldn't put his hands over his ears, because he needed them to cling to the rail as the ship slid sharply, once again, into a gray glistening trough.

* * *

A week without Gaius about was oddly disturbing. Apart from his master for the first time in twenty years, Faustinus paced around the private quarters in the praetorium scraping up things to do. He had the floors swept and washed, the door pins oiled, and the shutters of the praetorium windows scraped and repainted. He had the walls of his room daubed with fresh whitewash and, when nothing else was left to do, took out the "official" ledger and checked Merobauda's totals with the abacus. There was a never a mistake, apart from the ones he made. He put the ledger into the cupboard and closed the door with a bang. He snatched up his cloak, stepped out into the courtyard and strode toward the gate. Arverno came hurrying over. "Domestic Aquitanius! Where are you off to?"

"I'm going to stroll through the village. No objections, I take it?" He worked a little irony into his tone, as though he were talking to Gaius, but then realized it was pointless with Arverno.

"An excellent decision, Your Excellence! But alone? Remember your dignity!" He scolded Faustinus with the affectionate expression of a protective uncle, waved a pair of soldiers over with his staff and ordered them to accompany the Excellent Domestic. Faustinus resigned himself to the centurion's decision and went out of the gate followed by the soldiers, their long cloaks billowing in the autumn air, round caps set rakishly forward. Each carried a cudgel to show and, if necessary, to use, as proof of his authority in the village. It was a bit of a holiday for them. They swaggered.

Faustinus walked to the forum, where he stood indecisive—there was not really much to see in the village. Inspect the piggery at the northwest corner of the town? Look in at the smithy? Go out to highway and wait for a traveler to pass and ask what he'd seen down the road? And then, from the doorway of the little church on the north edge of the forum, a young woman stepped out. In the instant it took for her to put up the hood of her cloak, he recognized her. They nodded to each other as she approached him.

"Good afternoon, Cornelia Merobauda." He began to cross the forum, drawing her with him. "Is today a holiday? Have I missed something?" The soldiers kept back a polite distance.

"You don't know the holidays?" It wasn't so much a question as a mild criticism.

"My observance is rather spotty," he hedged.

She gave him a mildly censorious look. "I'll say. I've never seen you in the church."

"But today is special?" He pressed. He seemed to be heading toward the tavern; it was as though she were deciding their course.

"No." She looked down as they walked. She seemed discomfited by his persistence. After a few moments of silence, she stopped. "I said a brief prayer for the Tribune—for his safe voyage out and return."

Faustinus was felt a twinge of envy at the thought that this handsome young woman might care for Gaius. He couldn't help himself and said, "You know he's not a Christian."

She shrugged. "That doesn't matter. He'll be a better tribune than Martialis ever was, and if he doesn't return, then we'll all suffer." She looked down at her shoes a moment, as though she'd revealed too much. "So, I asked for his safety."

"Of course. Very wise." But he doubted that her prayers were entirely for everyone's benefit; he sensed a hidden personal interest. He looked up to the gray autumn sky. "I can't imagine what the sea is like this time of year." It was unkind of him to frighten her with this, but the moment it was out, he realized that he had been hiding from himself the dreadful possibility of Gaius's death and all the consequences of it: his sale to strangers, a life up on the barbaric German border, perhaps to work as a farm hand if his new master couldn't appreciate his talents. And, of course, he'd miss Gaius.

In a few moments they had come to Merobauda's tavern, where he and the young woman stood awkwardly at the door for a moment. He told the men to sit outside on the bench along the south wall under the low eaves. They touched their caps, drew their cloaks around them and settled down, happy to rest their feet. He followed Merobauda into the tavern—it seemed the only thing to do.

Merobauda called to Vilfrida—the old woman behind the counter—and ordered wine for Faustinus and beer for the soldiers on the bench outside. Then asked him, "Why are you here, Domestic?"

He looked around. "It's a nice place."

She gave him a guarded look as though she suspected irony. "Quite a compliment from a fellow who was living in Rome two months ago.

What's your reason, really?"

"I'm bored," he answered and regretted it. But Merobauda didn't take it amiss.

"It's just boredom? It seems more than that. I'd say you're worried. I can see it."

"You can see why I worry. If he—well…" To distract himself, he scanned the empty room, and chose a table to sit at. Merobauda sat across from him with her elbows on the table, leaning forward and looking quietly at his face until Vilfrida had brought his wine and wandered off. "You worry he might be lost at sea." she expressed his fear with matter-of-fact brutality. "Well then. You'd be floating around at the edge of the Empire and that doesn't appeal to you much, does it? Not after Rome? And you can't go home to Narbo either."

Faustinus was impressed at the appalling penetration of her insight, and he grimaced as he saw himself alone in a wilderness of military camps, petty farms, walled estates and half-Roman provincials. "It's true. I don't care to think of it."

"You've been with him, what? About twenty years?"

Faustinus nodded.

She continued. "It would be very hard for you if the Tribune never came back. Even with his faults." She smiled sympathetically, and it was a pleasant smile. "He's naïve and inexperienced. It shows. But at the same time, he's shrewd, wonderfully sure of himself, inconsistently arrogant and, altogether, rather exuberant."

Faustinus nodded and sipped his wine. There was nothing to say to this, really; it was all true.

"Don't you like that about him? I do." She turned her head away but looked at him from the corner of her eye.

"It all makes him difficult to…" He hesitated.

"To keep him out of trouble?"

He looked down at the table. "Yes. That's it." She could sense in him mixture of affection and embarrassment for his master.

"I can see he needs a lot of help in that direction." She looked directly at Faustinus, but he could tell she was thinking about his master. He finished his wine, set the cup down carefully in a ring left by another cup years before. She looked back at him. "Are you still bored?"

"I suppose a bit." He looked up, surprised at the change of subject.

"I don't keep girls here; I don't approve of it. But there's another tavern at the edge of the village. Sort of a tavern anyway. It's tucked back behind a market-garden in the southeast corner of the old walls. A little place, but they keep a couple of girls. I don't suppose I should tell you, but you'd find out soon enough: Martialis used to go there. He 'taxed' the place from time to time too."

He didn't need to think for long. Those girls would be pretty raddled after they'd been through half the garrison a few times. He shook his head. "Thank you for the local color, but I think I'll keep my eye out for a better prospect."

Merobauda gave him a look as though he had passed a test. And then she thoughtlessly made his situation clear to him. "If you were free, I could find half a dozen pretty girls who'd marry you."

"You among them?" He gave her a sour smile.

She looked at him frankly. "Oh, you'd do. You would. But then there's the Tribune."

Faustinus was brought up by a sharp stab of jealousy. He was a slave—educated, true—but still a slave. Even a provincial tavern-keeper was out of his grasp. "Aren't you aiming a bit high, Merobauda? Setting your sights on the Tribune?" His voice sounded peevish, even to himself, and he flushed.

"Oh, don't make it sound as though he rubs elbows with emperors. Remember that his father lost his property. So, what's his future? Twenty years of army camps and retirement outside of one. Oh, don't grimace—it doesn't look like a bad life if you've grown up here."

Faustinus looked down into his empty cup and turned it slowly. "And yet the Prefect Syagrius has some interest in him. That must mean something. But what?"

"Who can say why the Great Men do what they do?" Merobauda seemed uninterested in the question.

"The Tribune doesn't mean to spend his life on the frontier." He said it in the faint hope that Gaius really could find some way out of his situation, especially before his hijinks with the supplies and his legalistic maneuvers with the bureaucracy caught up with him.

"That means leaving the army." Merobauda's face clouded at this.

"Yes. He's taken the first steps toward moving up and out." Merobauda, who hadn't long experience of Gaius, didn't hear the irony in his tone.

"So he has a plan." She sounded disappointed.

Suddenly, a wave of animated talking worked its way through the tavern door. "There must be some news," Merobauda said, rising from the table. "It always starts here at the edge of the forum." She went to the doorway and looked out. Faustinus came up behind her to see the old peasant who had driven the wagon for them when they arrived. He was speaking and gesticulating to the soldiers on the bench as a crowd of villagers drifted up. He fairly glowed, flattered by their attention, and excited by his news. "... a burned farmstead. Bandits."

"Oh? Where?" one of the soldiers asked the peasant. He stood and hooked his thumbs in his belt and assumed a bored, brusque attitude. Bandits didn't scare him, and he wanted everyone to know it.

The peasant pointed west. "Over there!"

"Over where? How far, old man?" The other soldier stood up.

The peasant repeated himself.

The soldiers glanced at each other dismissively and then nodded respectfully at Faustinus as he stepped out of the doorway.

"It matters," Faustinus said to the old man. "Whose farmstead?"

The old man didn't know.

"Was it ten miles away, or twenty?" he pressed.

"Or a hundred?" one of the soldiers asked sarcastically, with a glance at Faustinus to be sure he hadn't overstepped.

The peasant, who couldn't answer the question, evaded it with colorful detail. "A cavalryman told me. Down the road two miles. He was watering his horse at the stream and we got to talking, him and me, about things. He was one of the boys seconded to the legion at Argentovaria—the horsemen they call the Argentovarienses nowadays. He was riding a bay," he added, with further irrelevance.

"How far away were these bandits?" Faustinus put the question this way, though without much hope of an answer.

The soldiers loomed over the old man to encourage him.

"Close enough, Your Excellent Domestic, that the trooper thought to tell me about them."

"And did you talk about the weather too?" one of the soldiers asked.

"Well, yes. Of course." The old man was rather diminished by the concession.

"There are always bandits somewhere, old man." The soldier turned to Faustinus. "Weather and bandits, Master Domestic." The juxtaposition trivialized everything—seemed to put it all into perspective.

The villagers were less confident than the soldiers—they murmured softly, uneasily. Faustinus listened to them mutter and then said with an assumed confidence worthy of his master, "Don't worry. We'll keep our eyes open. No bandits will dare come within ten miles of the fort. You know that, all of you." He scanned the crowd as he said it, looking into their eyes for emphasis, and when they'd fallen silent, he waved the soldiers to his side and strode back to the fort. The wind from the west gathered itself into gusts and flung fine drops of rain after him. He put up his hood and thought, as he neared the gray stone gateway of the fort, that it seemed, for the first time, welcoming.

* * *

Count Maximus looked Gaius up and down; he was a man used to measuring others, to judging them. He was stern, just short of fifty, clean-shaven. He wore the brush cut of a common soldier. The darkness of his complexion recalled his Spanish origin, and he gave the impression of hardness, as though to touch him would be like touching wood. He was very neat: his clothing, though not opulent, was pressed, and even his shoes were spotless. Gaius wondered how; he had seen more rain as he traveled up the estuary of the Thames to Londinium than he had seen even in Germany, and two weeks of travel had made him look half a sloven. He self-consciously rubbed his own chin, which bristled with a week's beard. With one hand he pulled uselessly down on the hem of his tunic to settle its rumpling while, with the other, he surreptitiously brushed at the dried mud on his cloak.

Maximus nodded curtly toward a semicircle of empty chairs at the end of the room, and Gaius followed him, waiting until Maximus sat before he took a seat. The Count leaned forward, clearly interested in Gaius himself. It was unsettling. "You have a letter for me from His Illustriousness Flavius Syagrius." Gaius noted the man's careful, perfect enunciation, all of a piece with his neat appearance.

"Quite, Excellent Count Maximus. I have it here. In fact, I admit to some embarrassment in following my instructions to hand the letter to you personally and to no one else. A busy man like yourself..." he trailed off vaguely. He knew that the Count had built his reputation restoring the northern border of the British provinces—drubbing the Scots and Picts. It was disquieting to sit face to face with an important soldier who had made his way solely on the grounds of military success—it was like something out of the past.

The Count said, "I am never too busy for a communication from the Prefect." As Maximus broke the seal, Gaius looked about, uncertain when he might be able to leave the Count's disturbing presence. He looked down the room to a pair of guards who watched him impassively. They gave him no indication. He turned back to Maximus, intently reading the letter and nodding to himself very slightly. Gaius politely averted his eyes and stared at the whitewashed walls of the room and at a patch of blue sky that surprised him from a high, half-opened window.

Maximus carefully folded the letter and put it aside on a table by his chair, one hand resting carefully over it.

"Gaius Obsequens Dolo."

"Yes?"

"That is your name."

"That's correct, Your Excellence."

Maximus repeated his name again quietly. It struck Gaius that he was memorizing it. "Are you among the Protectors at Court?"

Gaius was flattered by the question. It was natural for the Count to assume he held this rather exalted position since he was serving as a messenger for someone as important as Syagrius, the Praetorian Prefect, but he had to admit otherwise. "No, Your Excellence.

I command the garrison of a fort called Castellinum Ripae." Gaius added, "Of course, Your Excellence will never have heard of it." He gave a self-deprecating shrug. He shifted uneasily in his chair. "It's on the Rhine about midway between Argentoratum and Argentovaria."

Maximus looked at him intently. It seemed to Gaius from his expression that he was pleased with the answer. This struck him as odd. "I suppose Your Excellence wonders why I should be commissioned to deliver the Praefect Syagrius's letter."

"No. Not at all." Maximus took up the letter and folded it up. "It is quite clear from this that you are Flavius Syagrius's client." This fact did not, so far as Gaius could see, really answer the question— Syagrius had thousands of clients. Maximus went on: "The Prefect does not insist on a written reply."

"In that case..." Gaius shifted to rise, but was held back by a quick glance.

"This is what you must do, Tribune: upon arrival back at your post, send to Flavius Syagrius, on my behalf, a reply. In that reply, thank the Prefect for his letter, and state that I find what he says most interesting, if obscure."

"Interesting, if obscure," Gaius repeated, finding what Maximus said both interesting and obscure.

"That is all. But do not forget to do it." Maximus gave him a hard look and rose. The meeting was over.

XIV

GAIUS GOES ON CAMPAIGN

* * *

"Wait! Don't give me any news yet." Gaius Dolo Obsequens limped into his quarters, thoroughly disheveled and sagging with fatigue. He smelled about equally of his horse's sweat and his own. He looked at the couch, looked at the mats of horse hair on his trousers and then lay down upon it anyway. He rested his forearm over his eyes and sighed deeply, utterly content to be home again. Faustinus rose and called down the hall for a calo to remove Gaius's boots. Whatever he might say about army life, at least he no longer had to do the scut work. "That'll do." Gaius said after the calo finished. As he slipped out, Faustinus called after him to bring wine and a hot dinner.

"I rode the last hundred miles along the tow-path to save time," Gaius said. "I wish I'd just floated upriver on a barge, but I knew riding would be faster. What a poor decision."

"But commendable exertion," Faustinus said.

Gaius rested his arms by his side. "All of my joints seem to have separated from each other."

"Very far?" He ostentatiously examined his fingernails.

"Not by much—by a half-inch, I'd say, but that's quite enough. I feel as though I've undergone one of those judicial procedures. You know, the sort they put felons through to extract a confession."

"Don't exaggerate." Faustinus said. "Anyway, they'll tighten up again." He made a slight concession: "And think how improved your horsemanship must be by now."

Faustinus took the opportunity to sit in Gaius's favorite chair and rest his feet on the footstool. Gaius turned his head when heard the chair creak but was too exhausted to remark on the impudence. Instead, he looked up at the rafters and then closed his eyes for a few moments. "You don't seem quite your usual sardonic self—not quite."

"I reined in my natural impulses when I saw you and the optios drooping through the gate. I'm surprised you didn't tumble off your horse. No snap and dash whatsoever. It actually evoked my sympathy."

"Instead of your customary—what? —sardonicism? Is that word? Anyway, I felt I had to move fast on the way back here. I thought I should get back to the fort to keep ahead of any important developments—in the lawsuit, for example. Or any reply from the Duke or the Vicarius about our requisition. That sort of thing. And, of course, I had to lead by example, and that meant I couldn't complain about anything. I can't tell you how frustrating that was." He sat up and looked at Faustinus. "Here's a piece of advice for you: don't lead by example if there is the least alternative." He lay back down.

"Duly noted." Faustinus folded his hands in his lap and sat back comfortably. "I take it you met His Resplendence, Maximus, the Count of the Britains?"

"Yes. It was rather an embarrassing experience—they took me in to see him without giving me the least chance to clean myself up. I looked as though I'd slept in the street."

"I can only imagine your distress."

"You might try a little harder."

"And then?"

"And then he took the letter, read it, and told me to reply on his behalf when I got back."

"What kind of man is he?"

"Hard and competent, I'd say. A dangerous combination, if you ask me, but he's in Britain, so that's not a problem for us. He ordered me to write a letter to Syagrius to say that he finds his letter 'interesting but obscure.' That's the exact language he insists upon. And then we're done with him."

"And Britain? Is it as picturesque as they say?"

Gaius winced at the memory of his crossing of the Channel. "I had to bob through a tempest to get there, equally in the power of titanic natural forces and of a crazed captain. Once there, I was treated to three days of low clouds and intermittent rain. Thank the gods that the return voyage was calm: it braced me for my little jaunt back here along the edge of the Rhine." He shook his head. "Why our friend Mus wants to go to Britain—the back end of beyond—escapes me entirely."

A pair of calos brought in supper on a tray and a jug of wine along with a pair of squat, brown-yellow glasses and left without a word. Gaius bestirred himself to sit at the table and stare at the food. Faustinus sat with him, poured wine and waited for his master to say something. Gaius, who found the silence trying, finally asked, "Well, what's the news here at the fort? Has anything happened in the last three weeks?"

"Three things." He held up three fingers. "Your brother Arcadius has sent you a letter about the lawsuit."

"I hope it displays enough anger and frustration to be worth reading several times."

"I think you'll enjoy it."

"Good. And what else?"

"Cornelia Merobauda would like to marry you."

"What?"

"And," Faustinus continued smoothly, "the Duke of Upper Germany has ordered you and the men to go out on campaign."

Gaius stared at Faustinus, the spoon halfway to his mouth. "Wait!" There was a tinge of unease in his voice. "That Merobauda woman wants to marry me?"

"That's my strong impression from a recent talk with her." Faustinus went back to his third point. But let's get back to your job. The Duke expects to you to lead the men on a campaign to the west of here." He got up and found the relevant tablet. "The full details are here. He expects you to join forces with other units about twenty miles west of here by the end of the week." He resumed his seat at the table. "It's good that you hurried back; if you hadn't arrived in time, Arverno would have had to take command." His comment had the intended effect—Gaius swore.

"I could have lived with that." He put his spoon down. "I see now that I should have rested my arse in a barge and taken in the scenery on the way back."

"But this way the glory will be yours alone."

Gaius rubbed his face with both hands. "I see a serious problem— two, in fact. What if I'm supposed to engage in a bit of fighting with the Alamans across the river?"

"Surely it can't be the danger that puts you off." In fairness to Faustinus, he was uneasy about the dangers, but the remark had been too good to forego.

Gaius ignored the cheek. "The fight had better not be against the Alamans. I was hoping to do a bit of trading with Adelgar's people in the spring, when the provincial supply officer grants my request for extra supplies in place of the ones Martialis took."

"The supplies you've already replaced."

"Don't drift off the point! The fact is that a war with the Alamans will be bad for business." He shook his head. "Those supplies might have come to a hundred solidi. With a hundred more solidi I could really have pummeled Arcadius in the lawsuit." He threw his hands in the air. "What a bloody nuisance wars are." He picked up his spoon and stared at it resentfully.

"Don't worry." Faustinus pointed to a line of text. "No Germans are actually involved."

"Well, that's something, anyway." He seemed half mollified. "Who's supposed to feel the brunt of our fulminating military force? And, by the way, there isn't enough fish sauce for this dinner."

"We've run out. Shall I send for mustard?"

"No. I'll suffer in silence." He broke a piece of bread in two and studied its coarse grain critically. "What are we being called up for? Not for one of those silly contests with Persia, I hope. You know the sort—the Emperor and the Great King amusing themselves by fighting to a draw over Armenia and passing the costs on to everyone with a special tax the next year."

"No. Actually, the Duke wants you to help put down some—minor, I think—insurrection of bagaudae."

"So, we're campaigning against our own provincials."

"Apparently. And the second problem?"

"I don't actually know how to lead troops in combat."

"Can't you just rely on Arverno?"

"I could rely on him to explain his approach, but you know how he talks. What with all of his divagations, he might still be explaining foraging or camp sanitation by the time we need to go into action. Isn't there a helpful treatise somewhere around here? Something for officers like me chosen not for their experience, but for their general accomplishments and character?

"And their connections?"

"Yes, of course. Those too."

Faustinus rummaged through a cupboard in the corner full of oddments: extra blankets, a half-dozen glass beakers, old writing tablets with cleared surfaces ready for writing, and a half dozen books, mostly of Milesian tales. He fished out a small volume from the back, wiped dust from the cover, and offered it to Gaius, who opened it and glanced at the title page: ***Liber Tacticorum ad Usandum Tironum in quo est Totius Sapiendum Ignorantibus***[44]. He handed it back. "I'll start my course of study tomorrow. But first, you read it and tell me what to concentrate on."

Faustinus thumbed through the volume with practiced resignation. "All right, Master. I suggest that we start with the section on basic commands for use in the field." He put the book down and smiled with the merest touch of malice. "I'll get you up at sunrise so we'll have hours and hours to go over the instructions."

Gaius glowered at Faustinus, but he affected not to notice.

* * *

Two days later the half-rested Tribune Gaius Obsequens Dolo,

---

[44] ***A Book of Tactics for the Use of Beginners in which is Everything the Ignorant Must Know***. This undoubtedly useful work has, unfortunately, not survived to our time.

mounted on his ill-tempered jade (Faustinus, with his usual irony, had named her 'Dulcina' and the name had stuck), led his troops out on campaign, passing west out of the village in the cold gray light of an October dawn. He was wrapped in a heavy cloak against the steady west wind, which worked its best to chill him where it could. He rode at the head of thirty horsemen. Sixty foot soldiers trudged behind. Their shields were quartered in red and black and slung over their backs; their helmets hung on thongs from spears over their shoulders. Fifteen spare horses loaded with provisions and equipment trailed at the rear. The whole village turned out to see them go—it was the great event of the season. Gaius had obeyed the summons with as few men as he could; a hundred and twelve were left to man the fort, mostly the older men, and those married men who, he suspected, had contributed to a modest sportula to the centurions to receive guard duty in place of field service. He would look into that; yes, he would. He disapproved but, as long as it had been done, he'd take a cut. Would half be too much? Probably not.

The column reached the rendezvous in the late afternoon of the third day, and the men and horses were tired. A good deal of time had been wasted in trying to determine where the place was; the official directions differed markedly from the geography of the area. Gaius was heartened, though, when he finally came upon it: a large, rough walled enclosure built out from a villa.

"It looks to have been built during the campaign against the Lentienses," Gaius hazarded as they approached. The work had the rough look of something put up in a hurry.

Arverno nodded. "Most likely. And good luck for us—we won't have to make our own camp. Those walls will do nicely for us."

Gaius's looked around him at the muster; it numbered about three hundred now that he had arrived. The shield blazons, some yellow, some white and blue, told that men from two other units had arrived. He slipped down from the saddle and found the commander in the main hall of the villa. The owner and his family had made themselves scarce in another wing of the building.

He was a young man like Gaius, and he stood leaning on his

hands over a table on which rested a large sheet of palimpsest. He concentrated on it trying to winkle out the meaning of the curves, ovals and jagged lines drawn over it. When he heard Gaius enter, he straightened and said, "You aren't Probus Martialis." He didn't seem at all disappointed.

"No. Gaius Obsequens Dolo."

He looked questioningly at Gaius, but said nothing.

"I'm Tribune at Castellinum Ripae, in command of the Second Pannonian Horse and the Milites Feroces."

"So, the command has changed at the fort." He nodded to himself. "What's become of Martialis?"

Gaius frowned. "He's moved up in the world." The stolen wagon still rankled.

"Ah. I recall some boasting when I met him last time. It seems he's achieved some of his ambitions. I wonder where he found the money."

"Who knows?" Gaius said, evading the question. Meanwhile he assessed the other man; though his light blue tunic was particularly fine and the needlework on his badges quite skillful, he was too young to be the Duke. His diction suggested that he came from a Spanish province.

Gaius asked where the Duke might be.

"Not here. Augusta Treverorum, most likely."

"So he's not commanding this expedition?" Gaius realized his blunder at that instant and grimaced when the other smiled at his naïveté.

"This petty job? I don't think so." His grinned a moment indulging Gaius in his innocence. "No, the has Duke decided that I need a little exercise for my talents—or that he himself doesn't anyway. So, here I am chasing after peasants in revolt over taxes. There'll be some fleeing slaves too, and probably a handful of deserters among them to leaven the mix—a typical gang of bagaudae." His expression grew serious as he reflected on this.

"You're in command, I take it?" Gaius tried for the correct blend of deference to the other's position and pride in his own.

The other nodded. "I'm Magnentius Terentianus, Tribune on the Duke's staff.[45]" His manner grew suddenly brisk. "Now, how many

---

[45] In Latin, *Tribunus Vacans*. It sounds rather like such an officer is always on holiday.

men do you have and what sort?"

"Thirty cavalry and sixty infantry."

Terentianus looked dissatisfied but said only, "You're lucky we're only chasing bagaudae. If it were a proper campaign the Duke would be quite unhappy that you brought so few men."

"I do have a fort on the Rhine to hold," Gaius answered defensively. "I reckoned ninety men would be enough for this.

"Quite likely." He gave Gaius a meaningful look. "But in the future you might want to remember what they say: *Victoria malet cohortes magnas*[46]."

"What other units are here?" Gaius asked, to redirect Terentianus's attention.

"Some of the Third Batavian Horse and, for infantry, some of the Milites Lugdunenses[47]."

"And how many of them?" Gaius pretended it was idle curiosity.

Terentianus hesitated, sensing a trap. "Thirty of the cavalry, fifty of the foot." And then he smiled thinly. "I'll give you this: you came yourself—it's more than the commanders of the other units did. They sent optios and 'commended their troops' to my care." He looked down at the map again—the subject was over. Gaius approached the table. "Do you happen to know the country hereabouts?" Terentianus asked him. His tone showed it was a thin hope.

"I'm afraid not." Then, thinking he must say something further, he added, "And yet, a thorough understanding of the terrain is paramount." This was a vacuous statement he'd picked up from the *Liber Tacticorum*.

"Well," Terentianus said, without looking up, "At least you've been brushing up on the *Liber Tacticorum*." Gaius reddened. "I can't say it will lead you astray," he continued and looked up, "But the advice is, on the whole, too general to be very useful. Just what you'd expect from the author—some courtier under Alexander Severus, I think. Lots of advice taken from old treatises on how to maneuver twenty thousand men on an open field. That sort of thing. You'll have

---

[46] Terentianus curiously anticipates Napoleon: "Victory goes to the big battalions."

[47] The Infantry cohort of Lugdunum (Lyon).

noticed that we won't be doing that." He slapped his hand down on the map. "This thing's useless." He turned away from it and strode to the end of the room, Gaius following him. When they reached it, he turned and stopped. "Here's what we do, Tribune Dolo."

XV

GAIUS COMES TO GRIPS
WITH THE ENEMY

* * *

Terentianus's plan was simple. The bagaudae, about a hundred of them, were hiding in a swampy, tangled wood about three miles from the estate. Bordering the northern fringes of the wood was a small, gently sloping plain, quite open and with nothing to offer cover. Gaius would lead his foot soldiers—the Feroces—into the woods along a trail from the southeast, and Arverno, as the only centurion present among all the troops, would lead the other foot soldiers, the Milites Lugdunenses, into the woods from the southwest along another path. The two troops would join each other near the center of the forest. As the two troops neared each other, they would approach the bagaudae from two sides and menace them into retreating northwards and out of the wood. During this maneuver, Terentianus expected little or no fighting (a relief to Gaius)—a display of their strength should suffice. As the bagaudae fled from the woods and into the plain, they could be run down by Terentius in command of the cavalry, the Batavians and Gaius's Pannonians. Any retreat into the woods would be blocked by the Feroces and Lugundenses behind them.

"They ought to flee the moment they realize you're onto them,"

Terentianus said. "Some bagaudae have attacked estates successfully—in fact, they burned two of them about twenty miles west of here—but they never successfully face troops. It shouldn't be any different today."

Gaius kept this in mind as he advanced into the forest, a densely grown wood fringed by dark pines and, beyond them, trees that flourished in damp soil, as the path, hardly wide enough for two men abreast, tended downward, often with swales on either side. Low branches made it impossible for him to ride, so he trudged at the head of a column of sixty men while Dulcina was led at the tail of it, followed by the optio bringing up the rear. He wondered whether his men were as uneasy as he was, or merely as uncomfortable; his helmet was insufferably hot, sweat dripped into his eyes, his jacket of iron scales grew hotter with each hundred yards—and it seemed to grow heavier too, as though it were gathering extra scales along the way. His big oval shield was really quite trying. He wanted to hang it over his shoulder from the strap, as on a march, but he had ordered the men to be ready instantly for a fight, and he had to set a good example. Despite the ear-holes in his helmet, he didn't hear particularly well, and the edge of the bowl above his eyes restricted his vision upwards. The wood grew darker as the path went down, and the sky, mere gray flashes through high branches above, seemed farther away than it should be.

Behind him the men walked without speaking. Terentianus had not insisted on a silent approach—after all, the purpose of the maneuver was to flush the bagaudae out of the woods. All the same, Gaius had ordered silence, so that the men wouldn't distract each other with chatter and leave themselves open to attack, however unlikely that might be. The advance was quiet apart from footfalls, the occasional thump of on shield, and the brush and snap now and then as a branch passed over a helmet. Now and again men grunted as they slipped on the path, which grew slicker as it sloped down and was churned up by so many feet. From the end of the column sixty yards away Dulcina snorted. Gaius adjusted his grip on his shield, bravely painted in red and black, and he drew his sword an inch or two and slipped it back, checking to be sure it was still there. Meanwhile, his feet had grown noticeably heavier—his boots were now thoroughly caked with mud.

Eventually the path leveled out but was muckier than ever as it skirted a long swale shaded by weedy trees. Gaius wondered idly why the path was even here, where it led, who would use it. He raised his arm to call a halt. The swale lay on the right. Though canopied by overhanging branches, it was fairly open, and the ground was spongy. No one with any sense would approach from that side. By contrast the ground to the left of the path was drier—it rose gently and was thick with underbrush springing up among tree trunks.

"Well?" Gaius asked the optio beside him, who was taking in the terrain with a practiced eye. The optio took a final glance around to the left and disturbed Gaius by saying, "I don't like all of the cover to the left, Excellence." The optio was a veteran, so his opinion mattered. Dulcina whickered—a sinister sound like laughter in a dark room. Gaius said, "We must have come a good two miles by now, so we ought to meet up with the Lugdunenses very soon." The optio nodded, but he kept looking off to the left. Finally he shrugged and said, "If they're that way, then they are to our shield side." Not much comfort, Gaius thought.

Gaius stood listening, hesitating to give the order to proceed; he was soaked in sweat under his armor, and the cold breeze that rattled the brown autumn leaves was chilling. In that instant the recollection of an afternoon in Rome came to him, of sitting, comfortable, rested and clean, on a bench in a whitewashed room idly listening to Enthymemus maunder on about some niceties of rhetoric. It had been zeugma—or had it been anaphora? He couldn't remember exactly, but he did remember the blazing Roman sun streaming through the windows, and the racket of the crowd in the street outside: shouts, whistling, a donkey braying. All very ordinary and comforting. But now? Soaking feet in muddy boots, stinking in cold sweat under his armor, a clammy cap under an iron helmet—and who knows what in the woods? Still, it was obvious, even to a military duffer like him, that they couldn't just stand about along the path, that there wasn't much to do apart from following it until it led to some higher, safer ground.

Still, he hesitated to order an advance. He set his shield down in front of him, undid his helmet and took it off to hear better, but he heard nothing, no animals scurrying, no birds. He wondered for a moment whether, perhaps, the bagaudae did indeed lurk behind the screen of brush to the left. He replaced his helmet and glanced back along the line of men behind him. They were closing up a few steps at a time, unconsciously drawing close to each other; some stood with their shields edge-to-edge—they were uneasy and cautious. Gaius threw the dice and ordered the advance. At least, as the optio had said, the men would present their shield side to any bagaudae hiding there.

As the column went north along the sticky narrow trail at the edge of the swale, broad puddles reflected the steel-gray sky above like the shards of a dusty mirror. Fifty yards on, the path began to climb and dry, though Gaius reflected that it was too late to be of much help—his sodden boots seemed to have each added a pound to their weight, and his feet were cold. He wondered idly whether they could be restored to their beautiful deep blue. Maybe they could simply be dyed black and used on the next campaign. Next campaign? He was vexed to think that he was the only tribune naive enough to lead his men in person on such a paltry exercise. He would know better next time; he would send Arverno in his place. He pushed his helmet about to get it settled better and tried to see past the rise in the path, when he heard a soft rushing noise, much like a half-dozen whispers all at once. A *thwack* followed, and one of the men shouted. Gaius could hear the surprise in his voice. He stood stock still and heard a thunk and felt a bump against his shield. In his surprise, he foolishly grounded his shield and looked down over the rim at the face of it. An arrow stuck out of it and, while he was reflecting on this, another arrow struck him in the chest. It bounced off his armor and turned in the air as it fell away. He hoisted his shield up in a flash and crouched behind it, searching his mind for the command to bring the squads into formation, but the optios were already bawling, and the men at the rear of the line were jogging up to form up a line facing left toward the bushes through which the arrows had come. The men leveled their spears and huddled behind their shields, just peeping over the tops of them, offering the enemy almost no target. In the meanwhile, a thin, intermittent barrage of arrows continued to pass through the bushes; a dozen archers were shooting at them from somewhere behind the scrub.

Gaius floundered to the middle of the line, now four men deep. "Shoot back!" he called, to no one in particular (and it seemed a rather unmilitary way to put it), but the optios were already bringing up a half a dozen men with crossbows, who spanned their weapons and stepped forward to stand just behind the men in the front rank. They sheltered behind the big overlapping shields and shot now and over them. After a dozen shots through the brush, one of the optios called for them to stop. Everyone stood tense; everyone listened for their attackers, who could be heard shouting indistinctly in the distance. Gaius drew his sword (he had forgotten all about it in the excitement) and glanced left and right to see whether anyone had been struck. A half-dozen arrows stood out from shields, and a single arrow sprang out of a tree just behind him, but no one had been wounded. There was some jostling along the front as some of the bolder men stepped forward and shouted insults at the enemy hidden in the brush, but they were called back into line. Now and then the brush spat out an arrow. Both optios looked at him for orders. Here was his chance to demonstrate his tactical cunning, his military know-how, his bravery. As a tribune, they knew he must be possessed of all these things. Gaius found this a very distressing position.

All the same, he was on the spot and couldn't dither. But what to do? Advance through the brush at the unseen enemy and thereby struggle through a tangle of undergrowth toward what might be a hundred bagaudae? Two more arrows struck shields—little provocations—and one of the crossbowmen shot back into the brush and was scolded for wasting a bolt. Something seemed odd to Gaius about the situation, however. Why should bagaudae fight Imperial troops when they might easily have slipped away through the woods? Or were Arverno and the Lugdunenses squeezing the bagaudae so hard from the west that, inadvertently, they had forced them east and into an attack on Gaius's men? But that didn't seem likely. When attacked, wouldn't peasant rebels just melt into the woods and disappear by ones and twos in different directions? That's what he would do.

As Gaius turned the advantages of this tactic over in his mind, he noticed the fletching of the arrow sticking out of his shield. It was nicely done. He peeped once more around his shield at it. The whole arrow was well made, not just the fletching. In fact, it looked just like the arrows in the armory back at the fort, arrows made in an Imperial arms factory. He took a step ahead of the line (but kept his shield up—no sense in being foolhardy) and glanced back to the men to his right and left. The arrows in their shields and the arrow in the tree behind him—they were clearly all from an Imperial factory. He felt a sudden immense relief—he had a plan now. He shouted: "Optios! Command the advance. Tight formation. Keep your heads down."

"Very good, Excellence," they acknowledged him in unison.

"This will be over in a few moments," he added boldly.

"Very good!" the optios shouted, without the least indication of doubt in Gaius's leadership, and they ordered the men to form a rough half-circle of shields and to level their spears. The half-dozen men with crossbows stood behind in their shelter, the second optio stood ready to bring up the rear, and the soldier leading Gaius's horse stood behind him. Just as the line began to advance, Gaius slipped himself into the front rank and held his sword up as though ready to strike. This was safe enough because, if he properly understood the situation, he would not have to hit anyone with it. All the same, he reflected, he should have taken a lesson or two on how to use the thing, but there had always been so many other things to do at the fort, like seizing supplies, suing his brother, squeezing a little money out of the Nebulosi with the threat of the assize court. He stumbled over a rock, caught his balance, continued his advance, and tried to force his way straight through a thicket so that he could keep in line with the men to either side. He leaned into his shield and pushed for a few moments, but tangled branches held him back. He slashed at them a few times, but they resisted his swordsmanship. Eventually he found a way around and scrambled to catch up with his men, careful to skirt the next challenging shrub.

As it turned out, the struggle through the screen of bushes was the most difficult part of the advance. After that, the undergrowth thinned, and the men had some success in keeping formation as they moved past trees or over fallen limbs scattered like traps along the gentle rise. Gaius could hear Dulcina protesting the advance with grunts. The optios shouted as they kept the men advancing in fair order, and Gaius was heartened to hear the Latin. ***The shouts should help a great deal,*** he thought. After struggling to cover thirty yards, Gaius and his men caught glimpses the enemy moving down the slope toward them, groups of them slipping around tree trunks and reforming loosely where the ground permitted. Their steel helmets glinted behind their shields, each white with a blue disk in the center. After they had advanced ten yards, their line wavered, slowed, and came to a complete stop. They were, of course, the Milites Lugdunenses. Gaius forced his way out of the line and advanced boldly up to them, waving his sword for rhetorical effect. "You stupid ass, Arverno!" Gaius called when he saw the centurion. "You could have hurt us!"

* * *

Gaius freely gave Arverno the rough side of his tongue, as much out of relief as to display his authority to the other troop of infantry, who did not know him. It was important to establish his authority quickly and, because he outranked everyone, Gaius knew there would be no mutual recrimination—it was quite a safe approach.

"It was the horse, Your Excellence," Arverno said, explaining everything with his usual indirection.

"What horse?" Gaius asked, irritably. Was the man's instinct for missing the point just some innate gift? He took off his helmet and cap to cool his head. Dulcina, coming from behind, nuzzled his shoulder and licked the back of his neck.

"Yours, Excellence." Arverno pointed helpfully. "Dulcina."

"My horse? Yes, yes. What about her?" He pushed her head away and she snapped at him, brushing her great yellow teeth on the scales of his armored shoulder.

"We heard her whinny and took the sound for a troop of bagaudae."

"You heard a horse, and so you shot through the bushes at hazard? Perhaps to see what would happen?"

"Quite right, Excellence." Arverno answered forthrightly.

"I'm not at all clear what you thought you would achieve," Gaius went on. "But, then, I don't suppose you were either. Perhaps sending a scout or two ahead would have been helpful?"

Arverno coughed deferentially at this and diplomatically declined to observe that Gaius had not sent any either. Instead he said, in a tone of cheerful satisfaction, "We have successfully joined forces, Excellence! Let's hope that our next steps are as successful as this one has been." Gaius regarded him for a second, suspicious of irony. But no, he reflected. Although it was a comment worthy of Faustinus, from Arverno it had to be entirely ingenuous.

Gaius sent three men under an optio to fan out to the north in the bushes on either side of the trail and report back at any sign of bagaudae. In the meanwhile, Gaius's men yanked the arrows from their shields and handed them to the archers among the Lugdunenses, and everyone rested, waiting for the report from the scouts. It was difficult to tell the time under the canopy of leaves, the sun was mostly hidden, but after perhaps a half an hour, the scouts came back with the news that, yes, there were footprints ahead and some recently broken twigs; clearly a band of men had passed that way not long ago. One of the scouts thought he might even have glimpsed a figure slipping down a declivity and into some brush, though he wasn't certain; he thought he'd caught sight of a bit of gray, like a rough cloak, and a single quivering branch. All over in an instant. Gaius reflected on this. If the bagaudae were drifting ahead of them, then they weren't likely to fight. As Terentianus had foreseen, they were moving ahead and there was nothing to do but press on.

Gaius and the men trudged north. It was impractical to spread out, so they advanced, as before, in a narrow column along the path, which rose gently and then, topping a wooded ridge, dropped again. After perhaps two hundred yards they came upon the footprints that the scouts had reported, the footprints of men who had filtered out of the woods and then taken to the path ahead of them. Unconsciously,

Gaius and the soldiers slowed their pace, at the same time straining to hear, straining to see whatever was ahead. Another hundred yards and the path forked: a branch led down and to the left.

Gaius called a halt and considered which way to go. Arverno pointed left to the descending path. "Excellent Tribune Dolo, it's clear from the marks on the trail that they've taken this branch." Gaius scowled as he considered the situation. He supposed that he might justifiably press north on the main branch in strict conformity with Terentianus's plan (and with luck avoid any encounter with the bagaudae), but to head that way would leave them somewhere on his flank, which was disquieting—maybe even dangerous. Unfortunately, it seemed safest and most in keeping with the intent behind Terentianus's orders to take the left branch after the bagaudae. He gave the order.

The path went down gently at first, hemmed in by trees, and then it dipped sharply and widened a good deal as the trees drew back from it. Gaius stopped above the dip, and Arverno and the optios clustered with a handful of men around him. They all looked down the path, which led into a hollow of about two acres overgrown with tall, rank grass. Here and there, hummocks stood out of the floor of the hollow, the thick grass growing from them still green in the early autumn. The floor of the hollow was slubbed here and there with mucky patches decorated by low, broad-leaved plants, and its margin was walled by tall dried bullrushes. At the other side of the hollow the ground rose steeply into a bluff fringed with brush and weedy trees among which a handful of men stood half-hidden. At the appearance of the soldiers, they began to jeer and shout taunts. One of them stepped to the edge of the bluff, whirled a sling and cast a stone at them. It flew in a flat arc, so fast it was almost impossible to see, and struck and bounced off a shield with a sharp crack. Two or three other stones followed and, before Gaius could quite decide what to do, a dozen of the soldiers had scrambled down the path, hurrying behind their shields into the hollow and advancing toward the bluff on the other side. The optios shouted for order, and the men reluctantly halted, forming a rough line. Gaius waved his sword vaguely, and the rest of the column descended into the hollow, all eyes on the men in the brush at the top of the bluff, who continued to rail at them and provoke them with the occasional slung shot. Gaius couldn't at first see a way to easily attack directly up the bluff and, by the time he had thought to order a squad to clamber up either side of it where the slope was gentler, his men were all down in the hollow.

Little matter, really, he supposed: the bagaudae were just a rabble that hardly dared come to grips with them—this demonstration of Gaius's should be more than enough to keep them moving north and out onto the open ground where Terentianus and the cavalry waited. Still, the usual question remained: what to do next? What, precisely? There hadn't been anything in the military handbook about this, unless Faustinus had missed it. That wasn't like him, but he'd ask. He sighed. He hated to be in this sort of position, but in the end he decided to order the crossbowmen to shoot a few times at anyone they might see—he and his men had to make some sort of demonstration—and it might drive the slingers back into the brush where they couldn't whirl their slings. He was about to give the order when he heard a dry whack. The soldier next to him shouted sharply, swore, and then turned to face to the rear. Gaius saw the impression left by a stone on the scales at the back of the soldier's armored jacket: he had been struck from the rise behind them—the rise down which they had just come. The bagaudae were obviously on two sides of them.

Here and there slung shot whisked through the dried stalks of the bullrushes with a dry menacing sound. Gaius called out the command to form two fronts; the optios took it up, and in moments the men started forming up—half to face forward—half to the rear. But as the carried out the order, Gaius saw a number of men move with a weird slowness as though their feet had grown too heavy to lift. Several stopped and shouted in alarm. Two on the left flank had inexplicably grown shorter—they could hardly see over their shields. Gaius stared in fascination, unable to believe what he saw—that their legs had shortened grotesquely. He heard a panicky yell from behind him and saw another man sinking slowly into the earth—in a few moments it seemed that he sprang out of the ground from his knees. The men around him milled about in a fear. Another began to sink but was able to struggle out of the morass, his legs coated with stinking mud to the knees. Gaius realized that they were all standing on a quagmire. He called out, "Throw down your shields! Crawl onto them! Your shields! Crawl onto them!" Arverno grasped the idea and shoved the optios toward the sinking men, repeating Gaius's command. Cast stones flew steadily into the mass of struggling men, stopped by armor, bouncing off of helmets, slapping shields or striking the sodden ground, but no one paid them any attention.

Sinking men threw their shields down and crawled to safety on them while others snatched at spear shafts and were dragged back to patches of solid ground. Gaius turned about quickly to see whether anyone remained in immediate danger and stepped back himself onto a soft spot that gave way beneath his feet. "To me! Quick!" He tipped his shield toward Arverno, who threw aside his own shield, grabbed the edge of Gaius's and pulled him out of the muck.

The men understood their situation now: they must to step carefully indeed to get out of the bog alive, but the jeering and slung stones reminded them that bagaudae were on either side of them. Gaius considered things: a frontal attack up the path to the top of the bluff was not impossible—with shields and armor, the soldiers would be hard to stop, but still it would not be easy, the path was too narrow to allow more than two men at a time to clamber up. That might be just enough and then it might not—at least not without some losses. Then again, it might be that the bagaudae at the top of the bluff were very few, or were even gone—the stones had stopped flying. On the other hand, there might be fifty of them crouching just out of view. They must be badly equipped, if equipped at all, but could he be sure? And the path back? It was the same situation. The bagaudae had led them into a trap. The afternoon was getting on, and Gaius and his men could not stay a night in the bog. The men were formed up in clumps where the ground was solid and turned their heads about, looking for a way out. Many were looking at him.

"Well, Your Excellence?" Arverno looked at him with alarmingly calm trust. As Gaius tried to improvise some solution, Dulcina (he had forgotten her in the excitement) squealed and bumped him with her shoulder, flinging him on his face. He struggled to his feet, his shield smeared with muck and the scales of his armor dripping with mud, and saw that his jade had broken free of the soldier who was leading her. She snorted at Gaius as he wiped at the mud from his armor. She seemed to scorn his wretched appearance, and then she plunged off to the right, apparently into the heart of the bog. Gaius had mixed feelings about her, but cringed to think of her floundering to her death somewhere in the marsh. But then he noted something about her progress as she went off. After first slipping into a patch of mud, she scrambled onto a narrow ridge of solid ground and then stepped carefully, weaving here and there, but apparently without difficulty as she went eastward. Gaius was inspired. He sheathed his sword, shouted, "Follow me!" and trotted off after his horse, hoping desperately that Dulcina knew what she was doing. The men fell in behind him.

Dulcina wound her way across the morass, delicately treading around the mucky pools, seldom or never even smutching her hooves. Now and then she halted to sniff, turning her head this way and that, her nostrils flaring but, once she had decided her way, she set off confidently, and Gaius followed, gambling that he would be credited with the happy (he hoped) results of her native pathfinding skills. At first he was uneasy, as he stomped after her, clumsy in his mud-soaked boots and puttees, his shield and armor now heavier than ever, but the further he went after the horse the rarer the mucky pools and, after a hundred and fifty yards, he was confident that she would lead the troop to safety. A quarter of an hour of careful trudging and he found Dulcina looking back down at him from the brushy top of a rise well above the bog. He struggled after her, the men from the two units following closely. Once at the top, the soldiers formed a loose circle facing outwards and awaited orders. Gaius set his shield down, straightened his cloak—from the hem upward was soaked for a good foot with stinking mud, and turned on his heel (rather elegantly he thought) and drove his head into a low tree branch. Arverno and half a dozen of the men looked away suddenly as though they hadn't seen anything, but Gaius's helmet did its work splendidly: he hardly felt the blow, though it left a small but impressive dent on the right side. It might prove useful to illustrate war stories, he reflected.

"Have the men call themselves off, so that we can see that we're all here," he ordered, to take up a little time while he thought what to do next. Really, though, there wasn't much choice but to keep heading north before the late afternoon faded into night. He reckoned they had come a little more than halfway through the wood, though they had lost an hour in the marsh, so it might be hard to reach its northern edge much before dusk, particularly if they had to press on without a path, as was clearly the case after their forced detour. He ordered the men with crossbows to move ahead as scouts. Unencumbered by shields, they slipped among the trees and showed the way north.

The going was slow, every tree and fallen trunk an obstacle. The men, tired and tense, looked about anxiously through the gloom under the canopy of autumn leaves. Gaius was as worn out as any of the men—probably more so—and he longed to ride Dulcina, but she had to be carefully led around fallen logs and dips in the terrain and couldn't carry him. He trudged on grimly, his exhaustion a sort of recompense, alleviating in part his anxiety. Finally, when he guessed that he had about another hour's worth of effort left, the crossbowmen slipped back from among the trees. They showed troubling enthusiasm.

"Now what?" Gaius asked. He didn't even try for a masterful tone.

"Their camp, Excellence!" one of the scouts called as he approached.

Oh, no, Gaius thought. He glanced at the men about him, footsore, muddied, ill-tempered. ***Must we really attack?*** He supposed so, sighed, and waved an optio over. "Get the men in order," he said vaguely, wondering what sort of order would do.

"No need, Excellence!" the scout said. "They heard us coming. They've fled!"

"Well, of course they have!" Gaius said—instantly bright and cheerful. Well, more bright and cheerful. "Let's see what they've left us."

Fifty yards further north the woods opened into a small round meadow of half an acre, and the camp was there. It was just a rough bivouac, the cold remains of a dozen small cooking fires, some roughly chopped underbrush piled here and there for beds, many covered by filthy old quilts or ragged cloaks to serve as blankets. A glance showed that the camp couldn't have served more than fifty or sixty men. There were no weapons to seize and and no reason Gaius could see to do more than note where the place was. He ordered the men to keep moving north until, at the end of the day, they came out of the wood, their mission accomplished.

* * *

Back at the villa that night Gaius sat with Terentianus over a dinner that he was almost too tired to eat. The other man was less fatigued by the events of the day and seemed rather amused—as though he knew altogether too much about what had happened in the wood.

"Covered in mud as you were, you really looked as though you'd been through a hard campaign. Quite convincing." He played with a piece of bread and smiled faintly. "I particularly enjoyed that centurion of yours. He was so eager to point out that dent in your helmet—but surprisingly vague about how it got there. He seemed to imply some sort of heroism on your part."

"It was nothing," Gaius said truthfully, hoping that Terentianus would mistake this for false modesty.

"Still, that handful of bagaudae inviting you to blunder into a swamp…" He looked sardonically at Gaius.

"It could have happened to anyone."

"Maybe." He gave Gaius a tolerant smile. "It happened to you anyway," he said, but there wasn't any judgment in his tone. He went on: "But extricating the men without the least loss or injury. I never would have guessed you were such an accomplished woodsman."

Gaius smiled modestly, just as though Terentianus had actually discovered some hidden talent of his. He expatiated a bit, to be more convincing. "As a boy, I often threaded my way through the woods near our old estate, slinking among the copses. One develops a rather refined sense of direction that way, you see—an eye for the lie of the country." He thought back to family picnics near the villa under a stand of trees when he was growing up. "One learns things." He waved vaguely. He'd ambushed his brother a few times at those picnics. Those were good days.

"So it seems. Frankly, I may have underestimated you. I apologize."

Gaius shrugged to show it was nothing. "Don't think anything of it."

"And your discovery of the bagaudae camp. That was unexpected too."

"Well, it had to be there," Gaius said with a tone that he hoped would invest it with real meaning. Terentianus nodded politely. "I'll report all of this to the Duke. On the whole, we've been quite successful—we've scared the bagaudae, caught a dozen of them on the meadow north of the wood, including the ringleaders, and we've recovered all their loot. Not that it amounts to much."

Gaius nodded. "And what now? I should get back to the fort—keep my eye on the Alamans and that sort of thing, you know."

"I won't send the slaves to Treverorum for trial—they're too valuable to their masters on the estates. The same with the peasants. Not that there's anything to try, really." He looked down at his cup of wine. "I don't much like chasing peasants anyway. They're often desperate, one way or another..." he trailed off, looking into his wine cup.

"The ringleaders?"

"Oh, they'll go off with me. They'll have to be tried and made an example of." Terentianus looked down thoughtfully for a moment. "What do you think is a fair cut of the loot?" Gaius was surprised at the question, surprised that he hadn't seen it coming, but there was something about Terentianus that hinted that he might not be warm to graft. An odd fellow, perhaps, but Gaius liked him.

"What is there? Apart from some food and a barrel of beer? Some clothes and hand tools? I can't say that these bagaudae have done very well for themselves."

Terentianus shook his head. "No, not really. But they don't really know what they're doing, when you come down to do it. They're just angry. And who can blame them? Taxes go up and rents too, when taxes rise. There's a bit of forced labor and maybe a barbarian raid now and again. And, when the army passes by, then it's time for requisitions. I understand their frustration—but burning estates? What does that get them?" The two men looked at each other for a moment in silence. Then Terentianus said, "I had an optio take a squad to search the camp. He found two clay pots full of coins and a solid silver dinner service cut up into pieces so it could be shared out. I'd like to return them to the owners, but…" here he hesitated, "Let me just say that the Duke would less than enthusiastic if he didn't get a bite of something."

So, just as Gaius suspected, Terentianus wasn't interested in taking a cut of the loot for himself. He rather admired the man for taking this novel attitude. As a gesture of friendship he said, "As for myself, I'll take nothing." He thought that was a pretty handsome concession.

Terentianus looked surprised, but he was shrewd enough to wait for Gaius to finish; he had noted Gaius's initial phrase—it suggested some qualification. Gaius went on: "Still, I would like my men, the Pannonians and the Feroces, to get something. Just a little, to reward them for their efforts. Say, a twelfth of the coins?"

Terentianus chuckled. "That means I must give everyone something—the Batavians and the Lugdunenses too. You've outfoxed me."

"But we—you and I—can be as virtuous as the situation allows."

Terentianus smiled ruefully. "These times aren't good for virtue, my friend. Maybe they never are. But that's what we'll do. So, one twelfth of the coins to your men and one twelfth to other soldiers."

"And let the Duke decide about the rest." Gaius said, smiling at Terentianus. "He ought to be pleased with you for that."

"It'll do. It'll do."

XVI

THE EMPEROR AND SYAGRIUS
HAVE ANOTHER TALK

MEROBAUDA AND GAIUS
ACT ON IMPULSE

* * *

Once again Syagrius was admitted to the Imperial Presence, and he found Gratian once again on the high loggia of the palace, his hands on the stone balustrade, looking past the red roofs of the city below him and north toward the mountains, purple-gray in the afternoon sun. Syagrius greeted the Emperor and stopped at a respectful distance, as much for the sake of the Alan guards as for the dignity of the imperial office. Gratian turned and drew his purple cloak snugly around him against the chill northern breeze; a few long, thin clouds flew in rags high above the mountains, like scouts from the northern provinces. Gratian waved the guards back. Syagrius bowed his head and approached.

"What is it today, Prefect?" He turned about and leaned back against the stone railing, his arms crossed. "The grain-dole in Rome? There were a few tons unaccounted for, as I recall." He glanced over his shoulder at the mountains again. He didn't seem much interested in his question.

"A hundred and twenty-two tons. I found them loaded on a ship in the Tiber. She was headed to Syracuse."

"And who was responsible?" Gratian asked in a flat voice, looking away into the distance.

"Ultimately, I'd say Marcianus Favolus, but there were so many cut-outs and some complicated bookkeeping. He's very well connected, as Your Serenity knows. Thus a prosecution would be awkward, both legally and politically."

Gratian looked at Syagrius. "I could order a little summary justice," he said darkly, but without enthusiasm. "But I suppose it might provoke the Senate. Or perhaps I should degrade him: I wonder how he'd enjoy life as a provincial town-councilman?" He sighed. "I can't believe I have to deal with these questions. And a hundred others every day. Trivialities…" He seemed burdened by the thought of them.

"There is no need at all for Your Serenity to deal with this. I took it upon myself to have a talk with Favolus about his future, and the two of us discussed frankly the different approaches that an enlightened and merciful ruler might feel constrained to take—purely for the edification of others highly-placed, you understand—against a peculating official. He agrees with me that the grain should find its way back to the imperial storehouse with an additional ten tons at his own expense to demonstrate his distress at the less than perfect accounting."

Gratian nodded vaguely, his mind clearly elsewhere.

"I regret that Your Serenity was even troubled about such a slight matter."

"Everything falls to me."

Syagrius stood in silence, waiting for the Emperor to bring up the topic that interested him. Finally, Gratian said, "It has been a month since we last spoke of Count Maximus…" His voice trailed off.

"We have received a reply of sorts. In fact, that is why I requested this audience."

"Of sorts?"

"A courier delivered a letter to me this morning."

The Emperor put out his hand and Syagrius gave it to him. The old man was placed so highly that he did not have to follow the usual court etiquette: he did not first have to wrap the letter in the edge of his sleeve so that he did not touch the imperial person. The Emperor read the brief text carefully and then handed it back. He drew his purple cloak around him again.

"Who is this Gaius Obsequens Dolo?"

"A minor tribune in command of a small force along the Rhine. He is one of my clients from the Gallic provinces. I had him deliver the letter the Maximus last month so that it would not pass through the Imperial Post. I gauged it would be more provocative and thus more convincing that way."

"Delivery is one thing, but why does this little man write on behalf of Maximus?"

"I think we must suppose, Your Serenity, that Dolo has done nothing more than take the Count Maximus's dictation, thus keeping the reply at a remove from the Count himself."

The Emperor pointed at the letter in Syagrius's hand. "Maximus finds your letter 'interesting and obscure.' But he says nothing more. The response is vague: he avoids taking any position. And it isn't his letter, so he can deny it if needs to. He's cannier than I expected. I don't like that."

"Has he denounced me?" Syagrius asked.

The Emperor looked at him in surprise. "Denounced you? Why, no. He hasn't."

"Then we have learned something, Your Serenity."

Gratian thought a moment and narrowed his eyes at the Prefect. "I see your gambit now. Or more of it than I did at first. You're a shrewd old bird, Syagrius. Maximus is keeping his options open. I was right to be wary of him."

Not only had they learned a little something, but Syagrius had introduced his client to Magnus Maximus. No one could say where that would lead, but it might prove useful someday, and that chance was enough for him.

* * *

Merobauda sat at Gaius's worktable carefully entering figures into the official ledger. The abacus sat at her right elbow and a pile of palimpsest and wax tablets at her left—all of it unused. She did not need either one to rough out her calculations. A glance at the receipts and the notes of the inventories from the granary and storehouse and the totals flared into her mind, sudden as flames from pine tinder. She inked them neatly in two dark brown columns, ruled a line at the bottom and wrote down the totals without a moment's hesitation.

Her mind kept turning back—despite her efforts to concentrate— to Gaius, off on his expedition against the bagaudae. Her cousin Liutgar was in the troop too—surely that was what was distracting her. She did not want any harm to come to him. Yes, that was it. Well, no. Well, yes, actually. She didn't want any harm to come to her cousin but, really, that last glimpse of Tribune Dolo kept returning. She saw him again on his sorrel horse at the head of the column, the faint early sun glinting on the droplets of mist on his dark green Gallic cloak, his face shadowed by the hood. She wished now that she could have seen his face clearly before he had passed through the old embankment and turned north and out of sight.

Better to double-check the figures. But why, really? They were never wrong. She shifted restlessly in the chair and sighed sharply. She ran her eyes down the columns of numbers and glanced at the totals. Correct, of course. Let Faustinus check the spelling; he could fix the *K*s and *C*s and whatnot. And he would do that without ridiculing her, unlike Gaius.

Ah, Gaius. Despite his pomposity and pedantry, she found that she couldn't stay angry with him. She leaned back in the chair and stared at the yellow flames of the triple-lamp that hung on a chain above the desk; they seemed to brighten as the light from the open window faded in the autumn afternoon. She couldn't draw the work out any longer; it was time to go back to the village.

She closed the ledger and the ink-pot and set down her pen but, instead of rising, she sat and thought, and dark thoughts came to her, unwelcome as the chill air shouldering its way through the open windows above her. Men were injured on campaign, or fell sick. It could happen even on a paltry jaunt such as this one that Gaius found himself on: a fall from a horse, bad food and, of course, fighting. She considered what had happened to Latro, the fort cook. Stories were he'd been one of the boldest of the men back when she was a little girl but, all the same, he'd come back from Valentinian's campaign without his right foot. Now he stumped around with a crutch or passed his time in a chair at the end of the kitchen hollering at the scullions. Well, maybe he was lucky in a way—he was a sort of mascot, and he'd never have to go on campaign again, never have to huddle behind a shield and face spears, never have to range through woods not knowing who lurked where. Before now she hadn't thought much about Latro, taciturn and stumping through life on his crutch.

Through the high windows above her a shout carried from one voice to another, as happened at the end of a watch: the soldiers were calling to each other. Merobauda wondered about this—the watch wouldn't end for another hour. She stood up and turned around, but the windows were too high for her to see into the courtyard of the fort. She snatched up half a dozen ledgers, stacked them below the window, and stood on them to see out. Rocking a bit on this footing, she steadied herself with her hands on the sill and looked across the courtyard to the gate. This late in the day its archway was shadowed, and it was hard to make out much more than the movement of the guards stepping back as they admitted someone on horseback: a dark, hooded figure wrapped in a cloak and riding a sorrel that snapped at the soldier reaching for its bridle. The rider slid from the saddle, staggered a moment with fatigue, and straightened himself with an effort that Merobauda could sense even this far away. Other horsemen followed, but it was the first one, Gaius Obsequens Dolo, on whom she fixed all her attention. She couldn't help it. Even though she couldn't make out his face in the dusk, she knew him by the way he moved, and this knowledge surprised her. When had she learned to pay such attention to him? Another figure, a bit taller, walked up to him—clearly Faustinus, and the two of them began to talk earnestly as they headed towards the praetorium. She slammed closed the shutters, blew out the lamps and stood in the doorway of the darkened room, looking down the hall. Absurd, really. Why was she waiting?

Ah! For the news of the little expedition, of course. Yes, that was it. Well, no, it wasn't. Any news be all over the village the next morning—she didn't have to wait long for it. There was no way to keep the soldiers from chattering, now they were home.

She heard the door to the courtyard open, just beyond the crook of the hallway, and she could hear talking. The words were too blurred to be understood, but she recognized Faustinus's voice. She leaned against the door straining to hear. Why didn't Gaius reply? She felt a pang of fear. Was there something wrong that she hadn't seen as he'd crossed the courtyard? But then, finally, he spoke. The words were indistinct; he sounded very tired—but he didn't sound unwell. This cheered her—she suddenly realized that she had forgotten to say today's prayer for his preservation. It would have showed a good attitude toward him.

But what, exactly, was that attitude? It seemed to have something in common with her old feelings for Rutuolf. She thought for a moment of her husband, struck by lightning. Not a bad fellow, really, though poor with figures. She hadn't really known him all that well when she got to thinking about it. Perhaps there hadn't been so much to know: he'd loved horses and talked about them too much. He could natter on about a horse's conformation for an hour, especially after a cup of beer. Well, we all have our foibles. Still, the lightning had spared her further equine disquisitions after a year of marriage. Funny that she'd be thinking of him now.

The outer door slammed; Gaius and Faustinus would come around the corner in a moment or two. Merobauda crossed her arms and leaned against the door frame with exaggerated casualness. As they came into sight she heard Gaius say, "Yes, I know I'm a bit grubby." He stopped and pulled a mat of horsehair from the inseam of his trousers and looked about ineffectually for some place to be rid of it. Faustinus looked at him sympathetically but didn't offer any help. The two of them stood smiling amiably at each other, Gaius with the mat in his hand, Faustinus with his hands clasped behind his back. Merobauda had the impression they were playing a little game, taking their parts in a contest that went back twenty years. Gaius was the first to relent. He rubbed his hands together and let the mat fall to the floor where he slyly brushed it aside with a muddy boot. "I don't envy the fort cobbler. He'll have to restore these. They were such a beautiful blue."

"It's good that you manage to keep things in perspective," Faustinus said. "I never realized how filthy soldiers on campaign could get."

"Honest dirt, as they say. But never mind that. I'm a hero around here. I took ninety men out and brought them all back. And gave each one a silver coin."

"Merobauda will be pleased with that."

"Why?"

"Half those coins will end up at her tavern. And the rest at the little tavern near the market garden."

"I hear there are whores there," Gaius said.

"Do you want me to confirm that for you?" Merobauda stiffened as she heard this.

"I don't think so. I've been lonely, but not that lonely." Merobauda relaxed. So he was lonely. Well, so was she when she let herself think about it.

Faustinus continued with the theme. "I thought perhaps you'd like to share in the life of the common soldiers. You know—a matter of solidarity. I'm sure they'd admire you for it."

She could hear Gaius laugh. "They already admire me; no one was killed. You heard how the village cheered when everyone returned. Some of the women even cried."

"Perhaps it's because everyone *did* come back," Faustinus said. "Or did you leave all the husbands here on guard duty?"

"You revel in cynicism, don't you?" Gaius was going to go on, but he noticed Merobauda at the end of the corridor. "Oh, hello," he said, suddenly abashed at his appearance. He straightened and absently rubbed his five-day beard and then smiled sheepishly and wondering why he worried about his dignity in front of her. Was he really as vain as Arcadius accused him of being? Well, probably. Or perhaps it was because Merobauda was quite handsome, really, when you got down to it. A bit on the thin side perhaps, and she had a censorious way of looking at him. But not at the moment.

She closed the office door behind her and turned the key.

"All done with the books?" Faustinus asked.

"Not quite." She handed him the key.

"Well, come back tomorrow morning. You can finish up then."

"That won't quite do. I need to look at the other one." She watched Gaius as she said this.

"The other one?" Gaius was too tired to do more than repeat her words.

"You know." She nodded at the door to his private apartments. "The other one."

"The set under the false bottom of the wardrobe."

"Yes, that one." She wondered whether he was trying to miss the point.

"Why now?" Faustinus intervened. "Can't you see the Tribune is exhausted?"

Merobauda fowned at him—he was just getting in her way. "It will just take a few minutes. I need to check some figures in it."

"Why?" Faustinus persisted. "We have two different sets of books precisely because they don't agree."

"I think there might be an error in the last set of entries." Gaius kept looking from one of them two the other, like a spectator at a handball game.

Faustinus gave her a suspicious look. "But you don't make errors. I even checked some of your work while the Tribune was in Britain, and it all come out right."

"You checked?" Merobauda was offended.

"Yes. Why not? As the Tribune's, domestic, I have responsibilities."

She thought fast. "I was talking about the spelling. I think there might be a problem with the spelling here and there."

Faustinus looked her incredulously, but Gaius missed his expression and said, "Oh, let her come in. She's determined." He swung open the door and entered the front room of his quarters. Merobauda followed on his heels, turned suddenly, and put a hand on Faustinus's chest. "You wait here." She hesitated and then added, "No—just go on. I'll call you when I'm done with the ledger." He looked over her shoulder at Gaius, who merely shrugged, so he walked off shaking his head. When he was gone, Merobauda closed the door behind him and quietly slid the bolt. Then she turned to Gaius, who had flung off his cloak and stood puzzled in his mud-daubed and sweaty clothes. He looked as though he'd passed the night in a stable somewhere. Perhaps he had.

"What's going on, Merobauda? This can't possibly be about spelling."

"Why not?"

"Because, if you cared about spelling, you'd have learned to do it properly by now. It's not that hard."

"Well, spelling isn't everything, is it?" she said, rather inconsistently and strode into his bedroom.

"Hey! Come out of there! I'll bring you the ledger." He hesitated to follow her because her imperiousness fostered a certain reserve, even prudishness, in him, but he put his misgivings aside and followed her. She squatted in front of the opened cupboard hunting in the bottom of it for the loop of string that raised the false bottom. When he got to her side, she had the heavy book cradled in her arms.

"Merobauda, I'm extremely tired." He tried to look even more tired than he felt, which was difficult.

"We'll see about that," she answered—oddly, it seemed to him. She glanced about, as though looking for a place to sit, and then, as though the bed were the only choice, she sat on that and opened the book at random on her lap. "Let's see…" She turned a page or two. She felt, paradoxically, a calm exhilaration, as though she had undertaken a daring, difficult, and satisfying task, a task at which she could not fail. She patted the bed next to her. "Here. Sit down. I want to show you something."

Gaius looked at her, dubious. He shifted his feet, rubbed his chin and took off his cap. His brown hair, stiffened with sweat, was plastered to the sides of his head, but stood up every which way on top, like an old paintbrush. He twisted his cap in his hands, then tossed it away and sat down. Merobauda kept her hands on each side of the book, as if mistrusting them if she let go. She stared at the rust-brown columns of figures, but Gaius's comical hair somehow stayed before her eyes. And he smelled strongly of sweat and horse. It should have put her off, she knew, but it wasn't the sour sweat of the poor and chronically unwashed. It was, just, what? Casual, as you might say. And a wash would take it away. She knew that from the days when she'd been married to Rutuolf and he'd come off-duty.

"So, what is it you want to show me?" Gaius sounded tired and suspicious, but wasn't there a trace of eagerness, of complicity in his voice? She thought so. It seemed as though she had taken the first step in a dance and he had joined her. Careful, careful.

She closed the book with thump and looked into his face, her gray eyes as wide open as they would go. "I was very afraid for you. Terribly afraid, Gaius." She was daring; she used his first name.

Gaius hardly noticed because he was just thinking how good she looked. And in fact, she did. He suspected for a moment that he was being maneuvered, but then, he thought to himself, that couldn't be: he was the one who planned and maneuvered. He was no mere pawn, no, he was the master of any situation. And so, he must be the master of this one too—in some way that he couldn't quite see.

"That little romp after the bagaudae was nothing. Nothing at all."

"You were so brave," she said quietly. Gaius suddenly loved the sound of her voice.

"You know, I was struck by an arrow." Perhaps she'd praise him further.

"An arrow! Where?" Could her eyes seemed get even bigger.

"My chest, actually. Here." He pointed. "But really, it was nothing at all."

"Let me see! I didn't realize you'd been hurt." She put a hand gently on his chest. A thrill went through him.

"Not really." He didn't care to admit this. "The armor, you know…" he trailed off, wishing he had a scar, even just a bruise to show her, but there was nothing—unfortunately the armor had worked splendidly.

"And I was just as terrified when I thought of you sailing off to Britain," she said, trying a different tack. "I hear the waves can be high as an oak tree."

"Yes, they are. Well, not quite all of them, but most of them. It's a sight many men don't live to recount." He shook his head slowly, dramatically. "In fact, it was all I could do at times to keep the captain from losing hope. At one point I had to advise him to belay the cleats and luff the freeboard to port." He wondered vaguely what this all meant, if anything, and how Merobauda would take it. She nodded, though, just as though she believed him entirely. He suspected she didn't—but was satisfied that she seemed to. Life is built of compromises, he reflected, and yet it works. "Were you really afraid for me?"

"Oh, yes." And, really, she had been.

"Well, thank you," he said. This seemed altogether inadequate but apparently not to her: she suddenly swung her arms around his neck and kissed him. And he kissed her back. Things moved apace after that. Gaius had never had to work his way through a provincial woman's clothes or puzzle out how to slip out of trousers wrapped with puttees and stuffed into army boots. He managed through great effort to slip a hand down the neck of Merobauda's tunic to caress her small breasts, but it was practically the work of a contortionist. In the end, they had to call a halt until they were undressed. When Merobauda awoke the next morning (first, of course) she felt her cheeks still burning from the stubble on Gaius's cheeks. She threw on her shift and tunic and sat on a chair gazing fondly at the sleeping Gaius. *Well, this will be a new chapter for us*, she thought. She glanced around the room. Yes, Una's bed could go right in the corner.

XVII

AN INSPECTOR COMES TO VISIT

* * *

As the autumn passed into winter, the sky was more often than ever gray, a light gray of no apparent depth except when a raft of clouds drifted in from the northwest to darken things further and rain on the sodden country or leave an inch or two of heavy, wet snow. The soldiers and villagers strayed about less and, when they did, they were hooded indistinct figures slipping through gray days. Gaius stayed indoors in his quarters as far as possible (less shabby now that Merobauda ordered the calos about their chores), and the heated floor made the winter just bearable. All the same, he deplored being cooped up. The choice between sitting in the fug of a dark, warm apartment (the windows half-shuttered against the outside breeze) or strolling outdoors in the gloomy damp made him long for the milder weather of Narbo or the sun of a Roman winter. Merobauda had gone off to look after the tavern, and she had left Una with him. The little girl, who was supposed to have been fobbed off with a doll, spent a good deal of her time staring at him and asking difficult questions.

"Where does the world come from?" she asked.

Gaius looked up from his book. He'd been squinting in the dim light at a Milesian tale he'd read a dozen times. He turned his head and shouted into the hall: "Faustinus!"

The slave came in a few moments later. "Yes?"

Gaius nodded at the little girl. "Una here has a question for you." He looked back at her. "Ask Faustinus. He's good at this sort of question." He turned a page.

"What is it, Una?"

She asked her question again.

"The world has always been here," Faustinus guessed. He waited for her to ask why.

"Why do you think so?" she asked instead.

"Because it's been here as long as I have."

"Have you been here a long time?"

"It seems that way sometimes."

Gaius interjected, "Perhaps we should move on before she asks about the nature of time." He stood and threw his cloak around him and set off on a tour of the fort. Faustinus and Una followed him. The three walked in silence, Gaius glancing about to see that everything (so far as he could tell) was in order. The men at their duties would stop and nod at him as he passed, all very good for his self-esteem, and when he'd had enough of that, he climbed the stairs to the parapet and strolled over to look across the Rhine toward the Alaman lands. He took a deep breath of the cold air and tasted it, hoping for a hint of early spring, and he studied the trees that lined the eastern bank of river and into King Adelgar's realm. The autumn had stripped many of them of their leaves, but in many places green and blue-green pines stood clear against the silvery sky. In the distance he saw a faint column of smoke rising from some settlement miles away. "Odd," he said with his back to Faustinus as he gazed over the wall. "I'm a highly trained advocate, forced into the army, sent to menace the Germans and I don't think I've seen one yet."

"Apart from half the soldiers. And all the ones living in the village."

"Well, apart from them. But, anyway, they speak Latin."

"If you start talking first," Faustinus said.

Gaius turned, leaned casually back against the wall. "Tell me again what my brother Arcadius says in his letter. I was rather too tired when it arrived yesterday to give it any real attention."

"The fatigue of attending to all of your duties as Tribune?"

"You could put it that way."

Faustinus took a moment to think back for a quotation or two from the letter. "Much of it was invective, when you come down to it."

"Good, good." Gaius smiled. He made a circular motion with his hand to prompt Faustinus.

"What is 'invective'?" Una asked. She had been standing quietly watching them both.

"It's something interesting, Una." Faustinus patted her head. "Listen closely to what I tell the Tribune and you'll find out." He turned back to Gaius. "Arcadius offers to compromise, but first he levels a good deal of harsh criticism about your character. He takes a great deal of trouble to exhaustively catalogue your faults. Or should I say, what he claims are your faults."

"Everyone has faults," Gaius conceded generously. He was mostly thinking of other people.

"'Shallow as a salt-pan' is, as I recall, the way he described your character in general terms. 'Unable to appreciate the inarguable justice of your miserable situation,' and, let me see—Oh, yes, he says your actions toward him show 'an utter disregard for your father's wishes and, thus, a callous attitude toward him that you had craftily hitherto hidden.'" Faustinus looked down at Una's upturned face. "Do you see now what 'invective' is?" She blinked and nodded.

"Of course he's wrong about all three points, but that doesn't matter. I've made him as angry as I ever did when we were growing up, and there's some satisfaction in that, isn't there?"

Faustinus didn't reply to this. But he went on: "He further accuses you of pomposity, vanity, greed, a certain pedestrian taste in clothing—"

"I think we've had enough of Arcadius's maunderings. What does he suggest as a compromise?"

"What is a compromise?" Una asked.

"It's when someone offers you something you don't want," Gaius answered. " Let's have it, Faustinus. How much?"

"A hundred solidi. For a hundred solidi you relinquish any claims against the estate."

"What?" Gaius scowled. "A hundred solidi? I've spent more than that just to get his far against him. Are you sure that's correct? I am his brother, after all."

Faustinus said with some restraint, "He's quite aware that you're his brother. Your fraternal relationship clearly inflames the entire situation and inclines him to a certain frugality."

"He should be used to our relationship by now—we grew up together. A hundred solidi." Gaius scowled.

"If you don't compromise, he threatens to seek a dismissal on the ground that you haven't stated a claim."

Gaius narrowed his eyes and put his hand on his chin, thinking furiously. Faustinus watched him uneasily as he paced for a few moments in silence. He drew up suddenly with an alarmingly crafty smile. "Ah, but I do!"

"You do?" Faustinus raised his eyebrows in disbelief. "How?"

"By the customary law of the Gallic provinces! Well, I imagine that I do. I seem to recall hearing something about how property is divided equally among sons somewhere in Gaul. I'm pretty certain it was the law in at least part of Gaul a few years back."

"How many years back?"

"A hundred. Two hundred." Gaius seemed blithely indifferent to this detail. He smiled as he watched a crow sail high over the fort and head across the Rhine. He put a hand on Una's shoulder and pointed to the bird.

"So, you're just guessing," Faustinus said. "And wouldn't Roman law take precedence anyway?"

"I doubt it." He turned back to Faustinus. "Besides, this approach raises a question of the conflict of laws." He glowed with enthusiasm. "We'll plead Gallic customary law. You see, the customary law itself will have to be proved, and there won't be any record or copy of it in Milan, so it will need to be done by showing some musty old decision or decree from who knows where in some Gallic province—something that might be found in a municipal library somewhere. We'll claim the authority is in a library that's hard to get to. Burdigala sounds good. That'll tie up the case for a good six months more—maybe a year. That'll make Arcadius think a little harder about compromise."

Faustinus patiently restated Gaius's plan to him. He hoped the restatement would show its flaws. "You're going to have your lawyer to make a legal argument based on something you don't know even exists."

Faustinus waved dismissively. "He won't mind."

"I think you're missing the point." Whether on purpose or not, Faustinus couldn't quite decide.

"I can see this approach worries you, but don't be uneasy. I'll compose that part of the—ah, 'customary law'—in appropriately archaic Gaulish. Or what would look like it anyway. I could, for instance, fiddle a bit with the grammar. That's always persuasive. I suggest we add a different vowel to some of the dative endings of the nouns, for example. I think that would be convincing, don't you? I'll modify a couple of verb endings too, while I'm at it. So, don't worry—all you'll have to do is write it out in a fair copy."

"So, you scribble a bit of fake antique Gaulish for the judge and hope this scares Arcadius into raising his offer."

"Most brilliant ideas are simple."

"Doesn't it ever occur to you that chicanery might not be the best approach?"

"What's chicanery?" Una asked.

"Keep watching the Tribune," Faustinus said, "and you'll learn."

"Of course it's the best approach. Father should have given me half of the estate. I'm just correcting his error. In fact, it's much like fixing the problem Probus Martialis left us with: the supply shortage."

"I don't find the analogy at all convincing."

"Let's not worry about how well you grasp analogies. Instead just think how well we're doing (Faustinus winced at the 'we') with that little requisition from the supply boat. What's been the result so far? Just a raft of correspondence. And the upshot of that? The tribune of the Second Legion has squealed to the Governor, but he isn't sure who's in the right, and he can't find out what happened to Probus Martialis. The provincial supply officer is still trying to decide whether we should get the supplies I asked for in place of those Martialis sold. So that part of the bureaucracy thinks we're short on supplies, so the idea that we've seized anything seems like an error on someone's part—or it will if they ever think of it. Meanwhile, the Duke is too busy with something (who knows what?) to reply. Because he isn't communicating, the Governor can't take any action on the complaint from the tribune of the Second Legion, who still thinks Martialis is behind things. The Vicarius is trying to decide whether he wants to take jurisdiction, but he hasn't done it yet, so even if the Duke finally gets around to paying attention, he can't make a decision until that question is settled. The same is true of the Governor, who is under him. And if the Vicarius decides that it is his business, then neither the Governor nor the Duke can take charge of it.

"What an utter mess."

"It is, isn't it? It's really a rather splendid accomplishment. I think you should be proud of me."

"I'll wait to applaud until I see what happens after the whole thing unravels."

"But will it?" Gaius held up a finger didactically, unconsciously imitating Enthymemus. "This tangle would take the better part of a year to resolve if anyone really cared enough to concentrate on it. But in spring the new supplies will arrive, and then there'll be no point in unsnarling things. And anyway, by then something else will be attracting the administration's attention. Maybe some Franks will make a raid, or another bunch of bagaudae will erupt. Maybe Persia will declare war—that's always a big distraction. And remember, we did it for the men. We couldn't let them starve, could we? We firmly hold the moral high ground."

Before he could reply, Faustinus heard shouting from down in the courtyard. Gaius came to his side and they saw a small party come through the gateway. The party seemed to be made up of an official of some sort and his small escort: four cavalrymen and another fellow—a secretary?—on a gray mule. Gaius nodded across to them and said to Faustinus. "Find out what they want and let me know before they're admitted. I'll receive them in the praetorium office."

Faustinus nodded.

"And send me Arverno. You know, to enhance my dignity."

"Can he do that?"

Gaius stared at him narrowly, sensing sarcasm. "If he keeps his mouth shut." He looked down at Una. "And don't forget to look after this little princess." He patted her head affectionately and walked off.

* * *

Gaius sat behind his table in the praetorium in his best tunic: brick-red with blue embroidered strips over the shoulders and blue matching trim around the neck. His military cap sat on the table next to a set of wax tablets, a ledger, and a stylus, all calculated to suggest military efficiency. He rested his elbows on the chair arms and sat with his fingers laced with, as he saw it, a certain languid yet commanding authority. He felt confident, if curious, about the visitors. Quite some time passed, and he was tiring of exuding languid authority when Faustinus stepped into the room and carefully shut the door. He was clearly unsettled. Gaius leaned forward.

"What is it? You look shaken."

"I am. An inspector is here from some office in Milan. He's an undersecretary. What if it's about the supplies?"

Gaius leaned back and waved casually. "That's nothing to worry about. I've just gotten done telling you why."

"He was very cold when I received him at the gate. Very distant."

"Not everyone responds warmly to you at first, Faustinus. It's your cynicism. It can show even when you're not provoked. I think you need to work on that." He leaned forward and gave Faustinus as avuncular an expression as a young man could. "I say that not merely as your master, but as your friend."

"Don't worry about me." Faustinus put his hands on the table and leaned toward Gaius.

"If all of these agencies are so tied up with each other, then why is he here?"

Gaius pursed his lips a moment and then, buoyed up by the return of his native optimism, he said, "You worry too much." But not quite all of his customary optimism had returned. He glanced at the ledger and shifted it an inch to center it better on the table. Faustinus caught the uneasiness in the gesture. Arverno's usual thunderous three taps rattled the door. The two men looked at each other, and Gaius called out, "Enter!" Faustinus came to stand at Gaius's side.

Arverno swung the door open and waved in a small, venomous-looking man. He was a puny fellow of about fifty, his nose and chin too close to each other from the loss of teeth. His hair was thin, his tunic hung loosely on his small frame, and his military belt—the mark of his office as a civil servant—was too wide on him, as though he were a child. He was followed by a cowed slave, a weedy boy of about sixteen, who carried a battered satchel. Last of all came someone Gaius knew slightly, but that was enough: Probus Martialis.

Arverno improvised an honorific with is usual aplomb: "His Reputedness Scaevolus Volusianus, Undersecretary in the office of Flavius Merobaudes[48], Master of the Infantry of His Serenity, Flavius Gratian." He didn't hide his disgust, though, as he stared at Martialis, who grinned wolfishly at Gaius, and he didn't bother to introduce him.

"Leave us," Volusianus said to Arverno without looking at him, but Gaius shook his head and the centurion stayed put. The little man made Gaius uneasy. Let Arverno stay and utter whatever fatuity he might; he and Faustinus lent him a little fortitude by their presence, and he had begun to suspect he might need it. Volusianus looked Arverno up and down and then shrugged. It was clear that Arverno's presence didn't matter at all to him. Gaius's apprehensiveness grew—the little man showed an unsettling confidence, a confidence all out of proportion to his size.

Gaius was about to indicate a chair, but Volusianus had already taken it. "To what do we owe the honor of your visit, Undersecretary?" This came out not so much suave as stilted. Gaius searched for another phrase that would project a confidence that was seeping away but, before he could turn one up, Volusianus said bluntly:

"I must hurry on to Augusta Treverorum, so I won't waste any time on etiquette. I am here to collect two hundred solidi from you."

---

[48] Gratian's chief general, Flavius Merobaudes, perhaps confusingly for the reader, shares his name with a major character in this book, but he is not related to her, or to her father of the same name.

Gaius looked at him blankly for a moment. The amount was staggering—and he didn't have it. And he couldn't think why this repulsive little man was demanding it, but he suspected he might somehow be on the hook for it. The thought flitted through his mind that he would have had the money if only he hadn't sent so much last month to Crastinus to pay the judge, though it had seemed a good investment at the time. Volusianus was watching him silently, his bony fingers laced under his chin, and his gaze turned Gaius's mind back to the problem at hand. He cleared his throat importantly. "By what authority—"

Volusianus cut him off. "Authority?" He snorted. "I'm much too tired to palter with you, Tribune. I'm an Imperial Undersecretary from Milan. That is my authority. You have fifty phantom soldiers on the muster roll here at…" He turned to Martialis. "What's this dreary place called again?"

"Castellinum Ripae." So, that was it. Gaius began to see the situation.

"How inventive." Volusianus turned back to the Gaius. "You have fifty phantom soldiers on the muster roll here, and now the time has come to pay for them."

"Undersecretary Volusianus, I can only guess that you are laboring under a misapprehension. Phantom soldiers! The very idea… " Gaius looked at him loftily. Martialis, standing by the door, chuckled darkly. Of course he would—he had carried out the same fraud himself. But, still, there was false ledger—how could they get around that, no matter what Martialis might claim? Let them search the chest with the false bottom—they would find nothing. Gaius had turned the custody of the ledgers over to Faustinus months ago.

Volusianus clucked his tongue. "You are being tiresome, Tribune." He looked at Martialis. "These new commanders. Why are they so slow to learn?"

Martialis, leaning against the door, shrugged at the mystery.

Volusianus turned back. "We'll do this then: you pay out a hundred and fifty now and the balance after the next donative. But I'm only offering this solution once and because you're a novice."

Gaius rankled at the characterization. And he did not have a hundred and fifty solidi. No, he did not. But he did have the helpful ledger. "Secretary Volusianus, you will find that the official complement is quite correct."

Probus Martialis snorted.

"Tribune Probus Martialis, former commander of this 'crack unit,'" Volusianus chuckled derisively at the epithet, "assures me of the fraud."

Martialis shook his head sadly. "It's all too true, Undersecretary Volusianus. I vouch for it." He turned his vicious smile on Gaius.

Gaius rested his hand on the ledger, raised his chin and replied, "Tribune Martialis's accusations are entirely baseless." He used his iciest tone.

Volusianus flapped his bony hand. "And don't try to squirm out of this by claiming that you've sent these rather 'transparent' soldiers off on maneuvers or across the Rhine to chase raiders."

"We've heard that all before," Martialis said. "I tried it once when I was a young cub. It cost me an extra twenty solidi."

Volusianus chuckled at the anecdote. He sounded like a dry hinge.

"I stand by my earlier statement," Gaius said with simple dignity. Both Faustinus and Arverno nodded solemnly in support, the centurion with complete trust in Gaius, Faustinus hoping grimly that the ledger would defeat the Imperial official. With Martialis informing against him, only the ledger, if that, could protect him.

Volusianus sighed, as though at an obstructive child. "All right then. You force me to conduct an audit, and when everything is reckoned up, it will go badly for you."

"Very badly." Martialis shook his head lugubriously and then grinned.

"The punishment for peculation—well, let's not dwell on it," Volusianus said with a smile as he dwelt on it. "It's awful enough without the amplification of anticipation. Let's begin." He put his hand out to the weedy young slave without looking at him, and the youth rummaged quickly in his satchel and brought out a sheet of figures. Volusianus brandished it at Gaius. "The comparison of a handful numbers will quickly disprove your claim. We'll compare the official numbers of the rations given to the unit—I have these here—to those in your ledger and find the disagreement. It will be there. We'll find it quickly enough." Volusianus studied his sheet much longer than necessary and, when Gaius had begun to squirm, looked up. "How many rations have you claimed during the last quarter?"

Gaius lounged back in his chair and flicked his hand as though casually. He could afford bravado; he had the ledger to back him up. "About two-hundred and eighty rations, more or less, given the size of the unit, the number of officers and a few pay-and-a-half men."

Volusianus clucked his tongue again and smiled. He didn't believe the number and he looked forward to disproving it. "I admire your brass, Tribune. Really I do. But it won't survive the audit." He tapped the sheet in his lap with a bony finger. "I shall make a close comparison of your account to the numbers in this return. So, the ledger, Tribune Dolo. Let's get to it."

"If you insist, Gaius said with the tone of one unjustly accused. He slid it over from its place near his right elbow and, in that moment, saw that it was the off-book ledger: the one that accurately stated the unit strength at two hundred and two, the one that constituted an admission in black-and-white of the fraud. Volusianus reached across the table to take it and brushed Gaius with his cold hand. Gaius shuddered and was seized by a momentary sensation of unreality as he wondered why this ledger, and not the false one, was on the table. It came to him in a rush—Merobauda had left the book out for him to approve, yes, he remembered it now. Just as she always did. And he hadn't given it to Faustinus to put away. The ledger would never match the Imperial record which must imply a garrison of two hundred and fifty two. He closed his eyes and began to sweat.

XVIII

THE UNPLEASANTNESS CONTINUES

* * *

As Merobauda walked back to the fort that afternoon from the tavern, she noticed a knot of soldiers standing in the gateway, heads together in unnaturally quiet conversation. When she came up to them she asked sharply, "Is something wrong here?" No one answered, but the optio signalled with a thumb over his shoulder. She looked across the courtyard at a tall officer lounging in the open doorway of the praetorium. His cloak was very fine, his tunic a rich red, and silver glimmered on his belt; he was no border soldier. She recognized him and scowled—she hadn't seen Probus Martialis since he'd left the fort eight months before. Not one to hesitate, she strode across the courtyard. When he saw her approach, he leaned casually against the door jamb.

"Well, Merobauda. Come to handle the books?" He seemed pleased with himself—as though he had never come up with a witticism before. Perhaps he never had.

"What are you doing back here, Martialis?"

"Don't be too familiar, Merobauda. 'Protector' is the correct form of address."

She snorted. "You wanted to be familiar the last time I saw you." She didn't hide her disgust.

He smirked. "You flatter yourself, girl. Not that I wouldn't have minded you, but there were plenty of other girls in the town who were interested in me."

"Most people have poor taste, when you come down to it."

"Maybe you should have judged a little better. As I just said, I'm a Protector now."

She shrugged. "I'm not any more impressed now than I was when I heard you'd bought your way into the Field Army."

"You could have come with me." He sneered. "You'd be more than a jumped up provincial barmaid now. Haven't you ever wondered what Milan looks like?"

"From time to time. Full of men like you, I suppose. It must be lovely." She looked at him with such open contempt that he winced. She stepped forward and tried to pass, but he blocked her way with an arm across the doorway.

"Let me by," she said sharply. He shook his head.

"Official business, Merobauda. It doesn't concern you."

She looked uneasy. "What business?"

He nodded back through the doorway. "Accounting irregularities. The Undersecretary isn't pleased."

"There can't be any accounting irregularities. I'm still keeping the books."

He grinned maliciously. "I'd guess the numbers all totted up just fine, girl, just fine." He wrinkled up his forehead and pretended to think hard. "But maybe what's being counted isn't quite what's there."

"What do you mean?" But she knew exactly what he meant: the phantom soldiers. She clenched her hands and then relaxed them, trying to hide her unease. The false ledger should have done the trick…

He went on: "Your little tribune Dolo—he seems to have overreached."

"You tipped this auditor off, though, didn't you? You bastard."

"It was painful, let me tell you, but I had my duty to do." He chuckled offensively.

She gave him a dark look.

"Why the face, Merobauda?" He looked at her ironically. "Oh, the two books? Is that it? You thought that would help?"

"They always did; that's why I set them up for you."

"Your new tribune's an innocent." He shook his head sadly. "He doesn't really know how to play the game." He tapped his chest. "Back when I commanded here, I openly admitted to twenty phantom soldiers. I'd use the ledger to hide the other thirty, but I'd shunt the notary a twelfth of the pay on the twenty phantoms I'd admit to. You remember how it was."

"What's the notary asking for? Ten solidi? Twenty?"

"Oh, no. Oh, no. Two hundred."

Merobauda opened her eyes wide.

"That fool of a tribune was caught with the true ledger on his desk. We didn't even have to search for it. I enjoyed that I must say, after what that bastard tribune cost me with his trick. It's funny how things just work out sometimes."

Her mind was racing as she tried to assess the danger, but she didn't have all of the facts. "A trick? Cost you? What are you talking about?"

"There was a hell of a lot of unpleasantness back in Milan about a requisition from a supply barge that stopped here last autumn. Somehow my name was signed to it."

This was news to Merobauda, but she did not care a whit for any trouble Martialis got into. "You would have let the garrison go hungry to pay for your commission. You deserve any misery you got."

"Well, aren't we the little scold? I never liked that in you, Merobauda—that superior moral streak. I think that's why I enjoyed threatening Rutuolf with demotion so you'd come up with the second ledger. It offended your sensibilities." He turned back to the subject at hand. "Dolo must have signed my name to the requisition, and it cost me fifty solidi to pay my way out of trouble. I'll get that back from the notary when he's done with your little Tribune."

Merobauda understood the situation now. "So, both you and the undersecretary are squeezing him for the money."

"Two hundred solidi—that's what we're asking, but Dolo says he doesn't have it, not anything close. But where is it?" Martialis looked away in thought. "That's what I want to know. All that skim? What could he be doing with the money out here? There's nothing to spend it on." He shook his head. "So, the audit. Well, of course, that didn't turn out well. I hope he enjoys his arrest."

"He's arrested? Let me in."

"No one sees him but his household."

"His household?" She thought quickly.

"And what does that come to?" Martialis asked. "Just that slave of his."

"And his wife."

"He's got a wife? He didn't say anything about a wife."

"I'm his wife."

He looked at her in dumb surprise.

"Why should he stoop to tell you?" She looked him in the eyes to distract him and shoved him hard in the stomach with both hands. She slipped past him and put half the corridor behind her while he was still staggering. In the end he let her go. He had never been able to get her to cooperate on anything but the ledgers anyway.

Merobauda pulled up the hem of her shift as she sprinted down the hall toward Gaius's quarters. A pair of soldiers she didn't recognize—Martialis's obviously—leaned casually against the wall across from the closed door. They straightened up for an instant when they caught sight of her, but then slouched back. She ignored them and went straight to the door. "Hey!" one of them called, but she only turned long enough to glare at them and say: "If you're on guard duty, then look the part, you buffoons," She turned her back on them and entered the room, slamming the door behind her. Gaius, who had been pacing nervously back and forth turned suddenly. "How did you get in?"

"I'm your wife."

He stared for a moment, at a loss. "You are?" The statement had a disconcerting effect on him, as though in a dream he had learned something important, something unlikely and yet somehow true.

"So they can't refuse me entry, you fool."

"Wife," he said again, vaguely, trying to work it out.

Merobauda glanced about the room. Faustinus leaned despondently against a wall with his arms folded, looking at his feet. She pointed at him. "Tell me what's going on. Give me the straight story."

She glanced at Gaius and said, "You keep quiet!"

Faustinus began: "An Imperial undersecretary is here to check the books against the official ledger. It seems that…" He hesitated and glanced at Gaius.

"Oh, speak up. This isn't the time to spare anyone's feelings." She glanced crossly at Gaius.

"Well, it seems…"

"It's only house-arrest, Carissima," Gaius interrupted, in his best chipper tone.

"Oh, hush." It was the sort of thing she might have said to Una who, as it happened, was sitting silently on the floor in the far corner, looking grave.

"It seems that the Imperial ledger and the cohort's ledger don't agree." Faustinus said.

She turned to Gaius. "In other words, you showed him the wrong book."

"Strictly speaking, it was the right one, you know. The one with the accurate accounts."

"In other words, you showed him the wrong book," she repeated implacably.

"In my defense, Carissima, there was no reason to expect anyone in authority would ever insist on seeing that ledger."

"Whatever you thought—or didn't—you shouldn't have shown him the off-book. You should have showed him the false ledger and then offered a little money if he was suspicious. That's what that ledger's for. Honestly!" She waved her hands in the air in frustration. "You knew this was a dangerous game. If you were going to play it, then you should have been careful."

Gaius reddened.

Faustinus said, "He'll take a pay-off, but we don't have the cash."

Merobauda looked up at the ceiling in frustration. "Don't tell me all that money went south to fund your damned lawsuit."

"Not all of it," Gaius said defensively. She glared at him. "Well, most of it, yes," he admitted.

"And Probus Martialis is in charge of the official's entourage!"

She said his name as though it tasted bad.

"That hardly seems an accident," Faustinus said. "I wonder if he informed?"

"Of course he informed! Are you as naive as Gaius?" She put her face in her hands for a moment in exasperation. Then she asked, "So, what's next?"

Faustinus glanced at Gaius and saw him hesitate to answer, so he said, "They're taking Gaius to Milan under arrest to investigate the case. They'll try him for peculation."

"Is this true?" Merobauda gave Gaius a sharp look.

He struggled quite unsuccessfully to look nonchalant. "Faustinus is right, in outline. But, of course, there are any number of details that could make a difference."

Merobauda looked utterly unconvinced.

"For example," Gaius said, spreading his hands. "Faustinus won't testify against me."

"I'm afraid that I probably will," he said.

Gaius turned to him in surprise. "What?"

"You forget I'm a slave. By law I must testify under torture. I'll do my best for you, but who knows what they'll do to get the answers they want?"

"I freed you in my will!" Gaius said, but then put his hand on his chin. "I never told you, though, did I?"

"Thank you, Master. But, of course, you're not dead yet. If I recall my Enthymemus, a conviction for peculation will result in that condition. Or is it torture and death? I'll be free then, I suppose. I hope they won't have tortured me too far to enjoy my freedom." He immediately regretted his mistimed levity. "I'm sorry," he said quietly and looked down.

"Perhaps we can whip up a document to free you and backdate it." Gaius brightened a bit at the thought a scheme. "We'll get writing materials from the office. Vellum, pens, ink, seals."

"Oh, shut up!" Merobauda said. "They've already got the true ledger. You're just blithering."

"And then there's Flavius Syagrius, my patron. Surely he'll intervene."

"Why should he?" Merobauda asked and pressed a cruel logic: "Why should he concern himself with a client who's a felon? And one who's small? What's in it for him?"

"Well, he got me into this position, didn't he? I was just a student in Rome a few months ago."

Merobauda and Faustinus exchanged exasperated looks.

The three of them stood silent for several moments, and then Faustinus looked up abruptly, took a sharp breath, and said, "Master, why don't you sell me? I can read and write and I have legal training. With a little puffing you should get close to fifty solidi. Volusianus might take the rest on account." He smiled with a certain bravado but it was painful too see.

Gaius turned to Faustinus in shock as though he had said something altogether obscene. "Don't talk that way!" His slave flinched— Gaius had never shouted at him before. But Faustinus persisted: "The risk—the penalty..." His voice failed him as he envisioned it.

"To hell with the penalty." Gaius seemed really angry for a moment. Merobauda looked at both of them with a new respect, and in that instant an idea began to come to her, small at first, and then growing, edge on edge like the facets of a crystal, gleaming and flashing, elegant, attractive and false. "Where is this official?"

"In the office, I suppose."

"You haven't admitted anything, have you?"

"Certainly not."

Merobauda sighed in relief. "Then come on—we're going to see him."

XIX

MEROBAUDA CONFRONTS VOLUSIANUS AND PERFORMS A LITTLE SLEIGHT-OF-ARITHMETIC.

***

"Who is this woman?" Volusianus asked sharply, glaring at Merobauda. He had taken Gaius's place behind the table and was dictating a report to the slave boy, who sat balancing a wax tablet on his knees. The boy glanced at Gaius and winced, as though he could see the future.

Gaius took a deep breath and began: "As your Excellence will suppose—or, in fact, has already noted with that perspicuity for which high officials are a matter of remark—up here in the rough-and-ready districts along the frontier..."

"Don't bother to flatter to me." Volusianus gave him a poisonous look. There was a moment of dead silence. "And don't beat around the bush. I don't have the time or the patience for it."

Martialis, sitting on a stool in the corner, sneered. "Perhaps she's here because the Tribune wants to offer something." He nodded at Merobauda.

Volusianus gave Martialis a black look. "Spare me the camp humor." Martialis reddened and Gaius was startled by the little man's prudery. Volusianus turned back. "So, why have you brought this woman here?"

"I am the garrison's bookkeeper, Your Excellence." She was instinctively repelled by the little man and grimaced at using an honorific. It felt like soap on the tongue.

Volusianus sat back, his eyes narrowing. "Really?" He glanced at Martialis, who nodded in confirmation.

"Well, well. Odd things happen north of the Alps. What an interesting fact." He gave Gaius a look of irritation. "But don't think that you can wriggle out of this mess by blaming your situation on the incompetence of a woman. It's a pitiful ploy."

"Pitiful," Martialis repeated.

Volusianus waved his hand at them. "Now get out—both of you."

Merobauda bridled at this but in a cool level voice said, "I am told that you believe our books and your accounts don't agree," She made no move to leave the room.

"I don't just believe it, young woman, I know it. They don't." The little man looked at her closely for the first time, balanced between annoyance and mild amusement. Gaius wanted to interject something but couldn't think of anything useful to add. He felt Faustinus squeeze his arm for silence. "Be quiet. Let her do the talking," he whispered, almost inaudibly, in Gaulish.

"Begging your pardon, Excellence"—this was the hardest part of the sentence for Merobauda—"But they're in perfect agreement."

"Perfect agreement?" The claim was so bold, so shocking, so contrary to what Volusianus knew, that he wondered, despite himself, if there was some odd little truth hidden within it, something he should, after all, consider. And besides, this rustic girl amused him and he'd had no amusement since he'd left Milan.

"I'm only a provincial, but it seems to me if the Tribune is taken to Milan and the books are fine… Well, certainly there'd be some trouble, even for a man of Your Excellence's standing."

"Perhaps some small inconvenience," he conceded.

Gaius, who could not help himself, blundered into the conversation. "In such a case—and it is the case—my patron, His Eminence

Flavius Afranius Syagrius, would surely wish to, ah, balance the accounts. Metaphorically speaking." He had been bursting to speak. Faustinus squeezed his arm so hard he almost yelped.

The amusement drained from Volusianus's face. "Don't threaten me!" He turned to Martialis and nodded to him to show them the door. Gaius's heart sank and would have sunk further, had Merobauda not stepped up to the table and, as she prepared to address Volusianus, delivered a sharp kick with her heel into Gaius's shin. Faustinus's painful grip on his upper arm kept him from jumping.

"I'm afraid the Tribune is rather disturbed at the moment," Merobauda said, "And therefore, as I'm sure you'll agree, it's natural that he might speak a little heedlessly." She forced a modest smile at the Undersecretary and glanced at Gaius out of the corner of her eye to see whether he needed a second kick. No. He couldn't get a word out—he was gritting his teeth.

"He ought to be disturbed," Volusianus said.

"But even so, it would seem prudent, wouldn't it, to spend a moment glancing at the ledger again? I know that to a man of your Excellence's standing, my concern is really of no importance, and yet I feel it my duty to clear up this misunderstanding and head off the difficulty and embarrassment that you would encounter at Milan if this isn't done. Surely it's worth a few moments to see whether I am correct?"

Volusianus clamped his mouth tight as he thought about it; his nose and chin practically met. He could not be wrong about the ledger: it was all there in black and white. The slave boy had assured him of it, and the boy was good reckoner. Volusianus himself was not an accountant—like most Imperial bureaucrats, he had only bought his position and let others do the scut work—but this was an easy case. Still… "All right. But don't take long." Her effrontery was refreshing but, all the same, he was tiring a bit of her forwardness.

Merobauda pointed to one of the cupboards. "Faustinus, get me the abacus." He nodded gravely and fetched it. She opened the troublesome ledger and reached out to Volusianus for his document. She glanced at it, found an appropriate page in the ledger, swiped the beads to their starting positions in the slots of the abacus and began.

"This document of yours indicates one thousand five-hundred and sixty-two rations for the six month period beginning on the kalends of September."

"Too many for a unit of this size. Quite a few too many."

"Well, I respectfully suggest not. I think there's an honest mistake behind your suspicions." Gaius had never heard her speak with such deference to anyone before. She drew a wax tablet over to her side of the table and took up a stylus. She wrote MDLXII and drew a line below it.

"The first month, we deduct two hundred and twenty-two rations. This covers the rations of the common soldiers and the officers."

Volusianus nodded. It seemed right. Not debatable at all, really.

"This leaves us with one thousand three hundred and forty.

"All right," he agreed.

"And, of course, there is the legal skim of one twelfth of the remainder for the tribune."

"Yes, yes. It's statutory."

"And we take that away, and that leaves us one thousand two hundred twenty-nine." She absently moved some beads on the abacus—not for herself, but to prove the subtraction to Volusianus. She went on: "In month two we take away another two hundred twenty-two rations and one twelfth from the remainder, and that leaves us with one thousand and twenty-four. We do this for the third month: the distribution of rations for the men and the tribune's twelfth of what's left," she slid the beads to show her work, "and the remainder is seven hundred and forty. And now for the fourth month. We do the same and the balance is four hundred and seventy-five." She inscribed this carefully in the wax and pointed to it. For the fifth month we do the same: two-hundred and twenty-two rations for the men, a skim of one twelfth for the tribune and we are left with a balance of two hundred thirty-two."

At this point even Gaius could see that the arithmetic was going to work out. It made no sense. And yet it was about to work out. He glanced covertly at Volusianus, who looked puzzled, uncertain.

Faustinus shifted his grip to Gaius's other arm and gave it a painful warning squeeze. There was the hint of a smile on his lips.

Merobauda went on inexorably: "Sixth month. Two-hundred and twenty-two rations for the men, a skim of one twelfth of the remainder for the tribune. This adds up to exactly two-hundred and thirty-two, and nothing is left over. The two columns balance perfectly."

Volusianus blinked hard at the tablet but, of course, none of the figures changed. He glanced over at Martialis, who half stood up and the relapsed onto the stool, shaking his head in puzzlement. Volusianus glanced over at the gangling boy, his assistant, who had been watching the demonstration with a mixture of surprise and alarm. Well, if the boy said nothing—if he was convinced... Volusianus looked back at the table, quite obviously disconcerted, but entirely at a loss to dispute the result. He glanced meaningfully at the boy, whose face went white, but he kept quiet.

Merobauda continued: "Your Excellence, you can see, it all works out exactly." She tapped the bottom of the columns with the stylus.

Volusianus squinted at the figures doubtfully for several moments, but finally conceded. "Yes, so it seems, and yet..."

"I take it, Your Excellence, that you are not entirely convinced?" It was a dangerous gambit to allow that Volusianus might have doubts, but she had correctly judged that he was too proud to dispute with her when he was entirely at a loss.

He frowned at the tablet and rubbed his chin. "Something seems amiss." He stared at the columns for another moment. "And yet..."

She interrupted his thoughts before they went too far. "As you can see—master accountant that you are—that the solution is simple to such as yourself but, to the untrained?" She smiled in pity for the untrained. "But figures lead the untrained into all sorts of errors." She watched him every instant to see how he took her flattery.

"The untrained, yes, well..." Still, a trace of doubt lingered in his voice.

"But to you, Your Excellence—Well, I think the correctness of the account is obvious.

The little man squirmed slightly, shoved about alternately by flattery and lingering doubt. Merobauda went on: "And, of course, it's arithmetic. As we all know, only fools argue with it." She smiled brightly—and deceptively. "And, when they do, they lose."

Volusianus, who was not one to make concessions easily, particularly to a mere woman, grunted a final grudging assent. "It does seem that there has been an error." He glanced at the quailing boy again.

"And the order for my arrest?" Gaius dared.

"Lifted," Volusianus said and shook his head, as though to clear his vision. Then he waved them away. "Tribune Dolo, my party and I will leave in the morning. Be sure to have our horses ready."

"Of course, Excellence."

Merobauda, Faustinus and Gaius left the room with all of the assumed calm that they could muster. Merobauda held the troublesome ledger unobtrusively under her arm and thought about how soon she could burn it.

XX

GAIUS RELAXES
THE EMPEROR WORRIES

* * *

"What I can't figure out is why I was so worried about Volusianus and the ledger. I mean, all the figures come out exactly right."

Merobauda, Faustinus and Gaius were all back in his quarters, the first two sitting uneasily on shabby old chairs while Gaius stretched out comfortably on the couch with a glass of wine. Merobauda looked meaningfully at Faustinus, who shrugged to show his sympathy with her.

"I mean," Gaius went on fatuously, "why couldn't Volusianus see there was no problem in the first place? All that threatening me with death and so on, and he didn't have a leg to stand on. Though he seemed to enjoy it." Gaius looked into the glass and swirled the wine. "It's a good thing it all worked out properly because I didn't have enough cash to pay him off." Merobauda and Faustinus gave him stoney looks. Gaius went on happily: "I can tell that you're both dubious about so much of my ready money going to Milan to prosecute the lawsuit, but there really wasn't any choice." He looked down for a moment, musing. "Still, I hope Crastinus doesn't keep too much of it for himself."

"Yes. We can only hope." Merobauda's tone was very cold.

"It's a fine line, I suppose. One the one hand, he can enrich himself at my expense while prosecuting the case—I expect some of that, of course—or he can enrich himself by winning the case. Which will pay better? Or which will he reckon pays him better? That's really the question."

"You might have thought of that first." Her tone was icy.

"Unfortunately, I have to trust him." He said obliviously and took sip of wine. He leaned back against a pillow, and reflected on the questions before returning to the original subject. "Frankly, I just don't see why we need a second set of books if the figures all tot up correctly. And yet, it can't be as simple as that, can it?"

Merobauda winced and looked up at the ceiling in exasperation.

"I mean, we really have been operating as though we have fifty more soldiers than we do. It's so puzzling. In fact, I'm just as puzzled as Volusianus, now that I come to think of it."

Merobauda said, "You're worse than my first husband."

"First? Is there another?" Gaius, who had forgotten about the late, lightning-struck Rutuolf, glanced about the room as though there might be another husband somewhere—possibly lurking in a corner.

"You're my second husband. Or you will be if you have any sense."

"Well, I suppose..." he drifted into silence.

"Honestly. Sometimes I think you need a keeper."

Faustinus coughed gently and said, "Master, it was all just a trick of Cornelia Merobauda's."

"Really?" Gaius sat up and put his wine glass down. "Well, of course. Yes, of course it was. Anyone can see that."

"You couldn't. And, more to the point, Volusianus couldn't," Merobauda said.

"Mistress, I'm just as lost as the Tribune here about how you did it," Faustinus said. "The figures can't all add up. And yet they did. You're a wonder."

Merobauda, flattered, gave Faustinus a fleeting smile. "It's simple, really. All I had to do was subtract one set of figures from the other until they both came out to nothing. I could tell at a glance—you know how it is with me—that by subtracting the skim—reduced each month as a twelfth of what was left—as well as by the number of rations, it would all balance out over six months. But the real trick is to put the two columns, which have nothing to do with each other, side-by-side.[49] That gulled Volusianus into thinking they were related. Fortunately, because he's a mere bureaucrat, he doesn't know how to keep accounts."

"Brilliant!" Faustinus said. "So elegant and simple. And you did it on the fly."

"Why, thank you, Domestic!" She inclined her head.

Gaius frowned, struggling to grasp exactly what she had done. He gave up. "So, we do need the second set of books?"

"Honestly, Gaius! It was just a trick." Merobauda anxiously glanced over her shoulder at the bolted door and then went to the window. She pulled the shutter back an inch or two, stood on her tiptoes to peep out—uneasy despite her successful subterfuge and not sure what she was looking for. "The sooner that official is gone, the better off we'll be." She closed the shutter carefully and turned back to Gaius. "Make sure everything is ready for him to leave in the morning."

"Yes, of course. I'll see to it. And I suppose I should free you, Faustinus. Just in case, some time in the future, you're faced with," he hesitated, a "legal 'procedure.'"

"Thank you, Master."

"Your motivation doesn't flatter you," Merobauda said with her usual bluntness.

"Just get me some papyrus and two witnesses—you can impugn my character later."

Faustinus stood up to go but stopped when Merobauda said: "Bring another sheet."

"Yes?"

"For a marriage contract." She nodded toward his master. "Gaius here needs more help than even you can give him."

---

[49] Although the ancient sources are silent on this question, it would seem that Merobauda invented the ploy "*Quomodo Evanescit Denarius?*" which is generally known nowadays as "Where Did the Missing Dollar Go?"

* * *

Gratian sat forward on his throne, his chin on his right fist. His Consistory stood at a respectful distance before him, a half-circle of men in robes of deeply-saturated claret, green and violet that complemented the mosaic of the throne-room floor, a fantastic expanse of squares, curves, circles and allegorical figures in glimmering tile and glittering glass, claret, olive and cerulean. Behind the Consistory and across the room, dividing it in half (to keep the Emperor from the rude gaze of the lower aristocracy), a tall curtain of heavy purple stuff hung from a gleaming, gilded rod loaded with further swags of purple. In each of the four corners stood pairs of Alan soldiers in the spotless white tunics of the Imperial Guard. After several minutes of silence had passed, the Emperor straightened and waved dismissively at his Consistory. "Leave me." The men bowed deeply and backed slowly toward the curtains, which ushers held open. He pointed to one courtier. "You remain, Prefect." Syagrius bowed again and kept his place, placidly indifferent to the jealous glances of the other great men as they silently slipped out. The ushers disappeared, the massive drapes fell to, and the two were alone in the great, hollow room—apart from the white-clad guards, who watched Syagrius with an almost inhuman fixedness. The Emperor waved Syagrius up to the throne, waited a few moments longer until the courtiers' footsteps had faded away, and then spoke.

"I cannot hide from you that I am rather uneasy."

"Indeed, Your Serenity? It troubles me to hear this. If Your Magnificence might condescend to tell me what concerns you, I would certainly do my poor best to ameliorate the situation if that should be within my small powers." He kept his hands clasped and respectfully hidden in the sleeves of his dark red dalmatic.

"It's Britain about which I'm apprehensive," Gratian said.

Syagrius stood motionless and silent, his eyebrows raised. Perhaps the Emperor knew something he did not—unlikely as that might be. He waited patiently until Gratian went on: "It's difficult to put a finger on." He looked all about the room, at the walls clad in light-grey marble shot through with streaks and islands of dark green, at the wan spring light that poured past the gilded network of the high windows of colorless glass. He swept his eyes over the furnishings of the room: the gilded lamps, the ebony tables, the chairs where his secretaries sat to take dictation, their finials intricately carved and covered with gold leaf. Above him, the ceiling was covered in mosaics: putti flew about and peacocks strutted among fantastically ornate foliage. The margin of the mosaic ceiling was defined by thousands of gold tesserae that winked in the yellow light of dozens of silver lamps hanging from slender chains.

"This is a prison, Syagrius. Rather floridly decorated. The decoration and furnishings—they deceive everyone. Some fools even envy me." He waved a hand. "But I'm a prisoner, when you come down to it."

"I must protest, Your Serenity," Syagrius said, as a matter of form. But he agreed.

"Certainly, I can step out. Hunt if I please, or visit one of my villas, but…" he hesitated, thinking. "Even then I carry the prison on my back wherever I go."

"Perhaps your Serenity overstates the case."

"I don't. And, of course, you know I don't." He sighed. "This is a comfortable prison, as prisons go. The difficulty is to know what goes on outside this gilded jail. There are so many bureaus, so many administrators at so many levels in so many provinces. No one tells me what's going on. Or, well, they'll tell me things, but as they think it favors me. And as it favors them—as it advances their interests or those of their family and friends and dependents. It comes to the same thing, really. And then there's the money flowing all around, a sort of underground river carving hidden channels all about me and…" He lost control of the metaphor and went quiet.

"Has Your Serenity heard something?" Syagrius asked in his most soothing tone.

"No, Prefect. But that's just it. It seems to me—it feels to me—that there is less word than there ought to be from the British provinces. From some of the Gallic ones too. Fewer reports or…" the Emperor thought for a moment how to express himself, "… or fewer reports of any real substance."

"This is an impression then, Your Serenity. Nothing has been directly reported?"

"Say that, if you like." Gratian was defensive. "But an Emperor doesn't live long if he can't sense a change in the weather."

"I defer to Your Serenity's judgment, of course." He bowed. "We are speaking of Count Maximus?"

The Emperor nodded. "And yet, without some proof, or some colorable accusation, it's difficult, even dangerous to act against him."

"Because he is a client of His Serenity of the East, the Augustus Theodosius?[50]"

"That will not protect him in the event of treason but, short of that, he must be handled carefully. Particularly if he is innocent."

"You entertain that possibility, Your Serenity?"

"That possibility, yes." He stood, went behind the throne, laid his hands on the back of it, and looked over it at Syagrius as though he were protecting himself. "You have many clients in Gaul. Do they tell you anything?"

"I have many clients there." He nodded. "Their real value, however, lies in this: should your suspicions prove true and Count Maximus attempt an usurpation, he will unknowingly have a number of them in his own circle. And that will be helpful to us. In the meantime, they quietly serve the Empire, and thus you, in their—shall we say—ordinary capacities."

"So, no news."

Syagrius shook his head.

XXI

GAIUS IS BACK IN TROUBLE

MEROBAUDA CONTEMPLATES A RADICAL SOLUTION

* * *

Faustinus hurried to the tavern the next morning immediately after Gaius had been arrested again. He cast about the great dim room looking for Merobauda. Vilfrida, behind the counter, guessed what he wanted and pointed to a rear door that led out on a fenced yard enclosing a vegetable garden and a pair of apple trees covered with white blossoms under which a half-dozen rusty-brown chickens scratched. Merobauda stood in the far corner stirring a pile of smoking ashes with a stick. She turned as he approached and pointed to the cinders with it. "The off-book ledger. I don't trust Gaius with it. I'll come up with another when Volusianus is good and gone. By the way, how are you enjoying your first day of freedom, Faustinus Aquitanius?"

"I don't know—I haven't had a chance to think about it." He pointed at the smoking ash-pile. "That doesn't matter anymore."

"No? Why not?" She stirred the ashes vigorously.

"They've arrested Gaius again."

Merobauda scowled, broke the stick in two and tossed it on the

200

embers. She rubbed ashes from her hands on a rag hanging from her belt. But, despite her deliberate actions, Faustinus could sense a welling anxiety in her.

"The same charge?"

Faustinus nodded.

"I was afraid of that. It was that slave-boy of Volusianus's, wasn't it?"

"I think so. They beat him last night. We could hear the screams."

"I could tell he was sharp. He must have seen what I was doing, but couldn't keep it to himself when they flogged him."

"So, what's left now, Mistress? If you come up with another trick, it'll be seen for what it is, even if Volusianus isn't clever enough to see how it works."

She folded her arms and looked down, thinking. "What's the penalty for skimming? As much as he's done? Death?" She hardly knew why she bothered asking.

"Very likely. Or at the least flogging, branding and destitution. Who knows, really, what the law is these days, except that it's hard if you can't pay your away around it." He looked up at the sky. "Why did Gaius have to spend so much on that damned lawsuit? If he'd kept the money, he'd have had enough to pay Volusianus off." He paced nervously. "All this bloody corruption! It's, it's…" He couldn't think how to finish, he was so distraught. "I suppose it's just the way of the world. But if he was going to wade into the phantom soldier business, why didn't he use some foresight? He's a charmer, really, but he seldom watches where he's going."

Merobauda had been regarding him silently. "Let's not worry about what's done. Let's see what we can do."

Faustinus looked at her miserably. "I can't think of anything."

"Just give me a few moments." She twisted her apron in her hands, her eyes focused on the middle distance.

Faustinus waited, hoping devoutly that she would pull a solution out of nowhere, as a conjuror pulls an egg from behind a peasant's ear on market day. After a few long moments she nodded to herself and turned to him. He felt a wave of relief; ever practical, Merobauda had found a solution. He pulled a handkerchief from his sleeve, wiped his forehead and smiled at her.

"We'll have a mutiny." She said it in such a matter-of-fact way that he couldn't believe he had heard correctly. She saw this by his expression and repeated herself. Faustinus stood thunderstruck for a moment. The enormity of the suggestion staggered him. She could only be joking and yet, at a time like this? But then, he reflected, it wasn't in her nature to joke. Perhaps her suggestion deserved to be considered, so he considered it. Merobauda smiled at him guardedly, and he was half won over.

"Well, the soldiers like him," he conceded. "And I'd reckon that half of the Alaman ones are cousins of yours…"

"Second or third. But that will help."

"And the other half would listen to you now that you're the wife of the commander…"

Merobauda said, "Gaius is popular, and they're high-spirited boys, most of them, so they'd enjoy it, don't you think?"

Faustinus still had reservations. "Won't the army just send troops to—well—settle things later? And would Gaius survive that?"

"I can't say, but it'll buy him time."

"And that's enough?"

"Maybe. Maybe not. But that's our only choice, as I see it." Merobauda hurried on before he could think of an answer. "Let's not waste time." She had become her usual no-nonsense self. They turned as they heard the back door of the tavern open and saw Probus Martialis step into the yard.

"What are you doing here?" Faustinus asked bluntly. There was no trace of deference in his tone.

Martialis smiled smugly. "I've stopped by as a courtesy to Merobauda."

She looked at him scornfully. "Courtesy. A new experience for you. How does it feel?"

He sneered at the gibe. "I've come to tell you that the Tribune Dolo has been arrested again." He hooked his thumbs in his belt. "That performance yesterday." He shook his head in respect. "You're a clever girl—I'll give you that. But your trick's been worked out."

"Though not by you or that awful creature Volusianus."

"I wouldn't slur him, Merobauda. If you provoke him, he can make things more unpleasant than they need be."

Faustinus risked a question. "Does he have the power of summary execution?"

Martialis grinned at him. "He'd get away with it, if that's what you mean." He savored Faustinus's obvious dismay and watched him quietly for a moment to draw it out. "But that's not what he wants to do. He wants to take the Tribune back to Milan as a trophy."

"What does that mean?" Merobauda advanced on him a step.

"Volusianus wants to prove he's been diligent in cleaning up corruption on the frontier. Dolo's trial—and execution—will show that he's doing his job keeping the commanders of the units honest."

Faustinus felt sick and spoke with bitter cynicism. "That's what Volusianus does, then? Tours the Gallic provinces reinforcing the integrity of the Imperial system?" It had no effect on Martialis.

"Don't play dumb, Domestic. You know—or you should—how the game is played. Volusianus visits the camps, checks the accounts, determines by how much the skim exceeds that allowed by law, or finds out how many phantom soldiers are on the rolls."

"Then he takes a grift of the skim and the pay of the phantom soldiers and moves on to the next camp."

"That's right. That's exactly what he does. Unless the commander hasn't saved enough to pay, in which case it's arrest, trial and death. Or sometimes just a thorough flogging with iron rods—and that might be worse. But usually it's just a sizable payoff. After all, he has to pay back the investors who lent him the money to buy his position as Undersecretary, and he can't do that on his official salary."

"So, how did you avoid his demands when you were commander?" Faustinus asked. "You're as guilty as Tribune Dolo."

"More," he said smugly. "But I was smart enough to keep money aside. Your fool of a Tribune didn't do that. Though what he's spent the money on out here I can't figure out."

"Why are you here with that old vulture?" Merobauda asked.

"In return for a small bribe in Milan—we call them "emoluments" there, you know—in return for an emolument, it was arranged that I be assigned as Volusianus's aide and commander of the troop protecting him. In return, he gives me a twenty-fourth of his rake-off, but I've agreed to forego my cut until he's made two hundred and fifty solidi. After that I'll start getting my share. Everybody's happy."

"Everybody's happy," Faustinus repeated with dull irony.

"Everybody." Martialis raised his hand and counted on his fingers. "First, I'm happy—I stay out of trouble and keep my position as a Protector. Second, Volusianus is happy because he makes a good living and pays off his investors. Third, the commanders of the cohorts and legions are happy because they only have to give up part of their skim, and, fourth, the Administration is happy because it looks like the army is up to strength."

Merobauda said, "I can give him ten solidi for Gaius. Give me a week and I can get another five."

"Fifteen solidi to buy the Tribune out of this?" Martialis was incredulous. "Once your little tribune is dead and the news of it gets back out here, Volusianus will get twice the usual rake off from the other provincial commanders next year. You think he'd throw that away for a pittance? I thought you were sharper than that, girl."

Merobauda scowled ferociously but said, "What's this courtesy you were talking about just now?"

He looked around the yard and turned to give the tavern an assessing look. "How many beds for travelers do you have up there?" He pointed to the second floor.

"Don't play games. You know the answer. It's ten. You made up that tax on my property just before you left. Thirty-two folles: three for each bed and two for the great room."

"Ah yes, I remember now." He rubbed his chin as though he had to think about it. "And I've seen you feed as many as fifty in an evening, apart from drinks. So, what's your income in any given year?"

"Get to the point."

"Maybe, just maybe, I could convince Volusianus to take over your property and the ownership of this slave," he pointed to Faustinus. "I'd need a little encouragement from you too, Merobauda." He leered. "I've been a little lonely on the road and I've always wondered what you'd be like…"

"You're scum," Merobauda said in a flat tone as though she were remarking on something beyond dispute, like the length of her foot or the color of her shift. Martialis didn't redden; he was too brutal or too complacent. She added, "And Faustinus has been freed."

Martialis glanced at him and then turned back to her: "Freed, eh? Well, that tribune of yours—he just makes one mistake after another, doesn't he?" He shook his head. "Freeing an educated slave? Throwing away what? Thirty or forty solidi? Just like that!"

Merobauda turned away abruptly and strode off, waving Faustinus to follow. Martialis called after them: "Don't bother with his quarters." He paused a moment for effect. "You might try the jail!"

* * *

The jail was an intensely dark room in the cellar of the fort, closed with a door of age-blackened oak planks and fastened with a crude iron bolt on the outside. In the center was a single small iron-barred window through which Merobauda and Faustinus could smell fermenting straw, mildew, urine, sweat and feces. A pair of Martialis's men stood guard.

Merobauda ignored them and, because she was tall, was able to squint through the window into the dark cell. She wrinkled her nose at the smell and called out, "Gaius!" He was there in a flash, grasping the bars and pushing his pale face out between them as far as he could. Faustinus, who had known him so very long, had never seen him look so frightened. Gaius's knuckles, as he grasped the bars, were white.

"Hello," he said, in a barely steady voice. Well, he was still game. More or less, anyway. Merobauda looked at him closely for a moment or two, searching his eyes, at a loss for what to say. "I can't tell you not to worry," he said to her. "That would be stupid." He looked away for a moment, unable to speak. "But don't worry for yourself—after that brilliant demonstration of yours, Volusianus won't embarrass himself by arresting you and showing himself to be your fool. So…" He hesitated, too distracted to gather his thoughts. "I'm going to Milan. So, if I don't get back—you know there's some chance of that…" He said it with a forced smile. "Just forget about me." He rose on tiptoe to look over Merobauda's shoulder at the guards and said sharply to them in Gaulish: "Come over here!" They looked at each other and frowned, but neither stepped forward. One called back, *"Quo dici?*[51]" in a thick Illyrian accent. Relieved that the guards didn't understand, Gaius said to Faustinus in Gaulish: "I've kept a few solidi behind. Five or six, something like that. In the false bottom of the chest."

"I know." Faustinus looked as pained as Gaius.

"Oh, you do. Well, they're yours. Take them now while you can. You'll need them. At least Merobauda's got the tavern. You'll need something. Now, listen: I don't think the soldiers know I'm arrested yet, and maybe it doesn't matter. Take one of the boats at the dock and get across the Rhine. Take one of the boys who speaks Alaman to help you—maybe Celer or Theudomar. Merobauda must have cousins over there who'll help you till things blow over."

Faustinus sighed so hard he sounded like a horse chuffing.

"And don't come back until Volusianus and Martialis are gone. Think of me sometimes—it's been a good run, old friend."

"Don't talk that way!" He looked down, afraid that he might show tears.

"Shut up, you two!" one of the guards said sharply, suspicious of the conversation they couldn't understand.

Merobauda couldn't follow the Gaulish either, but that didn't matter—she was concentrating on her plan, firming it up. She kissed her hand and touched Gaius's forehead through the bars. She said quietly in Alaman: "We'll get you out. You'll see." He wondered what she'd said, but was happy just to hear her voice one last time.

The guards chuckled as Merobauda and Faustinus went out.

---

[51] Vulgar Latin: "What are you saying?" More properly "Quod dicis," but the soldier didn't have the advantage of a classical education.

XXII

MEROBAUDA AND FAUSTINUS TRY THEIR HAND AT MUTINY

* * *

As she left the jail, Merobauda took the dank stone steps two at a time, her skirts flying about her long legs. Faustinus jogged behind her. "You've got an idea about how to do this?" She nodded but said nothing until they had reached the center of the courtyard where she looked around to be sure there was no one nearby to overhear.

Faustinus said quietly, "You've settled on mutiny, haven't you? Absolutely settled on it?"

"It's the only way," she replied in a remarkably even tone, as though she were talking about how to do some household duty, like patching a wall or making soap. "You'll have to rile up the men, Domestic. That's your job, but I'll help you with it."

"What about afterwards?"

"There'll be more trouble then, of course. But that's a problem for another day."

"That sounds remarkably like something Gaius would say."

Merobauda looked at him sharply. "It's different for you and me. He chooses to do things that way. We don't have a choice. No more talk! It's time to get to work."

"How?"

"Go get Una and bring her to me." She pointed to the tribunal in the corner of the courtyard from which the centurions (and Gaius, when he felt like addressing the men) gave orders. "I'll meet you there."

* * *

Faustinus found Una playing jacks by herself in a hallway of the praetorium. Faustinus swept her up and carried her off at a run, scattering counters across the tiled floor and leaving the ball to roll into a corner. Una held him calmly around the neck, a bland expression on her trusting face—she and Faustinus were great friends: nothing he might do was alarming. By the time they had reached the tribunal, half a dozen curious soldiers were gathering before it, Arverno among them. They all watched Merobauda, who stood on the platform crying out and waving her arms over-theatrically, as it seemed to Faustinus. On the other hand, she might be correct in her approach. He couldn't judge: he'd never tried to foment a mutiny before—perhaps this was how it was done.

Merobauda continued to call out in melodramatic distress in Latin and Alaman, "Vae! Vae! Weh! Weh[52]!" As he mounted the platform, more soldiers approached, some drifting slowly, others jogging. Merobauda took Una from him and put her straddling over her hip. Faustinus looked about. Two figures darkened the doorway to the praetorium, one big, one little and stooped. He put a hand over his eyes and squinted to get a clear sight of them. Martialis and Volusianus.

Merobauda said quietly to Una, "In little while I'm going to squeeze your leg. Every time I do that, you must shout "Daddy," as loud as you can." Una nodded solemnly. "Daddy," she said. "But very loud, " Merobauda told her and then turned to Faustinus. "Get on with it, Domestic. Gaius's life is in your hands."

Faustinus would usually have flinched at the cliché—he was, after

---

[52] For a full appreciation of Merobauda's exclamations, readers should note that, by this time the Latin "v" (originally pronounced "w") was pronounced "v," and the Germanic "w" was still pronounced "w" (and not "v," as it was later.) So, no mental adjustment is required of the modern reader. Convenient, no?

all, no less Enthymemus's student than Gaius was—but this was no time to judge style. And she was right: he was about to juggle with Gaius's doom, so he thought back to what Enthymemus had taught about addressing crowds. The old teacher's precept came back to him: "Crowds are not susceptible to reason, but only to images, slogans, affirmations and repetition." He took a deep breath to help clear his head and tried to think calmly, despite the approach of Martialis and Volusianus. ***Don't let them shake you***, he told himself. ***Don't let them spook you! Don't stumble!*** He scanned the crowd, a good thirty men now, and the sentries along the wall were peering at him. He waved them to come down.

"More men!" he told Arverno. "I want everyone here! Everyone!"

"The women too!" Merobauda shouted at him.

Arverno, who couldn't tear himself away from the scene, barked at an optio. "You heard! Get everyone out here. Everyone!" The man set off at a trot, shouting, but it was hardly necessary because the excitement of the unusual event had flashed through the fort, and soldiers, women and calos were running up. Even the cook, Latro, came stumping over, supporting himself on one side with his crutch and on the other by a scullion's shoulder.

Volusianus and Martialis had pushed to the front of the crowd, and the Undersecretary scowled up at Faustinus and Merobauda. "What is this business?" His voice was thin and sharp.

"You'll hear!" Faustinus replied in a grave tone. Enthymemus had taught that vague threats were the most effective, so he added nothing more. Instead he waited until most of the men had gathered—and the two-score women who lived in the fort. In a knot in the middle of the throng Martialis's escort clustered defensively, six splendidly-dressed cavalrymen ostentatiously resting their hands on their sword pommels. But only six. Faustinus waited a few moments longer, fanning the excitement of the crowd with his silence. He waited until he could see the men at the back of the crowd shifting about for a better view like wavelets in a choppy bay. Good. He had their attention.

"Soldiers!" he shouted. "Listen to me! I have news of great importance to all of you! And more than this, it is appalling news!" He waited a moment, a long moment until many of them leaned forward or turned their heads slightly to hear better. Excellent—he'd hooked them. Now it was time to draw them like a fish on a line. "Soldiers, you are among the most unhappy of men, though you do not yet know it." That was good start—it had the attraction of mystery. Faustinus shook his head to show that he was unhappy too. He looked out at the crowd until all eyes were on him. It was time to reveal the situation. "And I am as unhappy as any man here. More so, indeed! My patron, the Most Excellent Tribune Dolo, the man who has supported me, protected me, counseled me, treated me as an equal because he is confident in his station, has been arrested!" Everyone looked surprised, and Faustinus gave the men a few moments to turn to each other and exchange remarks. "Oh, yes!" Faustinus looked the crowd over, choosing a man here and there to look in the eye. "Arrested! And what for?" He waited as though for a reply, but when Volusianus piped up with "Peculation and…" Faustinus interrupted with a scornful laugh. "'Peculation,' you call it. I call it 'Duty!'" Faint murmurs from the crowd. Good. "Is it not dutiful, nay honorable, for Our Excellence the Tribune to look after the troops which His Serenity the Emperor has entrusted to him?" The crowd murmured that it was. "And has he not done that?" There was general agreement that he had. "I say to you that he has done it—and done it well indeed!" He put his hands on the railing of the tribunal and leaned forward, warming to his oration. He repeated even louder: "I say that he has done it well indeed!" There was agreement again, this time more enthusiasm. Faustinus pulled a silver coin from purse on his belt and held it up before the crowd. He walked slowly from one side of the tribunal to the other with the glinting coin aloft. "When our Tribune led you brave men against the terrible bagaudae, a threat to the entire province, did he not stand in the front ranks with the bravest of you?" They agreed that he had, and there was great excitement in their voices. "And did he not lead you safely out of great danger while under deadly assault from those vicious men?"

"He did!" the men shouted, becoming part of the event, part of the theater.

"And did he not lead you, sword in hand, on a successful assault of the bagaudae camp, utterly heedless of any danger to himself?" They agreed, despite the facts, that he had.

"Of course he did! Of course he did! You remember it well!" He scanned the crowd nodding back at those who nodded at him. "And you recall his dented helmet, mute testimony to his valor—the equal of yours!"

The soldiers replied with enthusiastic cheers. Faustinus nimbly tossed the silver coin from one hand to the other and back again as the soldiers watched. He held it up once more, and it winked in the sun, which had just then agreed to slip from behind a cloud.

"And did he not forgo any share of the booty for himself and give it all to you, without thought for himself? All to you, his comrades-in-arms?" He flung the coin into the crowd, where a hand snapped it from the air. "He thought no more of those silver coins than that! He gave them all to you. All to you!" He paused a moment and regarded the crowd. They were simmering with excitement. "And, tell me, how many of you went on the campaign with him?"

"Ninety!" the soldiers shouted.

"And how many returned?"

"Ninety!"

Faustinus nodded at them. "Ninety went to fight and ninety returned! And this is the commander that these," and here he paused dramatically, "these strangers from Italy—" he pointed to Volusianus and Martialis—"have imprisoned."

"But men!" Martialis said, turning to the crowd. "I am no stranger to you…" But he was drowned out with hisses and whistling—they remembered him all too well. He stepped back in dismay and bumped against a garrison soldier, who shoved him. Martialis's escort started unobtrusively backing out of the crowd.

Faustinus went on, no longer doubting his power over the men. He was instead fascinated by it. "And yet your excellent Tribune is wrongfully arrested and languishes in that stinking jail on a pallet of rotting straw, without light enough to see his hand before his face." The crowd rumbled unhappily. Faustinus nodded at them. "Does he deserve this? I say, 'No!'

There were some shouts of "Injustice!"

"Injustice indeed! Let me ask you this, fellow soldiers of the Tribune: how many of you have eaten today? Shout it out to me!" Everyone had eaten and they shouted that they had. "And you ate yesterday and the day before. And you ate well. And you have eaten well since the day our Tribune Gaius Obsequens Dolo took command. And this is no small thing." He pointed to Probus Martialis. "That man meant to let you starve! Did you know that? Perhaps you are unaware of his treachery! Would you care to learn of it?" Indeed they did. They pressed closer to the tribunal. "Recall how you unloaded that barge under the direction of the Noble Tribune Dolo? Oh, that was just a day's work for you. Little did you know that he was acting on your behalf. Oh, yes! On your behalf! And he was risking punishment—severe punishment from such as these"—and here he pointed at Martialis and Volusianus—"Risking punishment, even perhaps an ignominious death at the order of villainous officials—yet he dared to put his hands on the supplies that you men require as you stand your noble watch on the frontier. And what prompted him take such a risk? I will tell you! That man, who calls himself 'Protector,' and called himself your tribune had sold your food—taken the very food from your mouths—and sold it for the money to buy himself a high position. Was ever a man so vile? He parades in fine clothes and amuses himself in the Imperial Capital while you might have starved up here. Indeed, I say, he meant you to starve so that he could preen himself and live at ease in Milan! And for the crime of providing for you and your wives and children, your Noble Tribune Dolo lies in the stinking jail." The crowd rumbled in anger with a sound like thunder in the distance. The sound might have disconcerted even Faustinus, who had conjured it, except that he was elated, flush with his power of his oratory. "And, if you desert your commander in this, his most desperate hour, what can you hope for?" He pointed again at Martialis and Volusianus. "Expect a new commander strange to you, as corrupt, as dishonorable, as unjust and as brutal as Probus Martialis, whose character you know all too well!"

At that moment Una shouted "Daddy! Daddy!" And Merobauda

called out to the men, "Honor requires that you have mercy on your commander's wife and daughter, who would otherwise perish from want. Free my husband Tribune Dolo!" Merobauda squeezed Una's leg for an additional "Daddy!" Faustinus noted that Merobauda had managed in the excitement to unbind and dishevel her hair. The soldiers' wives and other camp women gathered at the back took up wailing, and Martialis and Volusianus, who had been unobtrusively drifting out of the crowd, gave up any attempt at subtlety and forced their way through. As they squirmed and shoved, the soldiers jostled them, gently at first, then gradually with more violence, until they reeled and bobbed like corks in a flood. Volusianus shouted ineffectively for his guards, but those six men stood in a defensive half-circle, their backs to the west wall of the courtyard, their swords drawn. Martialis drew his blade in a single, practiced action and slashed in front of him in a flat arc. It swept against the chest of one of the sentries from the wall. The blade was turned harmlessly by his jack, but the soldier recoiled and Martialis stepped into the opening, dragging Volusianus behind him by his collar toward the protection of their guards by the wall.

Faustinus reckoned the moment had come to order Gaius freed, but even has he spoke he heard a muffled shout from his left, and turning that way, saw Gaius, riding toward him on the shoulders of half-a-dozen cheering soldiers. He blinked in the sunlight and turned his head about, clearly confused at the turn of events. When they had deposited him on the tribunal, the men gave a tremendous shout, in answer to which Gaius, who had begun to grasp the situation, waved both his arms. While smiling at the exuberant soldiers, he said to Faustinus and Merobauda, "Good work. I think. And how did you pull this off?" He clasped his hands together and waved them over his head like an athletic champion. The men roared.

"It's all a matter of education, Gaius. I think you should write a letter of thanks to Enthymemus."

"I see. And what happens now?" he said out of the corner of his mouth while smiling and nodding at the crowd.

"We haven't gotten any further. Try to be satisfied with this," Faustinus said.

Gaius observed: "I think you may have to suggest something to the men or we may have a lynching." He pointed to a soldier running out from the storerooms with a coil of rope. Faustinus had lost control of the men—the crowd had taken on a life of its own. Martialis realized this too and saw where things leading. He had joined his little troop by the wall, and now he had them form a ring around Volusianus. With their swords out, they menaced any who approached and walked quickly to the main gate, careful to maintain their formation. A dozen of the garrison followed them menacingly but, enthusiastic as they were, satisfied themselves merely by driving them through the gate. Someone threw the levers of the portcullis and, with a rattling of the dogs on the gears, it came crashing down behind the fleeing Imperial officials, who shouted threats and brandished their swords as they went off. One of the garrison ran up with a crossbow and shot through the portcullis and into the ground behind them, to speed them along. Faustinus wiped his forehead looked around, dazed at his success.

Gaius looked at the cheering, rambunctious men, clasped his hands behind his back and rocked on his heels, proud as if he'd pulled off the coup himself. He asked Faustinus again, "What now?"

Faustinus was already thinking ahead about how to handle the men, now that they'd been riled up. "I think the men need of a holiday, Master. Footraces, wrestling, bowling, some musicians from the village—and lots of beer."

"Get me a cart and six men and I'll get you lots of beer," Merobauda said.

"And then after that?" Faustinus asked, looking further into the future.

"After that, more trouble, I suppose," she said wearily. "Those two vultures and their men had to leave their horses and baggage behind, but even on foot they'll Argentovaria in about three or four days. After that? Who knows? But we'd better be prepared for it."

XXIII

GAIUS, FAUSTINUS AND MEROBAUDA FIND CIVIL WAR HELPFUL

* * *

The next day things around the fort ran raggedly. The soldiers were all hung over; most slept very late, and Gaius, sensing that cajolery was called for, gave no one any real duties for the day apart from manning the walls. Even so, the soldiers on the parapet half leaned on their spears or slouched against the battlements, or sat with their backs against the wall and dozed. Gaius ordered the gates kept closed and the portcullis left down for the day. He nodded happily at the situation as he strolled about the courtyard with Faustinus. They stepped around empty beer barrels and a chalked circle in which there had been wrestling (a battered army boot lay in the middle of it), past an old mattress peppered with crossbow bolts propped against the wall as a target for drunken marksmen. Two of the marksmen were sleeping uneasily in the shadows against the wall. Gaius considered them in silence for a moment and then went on, keeping an eye out for the half-dozen lawn-bowling balls scattered across the courtyard where they might trip up the unwary. Here and here illiterate and obscene doggerel had been scrawled in charcoal on the walls. Gaius checked each verse to be sure that he was not the subject of any. No, it was mostly the optios who came in for colorful criticism. He continued on with his stroll but stopped when he noticed some movement under a wagon parked in the far corner of the courtyard. He went over to it and knelt down, turning his head to see better. Volusianus's slave boy peeped out at him from the shadows.

"Come out of there." Gaius stood up and brushed off his knees. The boy crawled out and straightened up, working the stiffness out of his limbs.

Faustinus asked him "What's your name?"

"Archelaus." He ducked his head. "Your Excellence won't send me back to the Undersecretary?" He looked terrified. "I, I..." he trailed off. He squinted and turned his face away, raising a hand involuntarily as though he expected a blow. "I had to tell him about the trick." His face flushed and a pair of welts stood out on each cheek. "I didn't want to, but..." He stood there shaking.

"No one's going to beat you." The boy's terror of Gaius had brought out an urge to protect him. "You're not alone in wanting to see the last of him. The Domestic here will find something for you to do around here. Now go get cleaned up." The boy ran off.

Gaius said, "Well, then, we are in a bit of fix. All the same, it would be churlish if I failed to compliment you and Merobauda on provoking the mutiny." Merobauda came up to them at this point and he continued, "But I must say, your plan doesn't seem to show a lot of forethought. The consequences afterward—you two don't seem to have properly considered them." It was important to him to express some criticism; it showed he was back in charge of things.

"I know," Merobauda said. "It's just like one of your schemes in that way. The difference is that *we* had no choice."

"I wonder if there's any way we could pay our way out of this." Gaius put his hand on his chin. "Do you think we could sell the horses? The ones Martialis's troopers rode in on? And the remounts? That would be what—ten? To Adelgar, maybe? Or maybe to that troop attached to the legion downriver? You know, the Argentovarienses? It would save us the trouble of getting them across the Rhine." He began to wander off the point in his enthusiasm at working out a scheme.

"We'll keep their shields; we wouldn't get much for them anyway. I'll just have them re-painted in one of our designs. And there's the rest of the baggage they left behind; who knows what's there? But we ought to get a few solidi for the clothing and saddles. Now, those we could get over the river easily—maybe sell them to the Alamans…" He trailed off, trying to rough out in his head what it might all come to.

Merobauda put her hands on her hips. "No, Gaius. We can't pay our way out of this with the price of ten horses!"

"They're good ones, you know. From the Field Army."

"Are you listening to me?"

"Yes, I am, Carissima, but I do wonder whether, if we sold them and used the money for a really fine gift for Syagrius and then asked for his intercession, we might just get away with the mutiny. We'll tell him it was all a mistake. You know—that sort of thing.

"There wasn't any mistake."

"Well, you caused Volusianus to make a mistake. You know—about the ledger."

"About the ledger, but not about the mutiny, I didn't."

"I'm Syagrius's client," he persisted.

"So are thousands of other men, high and low—so how are you unique? I'll tell you how you're unique: he gave you this position and now you're in open revolt against the Empire! I bet he doesn't have any other client in open revolt against the Empire. Not one! I'm sure he'll rush to help."

"That's putting the worst face on it, Merobauda, I must say. It isn't as though I'm some sort of imperial usurper. And besides, I didn't provoke the mutiny." Gaius sounded petulant.

"All right, then, Faustinus and I provoked the mutiny. But you're in command."

"I'm not so sure sometimes," he said looking from one to the other.

"We're getting nowhere," Faustinus observed the obvious.

Merobauda turned to him and said sharply, "So, we're getting nowhere. What's your suggestion?"

"Well," Faustinus said, trying for a joke, "nothing would help us more than some sort of ***deus ex machina***[53]."

"What's that?" Merobauda asked, suspiciously.

"It's something in the theater, Carissima," Gaius said.

"Theater? Like that troupe that came through here two years ago with their dirty skits and coarse songs? Can't you two keep to the point?"

"Not that kind of theater," Gaius said.

"He means 'High Art,' Merobauda." Faustinus put his hands up in a gesture of mock respect.

"Oh, like they have in Rome." Her mouth went down at the corners.

"Yes," Gaius said. "Aeschylus and that sort of thing, you know."

"No, I don't. Who is he? Some slippery Greek friend of yours back there? I've heard about them."

"Anyway," Gaius went on, "The idea is this: when there's a plot problem in a play that can't be easily solved, they lower an actor dressed as one of the gods onto the stage, and then he sorts out the situation in the last act."

"That sounds like cheating to me," Merobauda said.

"Well, you see—" Gaius went on pedantically, but he was cut off by a shout from the sentry over the main gate. All three looked up.

"Your Excellence! A troop of horsemen!"

"What now?" Faustinus asked, with a sudden stab of fear. "How could Martialis and Volusianus have reported the mutiny so soon?"

"They can't have," Merobauda said. "These men must be on some other business."

"Still, I'm not eager to find out what it is," Faustinus said.

"Well, we have to," Merobauda said with her usual practicality. She hurried up to the stairs to the top of the wall, lifting her skirts as she went. Gaius and Faustinus followed warily. When they reached her, she was gazing down at Magnentius Terentianus at the head of a small troop of cavalrymen and a string of remounts and packhorses. He was not the neat figure Gaius had seen at the villa: his windblown hair stood up, and there were white salt rings under his arms. His gray horse shifted restlessly under him, as though tired of the saddle.

---

[53] You can look this up in a reference book, or just read on until Gaius explains the term.

His men looked worn out and grim.

"Tribune Dolo! I see the gates are shut. So, you've already heard the news!"

"No. What news?" Gaius leaned over the parapet to hear better.

"Magnus Maximus, Count of Britain, has declared himself Emperor. He's landed near the mouth of the Rhine, and the Duke of Lower Germany has gone over to him. The Duke of Upper Germany—our duke—remains loyal."

"Come in and we'll talk!" Gaius shouted down.

"No! There's no time and not much to say. The Master of the Cavalry for Gaul orders all the forts along the Rhine to hold firm and oppose Maximus. Further to that, the garrisons are to ready themselves to join His Serenity Gratian's forces when they arrive from Italy. Until then, await further orders. I have to get on to Argentovaria with the news." He waved, turned his horse about and trotted away from the gate.

Gaius turned back to Merobauda and Faustinus with the beginnings of a smile. "Well, I think we can safely regard the little matter of the mutiny as closed."

"But what about this civil war?" Faustinus looked glum.

"I thought that theater trick you were talking about would work out better than this," Merobauda said.

"It depends on the playwright." Faustinus gazed north toward Lower Germany, where the mouth of the Rhine was, where the usurper's troops were gathering. "Really, some are much more skilled than others."

XXIV

ARCADIUS IS UNHAPPY WITH THE PROGRESS OF THE LAWSUIT

THE EMPEROR PREPARES FOR WAR

* * *

Arcadius approached his advocate's house unannounced. He was in a particularly foul mood: he had traveled up the highway north to Milan in a coach in which he had been bumped and jarred and chilled by the damp spring weather. He had meant to do some banking and, while he was in Milan, drop in on his lawyer and complain about how the case between his brother and himself was dragging on. He tipped the doorman at the entrance to Silvanus's townhouse and was met in the hall by a servant who escorted him to a small office off the peristyle and stayed to watch him until Silvanus appeared and sent him off.

"Do you always have your clients watched?" Arcadius sat down in a huff, determined to start the interview with a bit of aggression. "I might suggest, Advocate, that you might try serving a better class of litigant."

Silvanus straightened his robes with dignity and took the chair across his worktable from Arcadius. "I am often constrained by circumstance to lower my standards." He looked sharply at Arcadius, who squirmed and, to avoid Silvanus's eyes, glanced around the room, which was crowded with cabinets and shelves filled with petitions.

"Well, let's not talk about that now," Arcadius said, looking back at him. "Let's talk about your failure to have my brother's lawsuit dismissed." Silvanus laced his fingers together on the table and looked at him mildly.

"There was never any guarantee of that. I told you so."

"But my brother has no case!"

Silvanus regarded him blandly. "I told you at the start that his suit, though spurious, might prove to have, at least for a time, a certain vitality. And so it has."

"I didn't hire you to lose the case!"

"I don't appreciate the overstatement. We have not lost the case."

"You haven't won it."

"No. We have had only a setback, and setbacks are to be expected."

Arcadius ran his hands through his hair in frustration. "What is this damned setback, as you call it?"

Silvanus explained the situation with an annoying calm. "In response to our request to the court (and an adequate emolument for consideration of the question) to dismiss your brother's suit for failing to state a legal claim, he—that's to say, his advocate Crastinus—asserts that Gaius has a claim under customary Gallic law."

Arcadius surged up from his chair in frustration. "That smacks of Gaius!" He waved his arms in uncontrolled frustration. "It's exactly the sort of thing that crafty little bastard would cook up."

"Quite possibly," Silvanus said. "I can't see how Crastinus would know about customary Gallic law, though possibly your brother might. Please, sit down."

"And this means?" Arcadius stood glowering at Silvanus, who refused to speak until he had resumed his seat.

"Just that the suit continues." Silvanus picked up a stylus and turned it about in his hands, clearly bored with the conversation. "When the judge learned of the claim that Gallic customary law lent some color, shall we say, to Gaius's claim for half of the estate, he was constrained to deny our request to dismiss the action. At least for now."

Arcadius looked sullen. "Let me see what Gaius is claiming." He put his hand out rudely. Silvanus shrugged and pulled a document from a pigeonhole behind him. Arcadius unrolled it, turned to the light and read it slowly. Finally, he said, "This smells of fraud to me—and it should to you too." His tone was sharp and accusatory. "The 'archaic' language doesn't ring true. Those dative endings are awfully suspicious."

"Let's leave questions of Gaulish philology aside."

"I insist that you address this and soon!" He tossed the document onto the table in his frustration.

Silvanus ignored the gesture. "I don't know customary Gallic law. And—" he put his hand up to stop Arcadius, who had started to bluster. "I don't know customary Pannonian law. Or Illyrian law either. And I don't have to." He sat back comfortably with his hands in his lap. "First, your brother has to find that Gallic law somewhere (if it even exists) and second, if he can do so, he must prove that it takes precedence over Roman law. Third and finally, he has to prove that it applies to property in Italy. Finding and proving that law here in Milan (again, if it exists) could take a year, so you must prepare yourself for that."

"I don't like the uncertainty, though. I really don't." He seemed to have forgotten that he thought Gaius's latest ploy was a sham and subject to disproof. "And the delay."

Silvanus shrugged unsympathetically. "What is another year to you? And what is a little uncertainty? You hold the property now, and that—what shall we call it? —that inertia is hard to overcome. Especially with the right gifts."

"You make it sound as though things are going to get expensive."

"Yes, they are. I've told you that before. But you have more money than your brother, and for that reason, if for no other, delay works in your favor, not his. So, as I've told you already, the trick is to balance what we pay to the courts with what it will take to settle and hope meanwhile, that you will win." He sat back and looked Arcadius in the eye. "As your brother, Gaius must know how you well. He must realize how much uncertainty distresses you. So, you have to remain strong." He rolled up the document and returned it to the pigeonhole. "Now, if you'll excuse me…"

As Arcadius jounced in the carriage back down to his estate, he distracted himself with thoughts of how he could revenge himself on his brother whenever he might have the chance.

* * *

Spring light flooded through the windows of the Council Chamber of the Imperial Palace in Milan. The late morning light had overtaken the glimmer of the hundred lamps lighted when work had begun before dawn. The great men of the Consistory stood quietly, almost motionless against the walls, echoing in their immobility the statutes on plinths in the corners, figures of earlier emperors—Hadrian, Diocletian, Alexander Severus and Valentinian. Down the center of the room ran a long table of oak, polished to a deep sheen and loaded with documents. Gratian, followed by a secretary, circled the table, glancing at each document. Where needed, he signed one, where needed, he pressed his signet into a seal. Now and then a messenger advanced, his glance down out of respect for the Imperial dignity, with a document to be signed, or read, or summarized. A second table was covered with itineraries and a map showing Italy, Raetia and Gaul. A dozen tribunes of the Protectors huddled near the entrance of the room, Gratian's Master of the Cavalry at the head of them. As orders were signed, tribunes went off with them. Another dozen officers of the Palatine Legions and Auxilia were ranged down the hall, waiting to be called in for orders. As Prefect of Italy, Syagrius had, among other duties, the supply of the army. He trailed the Emperor at a respectful distance.

"Speed is the thing, Prefect," the Emperor stopped and said. "I must get well into Gaul before Maximus can supply himself adequately and before he can sway more of the provincial aristocracy into supporting him than he already has."

"Indeed, Your Serenity." Syagrius nodded.

"I will depend on the Field Army of Gaul for most of the infantry, and I will join the troops that accompany me to his forces. Several

Palatine Legions and Auxilia will follow from Italy as quickly as they can, but the matter may be decided before they reach the Gallic provinces." The prospect of military action seemed to elate the Emperor, to free him from the anxiety and uncertainty in which Syagrius had been accustomed to seeing him.

"I will be happy to relieve you of whatever duties I may." Syagrius pointed at the documents arrayed as neat as soldiers in formation along the table. "These orders for requisition hardly require Your Serenity's personal attention. Surely the conflict requires you to turn your attention to more martial activities."

"Every battle, every campaign, turns on supply," Gratian said, walking over to the table where the map lay. "We'll commandeer grain in Raetia and Upper Germany and send it down the Rhine to Argentoratum." Then he pointed on the map to Arles. "I want three ships loaded with soldiers' biscuit and on their way here by the end of the week. From Genoa if you can find them there. From Rome, if not. Their cargos will go from there up the Rhone on barges as far as we need them."

"Very good. And the Master of the Infantry?"

"Merobaudes already has left with two troops of Moorish cavalry and six Auxilia, mostly light troops." He looked up from the map. "I will follow in two days at the head of my Alans and two other cavalry troops, the Scutarii and the Marcomanni."

Syagrius did some quick calculations in his head: *two thousand cavalry, three thousand infantry, say, a total of four thousand men in reality (they were Palatine troops, so perhaps not too much under strength). The Master of the Cavalry in Gaul would have what? Another three thousand men (about half of what was stated in the records), for the most part infantry. With luck, Gratian would meet his enemy with seven thousand men—a few more if some of the border troops were brigaded. It might do. It just might.* "And victory will follow Your Serenity as a matter of course." He bowed politely and wondered, if things went badly, whether his Gallic estates would be largely spared. Quite probably: after all, that tribune of his—that little client—had met

Maximus, and Maximus would be uncertain where Syagrius's loyalties lay. That should help. He ought to come out well enough no matter how things turned out.

XXV

GAIUS PLAYS HIS PART
IN A CIVIL WAR

* * *

The first of the supply barges came downriver two weeks later and two more followed the next day. Gaius sauntered about the dock watching Faustinus oversee the unloading of the cargos, mostly soldiers' biscuit and sacks of grain, which were hoisted by the crane up the face of the bluff and stored in the fort's warehouse.

Following orders from the Master of the Cavalry, he commandeered twenty horses from the neighborhood (sparing those in the village around the fort, of course) and had them pastured in the garrison's paddock at the edge of the village. Gaius and Faustinus went to see them while the boy, Archelaus (an able and willing clerk), wrote down the particulars of the animals for the garrison records—except for those left behind by Volusianus and Martialis at their sudden departure. Gaius had other plans for them. As he watched the boy note down the colors and blazes of the requisitioned horses, he said to Faustinus, "I have to say I feel a little guilty about them."

"Yes?" Faustinus looked over at him in mild surprise.

"It didn't trouble me to commandeer a half-dozen from the Nebulosi. That was rather satisfying, actually. But from the others? The owners were paid for the animals in scrip to be presented to the provincial supply officer for cash—at the government's price, of course, and you know what that means—with coins so debased they might as well be hammered into door hinges or made useful in some other way. And they're supposed to do it after this little matter of civil war is over."

"So, if the war is won, they're paid in worthless coin, and if it's lost they never get paid at all."

"I wish you wouldn't talk that way. Though I'm used to your cynicism, the idea of losing the war is moderately unsettling."

"What would it mean to lose, really?" Faustinus asked.

"What sort of question is that?" Gaius looked puzzled.

"No. I'm serious."

"I don't see what you mean."

Faustinus spread his hands. "Gratian fights, Maximus fights. One of them will die." He shrugged. "All right. So be it then—they undertook it. But the soldiers? Some will fight and die. And why?" Faustinus pointed toward the Rhine. "Every ten or fifteen years some barbarians cross the river and raid. Sometimes they come in force, a real invasion. So then the army has a job—to run them down, stop them, drive them back. That sounds commendable, doesn't it? And yet what's it for? To protect the big men, the aristocrats and, maybe along the way, their peasants. And, of course, the peasants are stripped bare to supply the troops. And sometimes it's worse. Sometimes the Emperor just strikes a deal and settles the raiders in the provinces. Cynicism is exactly what's called for." Faustinus grew unusually heated by as he talked. "And why do the armies fight each other? So that one faction can rule instead of another? Or do the factions even change, really? The same families, they seem to be in power no matter what." He turned away and gazed into the distance.

Gaius looked at him for a few moments and then said: "You think too much about all of this. We have other things to worry about."

"Do we?" he asked darkly.

"Look, all we need to do is get through this war without getting killed. As you imply, let the Great Men worry about things after that."

A troop of cavalry came up the road from the south with a thumping of hooves and a grinding of wheels. The scales of their armor glinted like silver in the spring sunshine, and the purple tail of their dragon standard fluttered above them. A half-dozen wagons rumbled along behind, followed by two hundred light foot soldiers.

"Don't fret." Gaius folded his arms like Faustinus and nodded at the passing column. "It's those boys who are headed north. You can see they're Field Army troops. They're more likely to have to fight than we are. Our job so far has been to gather supplies. With any luck, we'll be ordered to stay in the fort to discourage the Alamans from crossing the river while the armies scuffle."

"Scuffle, you say." Faustinus seemed to scorn the word. He scowled at the passing soldiers. "They've got their armor on this far south. I don't like that. But you don't worry too much about the future, do you?"

"Difficilis est augere. Imprimis de futuro.[54]*"*

Faustinus shook his head at this but said nothing. He just stood there watching the column head north up the road.

* * *

It turned out to be easier to talk about avoiding danger than to actually avoid it. A despatch rider from Argentovaria soon brought orders: bring the Pannonians, the twenty requisitioned horses, and sixteen hundred pounds of biscuit to His Serenity's camp on the outskirts of Lugdunum. And be prepared to be brigaded to the Field Army upon arrival.

But Gaius fretted about Merobauda. Usually so annoyingly level-headed, she had suddenly become distraught. She inveighed against the war (she took the same view as Faustinus), and the fear of losing him. The prospect of losing him was bad enough, but it was sharpened by the thought that his death would be a pointless incident in a contest between distant Great Men tossing dice for the throne. Of course she had a point, Gaius reflected, when she'd expressed

---

[54] Latin for "It's difficult to make predictions. Especially about the future." Gaius has coined an aphorism that seems to have resurfaced in the twentieth century. Yogi Berra comes to mind.

herself, as usual, in no uncertain terms. The whole damned affair was pointless, but focusing on that just distracted him from the most important questions of the war, the ones that overshadowed all others: how could he survive the campaign and, if he could do that, how could he protect the men? He'd grown extremely fond of them—they had shown such commendable loyalty when they mutinied. He felt the needed to reciprocate as far as he could.

"You have to wear your armor from the moment you leave the fort," Merobauda told him. She took a very stern tone with him, as though he'd caused the war himself. "No arguments. Even the helmet." She paced the sitting room, wringing her hands. He looked over unhappily to the top of the cupboard where it sat with its brave little dent from the tree limb.

"Maximus's troops can't be within a hundred miles, Carissima." Una sat on his knee and looked at him solemnly. He patted her head. Merobauda's concern was touching, but her agitation upset him. He realized in that moment that he loved Merobauda more than he'd known.

"No arguments, Gaius!"

"Of course not, Carissima." He agreed immediately—he couldn't remember ever winning any arguments with her anyway.

"And did you have Arverno give you those lessons on how to use your sword? I'm always afraid you'll hurt yourself with it."

"Yes," he lied. "He says I'm a very quick study. He's very complimentary. He's a proponent of using the edge more than the point, at least on horseback." He added this detail, which might even be true (he reflected), to make the lie more convincing.

"Mmmm." Merobauda paused in her pacing and looked at him closely to judge whether he was telling her the truth. In the end she decided that she felt better with the question unresolved.

"I'll wear the armor," he said. It was an easy concession—he could take it off a mile down the road. And that's what he did.

A week later he was well on the way to join Gratian's forces, riding at the head of the sixty Pannonian Horse. He'd compromised with Merobauda (at least in his head) by wearing a canvas jack and hanging his helmet from the saddle—he could snatch it up if things got exciting. There was a little way to go yet to reach Lugdunum, but plenty of time to load himself with armor if he really had to. The soldiers' biscuit was slung on the backs of the column's remounts and the twenty commandeered horses. Arverno rode beside him, maundering on about his experiences fighting the Lentienses fifteen years before. At first, Gaius had dreaded listening to his stories—he thought they'd be terrifying—but in fact, they were shot through with a calming tediousness. His latest was typical.

"Yes, about twenty of us Pannonians were seconded to His Serenity Valentinian's field troops as scouts. The idea being, Your Excellence, that since we were, by and large, locals and not actually Pannonians, we'd know the country."

"That seems reasonable," Gaius said, without much interest in the details. He took his straw hat off and fanned himself with it. The late August heat was oppressive. As he fanned his face, he looked about the countryside, empty hereabouts as it had been for the past several days. It was to be expected; the peasants had driven their livestock far away from the army's path, and they'd taken their goods off in bundles. Those canny peasants were sitting out the war hidden in woods and marshes. No levies or exactions for them. Gaius knew it was hopeless to try to convince a peasant that unpaid requisitions were different from barbarian plundering.

He shifted in the saddle and tried to loosen his sweat soaked tunic, but it was hopeless; it clung clammily to him under his jack. To distract himself he asked, "And did you know the country?" He looked vaguely around. They were approaching Lugdunum, were in fact on the outskirts of it, and the city's walls stood somber and gray a quarter-mile ahead. They had been built a century ago against barbarian raids and enclosed only about half of the city; the rest, unprotected, had been abandoned. Thus, as Gaius led his little column toward the walls, derelict houses on either side looked eerily at him with empty windows and gaping doorways. A few had slumped over, and bushes grew around and atop the rubble. A hundred yards further down the way the column passed half a temple. The front of it was sheared off, as though struck by lightning. Gaius stared into its crumbling interior at weather-stained fading frescoes. He knew its columns, pediment and entablature and been stripped away to be fitted like the patches of a crazy quilt into the city wall, a sad exchange for grim survival. Arverno maundered on, indifferent to the ruin.

"Did we know the country? Not particularly. You know the army— they sent us out north of Treverorum, which was a new country to us. So, we were locals, as you might say. But not locals there. So maybe we weren't locals, now I give it some thought." Arverno considered for a moment, perplexed. But he went on inexorably. "One the troopers was a Frank. Now what was his name?" He looked away in thought and then smiled. "Bauto. No, wait. Tibatto. Or…"

Gaius closed his eyes, too weary to work up a crushing remark. He wished that he'd thought up a dozen of them before leaving the fort, just so that he'd have had them ready.

Arverno droned on: "However he was called—and he deserted after the campaign, so maybe his name's not important—he'd been up that way years before, but he didn't recall much besides visiting some taverns in a settlement along the river. Still, it didn't matter: the fighting turned out to be mostly to the south, and we weren't hardly involved."

"So, what did you do?" Gaius asked, wondering to himself why he did anything to keep the pointless monologue going.

"Mostly bullied landlords to get supplies and fodder."

"So, no fighting?"

"Only once. A few peasants fought the requisition, but nobody got killed. That's where Latro lost his foot, though. He was…"

"Don't tell me about it." He wiped the sweat from his forehead and settled his hat. He glanced over his shoulder at his column and reckoned it had gotten a bit strung out. He reined in Dulcina and she consented to stop, though she tried to bite his right foot. He agitated it to discourage her. He was about to order the column to tighten up when he noticed a smudge, gray and indistinct, rising from the road behind them. He pointed. "Do you see that?"

Arverno turned his horse about and north down the road. "Dust." He watched a moment longer. "It's a troop of horsemen."

So, now what? Arverno would expect him to make some sort of military decision. He hated making military decisions—things could go so awfully wrong. He'd read about military blunders any number of times and wasn't entirely sure he wouldn't commit one if given the opportunity.

The cloud thickened perceptibly as they sat their horses and watched. No, it wasn't exactly that—it was just that it had grown closer, and Gaius could just make out the growing figures of four horsemen trotting abreast, two on the highway and the others on the shoulder at either side. The dust cloud was wide; those horsemen were not alone—they were the outriders of a column moving quickly toward them, toward Lugdunum. So, should he join them? Oppose them? Whose men were they? He could just see the purple tail of a flashing dragon standard and, a moment later, the gleam of the leader's golden armor—a thousand fine scales glinting in the late afternoon sun, gems winking on his helmet. The men about him glimmered as well—the scales of their armor not merely tinned, but silvered.

"That's odd," Arverno said, watching them approach. "None of them have got their lances. I don't see any shields, either. They've lightened themselves." He took his helmet from the saddle, settled it on his head and tied the straps.

Gaius stared. He stared at the glinting armor, the conical helmets, the white of the trousers and the sleeves where the armor didn't cover them, and he thought suddenly of the white uniforms of the Imperial Guards—though not quite believing it—and realized in that moment that His Serenity, the Augustus Flavius Gratian himself, rode toward him. He watched from the road, unable to quite grasp the import of Arverno's observation about lances and shields until the advancing column broke into a canter. It was time to get off the road.

He raised his right arm, signaled the troop to follow, and led them into the adjoining field. They managed to get off the highway in time to let the Emperor and his fifty horsemen canter by. Arverno was right: none had spears or shields. At their rear, a horseman led a single string of a dozen pack-horses, foaming with sweat on their flanks, exhausted and slowing the column. He tossed aside the lead-line, and those horses stopped, staggering and chuffing. He seemed to see Gaius's men for the first time. He looked grimly at them and then shouted, "They're coming!" He nodded at the dust cloud in the distance and added, "Maximus's men!" He broke into a canter after the rest of his column, abandoning the pack-horses. A little court bureaucrat who had been riding along beside him, indistinct and gray with dust, turned his horse about and stared with wide eyes up the road. He sat stupefied for a moment and then sprang from his horse and scuttled off like a spider among the ruined houses to the left of the road. In a moment there was no sign of him.

Gaius looked north up the road where another smudge of dust was rising—Maximus's men in pursuit. Well, no sense in sticking around. He was suddenly inspired; he knew exactly what to do.

"Seize those pack-horses. Get them into those trees over there." He pointed to a wood a half-mile to the east of the highway just visible in a break between tumbledown houses. "The campaign's over, boys. We're heading home." An optio took the lead line, and the column headed as fast as the pack-horses would go between the abandoned houses, through a field of rank grass and into the shadows of the trees.

Meanwhile, from his hiding place behind a half-collapsed house, Scaevolus Volusianus peeped out at Maximus's approaching cavalry—and at the troop that had led off the Emperor's horses. The troop was a little shabby—border soldiers with shields quartered in red and black. His immediate concern was to slip off to safety somewhere, but his ordered mind made a note of the shield pattern and tucked it into the back of his mind with other information that might someday be useful.

* * *

Gratian rode hard, leaning forward in the saddle, almost one with his horse, so smoothly did he ride after a childhood and youth spent in the saddle. This last flight seemed dreamlike: he had never ridden so well, so gracefully, so fast and, just as in a dream, he seemed to know—and yet with calmness—that he rode to his doom. His Alan horse guards floated to either side of him and trailed him for a hundred yards as they passed along the highway, the percussion of hundreds of hooves echoing from the walls of slumped houses and drifting across the fields on either side. After they had swept past the troop of border cavalry on the side of the road, the column had broken into a gallop, hoping to reach the gates of Lugdunum before the horses were spent. Two miles behind them a column of Maximus's cavalry followed, just visible from time to time, depending on how the road dipped or veered. They did not have long.

Gratian spurred his horse and led his men toward the city walls and, as they closed the distance, the highway became a street flanked by huddles of decaying roofless houses. He and his guard passed through the dilapidation in splendid armor that glinted and winked orange in the setting sun.

But beyond the decay, the heart of the reduced city huddled safe behind strong walls, and there lay his chance. The diminished circuit of the shrunken town could be defended by the Alans and by the—what was the unit?—by the Milites Lugdunenses, he seemed to recall. His men and the Milites could hold the walls until help came, even if that help must come from Milan.

Gratian was soon in the shadow of the wall, a dozen of the foremost horsemen about him, the horses turning and milling about in their excitement. The gate was shut, but that was to be expected during civil war. The standard-bearer drew up next to him and, taking the haft of the standard in both hands, turned it in figures-of-eight to emphasize to the spectators upon the wall the purple of its whipping tail. The Emperor looked up at the battlements, at the soldiers gazing back down at him, seemingly without expression, their eyes shadowed beneath the rims of their gray iron helmets. "Open the gates!" he called, with such majesty as remained to him after a flight of two days. The standard-bearer jumped from his saddle and called in a thunderous voice for the gate to be opened. He drove the butt of the standard against the portals to hammer home the command but, against the massive wooden portals, the sound, despite the glamor of the gilded standard, was a mere tapping, a rap on a door. The gate stood shut against the Emperor.

Gratian wheeled his horse about to look back down the road, past the slumped houses and debris to that point where it became the great highway of the Via Agrippa, and he saw the approaching cavalry, their numbers hard to reckon at this distance, but likely two hundred. He looked back to the city wall, to the silent soldiers crowding high above him, their helmets dappled gray and orange in the setting sun, the rings of their armor seeming to shift about as the shadows played over them, the tips of their spears winking in the setting sun. None said a word to acknowledge him. Gratian did not demean himself by shouting again for entry: the town was against him, the soldiers as disloyal as Merobaudes, his Master of the Infantry, had proven. He looked back at the approaching cavalry and watched it fan out as it approached, forming a half-circle whose wings swept forward to either side. Gratian's men looked to him. So many had tossed their helmets aside during the flight that their expressions were plain to see, their eyes electric with a final, hysterical determination. These fifty men from north of the Danube, they at least were loyal, and he ought to save their lives. And there was only one thing he could do to save them, for it was clear that they were taken with a wild enthusiasm to give them up for him. Gratian raised his hand and ordered them to sit their horses until the enemy approached closer. He would give the order to advance, he alone. They nodded, drew their swords and waited as three hundred of Maximus's cavalry halted and leveled their lances and prepared to charge. Gratian drew his sword, noted its edge a faint red in the last of the evening sun and, before his men could react, kicked his horse into a gallop toward his opponents. Best to get things over with before his Alans could react and engage. With luck, after his death they'd be spared. He chose an opponent in silvered armor—an officer of some sort—and swung his sword down upon him in a glimmering arc as he came alongside. It was the last thing he did.

XXVI

GAIUS SELLS THE ARMY ITS OWN HORSES AND DISCOVERS HE IS SUDDENLY VERY RICH

* * *

Back at Castellinum Ripae, Gaius and Faustinus strolled at the edge of the paddock and watched Arverno and the decurion of the the cavalry troop from Argentovaria as they walked among the horses. The decurion was a wiry little man with a shrewd face. He passed among the horses, patting their flanks and studying their yellow teeth as though he were deciding the price of rubies. He didn't say anything, though—just grunted from time to time, so it was impossible to guess his thoughts. When he had spent a good hour at it, he and Arverno paltered for a while and then examined the horses once again, this time to settle the prices more precisely. Gaius was impatient; he wanted the business over with, he wanted the Emperor's pack-horses and those of Volusianus and Martialis little troop—sold and settled at Argentovaria before he had to explain where they had come from. All were uncommonly fine horses, even the pack-horses, which wasn't lost on the decurion; his face stony face paradoxically betrayed how much he admired them, how much he would like to have them.

"Frankly, my unhappy experience with Volusianus has made me uneasy." Gaius stooped and plucked a stalk of grass and bit the stem as he thought back. "I was rather surprised to see the Imperial Administration actually doing its job. More or less. Or some sort of job, anyway."

Faustinus agreed. "Some sort of job, yes."

"And so, as we discussed earlier this morning, we need to see the last of those horses. After all, it's just possible that His Serenity Gratian might trouble himself to track down his baggage and those horses of his would be rather an important clue to its whereabouts." He nodded toward the paddock. Arverno and the decurion were arguing over the precise age of a stocky sorrel. They haggled like a pair of villagers on market day testing their skill and amusing themselves. Gaius shouted put his hand around his mouth and shouted. "Get on with it!"

"You'll bring the prices down, " Faustinus remarked.

"I don't mind that at all." He wiped his hands together absently, as though getting rid of something. "A low price will make the decurion—how shall we say?—complicit."

"Arverno wants a good price; he expects a cut of it."

"I know he does. We've already discussed it. I'll see that he's taken care of whatever the horses go for. But I want that decurion to accept that we found these animals wandering in a field, to accept that they're strays."

"Strays. And not—this is just an example—horses from the Emperor's own Protectors."

"Yes, strays." He looked vaguely over the countryside. "You know how horses are—they're apt to wander off just about anywhere."

"Like the ones Martialis and Volusianus left behind," Faustinus said drily.

"You're being tiresome."

"And the Emperor's baggage?" Faustinus asked.

"We'll dispose of that later. We need to look through it carefully though—there might be something of interest in it."

Faustinus made a wry face. "Master, although I know it won't cause you for a moment to swerve from this scheme of yours, I just can't stop myself from pointing out that you are selling the army its own horses."

"I see you appreciate the elegance of my approach. And besides, who needs the horses more than the army? Who will pay? The army. And who will be paid? Why, myself, an officer in the army. The whole thing seems rather virtuous when you reflect on it. And, furthermore, it partakes of that wonderful and simple symmetry that is the circle. Parmenides, I think."

"I believe he reckoned that the sphere was the most perfect shape. Something like that."

"Well, we do what can here in the world." He turned to see Arverno and the decurion crossing the field toward him. The deal was done.

* * *

When the Gaius reached the office of the praetorium, he bumped his shoulder against the door when it didn't open. He stepped back in surprise and tried the latch.

"Well, it seems it's locked," he told Faustinus unnecessarily.

"Who's there?" Merobauda's voice came through the door. She sounded uneasy.

"Just me, Carissima."

"That means Faustinus too, right?"

"Well, yes, of course."

"Anyone else? Or just the two of you?"

Gaius looked around. It was just the two of them. "Carissima, why do you care?"

"Anyone else? Answer the question!" Her tone was peremptory, even for her.

"No. No one else." After a moment he heard the bolt drawn back and saw Merobauda's right eye peeping out as she opened the door a crack.

"All right. You can come in."

"Thank you," Gaius said, nodding his head in a slight mock bow as he and Faustinus stepped past her.

Merobauda ignored the levity. She bolted the door behind them with great care and leaned against the door as though her lanky frame could strengthen it appreciably. Gaius glanced about the office looking for whatever it was that was upsetting her, but all he could see out of the ordinary were three leather sacks sitting on the work table. A half-dozen horse-packs lay on the floor near the open door to the strong-room. The shutters of the window were closed and the bolts shot as though it were nighttime.

"I see you've been looking through the bags the pack-horses were carrying."

"You told me to," she said, fiddling a moment with the bolt on the door to be sure of it. She crossed over to the table and looked dolefully at the sacks.

"Oh, that's right—I did tell you to. Well, anything good? Oh, by the way, we've turned a good eight solidi on the horses. I've got to give Arverno what?" He glanced at Faustinus.

"A twelfth," he said.

"So, Merobauda, what does that come to?"

"One-and-a third solidus," Merobauda said automatically, not looking at him. She kept her eyes on the sacks and looked glum.

"Oh. That's rather a lot." He rubbed his chin and looked down. "Still, I have to give it to him. It's only fair. And the money will encourage his silence."

"Nothing will encourage his silence—you ought to know that by now." He was surprised to be scolded out of the blue—there must be something amiss, but what?

Gaius smiled to lighten her mood. "So what if he talks? It only matters if someone troubles to look for the horses. But, really, in the context of a usurpation, they're a small thing." He looked at Merobauda and Faustinus. "Really, you should have seen the Emperor sweep by—it was disconcerting. People like us, we never expect to actually see an emperor. Well, perhaps in the Imperial box at the Circus in Rome but, even then, only from a great distance. You look across the spina of the racetrack and see a smudge of purple in the crowd of courtiers and reckon it must be him. So, seeing him race by with his train of guards as though he were just some... some..."

"Some minor provincial tribune scurrying away from a defeat?" Faustinus suggested.

"That's a sharpish way of putting it." But Gaius smiled indulgently at him; he'd come through the war unscathed and had been in a sunny mood for days.

Merobauda added, "And you're relying on his flight to get away with seizing his horses."

"Not necessarily. After all, he let them go. And remember what I told you: the army's getting them back." He smiled as though he'd pulled off a coup.

"Of course. A virtuous circle. But you're assuming Gratian has been defeated, and you're hoping that will muddy the waters."

"It seems reasonable to me. Well, both things really: the Emperor's defeat and the muddy waters."

"We'll know soon enough how things turned out," Merobauda said, still staring at the sacks. "And there's something else that should worry us."

"Oh?" Gaius asked insouciantly.

"It's money."

"Money never makes me uneasy except when I don't have enough."

"Among the baggage you brought back are three sacks of coin holding twelve hundred and ninety-two solidi."

Faustinus caught his breath and let it out sharply.

Gaius didn't think he'd heard right. The number dazed him. He blinked. "Twelve hundred solidi?"

"Twelve hundred and ninety-two," she corrected him. "That's almost thirteen hundred, Gaius." At another time he might have rankled at her tone, but he sensed that she was frightened at the discovery. But why? Couldn't she see recognize of luck when she saw it?

He struggled with some mental arithmetic. He hadn't a whit of Merobauda's talent, but he could tell that the figure amounted to something like the pay of two legions for a month. Or it was the price of an estate. A really fine estate. One with a goodly villa, acres and acres of land, a village and tenants. Frescoes and painted walls and heated mosaic floors with tasteful designs, glass in the windows—that sort of thing. "That's a good deal of money," he conceded, "But, for an emperor?" He spread his hands out as though the figure were a trifle.

"It's enough he'll send someone to look for it. And that'll lead to trouble." Merobauda turned to him with her fists on her hips.

Faustinus couldn't help himself; he went to the table and scooped out a handful of the coins. They were fresh, uncirculated, bright, sharply stamped, with the profile of the ever-triumphant Gratian crowned with laurel on one side and Victory personified on the other. Her figure was circled by the motto *Fides Exercitus*[55]. There were hundreds and hundreds of them. Twelve hundred and nine-two. Merobauda wouldn't be wrong about that.

"Oh, I don't know," Gaius said and rubbed his hands together for a moment. His pride kept him from the indignity of plunging his hands into the money as Faustinus had done—but only just. "No one has to find out about this. I prefer to take the view, and you'll excuse the pun, that finding this money is an unalloyed good." He looked around for approval, but Faustinus only stood looking distracted. He rubbed his hands together absently as though he were brushing gold dust from them.

"It's the emperor's money," she said, her hands still on her hips.

"You know, Carissima, I can see that argument, really, I can. He was carrying it about with him and all that. It was collected by tax-collectors and town officials unwillingly pressed into his service and extorted on his behalf. That certainly counts for something. But then, who is the emperor these days? Maybe it isn't Gratian anymore."

Merobauda answered coldly. "We may not know who the emperor is, but there always is one."

Gaius took a different tack. "It was plain when Gratian and his men raced by that I couldn't carry out my orders. I'm a tribune, you know. An officer. So, I am obliged and trusted to use my discretion at times. And at Lugdunum, well, it was one of those times. So,"—he spread out his hands reasonably—"I'm back here at the fort, ready for new orders and busy guarding the Rhine. Utterly blameless, really."

"Apart from taking the money. And the horses," Faustinus said, as if the latter were an afterthought.

Merobauda tried for a disapproving look, but it melted away. For

---

[55] "Loyalty of the Army." The irony was probably not lost on Gratian.

all her exasperation at his clumsy ventures, she found Gaius endearing. All the same, she faced up to the problem, as she saw it. "How are we going to get rid of the money?"

"Get rid of it…" He looked as though she'd slapped him.

"She's right, you know," Faustinus said.

"You're both against me!" He was dismayed.

"Quite the opposite," Faustinus said. "You want to come out of this situation alive, don't you?"

"Of course I do. But rich too, you understand. Wealth really has a way of improving things."

"You might just have to settle for life."

"I'm not sure I like the sound of that. There must be some sort of compromise." Gaius tossed his restraint aside and took a coin out of the nearest sack. He turned it about, admiring its glinting freshness.

"Why are you so obstinate?" Merobauda asked sharply.

"I prefer to think of it as a steadfast adherence to practicality."

"To revisit an earlier question," Faustinus said, "I wonder who the emperor is now." He stood, arms crossed and leaning against the wall.

"Upon further reflection," Gaius said, "I'd suppose it's probably Gratian. He was almost to Lugdunum when he passed us. Once inside, he'll hold out until Flavius Merobaudes—or whoever—can support him. I expect we'll hear of some troops moving that way soon."

"Let's say you're right. What about the money then?" Merobauda looked at him grimly. "You can't argue it isn't his if he's still on the throne."

She had him there. But he shrugged carelessly and said, "His Serenity will have other things to think about besides where the money was lost. And let's say he does wonder. The Via Agrippa's a long road. How can he be sure where he lost it?" He made a jaunty attempt to flip the coin with this thumb back into to the sack, but missed by an inch. It struck the table and bounced onto the floor with a beautiful, heavy ringing sound.

"Snap and dash," Faustinus said absently, looking vaguely about the room.

Gaius was irrepressible. "Who's to say that the pack-horses

weren't scooped up by Maximus's cavalry? After all, they're on their way to Argentovaria now they're sold. If Gratian comes out on top, we'll put the blame on Maximus. He started all of this nonsense, being a usurper and all. It's not as though he'll survive if Gratian defeats him." He looked at Faustinus. "I can't believe you didn't think of that. You're supposed to help me, you know."

"So, where do we hide the money?" Merobauda wondered out loud. She looked down at the coin on the floor. It was clear that she wouldn't be budged.

"But Carissima…"

"Where can you spend it anyway? Not around here. Not now. It will just bring you trouble." She stared at the sacks on the table.

"I'll risk it."

"If you risk it, we'll all have to risk it, and I'm not having that."

"She has a point." Faustinus turned to him.

"What's that noise? That shouting?" Gaius went to the window and began to draw back a bolt.

"Wait! Stop!" Merobauda ordered him. She turned to Faustinus. "Here; help me get these sacks into the strong room." They quickly shoved them deep in the back of the room, and then she turned the two locks set into the door with heavy keys from her belt. She tugged at the door handle just to be sure.

It wasn't long before Gaius jumped at the whacks of Arverno's baton on the office door. He looked at Merobauda, she nodded, and all three tried to assume a certain nonchalance, though Faustinus seemed the only one to entirely succeed. It didn't really matter: Arverno was only as observant as usual. Faustinus let him in.

Gaius leaned back against the worktable, trying for a careless posture. "I take it the sale of the horses went well? You've taken your twelfth?"

"Yes, thank you, Your Excellence." Arverno stepped to the worktable and put down the balance of money paid for the horses. He stacked the coins in two neat columns. Meanwhile, Faustinus stepped on the glimmering gold solidus on the floor to hide it.

"I heard some shouting a few moments ago," Gaius said to distract

Arverno from Faustinus's sudden movement.

"Indeed you would have, Your Creditableness. We have just received an important messenger. So, of course, the boys around the gate were a bit noisy. It's almost a sort of embassy, you might say."

Gaius felt his stomach tighten. "Oh?"

Merobauda glanced at the strongroom door from the corner of her eye.

"It's a handful of cavalry. And an officer of course, Your Wonder. Like you. Well, not exactly like you."

"Which is he? Like me? Or not? A tribune? Or not a tribune? Honestly, Arverno, at times your obscurity provokes a feeling of awe."

"Thank you, Your Wonderment." He beamed. "The man's a decurion of the Field Army."

The Field Army, Gaius thought. *That sounds alarming*. He glanced involuntarily at the door to the strong room. If worse came to worst, he could offer to return the money. He'd claim that he'd been holding it for Gratian, that he was merely acting as a bailee for His Serenity until the difficulties of the war had passed, after which, of course, he would return the money. In fact, he was more than glad to return it now. It was a colorable claim, perhaps not colorable enough to to encourage a reward for his services, but surely enough to help him avoid a death sentence. He looked at Merobauda and Faustinus; they had both gone very white. He tried to smile encouragingly. "Well, Arverno," he said, "Let's go and meet this fellow."

Gaius left the office and climbed the stairs to the top of the wall over the gate (still closed against the threat of civil war) and looked down on four grimy cavalrymen. Their officer waved a hand in greeting. "I have a message from His Serenity the Emperor for the Tribune Gaius Obsequens Dolo."

Gaius glanced at Faustinus and Arverno, who had just come up on either side of him. He must be after the money. What other business could the Emperor have with him, apart from recouping his money? Gaius felt suddenly chilled as his thoughts drifted to the prospect of a trial followed by an exemplary and painful public death. His knees softened like porridge, so he leaned against the parapet for support as he began to work out how to convincingly express his claim to have held Gratian's money in trust. After a painful silence he stammered out: "There is a legal doctrine, officer, with which you may not be familiar. It concerns the finding of lost property, or as we prefer to call it in law, *res inventa*—" Faustinus stomped on his foot and Gaius lost his concentration.

The officer stared up at him. His mouth was half open and his head cocked a bit to one side, as though he had stumbled unexpectedly on a foreign language. He started again. "Is the Tribune one of you?" There was a good deal of deference in his voice. This was mildly encouraging anyway. If the man was here for the money, surely he'd have used a brusque tone? And brought a few more soldiers? Gaius admitted cautiously that he was the Tribune Dolo. "And you?"

"I'm with the Taifal Horse."

"I'm afraid that I'm not familiar with the unit."

"We serve in the Field Army of Britain," the man said, with evident pride.

"Of Britain?" Gaius was so preoccupied with the danger of holding the Emperor's money that the implications of the statement didn't strike him right away. He called down, "But you say you come from His Serenity the Emperor."

"We do."

"So then, His Splendor has defeated the usurper and reasserted his rightful command over the Imperial Army, including, of course, the Field Army of Britain." Faustinus stepped on his foot again. Gaius wished he wouldn't do that.

The man laughed indulgently. "Your Excellence has apparently not heard the welcome news. The Tyrant Gratian is dead, vanquished. We come from His Serenity the Emperor Magnus Maximus."

Gaius was quite at a loss for words, so he said, "Ah," but he worried that he ought to have shown more enthusiasm, particularly since the problem of the money was unlikely to come up.

"His Serenity the Emperor has sent us specially to you."

"Well. That's thoughtful of him. Yes, thoughtful. Of course, one would expect no less from him. I met him once myself, in fact," Gaius rambled on, giddy with relief that the subject of Gratian's money was unlikely to come up now. With Gratian dead, surely he'd be left in peace. Gaius burbled on: "An impressive man, to be sure. I saw a bit of Britain too, while I was at it. Quite an island you have there."

Faustinus shut his eyes in embarrassment. The officer nodded politely.

"And your message?" Faustinus took it upon himself to ask the question, and Gaius was able to listen for the answer with some attention, now that he wasn't frightened for his life.

"Just this. His Serenity Maximus commands that the Tribune Dolo take up his new duties at Court."

"New duties?" Gaius asked. Things were coming at him thick and fast.

"Yes, Excellence." The officer patted a saddlebag. "I have here His Serenity's commission. Let me congratulate you, Excellent Dolo. You are now a Protector of His Serenity The Emperor Magnus Maximus."

"A Protector..." Gaius's voice trailed off.

The officer bobbed his head in a brief salute. "His Serenity awaits you at his capital."

"And that would be..." Gaius regarded with dread the prospect of another sea journey to Britain.

"Augusta Treverorum."

"Of course." That was a relief. He gave the man a weak smile.

"His Serenity would like you to present yourself at his court before the end of the month. You will then adore the purple." The officer waited until a soldier was sent out to take the commission from him, and then he waved, turned, and rode off through the village toward the highway.

XXVII

A NEW EMPEROR SECURES HIS BORDER, ARCADIUS WINS THE CASE AND GAIUS HEADS OFF TO HIS NEW COMMAND

* * *

Syagrius was given the signal honor of a seat in the salon of the Empress Justina, once a striking beauty, still a handsome woman of about forty-three with intelligent black eyes and dark hair shot with grey. Her son, His Serenity Valentinian, sat beside her, pensive and silent on the purple cushions of a gilded curule chair; he was a boy of thirteen. A half dozen functionaries stood quietly along the wall to either side of her chair, among them Flavius Bauto, the new Master of the Infantry.

"I imagine you know all that has happened," she said.

Syagrius inclined his head in a subtle gesture of respect. "In a broad way, Augusta Justina." He watched the boy—Valentinian—from the side of his eye.

"Perhaps, as a confidant of Gratian, you know more than I do." She studied his face but kept hers inscrutable.

"How could that be, Domina?"

She paused and then replied obliquely. "Your holdings in Gaul, your clients. Thousands of them." Even Syagrius, remarkably perceptive from decades of politics and intrigue, could not discern from Justina's face, tone or posture how she judged his loyalty. Well, Maximus held half of the Western Empire, from Lusitania to Britain and to the border of Italy. Whatever Justina's suspicions, circumstances forced her to unequivocally ally with him, and that was enough.Syagrius looked solemn, his natural expression after a lifetime at court. "All that I have, my possessions, my clients, my networks, are at the service of his Serenity Valentinian and yourself, Augusta Justina. He nodded gravely at the boy Emperor in a show of reverence and humility, but he was, at the same time, measuring him against Maximus.

Justina continued. "As we understand the situation, within days of His Serenity Gratian's arrival at the outskirts of Lutetia, he found much of the Field Army of Gaul disaffected." She spoke with a flat intonation as though discussing something abstract, something remote, like the economy of Bithynia or the geography of Armenia.

"I see." Syagrius nodded, neither too quickly nor too slowly. He was thinking of Justina though. She was clearly shrewd and yet was she strong enough to prop up the young Valentinian?

Justina went on. "Furthermore, His Serenity Gratian found that the Duke of Lower Germany had sided with the usurper Maximus, thus reinforcing his army with the border troops of that province, many of which he had withdrawn from their posts for that purpose. It stands to reason that there must have been negotiations between the Duke and Maximus long beforehand."

Syagrius agreed. Justina knew how such things were done. She had, as a young woman, been the wife of a usurper herself, one Magnentius. His rise and fall had taught her a thing or two.

"The armies did not face off, not really. There was some maneuvering, some posturing, but Flavius Merobaudes went over to Maximus with a number of the Palatine Auxilia—and then, of course, Gratian's army dissolved."

Syagrius indicated his dismay.

"It was all over in a less than a week. His Serenity fled toward Lugdunum but was caught below the walls and killed. Spain seems to have gone over to Maximus as well." She looked at him interrogatively, but he offered nothing.

"We have no idea why the army betrayed him!" The young Emperor spoke for the first time. His mother glanced at him and, for a moment, Syagrius thought he caught a glint of sour amusement in her eyes.

"Currents shift about, Your Serenity. Small runnels of intrigue may cut away at the foundations of the throne."

The young emperor slapped his palms angrily on the arms of his chair and shifted himself as though he couldn't find a comfortable position.

Justina took up the conversation. "What is more, the Master of the Cavalry has joined Merobaudes in his treachery. Deceit ran a good deal deeper than we expected."

"Command me as you will. I am here to help Your Illustrious Majesties."

"Indeed you are, Syagrius, and we thank you." Was there a faint trace of suspicion in her voice? Syagrius wondered. "And our wish is this: tell us whatever else you may know of this conspiracy."

Syagrius timed his response carefully; he did not hesitate, but he did not undercut himself by rushing to answer. He shook his head slowly. "I know nothing more than you have told me. In fact, before we spoke I knew only that His Serenity Gratian had somehow been defeated."

"It seems very odd, Mother, that I will never see Gratian again. Well, not odd, but..." He waved his hand vaguely. "I'll never see him again."

Syagrius was struck by the boy's sentimentality over his half-brother; he wondered to what extent sentiment would hobble him as emperor. His mother ignored the comment and continued. "Well, now you do know some things, principal among them that the troops that Merobaudes led north will, of course, not return to Italy, because they now form part of the traitor Maximus's army." She spoke with no bitterness and impressed Syagrius with her remarkable restraint. She was clearly one to keep her head; he would have to watch her.

Syagrius did some quick sums in his head. Those soldiers came to what? Three or four thousand troops—and of the better sort—but probably no more than that. If Justina and her son could hold on for a year, the number could be made up, for the most part anyway. "What is the state of the Alpine passes?" He turned to the Master of the Infantry.

"Blocked," Bauto replied. "Entirely blocked. I've doubled the garrisons and set light infantry to patrol the foothills against any detachments that manage to slip through the passes." There was a slight Frankish undertone to his Latin. "But we can't bring the fight to Maximus. Not now."

Syagrius nodded. "So, Maximus will be shut out of Italy until snow blocks the passes. Good. We have until the spring before he can offer any serious threat."

"Yes, we're safe enough here behind the Alps," Bauto said with bland assurance.

"What about his Serenity Theodosius?" Syagrius asked. "His assistance must be implored."

Justina nodded. "We have, of course, asked His Serenity Theodosius for troops, but any men that he can spare cannot be here before late spring, and perhaps even later."

"Theodosius has the Goths to contend with," Valentinian observed gloomily. "What if he has no have troops to spare?" He drummed his fingers on the chair arms. "And we cannot reinforce ourselves with more than a handful of soldiers from the Danube line—we'll need them in the spring to hold on to what we have there. And what is more, Maximus has sent an embassy to the east to seek official recognition from Theodosius. It's very hard not to take a dim view of things."

"Your Serenity must not despair. Instead, let us plan." Syagrius smiled sympathetically at the young emperor—after all, Valentinian's was the great danger, not his. Syagrius, as a great man in both Gaul and Italy, could expect to survive any struggle between Maximus and Valentinian; he could seem to have been behind whichever man came out on top.

* * *

Arcadius prepared to receive the advocate Themistius Silvanus at his villa. He was in a good mood—he had just learned that he had won Gaius's case against him. Three chairs were set in the shade of the peristyle. Nuts, dried fruit and wine sat on a delicate marble-topped table, water splashed refreshingly in the fountain of the ornamental garden of courtyard, and the sun shone approvingly on everything. He waited in some anticipation for the lawyer; after all, he wanted details, and Silvanus's letter had communicated only the broad result. Surely there were technicalities to savor, maneuvers and legalities that, though abstruse, would provide an afternoon's entertainment. Nothing warmed his heart like the thought of Gaius burning with anger somewhere up north. Maybe it was raining on him up there, too.

"Your enthusiasm over this little victory seems a bit unseemly, dear," Aeliana said, taking a chair. Like her husband she was soft and fleshy, but in a pleasant overripe way.

He stood looking out of the peristyle at the fountain in its center. "*Little* victory!" He shook his head.

Aeliana rearranged fruit on a plate. "Perhaps you should be gracious in victory."

"I don't see why. I don't see why at all. Gaius has cost me a hundred and seventy-eight solidi in fees, tips and sportulae. And I don't know how many sleepless nights. All to retain what's mine." He turned at the sound of footsteps and put out both hands in greeting. "Why, Advocate Silvanus! How marvelous to see you! Let me present my wife, Aeliana."

Silvanus nodded politely. "Domina." He took a chair and placed a document on the little table.

Arcadius sat down across from him and leaned forward in his eagerness, while Aeliana poured the advocate a glass of wine. "Don't spare any details! I want to hear them all."

Silvanus looked at Arcadius with mild exasperation.

"Well?" Arcadius urged him on after a moment.

"Frankly, Arcadius Macro, I think you should be satisfied with simply winning the case."

"I agree, dear," Aeliana said.

Arcadius frowned at his wife and turned back. "But it's so…well, sudden. You must have pulled off some cunning coup. That's what we want to know about," he said, trying to make his wife complicit in his enthusiasm.

"There isn't much to say about it from the legal standpoint." Silvanus took up the document and handed it over. "You'll want this. It's the judgment. The estate is unquestionably and entirely yours."

"Yes, but why, exactly?" he persisted. "The details, I mean."

"Oh, Arcadius!" Aeliana said. She looked away, embarrassed at her husband.

"There are no details," Silvanus said simply.

"No details? What do you mean, no details? Surely there were some feints, some subtle threats, a procedural gambit here and there."

"You'll recall that we're in a state of civil war." He took the tone one might use with a dullard.

"Yes, I've noticed." Arcadius missed the tone and took the comment for sophisticated understatement.

"It is the court's presumption that your brother is now an officer in the army of the Usurper Maximus."

"Ah." Arcadius leaned back, thinking. "Yes, I suppose he must be."

"You can see the court's reasoning. As an officer of the troops in Gaul, he's presumed to have gone over to the Usurper."

Arcadius began to grasp the situation. "Bloody traitor!" he said. It seemed the proper thing to say.

Aeliana undercut this with a soft, dubious snort.

"Perhaps." Silvanus was judicious. "But then, who knows what choice he really had."

"Well, I say he got what he deserved." He gave his wife a malicious grin. She looked away again.

"As to that, I can't say. The court thought it best to rule against a likely enemy of the State."

Arcadius nodded. "Of course. And quite right too!"

"Are you satisfied, dear?" Aeliana asked him.

"With the result, certainly. And yet, to think that I spent a good two hundred solidi to defend myself, all to have it resolved by civil war."

"One hundred and seventy-eight." Silvanus rose. "You might take some comfort in reflecting that your brother probably spent a good deal more—and lost."

After Silvanus had gone Arcadius said to his wife: "So, a hundred and seventy-eight solidi to the judges and lawyers, all to have the case decided by chance!" He headed into the house.

Aeliana called after him. "Where are you going?"

"I'm going to my office."

"What for?"

"To gloat."

"Why there?"

"Because, after I've gloated a while, I'm going to write a letter to Gaius and tell him I'm gloating."

* * *

"Why did Maximus make you a Protector? I'm uneasy about that. I think you should ask yourself that question." Merobauda stood at the gunwale of the barge and looked up the bluff to the fort. Gaius could see that, despite her question, she was thinking of other things. Her expression was sad.

"Why look a gift horse in the mouth?" Despite his tone, he was uneasy about it too. He worked up a certain enthusiasm for his promotion, but it was feeble. "I've told you again and again this is a good promotion. Anyone can see that."

"I don't see it's all that good." She kept watching the fort as though she could keep the barge moored below it with her gaze.

"The pay, for one thing. And we'll be in a real city, in a real house. You'd like that, wouldn't you? And you'll have servants if you want them—more than Vilfrida and Parvinus." The huge man and the old woman sat on crates in the prow of the barge.

"I like it here," Merobauda said. "It's my home. I've never been more than five miles away." She sighed and wiped a tear with the back of her hand. He'd never seen her cry.

He took her hands in his. "Look, Carissima. I couldn't have refused. Maximus is powerful and it's dangerous to snub powerful men. What else could I do? Toss away my commission and run south to the territory of Valentinian? They're still at war. And what would we live on? You said yourself that spending the money was dangerous. He shook his head. "Frankly, I can't see that I had any choice in the matter."

Merobauda looked past him at their possessions tied down on the deck: a bed, chairs, a table, several chests, a cupboard and, incongruously wedged into the middle of it all, a beer barrel, on top of which Una sat, her legs dangling, talking solemnly with Faustinus. Gaius thought idly about how Merobauda had insisted on including the barrel among their household effects. "There's beer up the river where we're going," he had said.

"I need *this* beer." She'd emphasized the demonstrative. "Don't argue with me."

"But why?"

She'd taken him by the arm and led him away as the barrel had been carried down to the barge. "I need it for the wort. So I can make my own when we get there."

"But why? Why make your own?" She had avoided his look. "Oh, you want to sell beer."

"Yes, that's right." She agreed so quickly she almost spoke over him. "And you like money."

"Everyone likes money, but there's a question of dignity involved here. Mine, anyway."

Merobauda looked suddenly frustrated. "I can't make you understand."

"What's to understand?"

"Never mind."

She's sad to leave her home, he thought. *That's why she's being difficult about the barrel. Well, of course she's sad; she'll never see this place again.* He thought about his home in Narbo. He'd never see that again. He put his arm around Merobauda's shoulders and she leaned her head against him.

He turned his thoughts back to other immediate concerns. "And that letter from Arcadius—he's beaten me out of the property, the gloating bastard. Even if we got to Italy, we'd have no place to go, so we have to make the best of things in Treverorum."

Merobauda looked up at the fort one last time, wiped another tear, and forced a smile and waved at it as though it were an old friend. They felt the soft jarring as the boatmen pushed the barge from the dock and into the stream. The patched tan sail was set to catch the gentle western breeze on a broad reach, and Gaius and his family floated north down the Rhine on their way to Augusta Treverorum.

XXVIII

387 AD

GAIUS IS SENT TO DELIVER ANOTHER MESSAGE

NEWS OF MORE CIVIL WAR

* * *

Protector Gaius Obsequens Dolo had a tidy little townhouse now. Not at all of the Mediterranean style: no passage from the street into a house built around a garden and tucked into the middle of a city block in a sunny southern city. But then the German sky lowered a good deal, and over the course of five years he had come to appreciate his snug brick house of a dozen rooms. A walled bricked court stood behind it with a small brewery and a stable for Dulcina and another pair of horses bought to support his dignity as a Protector. Gaius stood, hands clasped behind his back, and looked out of the second-story window of his office over the city wall a hundred yards away to watch the Moselle flow darkly by. Sparrows sang under the eaves of houses nearby as the spring rain fell gently for the fifth day.

"You know, Carissima, it's odd to think of the forts up that way…" he tilted his head to the north. "They're all pretty much like Castellinum Ripae—only now they're garrisoned by Franks. The border troops have all been pulled away to the towns. Now we have Franks along the frontier to protect us from…" He trailed off and looked into the featureless gray sky.

Merobauda sat working at a table set near the window to catch the light, where she glanced at figures and wrote down totals. "Franks to protect us from Franks," she finished for him.

"But, of course, they're allies. *These* Franks." The thought of them in the forts disquieted him, but in view of Merobauda's Alaman origins he didn't elaborate.

"Like Flavius Merobaudes? He's a Frank." She glanced at a column of figures and put the total at the bottom.

Gaius grimaced. Merobaudes had betrayed Gratian and gone over to Maximus with his troops. It was best not to think too much about it, though—after all, his betrayal had amounted that of one Roman by another; it had nothing to do with his being a Frank. Gaius turned back to the window, rested his forearms on the sill, and leaned out.

"I'm tired of all this gloom." He looked up at the light gray sky and the dripping rain.

"What gloom?" Merobauda wrote another figure into the ledger.

"You can't even see it for what it is! Until we got here, I don't think you'd ever been five miles from the Rhine."

"I hadn't. I told you that." She closed the book and put down her pen.

"And we're not far from it now." He leaned out over the sill to catch rain drops on his palm. "You'd like it where the sun shines."

"It shines here."

"From time to time. In fact, I can remember it happening several times. Anyway, you'd like a little sunshine."

"That's what we get here."

"I don't mean that." He leaned back against the window sill.

"You can't go home, Gaius. It doesn't belong to you anymore." Merobauda had a gift for frankly stating hard truths—as though it never occurred to her that her listeners might not be as stoical as she was. "And your brother has that estate free and clear."

"Don't remind me. He sends me a gloating letter on my birthday every year. I can feel the ill-will through my fingers before I open each one. They're almost sticky with it."

She ignored the metaphor. "Still, you're lucky: you're a Protector and have a Protector's income, and I've kept you to the legal skim so you won't get in trouble. You've got a house and the three children, and you've got me."

"Well, yes." He didn't agree with much enthusiasm; he chafed at her keeping a close eye on his business even though it kept him out of trouble. He had his pride, and her success in curbing his tendency to scheme sometimes rankled.

"And Maximus doesn't even seem to remember you," she went on. "He doesn't send you on missions. He just lets you loll about the house, and you send Arverno out to drill the men every couple of days. The Emperor Theodosius in the East and Valentinian in Italy have officially recognized Maximus, so we've got peace It's not a bad life for you."

"You make it sound like paradise."

She stood up and looked at him impatiently. "No, not paradise. But maybe as good as it gets, I don't know. We have some income from the tavern back at Castellinum Ripae and a little more income from the beer we make here."

"I wish you'd give up brewing. It's embarrassing to have a wife with a trade."

"I just direct things. It keeps Parvinus and Vilfrida busy. They do the brewing. Most of it."

"So, you're happy to just stay here?" He looked around and lowered his voice unconsciously. "And there's all that money buried under the fireplace in the tavern back at Ripae. Twelve hundred and ninety-two solidi."

"Look, Gaius, I know it's hard for you, but try to think before you make some plan about the money."

"You don't trust my plans," he accused her.

She looked at him frankly. "That's because I've seen how they turn out."

"That was years ago. This is now."

"You still haven't entirely recouped the investment in that little barge you set Mus up in."

"We get a cut of the profits each voyage. It'll get paid off soon."

"If the old tub doesn't wallow and sink first."

"But I had to help him: he's my client."

"Look, I'm really not complaining about that or the rate of return. It's just that you don't take the long view of things."

"Well, as to that…" He trailed off, unable to think of a reply. Evasion though, that would help. He snapped his fingers. "I've got to get to the parade ground!" He kissed the top of her head and slipped out of the room.

The rain relented and, if he could judge by the sky, it might hold back until the next day, so he was in a good mood as he rode Dulcina toward the parade ground. The city, its houses islands of grim gray tricked out with dripping tiles, glimmered in the watery spring light with a half-hearted exuberance, and Dulcina, older now, had grown more tractable—at least with him—and she went uncomplainingly down the paved streets, threading her way between the stepping stones that crossed the way from time to time. As he rode past the basilica he glanced at its tall blank wall and the line of windows just below the roof. He thought idly about Faustinus, who was probably inside filling out petitions and writing letters for illiterates. Gaius had encouraged him to do some lawyering too—to advocate now and then for small clients. It kept him busy, allowed him to support his wife, Catalania, and their son. Gaius thought about how things change for a man once he's freed. He sometimes wondered how free he was himself.

The street turned west and away from the river and left the houses and shops behind; long porticos flanked it on either side, now old and shabby. At the end stood the great triple gate and the road north. A half a mile down that road was the exercise field, a morass of churned mud after a week of intermittent rain and cavalry exercises. He rode to the edge of the field and sat on his horse next to Arverno, who was watching the troop from the saddle. Gaius nodded in satisfaction as fifty bespattered cavalrymen on steaming horses churned the mire. They trotted back and forth describing wide sweeps as they followed their standard. Their armor was spattered with mud and their shields smutched a dirty brown along their lower halves.

"They're remarkably dirty, Arverno." The muck called back his adventure with the bacaudae years before.

"Indeed they are, Your Fastidiousness. Indeed they are, and it's good to see, isn't it? Very satisfying. By the time they've finished they'll know they've been drilled."

The two men watched the troopers, remarking now and then on displays of skill or ineptitude. One of the troopers' horses slipped in the mud, went back on its haunches and recovered its balance, but its rider pitched out of the saddle with a cry and landed in a heap in the mud with his shield over him like a turtle shell.

"Good, good," Arverno said. "Experience is the best teacher." The two of them watched the cavalryman, now entirely bemired, struggle in mud up to his ankles to catch his mount, which kept backing up just out of reach. Finally, the soldier threw his shield into the muck and waved his fists in the air. Arverno clucked his tongue and shook his head. The troop circled back on its next maneuver and the man was knocked back into the mud by the flank of a passing horse.

"Well," Gaius said, "things seem to be going along as usual, Prae-positus[56]." That's was Arverno's title, now that the Second Pannonians had been promoted into the Field Army.

"Thank you, Excellence. Your compliment is, as always, an encouragement." He smiled benignly on the floundering troop. "I enjoy these exercises so much: they really make one appreciate being an officer." He pointed: "Look! There's another one down in the muck. That'll teach him to keep in the saddle."

"Quite right." Gaius watched the trooper struggle up from the mud. "Anything to report before I head off?" He'd been at the drill field a good twenty minutes; that was enough for the day. He looked up at the sky to see whether it augured more rain and began to swing Dulcina around.

"Just this little summons, Excellence." Arverno reached into his pouch and brought out a tightly folded scrap of vellum. "From the Palace."

"Did the messenger have anything to say?" He looked vaguely

---

[56] Arverno has a new title, but it amounts to about the same rank in this case.

away at the soldiers in the field to hide his unease at being the object of Imperial attention.

"Not really, Excellence. He seemed surprised to find that you weren't here to oversee the maneuvers. Of course, I told him that was my responsibility."

"Good man!" Gaius leaned out from the saddle and clapped him on the shoulder. He took the note with an assumed nonchalance and rode off. The note seemed somehow warm in his hand. He waited until he had passed through the city gate to snap the seal and read it.

> To the Protector G. Obsequens Dolo. He will present himself to His Serenity Magnus Maximus, Ever Victorious Emperor, at His Palace at the eighth hour of this day.[57]

Gaius's heart thumped. Apart from adoring the the purple four years ago, he had never yet been summoned to an audience with the Emperor. He glanced up at the sun, which of course was, as usual this spring, invisible behind the clouds, but it must have been nearly the eighth hour already, so he kicked Dulcina into a trot. He wished that he'd dressed better, that he'd worn a properly embroidered tunic rather than this cheap one with its printed patches, but at least he wasn't muddy. He thought back to the poor figure he'd cut before Maximus five years before and hoped the Emperor would be as indifferent now as he had been then.

The summons upset Gaius; it was a bit of a strain to meet an emperor, even one who had been a mere—though that seemed the wrong term—a mere military commander a few years before. And Gaius could not imagine what His Serenity wanted from him. It was unsettling in the extreme to think of meeting a man who could do, quite literally, anything he wished to one—and for any reason.

The Imperial palace at Augusta Treverorum was a palace fit for a soldier-emperor like Magnus Maximus. It was quite unlike the magnificent jumble of marble atop the Palatine Hill at Rome: three hundred years of palaces sprawling against each other, flashing white at

---

[57] More properly: *Tribuno G. Obsequente Dolone Protectorum. Se praesentet Serenitate Magno Maximo Semper Victore Imperatore in Palatio Suo ad horas octo huius diei.* Of course, Gaius could read this easily: it was in his native language.

midday and rosy at sunset, each shouldering the other for room and enclosing hidden gardens where hundreds of gilded statues stood on plinths along footpaths or lurked among the foliage to divert the Imperial attention. By contrast the Imperial Palace at Augusta Treverorum was the center of glorified military camp. Glorified, but a military camp.

Gaius rode down the Via Nomentana toward the tall triple gate in the high stone wall around the palace. Dismounting, he showed his summons to the optio of the guards and then followed him across the courtyard in front of the palace which, though it was tricked out with marble cladding and pillars, was built in the style of every camp headquarters Gaius had ever seen—only much larger. His unease grew as he approached the palace doors and the dozen Imperial Guards posted there, but they passed him in without ceremony apart from taking his searching him for other weapons. After that he was led by an usher through hallways whose floors were set with geometric mosaics in somber colors and whose walls were decorated in rust and dun scenes of military victory: Roman infantry and cavalry in vaguely Hellenistic equipment riding over bearded barbarians who scampered through stylized fields. At the third turn the usher stopped and turned to him.

"Perhaps you'd care for a little advice before you meet His Serenity."

"Well, of course, anything that you'd..ah...care to tell me about His Magnificence would be welcome. Quite welcome." Gaius, in his anxiety, was open to any advice.

The usher stood silently watching him, one hand poised on the polished head of his official staff. "A wise position to take," he said but didn't offer any advice. The two stood staring at each other until the usher said, "Advice concerning His Serenity is particularly valuable. Particularly valuable." He looked at Gaius meaningfully.

Gaius looked back at him with a vague intentness. "Yes?" And then he took the usher's point and reached into his purse. He fumbled out three folles and handed them over. The usher curled his lip at the money but shrugged as though at a minor disappointment, say, weather turning unexpectedly cold or a little money lost on a horser-ace. "It's not likely that he'll ask you, but if he does, I'd advise you to agree that the Son is of equal importance to the Father."

"I see, yes," Gaius said, though he hadn't the remotest idea what the man was getting at. He finally decided the usher was alluding to the Emperor's son Victor, whom he had made Caesar—in other words, his official successor. But everyone knew that. Gaius wanted his three **folles** back (it was the principle of the thing) but couldn't think how to ask without sacrificing his dignity. While he was still fumbling for an approach, the usher went on:

"His Serenity is apt to react most strongly at the smallest whiff of Arianism." He turned and strode off, leaving Gaius to trail behind, fretting. It must be something religious, he decided. He seemed to recall that there had been a stir when Maximus had executed a Bishop, though he couldn't remember any details. He'd had other things on his mind at the time. He wished that he'd paid closer atten-tion to Merobauda's Christianity. Why didn't she force it on him? That happened to husbands all the time. If he got out of this interview alive he'd have to have a serious talk with her.

At length they came to the audience chamber somewhere at the opposite end of the palace (Gaius could not, after all of the twists and turns, quite remember how he had gotten there). It was curtained off in purple, and more soldiers in white stood guard before it. The usher turned to him. "You needn't advance toward the throne on your knees." He looked him up and down, taking in his cheap tunic, and added, with a trace of irony, "Your dignity, of course, obviates that obligation." He nodded to the guards, the curtain was drawn back, and he added in an undertone: "A deep bow, and don't advance until you're recognized— and then not too quickly." He stepped ahead of Gaius and announced, "A Protector of Your Serenity, Gaius Obsequens Dolo, presents himself in obedience to Your Serene Majesty's Sacred Command."

Gaius stood at the threshold of the audience chamber, half bent over in his bow and staring fixedly at the mosaic floor, from which a small, decorative bird in tiny blue and gray tiles looked back at him with red jasper eyes.

"Let him approach." It was the voice of the Emperor.

Gaius kept himself obsequiously bent over as his station demanded and surreptitiously tried to look from side to side to be absolutely certain it was he who was to creep forward. He hesitated a bit too long for the usher, who used his staff to prod him in the rump with subtle and expert technique. Gaius snapped up to attention and then started slowly forward, smoothing his face into an utter blankness that he hoped would indicate tremendous respect.

His Serenity Magnus Maximus, grayer now, was yet more imposing than ever in heavy purple robes and a gold diadem set with polished rubies. He leaned impatiently forward on a marble throne inset with medallions of and carnelian and orange quartz, and he scowled as Gaius inched forward, finally snapping, "Hurry up, then! Do not keep Us waiting! We have other business to attend to."

Gaius glided forward as quickly as he dared, keeping the white-clad guards who flanked the throne in the corner of his eye. When he had gotten within a dozen feet of the Imperial Presence, he bowed again, waited for what he judged was a fitting interval, and announced the appallingly obvious: "I am here." And then he remembered to add, "Your Serenity." Grasping the fatuity of his announcement, he went on to worsen it: "As of course, Your Serenity realizes. And as You commanded. Which, of course, Your Universality also realizes." It struck him how much he sounded like Arverno hitting his stride, and he flushed red as a beet.

His Serenity frowned alarmingly at this greeting, apparently regarding the equally mixed tactlessness and obviousness a mild offence. Gaius quailed at the Emperor's expression, as he might have at a nearby lightning strike. He tried to calm himself with the thought that, though Maximus could do anything he wanted to him—even have him killed out of hand—Gaius was was unlikely to succeed in doing anything spectacular enough to call for it. Still, his mind strayed from the immediate situation and oscillated sharply between the execution of the bishop and the gold hidden under the hearth at the tavern. He suddenly wondered whether the latter somehow lay behind the summons, and his heart sank. He could not believe he hadn't thought of that. He prepared to trot out the excuse he'd concocted at the fort—the one about holding the money as a sort of trustee—though he suspected that, after four years, it would be less convincing than ever.

But he needn't have worried.

"We summon you here in order to entrust you to carry a message."

Gaius nodded, almost sagging in relief. His armpits were wet. "Of course, Your Serenity."

"A message and gift."

Gaius nodded again. The Emperor signaled to an attendant who materialized from somewhere. He handed Gaius a sealed packet of vellum and a small, highly polished wooden box and then disappeared like a ghost. Gaius marveled at his skill.

The Emperor was speaking: "We command you to deliver the gift to His Serenity Valentinian and the letter to the Excellent Flavius Afranius Syagrius."

"Syagrius," Gaius repeated for want of anything better to say.

"Yes, to Syagrius. You are his client. As you are also mine."

"Well, yes, Your Magnificence. That, of course, goes without saying."

"Do not presume, Protector, to judge what We ought to say or not say."

"No! Certainly not, Your Magnificence." He felt suddenly hot, and his earlier anxiety surged back. Perhaps the irritation he had caused the Emperor would somehow cause the conversation to veer toward Arianism—whatever that was exactly. Now, what had the usher told him again?

But the Emperor was, in the end, all business. "We command you to deliver Our gift to His Serenity and Our letter into Flavius Syagrius's hand, and into no one else's. And we further command you to return with any reply that the Excellent Syagrius might have."

"Very good, Your Serenity."

"Take a troop of cavalry with you—as many as you need—" Here Maximus's face darkened. "And comport yourself with more dignity than you have done today." He pointed an Imperial Forefinger at Gaius, but his tone reverted to that of an officer at drill. "And put on a better tunic! You're a Protector and Our envoy—be certain that you look like one."

"Of course, Your Serenity."

"Do not fail to deliver the message and gift, and do not fail to return with the reply." The tone was once more cold, imperial, impersonal.

Gaius bowed as he backed his way out of the hall and through the curtains. Once out, he wiped the sweat from his forehead.

XXIX

AGAINST GAIUS'S BETTER JUDGMENT, MEROBAUDA OPENS THE IMPERIAL LETTER, WHICH TURNS OUT TO BE QUITE ODD

* * *

"Was the imperial presence all that you'd hoped for?" Faustinus asked.

"I can't say I hoped for anything, apart from getting away unscathed."

Merobauda looked fixedly at the end of the table where the letter lay folded into a packet. The little wooden box rested next to it. She and Gaius sat at the table in the dining room, the snug little place with a view of the city wall in the distance and the Moselle sparkling beyond. Merobauda continued to look thoughtfully at the packet and box.

Faustinus was bold enough these days to draw a chair up and sit at the table with them. "How long do you reckon the mission will take?"

Gaius leaned across the table and patted Merobauda's hand. "What can you tell me about Arianism?"

Merobauda exchanged a look with Faustinus. He said, "Master Gaius seems suddenly to have developed some rather abstruse interests."

Merobauda said, "Forget about Arianism. I want to know what's in the letter." She looked at him steadily. "Well?"

Gaius said, "I don't know."

"Let's see it, then."

Gaius was scandalized. "We can't just open it! It's from the Emperor Maximus himself. It's to be given directly to Syagrius—he's one of the Great Men."

"Maybe the thing has something to do with Arianism," Faustinus said wryly. "Whatever that is, exactly."

"Do you want to open it, or shall I?" Merobauda was her usual dogged self. Faustinus got up and closed the door to the dining room in anticipation of the inevitable outcome.

Gaius was flustered—His Serenity Maximus had impressed him as a man not to be crossed. "Absolutely not, Carissima. We can't do that! Think of the penalty for tampering with it."

"What is the penalty?" Merobauda looked at him inquisitively.

"I don't know exactly, but I'm sure it's terrible. Criminal penalties are all terrible these days. And besides, we'd have to break the Imperial seal." He pointed to it.

Merobauda leaned over the table and stared into Gaius's eyes. It was distracting. "Think what we might learn something important if we look at it. It might be something very important. Maybe there's going to be another war—something like that. We could get ready for it." And while she had Gaius's eyes fixed on hers she whisked the packet from him and sat back out of reach across the table. She turned it in her hands, appraising it. "I think we could repair the seal. And if not, you just say that it broke on the journey. After all, you'll be traveling four hundred miles. Anything might happen."

Her intransigence upset him. "There's a ring, too." The instant he said it, he wondered why he'd mentioned it. Merobauda just had that effect on him: it was hard to keep things from her. Besides, he knew that she was going to ask.

She looked up from the packet. "A ring?"

"In the box. A gold ring with an amethyst set into it. It's a gift from Maximus to Valentinian."

"So you *have* looked," she said with a slight smile.

"Just in the box, Carissima. Just in the box."

Faustinus sat back and crossed his arms, smiling ironically. "Doubtless, you were only being cautious, opening the gift of one emperor to another—to be sure that you really have what you're supposed to deliver."

Gaius ignored Faustinus's tone but snatched at the excuse. "Exactly. Well put. Now give me back the letter."

"Not until we've read it." Merobauda held it in one hand and tapped the palm of the other with it. She sat back just far enough that he couldn't lunge over that table and snatch it back.

Gaius tried to curb her interest. "It's probably just some string of turgid diplomatic formulas. You know the kind of thing…"

"No, I don't, Gaius. People don't send me diplomatic letters."

"Really, Carissima, it won't make any sense to you."

Faustinus raised his eyebrows. "Lots of participles, datives of reference and a hapax legomenon or two? A little anaphora for the sake of diversion?[58]"

"Yes, exactly. That sort of thing exactly. I wouldn't be surprised if it's just bursting with future participles."

"And nonce-words," Faustinus added.

"Those too." He put out his hand for the letter. "Really, I'm sure it's a curdled mass of prose, a thicket of syntax…"

"A thicket of syntax. That's very well put, you know." Faustinus egged him on.

"Thank you. Now let me finish. A thicket of syntax," Gaius continued with growing pomposity, the usual symptom of his enthusiasm for his own diction. "A veritable thicket of syntax that would take a grammarian the better part of an afternoon to cut through, swinging mightily at the turn of every clause with all of the razor-edged tools of diction." Faustinus winced, but Gaius persevered, "The very best people, people like Syagrius and emperors and so on, they like doing that sort of thing. It confirms their social position and helps them pass the time."

---

[58] The reader who wants to put this book down for a while is directed to Allen and Greenough's *New Latin Grammar,* in which all of these terms are explained in detail and illustrated with helpful examples. Give yourself an hour or two.

"Between usurpations and wars with Persia," Faustinus added drily. "Those are, of course, merely illustrative examples." Merobauda looked at him crossly and he shut up.

Gaius put his hand out, but Merobauda kept back in her chair with the letter. He felt faintly ridiculous, so he put on his most masterful tone and said, sharply, "Cornelia Merobauda, give me that letter!"

She said, "No."

"No?" Gaius was aghast. To save him embarrassment, Faustinus studied the fingernails of his right hand.

"No. I think Maximus is up to something, and what could it be but war? Don't forget you're in the army." She looked at him humorlessly.

Gaius glanced at Faustinus for help, but he had moved on to the fingernails of his left hand.

He turned back to his wife. "Now look here, Merobauda—" But he didn't have a chance to finish. As he began the remonstrance, she slipped a thumb under the seal and snapped it open. His heart thumped, but she only said, "Well, Gaius, we'd might as well read it now, don't you think?"

Gaius gaped across at the letter wondering how to reseal it.

In a moment Merobauda had flattened it on the table and was working out what it said. She looked up. "It's a birthday greeting." She glanced down again and continued reading, her lips moving as she went along, her finger following the text.

"Now that's odd." Faustinus pointed across the table at the letter.

"What's odd about a birthday greeting?" Gaius said snippily. "Everybody has a birthday. Even you, though you don't know what it is." He made this little swipe at Faustinus because he hadn't sided with him against Merobauda.

Faustinus replied suavely, "I chose June 15 for my birthday years ago. I find it works quite well. He went on. "But what's odd is that the letter is on palimpsest. You can see where the earlier writing was scraped off."

Merobauda continued to read, murmuring as she went along[59].

---

[59] ThismayhavebeenencouragedbytheRomanhabitofoftenwritingwithoutspacesbetweenthe-words. Readers back then generally read aloud.

The letter was written in purple ink, the privilege of the Emperor, in the beautiful hand of a court scribe, and signed by the Maximus himself. After a few moments, she looked up. "Faustinus has a point. Why wouldn't the emperor use a fresh sheet? After all, he's going to the expense of sending you and a half-dozen horsemen all the way to Italy. Why save money on the vellum?"

"May I?" Faustinus took up the letter, went to the window and raised it so that the sun shone through the page.

"Be careful with that thing, Faustinus!" Gaius said sharply. "It's bad enough the seal's broken. Don't smudge the paper too."

"I'm trying to see what was written on the parchment before it was reused. It shows through if you look closely enough."

"It's probably an old tax receipt or something. Some scrap from the bureaucracy."

"What do you see?" Merobauda turned in her chair to watch Faustinus.

Gaius helplessly tried to control the situation. "Look, let's just reseal the letter. We're going to get into trouble—if we haven't already."

"Here's another odd thing," Faustinus said. "The old writing— there's not much of it and it's faint—but it falls exactly between the lines of the letter."

"It's obvious that the new letter was written between the lines of the old one so the new writing would be clear. Get something to mend that seal!" Gaius stood up for emphasis but, of course, neither Faustinus nor Merobauda paid any attention to him.

Faustinus went on, "What's particularly odd is that every word of the effaced text is five letters long."

"How can you tell?" Merobauda asked.

"The words are separated."

"How handy," Gaius said kneading a touch of sarcasm into his voice. "Now let's get to sealing it up again."

"Five letters long? But words are all different lengths—long, short, middling." She frowned in puzzlement. "Even when you see writing with spaces or points between the words like some people do it, they're all different lengths."

"Are the *C*s and *K*s and *S*s straight? Or is it written according to Merobauda's reformed spelling?" Gaius asked. He was feeling excluded and resentful that no one considered his views about sealing the letter.

"There's no way to tell." Faustinus answered the question as though it had been serious. "The words don't make any sense."

"Let me see it." Merobauda held it to the light.

"It must be some sort of puzzle," Faustinus said. "Maybe each letter stands for another one. Didn't Caesar do something like that? Back in the Gallic wars?"

"But why are they all the same length? That must be some sort of clue." She sat musing.

"I think the real mystery is how we're going to get the letter sealed without Syagrius noticing any tampering." Gaius leaned back with his arm over the back of the chair and scowled to show his displeasure.

"It must be some sort of pattern," Merobauda continued. She thought a moment and then counted the words that showed faintly between three of the neat lines of purple imperial writing. There were twenty of them. "You can see the whole page wasn't covered with writing before it was cleaned off and used again. There were just these twenty words on three lines." Faustinus came around the table to lean over her shoulder and see.

She glanced quickly over the letters, taking the first letter of each word and putting them together, but no, that came to nothing. And yet, and yet, she could sense a pattern. Not the same as happened with numbers, but still a pattern. It was there, definitely there, but what was it? She drew her finger along each line and narrowed her eyes at the letters forming the meaningless unpronounceable five letter "words." In her mind she substituted one letter for another in the first two words—"A" for "B," and "C" for "D" and so on, but that came to nothing.

She looked up quietly in thought for a few moments. Faustinus winked at Gaius and put a finger to his lips. Gaius slumped in his chair, resigned to letting her work on the letter. Merobauda looked back at the document, this time searching for repeated letters. Some letters are a good deal more common than others, she knew, but they tended to cluster in ways that these did not. And then it was all clear, like a bird flashing out of a leafy tree, one moment invisible, the next clear and distinct against a blue sky.

"Ah!" Merobauda looked up in delight.

"Yes?" Faustinus asked, clearly impressed. Gaius was impressed too, but he kept it to himself.

She laughed briefly. "Got it! But I need to write it down to show you two what's going on."

Faustinus brought her a tablet and stylus, but Gaius folded his arms and frowned to show he wasn't happy with her larking about with the Emperor's correspondence. The secret operations of the Great Men were not for such as they. He wished Merobauda could see that.

She turned the waxed tablet longways and carefully copied out the twenty words in a single line. Gaius could see her eyes flash back and forth over the text. She leaned back and shook her head.

"Well?" Faustinus asked.

"It doesn't look good."

"So, you mean you can't read it after all?" Gaius didn't hide his disappointment. As long as they were risking the danger of opening the letter, it would have been good to know what it said.

But Faustinus had great faith in her. "But you *can* read it, can't you? It's the news that's bad, isn't it?"

"It's not good news at all. Here. I'll show you." She drew a straight line dividing the text into two groups of ten words. "Now it's easy to see." Faustinus looked over her shoulder and Gaius, despite himself, stood up to see. She pointed. "Look at the first letter of the first word and then the first letter of the first word after the dividing line. Then the second letter of the first word, and then the second letter of the first word after the dividing line. And then the third and so on." She drew a vertical line and rewrote the letters in the way she had described.

It was upside down to Gaius, but Faustinus read it out slowly.

WE APPRECIATE THAT WHEN OUR ARMY COMES TO ITALY FOR THE GOOD OF THE STATE WE MAY PROVISION IT FROM YOUR GALLIC ESTATES AND COUNT IN OTHER WAYS ON YOUR COOPERATION RBUS

The three of them looked at each other in silence for several moments.

"So, Gaius," Merobauda said. "It's war again, and probably soon. Maximus is sending you because you're a minor client of Syagrius, and you've carried a message for him before. You're a surety that the message is genuine."

"A minor client," he repeated flatly. This minor client business might turn out to be rather risky.

"That explains why he sent you to Britain with that message years ago," Faustinus said, nodding to himself. "As a client of Syagrius, you'd be trusted."

"Exactly," Merobauda said.

Faustinus elaborated the point. "And Maximus appointed Gaius a Protector in his court to keep a line of communication open to Syagrius. And, remember, Syagrius established the relationship between Gaius and Maximus before the usurpation. I suppose that was in case he needed a personal connection with Maximus. He's a canny one, that Syagrius. I wonder whose side he's on?"

"His own." Merobauda said with decision. She smoothed out the letter absently.

"What's the '*RBUS*'?" Gaius couldn't help asking.

Merobauda looked at him as though he'd failed to see something obvious. "To make the number of letters in the message come out right. So that they could be divided by five with no remainder. Honestly, I don't know why division is so hard for you."

"For some of us, spelling is the long suit," he said, giving her a meaningful look.

"It wouldn't be a problem if people spelled things properly."

"Perhaps we can move beyond the question of whether spelling or division is the more important," Faustinus said, "and concentrate on the immediate situation, which seems to be impending civil war."

Gaius looked at him. "The immediate situation is that you need to pack a number of things."

Faustinus shook his head. "Archelaus does that sort of thing for you now."

"You misunderstand. *You* need to pack *your* things. We're heading for Italy in three days."

✕✕✕

GAIUS AND FAUSTINUS FIND THEMSELVES ONCE AGAIN IN ITALY.

* * *

His Serenity Valentinian was a slight figure swathed in heavy purple robes, the scarlet toes of his boots just peeping out below them. He perched on his gilded throne set high on a dais of porphyry, entirely immobile during Gaius's brief audience with him—really just a few moments during which Gaius had declaimed a florid formal greeting to His Serenity and delivered the box with the ring to an attendant. The young Emperor had inclined his head once, and slightly, in vague acknowledgment of the gift, but he had said nothing and, the gift given, Gaius had been shunted wordlessly from the audience chamber and sent on his way.

The encounter had been dreamlike, the recollection of it dissolving until there was nothing to it apart from vague fading wisps of color and wealth. Valentinian had been more splashed with gems than Maximus, surrounded by more courtiers, displayed in richer surroundings, and yet he exuded less power—in short, though splendid, he was not awesome. Not awesome at all, really. Odd, that. Gaius mused about these things as he followed an usher through the maze of hallways toward the portals to the grounds around the palace. Now and again someone slipped quietly by—another usher, a white-clad guardsman with a message, an undersecretary with a tablet, officials major and minor carrying out the vague work of administration. As Gaius and the usher were almost out of the palace, a soldier, in a friendly way, laid an arm over Gaius's shoulder and, leaning confidentially toward him, said, "Well, if it isn't the little bastard tribune from Castellinum Ripae!" Gaius looked around to see whether there could be another bastard tribune from Castellinum Ripae nearby, but there wasn't—just the usher, who was looking curiously at him. Evidently Gaius was the bastard—and the greeting made him uneasy. The soldier was a big man, and he steered Gaius with the pressure of his arm down the corridor a few yards away from the usher.

"We're old friends, Dolo and me," the soldier said, nodding back to the usher. "Aren't we? Very old friends. We go way back. Oh, yes." His voice held the trace of a growl. Quite disconcerting.

Gaius, shook himself free and studied the other man. Recognition took him a moment or two; he hadn't seen Probus Martialis since the mutiny years before, but it was him. Not much about him had changed, apart from the greying in his brush-cut hair, but the aggression and menace were as fresh as ever. Gaius unconsciously backed up a step, keeping his back to the wall, though he could see that Martialis carried no weapons—like everyone in the palace apart from the guards, he'd been disarmed.

"What brings you here?" Gaius said, as jauntily as he could manage. He noticed that Martialis held a pair of tablets with columns of writing on them, doubtless lists of names.

"Don't you worry about my business, Dolo," he said.

"Ah, carrying troop rosters, are you, Martialis? Seems rather a mundane duty for a Protector." Gaius regarded him narrowly and noted hints of straitened circumstance: the cuffs of his tunic had been turned, and a rip at the hem had been carefully, but quite evidently, mended from underneath.

Martialis looked around, fixed his glance on the usher until he looked away, and then whispered, "Praepositus."

"Just praepositus?" This was good; he wasn't a Protector any longer. "Of what?"

"The Milites Scyri.[60]"

"Ah, border troops. I see." He clucked his tongue with openly false sympathy.

"They're in the field army now." Martialis sounded defensive.

"Jumped up to the field army, of course. Pseudocomitatenses. But still, at bottom, border troops, wouldn't you say?"

Martialis glowered at him. But the usher was watching from the corner of his eye, so Gaius felt safe. He smiled at the bully's frustration. "I see you're descending to your natural level. It was bound to happen. Trust me—you'll be happier when you finally arrive."

"You bastard..." Martialis repeated, fumbling for something more cutting.

"Praepositus, eh? You'll forgive me if I have trouble telling your current position apart from…oh, say, the one you held years ago back at Castellinum Ripae." He shook his head sadly. "All that money you paid to be a Protector wasted. Still, I suppose someone got some good out of it."

"You bastard."

"Now, Martialis, I forgive you because it's evident you suffer from a paucity of invective, and that must be very hard on you. But in future don't forget your manners. You're speaking to a Protector in the service of His Serenity, the Emperor Magnus Maximus."

Martialis looked impressed despite himself and then, hoping Gaius was simply making this up, asked the usher, "Is this true?" The attendant nodded and looked politely away.

Martialis turned back. "You're still a bastard."

Gaius smiled smugly. "Let's move on to a new subject, shall we? One of more general interest." He feigned deep thought, and then said, "I know! How about your demotion?" He gave a curt nod to the usher to ensure his attention and smirked at Martialis. "Now there's a topic worthy of some exposition. How, exactly, did Fortuna, with her hand on the rudder, trip you up on the Road of Life?" He'd read that somewhere, long ago. The mixed metaphor still jarred, but Martialis would be insensitive to notice. "At least you're an officer—however

---

[60] Poor Martialis has had a setback.

lowly. Still, for someone who was once a Protector, well…" He trailed off for rhetorical effect, and he glanced once again at Martialis's belt to be sure he'd been completely disarmed. Better safe than sorry. "Yes, perhaps you'd care to tell me how you came down in the world? I'm sure it's a gripping story." He spoke loudly and clearly for the benefit of the usher. He folded his arms and rocked on his heels, enjoying himself.

Martialis glared at the usher, but he wouldn't look away. "Figure it out for yourself," he hissed at Gaius.

"Let me think a moment." Gaius put his hand to his chin and shammed deep concentration. He snapped his fingers. "Ah, yes! The lost horses, the lost equipment. Quite an embarrassment, I suppose—that little difficulty up at Ripae."

"You suppose!" Martialis gathered his fingers into a fist the size of a small ham but then relaxed it as a pair of imperial guardsmen passed them. "Volusianus saddled me with all the blame."

"He did? And why not? I'm sure you'd have done the same if you'd been in his position." Gaius was really enjoying himself now. "And what? You couldn't pay your way out of it?" He assumed an entirely unconvincing expression of sympathy. "I suppose not, what with your little shakedown tour cut short by Maximus's invasion. Gaius shook his head and clucked. "So, you must have been broke when you got back. And of course you'd bungled." The final sentence sat on his tongue as sweet as honey. The usher was now openly enjoying the exchange. "This fellow here is Martialis—first name's Probus, which of course means "upright." Funny, that name for him—the sort of thing that seems like a cheap literary trick.[61]

Despite the presence of the usher, Martialis surged forward and snatched up a bunch of Gaius's tunic, undecided whether to shake him or slam him against the wall. Gaius smiled blandly at the attendant and said in an even voice, "You may wish to call the guard before Martialis quite finishes his assault on an Imperial Envoy to His Serenity Valentinian." Despite his smile and off-hand manner, Gaius's heart had begun to pound like a hammer, but he couldn't help

---

[61] Which, of course, in this case it is.

himself from goading the big man as he thought back to his hours in the stinking cell at the fort.

Martialis held his grip for a moment longer and then released Gaius with a shove. He leaned close. "If I ever see you anywhere that I can do it, I'll kill you."

"Why, Martialis, such a barbaric ambition!"

"I'll kill you!" he repeated and strode off.

"Shall we go?" Gaius asked the usher, smoothing out his tunic, and assuming, so far as he could, a certain nonchalance.

XXXI

GAIUS VISITS SYAGRIUS

VOLUSIANUS CONDUCTS A BIT OF RESEARCH

* * *

"Apart from the death threat, how did things go?" Faustinus asked, as they rode away from the Imperial Palace. The three troopers, the calo and the two pack-mules of their escort fell in behind them.

"Quite well, really. If I'd goaded Martialis any further, I think he'd have exploded. I took pity on him and let up a bit on the taunts so he's still among the living."

"Your restraint reflects well on you."

"Well, the ring's delivered. Now for the letter to Syagrius. He's at one of his estates about ten miles south of here. Ten miles. The last thing I need is another three hours in the saddle."

* * *

This estate of Flavius Syagrius was one of his smaller ones, a villa of fifty rooms, a reception hall that would have done for one of the earlier emperors, a dozen outbuildings, two hundred acres under cultivation and three villages bursting with tenants. Enclosed by the walls around the villa was a garden of box-hedges and lawns planted with roses; classical statutes stood at the corners of perfect squares and triangles cut by paths of white gravel. At the gate in the wall and at the entry to the villa itself—tall wooden double doors with great brass rings as handles—Syagrius's private soldiers stood— tough Illyrians in blue tunics, each with a sword at his belt. At the doorway, Gaius straightened clothes to achieve what dignity he could. He had dismounted at the edge of the estate and thrown a dark blue dalmatic over his tunic, hoping it draped far enough down to hide his dirty trousers. He didn't cut much of a figure, but perhaps Maximus's letter would imbue him with a trace of dignity. Faustinus followed him into the great house, one guard ahead and two behind. Thirty yards down a corridor frescoed in a pastoral scenes they were stopped by an usher, a young but remarkably superior sort of fellow who, though shorter than either of them, somehow managed to look down on them.

"I understand that you are Gaius Obsequens Dolo."

"A Protector of His Serenity The Emperor Magnus Maximus."

"So we understand." The usher used the plural form as though he were an emperor himself. "Magnus Maximus.[62]" Somehow, despite its meaning, he made the name seem a diminutive. "And you?" He looked at Faustinus.

"I am fortunate to be the Protector's Domestic."

"Your name?"

What an opening and not to be missed! He gave himself a third name. "Faustinus Aquitanius Obsequentianus."

Gaius turned to look at him, startled but mildly flattered. Faustinus smiled blandly, and the usher headed off, leading the party to The Great Man's reception hall. Once in, they were announced, and Faustinus's new name, uttered before Flavius Syagrius, was legitimated.

The hall was floored in mosaic and the walls, too. Tesserae of a hundred colors covered the walls, many of them gold and glinting. The room—indeed, the entire villa—spoke of three hundred years of the very rich marrying the very rich. Gaius, even though he had lived two

---

[62] The name, of course, literally means "Great Greatest." Not very sophisticated, really, when you think about it. But there it is.

years in Rome and had seen things—had even seen two emperors in their palaces—had to keep himself from gaping. Syagrius, a private citizen, seemed not to suffer at all by comparison to Their Serenities.

The Great Man stood to receive them, conceded even to take a few steps toward them, and his eyes hinted, just hinted, at a smile. But at what? Was it of welcome, or was it turned inward, as it were, toward something that concerned Syagrius alone? Or did it touch Gaius? Was it the reflection of some other subtle stratagem in which Gaius would be forced to play a role? He felt suddenly resentful. In principle, there was no slight to his dignity in being sent as a messenger on important missions between such powerful men—quite the opposite, in fact—but his mission to Britain had drawn him along the edge of conspiracy, just as this one was doing.

Merobauda and Faustinus were right about Syagrius's apparently inexplicable interest in him and his career. With little more than a word to someone in the bureaucracy, he had, in broad outline, settled Gaius's fate for years. What, precisely (or even generally—Gaius was not particular), did Syagrius expect in the future? It dawned him that at any moment convenient to Syagrius, Gaius might find himself involuntarily tied to an unsuccessful adventure and conveniently ruined or even punished as an associate in the Great Man's disgrace. It could happen. Or might he be rewarded as an ally in the success of Syagrius's next maneuver, whatever that might be? But in either case, Gaius himself would not determine the outcome. This realization came to him very clearly. But this was no time for reflection.

Gaius bowed low, straightened, and waited to be spoken to. In that time, he studied Syagrius carefully, the slender old man in a plum-colored silk dalmatic over a dazzling white tunic. Delicate gold filigrees marked the toes of his shining supple white shoes as they showed below the long white tunic. The old man was nearly bald now, but his eyes were still a clear icy blue. Despite his age, he saw well; it was evident from his expression. He stood studying Gaius, judging Gaius as Gaius[63] was judging him, but with more perspicacity, Gaius

---

[63] The author apologizes for using "Caius" four times in a single sentence, but there was really no other way.

suspected, than he could muster.

"Good afternoon, Protector Dolo." Syagrius's voice was rich, the product of training in elocution. "I should imagine that your mission was tiresome in the extreme, but that His Serenity Maximus would not have so commissioned you, were it not important." Gaius noted the elaboration of Syagrius's diction, the careful placement of words, the precise use of flexions. He spoke a Latin more refined than any he had ever heard, like something out of a book. Gaius thought it best to simply nod once and slightly to show agreement and deference.

"I understand that you have a letter for me."

"Indeed I do," Gaius said, answering properly instead of saying "yes," as though he were from the lower classes or a mere soldier.[64] He held the letter out with a flourish. "I am commanded to hand it directly to you, Excellence and, as the command comes from His Serenity himself, I am obliged to trouble you with a personal audience which I would otherwise have sought to spare you." That sentence came out well, Gaius thought: just the right blend of deference and syntactic elegance. He looked out of the corner of his eye to see whether Faustinus had noticed.

The usher took a step forward to take the letter from Gaius, but Syagrius gracefully waved him away and took the letter himself just as though Gaius had been his equal—say, a consul or an aristocrat whose lands, all put together, amounted to half a province. Their fingers brushed lightly as the letter changed hands, and Gaius felt uncomfortable, as though he'd touched something dangerously powerful. Syagrius, a Great Man, lived as richly as any emperor and he and his kind outlasted them. It was something to think about.

Syagrius gave the letter the merest glance. A secretary drifted up from somewhere to take it from him, but he shook his head and the man disappeared. Odd how the minions of these high personages could appear and disappear like spirits. It was as though they partook of some supernatural power that emanated from their masters.

Gaius said, in his most polite tone, "I have been commanded to

---

[64] Latin has no word for "yes." But the common people used "sic" or "huic," words which became "si" and "oui."

return with any reply that Your Magnificence might deign to send to His Serenity."

"You will receive my reply tomorrow at the seventh hour. You may go now."

"Very good." Gaius turned his back and walked out. He didn't back out—after all, the man was not an emperor.

* * *

Volusianus was embittered—the loss of the Gallic provinces to Magnus Maximus had narrowed the scope of his duties and peculations to Italy. This was a serious problem, as he could not shake down the commanders of the Palatine troops as he could the provincial commanders, and that reduced the pickings even further. His income had been sharply curbed, and he still had his creditors to pay off— men who had helped him buy his office, men who didn't take well to excuses about changed circumstances. Changed circumstances were for small men to bear, small men like Scaevolus Volusianus. That thought rankled as much as the lost income.

But one day he had an inspiration as he trudged through the hallways of the administrative wing of the Imperial palace, nagged by his debts, vague thoughts of insolvency flitting through his mind like bats at sunset, turning away now and then but always swooping back. The idea had formed suddenly, and he stopped, wondering how it had not come to him before. Mulling over it, he changed his course, stopping at an office with the words **Biblioteca Officinarum** painted over the doorway. The sign was the first guidepost on his journey to recoup the money and standing he had lost years before. Here he would find a copy of **The List of Offices**. He straightened himself up so far as he could and assumed the haughty expression he inflicted on underlings and stepped into the office.

A pair of clerks sat at a table, one reading figures slowly from a pile of sheets, the other taking them down on a neatly ruled sheet of vellum. They looked up as he entered, and the younger of them, hardly more than a boy, stood up in respect. The older clerk frowned and kept his seat.

"Mere clerks should rise at the appearance of their betters, as, for example, an Imperial Undersecretary."

The older clerk sighed audibly (an insult, really to Volusianus, that sigh), put down his pen, but did not stand. Clearly the man had heard of Volusianus's difficulties and of his financial descent.

"Your wish?" the younger clerk asked with naive eagerness. The older clerk grimaced at the boy's polite tone, but then shrugged. The boy didn't know Volusianus's reputation.

"*The List*. I wish to see *The List*."

"*The List?*" The boy looked at the older clerk for help.

"He means the *List of Offices*," the older clerk clarified, referring to Volusianus in the third person as though he weren't there.

"I see your assistant is a blockhead. It must be trying for you."

The older clerk shook his head. "He's quick, in fact. He's just new." To irritate him further, he waited until Volusianus frowned at his lack of subservience and then added, "Your Excellence," in a tone that suggested that he was unsure Volusianus deserved it. He looked at the boy and nodded to an inner doorway. "The north wall. It's on the second shelf from the top. That's a good boy, fetch it for 'His Excellence.'" Again that ironic tone. And then he added, "Yes, fetch it for him, but—" and here hesitated for emphasis, " but do it, perhaps, in a moment." The young clerk turned back in the doorway, uncertain what the older clerk intended.

Volusianus scowled. "You dare to delay an Imperial Undersecretary?"

The senior clerk finally rose. "Not if he has an order. You have an order, or course."

Volusianus glowered. "I need no order! My status is sufficient." He searched his mind to think when it was that he might have offended this clerk, but he had stepped on so many men over the years, he could not recall.

"Maybe so." He took his time looking at Volusianus and then added, "And maybe not." He turned to the younger clerk and indicated Volusianus with a nod of the head. "Take His Excellence here to the office of the Head Secretary and confirm his permission."

"Wait." Volusianus scowled and then, to save his dignity, said, "No need for useless formalities." He reached into his purse, counted out five folles and set them on the table. The senior clerk regarded them gravely for a several long moments and then, when Volusianus was just on the point of speaking, he said, "Six." Volusianus gave him a vicious look but reached again into his purse, at which point the senior clerk added, "And one for the boy here."

Volusianus slapped two coins beside the others. The old clerk made no move to pick them up. He just glanced at them casually until he could sense that Volusianus was about to speak then forestalled him with perfect timing, saying to the boy, "This man is Scaevolus Volusianus. You would do well to remember him." He looked as though he had a bad taste in his mouth. He took up one of the folles and gave it to the boy. "Go ahead and get the book now." He left the other coins where they lay at the edge of the table like a subtle indictment.

Volusianus snarled after him: "See to it that it's a copy with colored figures. I must see the shield blazons."

"The top shelf then," the senior clerk called after the boy.

A few moments later the volume lay on the table, its title lettered in a neat line: *Notitia Dignitatum et Administrationum Omnium tam Civilium Quam Militarium in Partibus Orientis et Occidentis.*[65]

The older clerk asked, "Would 'Your Excellence' (how did he keep making it a slur?) care to have us look something up for you?"

Scaevolus tossed him a scowl and shook his head. He took a seat and leafed through its pages, searching for a particular section while the clerks watched him curiously. Those troops were listed here somewhere—those troops he'd seen near the walls of Lugdunum leading off the Emperor's baggage (and his little treasury). They were most likely listed somewhere among the troops assigned to the Duke of Upper Germany.

"How recent are these entries?" He squinted at the text. "The Gallic ones?"

"We don't get reports of the troop figures and postings from Gaul

---

[65] This was the official list of all civil and military positions in all provinces of the Empire. Rather an interesting document.

anymore. That's his Serenity Maximus's territory. So, those sections are about five years out of date." He swept the coins up from the table.

Volusianus looked back at the pages. Five years out of date. That was just what he needed, actually—the units in Gaul and their postings at the time of Gratian's reign. He turned the stiff pages over one by one, glancing at the headings and the illustrations of the various insignias of office until he came to the section for the Diocese of Gaul. On the left page the commands descended in order of importance from the Master of the Cavalry down to the various dukes. The office of the Duke of Upper Germany was there and, below it, a neat list of all the military units under his command and the places where they were stationed. But which one had taken the Emperor's baggage?

On the right, within a neatly ruled box, was an illustration of the shield pattern of every cavalry troop or infantry unit posted in Gaul, whether in the Field Army or among the Border Troops. The shields were shown as dozens of variegated and brightly colored circles, like the flowers in a lush disordered garden. Each design had been neatly inscribed with a compass, and these circles were filled with colors and designs, green, red, blue, yellow, black, or white. Some shields were of one color, some were divided into halves or quarters of contrasting hues. Some were painted with stars, others were solid circles, or circles with a contrasting center. Here and there a shield stood out, decorated with pairs of dragons' heads or a statue of Victory.

Volusianus bent over the page and narrowed his eyes to see better, taking his time over the patterns, running his finger over each rank of shields, searching through the garish thicket of symbols for a disk quartered in red and black. And there it was, midway down and to the right, no doubt about it: a disk divided into four: red and black, red and black. The name of the unit was written neatly below the image. He sat up in delight. The unit bearing that shield was the Second Pannonian Horse. He didn't have to look up their posting because he remembered them. Oh, yes. Yes, he did.

XXXII

SCAEVOLUS VOLUSIANUS COMES FOR A VISIT

* * *

Volusianus drifted down the Rhine in the shade of the barge's sail, which had been draped like an awning over the stern against the gentle, but steady, spring rain. Two soldiers sprawled dozing against the gunwale, a third sat on a crate near the bow, just under the edge of the awning. Though he wanted to, Volusianus couldn't sleep; his costs were mounting. Five solidi to the chief notary to pay for two months' absence, ten solidi for the hire of the three soldiers he needed as an escort and for scut work, three solidi to an official in charge of the post roads in Italy for a pass to stay in the Imperial mansios along the way. Finally there had to be a payment at each stop in Upper Germany, once he was in Maximus's realm. And he had to feed the soldiers, though he kept them on a cheap diet.

He shifted himself and looked up from under the sail at the fort of Castellinum Ripae as they approached and kicked one of the soldiers awake. It bothered him that the louts could sleep so easily. "I've hired you to look after me, not to sleep." He called to the steersman. "Remember, pull in here." Satisfied at showing his authority, Volusianus gathered his cloak about him and stared at the neat mending of a tear across the front. The mending was neat, yes, but there had been a time when he would have worn a new cloak; the mended one would have been given to one of his slaves. He'd come down in the world quite sharply, no doubt about that, but, if he was right, this coup would put him back where he belonged. The river was running fast with the spring rains, and when the steersman turned his oars, the barge seemed to sprint for the dock.

* * *

"Are you sure you read Syagrius's message correctly?" Merobauda sounded half doubtful. She paced back and forth while Gaius sat the table eating. He'd had enough army food, enough of the slumgullion from the mansios along the route on his way back from Italy. He'd really looked forward to a little something from the kitchen at home, even if it did taste much the same as the food in Merobauda's tavern. But her pacing put him off his feed, and she'd called Faustinus in too, so that dinner seemed more like a family council. Faustinus stood in front of the closed door as though to prevent Gaius's escape.

"Yes, Carissima." Gaius closed his eyes. He had memorized Syagrius's reply to Maximus. He recited it to her once more. "It read, 'I welcome the passage of Your Splendor's troops through my Gallic estates and will take pleasure in supplying them to the fullest extent of their needs." He sighed. "It took a while to work it out, I can tell you. I wish he'd made a simple refusal—we'd have been spared an hour of fussing to decode his message." He swirled the spoon thoughtfully in his plate of soup.

"We deciphered it the same way you did with that message of the emperor, Mistress," Faustinus said. "There's no doubt now that he's agreed to ally himself with Maximus."

"Working out the faint letters is one thing. Putting them in groups when you've got them—it's trickier than it looks." Gaius frowned as he thought back on the effort.

Merobauda crossed her arms and gazed out of the window. "So, it's certain to be war. Well, I suppose we should have expected it."

She turned back to the two men. "Syagrius's Gallic estates—where are they, exactly?"

"Everywhere—like a patchwork." Gaius waved his spoon in an extravagant circle. He pointed vaguely out the open window. "And he's got a lot of the in Italy too."

"The greater number of his Gallic estates are in the The Province," Faustinus said, stepping away from the door.

Merobauda nodded. "There must be a way into Italy from there, a good road or two?" Her knowledge of geography was limited to the Rhine Valley.

"Yes, Carissima. By the Via Aurelia down along the coast—or by the Via Cottia. That road goes through some low Alps."

"Which would you take, Gaius?" Merobauda asked him.

He looked up from his bowl and hesitated. He didn't consider himself much of a strategist, but five years in the army had taught him a few things. He put down his spoon and reflected. "The Via Cottia is the shorter way—it cuts a big corner. The diplomatic embassies back and forth between Maximus and Valentinian—they go that way." He thought another moment. "It does go through mountains, but they're low, as mountains go…" He nodded to himself. "Light infantry moving fast could go that way and then hold the way open for the rest of an army to follow. That's what I'd do."

"We know war is coming." She gave him a worried look. "If you hear about troops moving down that way—especially if they're good ones—we'll know it's about to start."

"Well, it won't matter."

"Why won't it matter?"

"I'm going to sell my commission and get out of this business. Like Terentianus did. He sold out and went home to Spain."

"You know it's illegal. Strictly anyway." But she sounded hopeful.

"It's illegal if you don't split the take with the next officer up. I just need to find someone interested in the position, and there has to be someone somewhere."

Merobauda still looked troubled. "There's another problem besides finding a buyer. How can we afford to have you give up your commission even at a good price? You've got the household to maintain and you're still shunting money to that Crastinus for the lawsuit against your brother. And yet, soon, we'll have to get out of here. We know there'll be war and we know it'll be soon."

Gaius focused on the lawsuit. "It was rather a clever move to seek to reinstate the case on the ground that I was no longer the officer of an enemy state." He put down his spoon. "After Maximus was recognized by Theodosius as a legitimate emperor, then the grounds for judgment in Arcadius's favor disappeared." He grinned in delight at the outcome. "So, it was easy to reinstate the case."

"Maybe so, but it cost a lot all the same." She looked imploringly at him. "And then there's the cost of going ahead with it now that it's reinstated. What if it's all been thrown away?" She looked out the window again, as though she could see the future more clearly that way. "And with a war coming…" she trailed off vaguely. She turned to him suddenly. "If you could get a hundred solidi for your commission, we can make out on what we bring in on my beer and what you could bring in arguing cases in the law courts." She looked determined, like someone who has made a hard decision and put it behind her. "We'll have to cut back at first, but that's nothing." She smiled at him and said, with affection, "We have each other, Gaius." She came behind and put her arms around him as he sat at the table. "I wouldn't mind a few patches on our clothes here and there; would you?"

Gaius squirmed; it was very unlike her to demonstrate affection in front of anyone—even Faustinus. He realized that she was worried for him, worried about how unhappy he would be to live a straitened, even poor, existence. Well, he had an answer. "Carissima, you forget the thirteen hundred solidi under the hearth of the tavern back at Ripae." Gaius never forgot it though. He'd thought quite a bit about it ever since they had buried it there before leaving Ripae.

"Twelve-hundred and ninety-two," Merobauda said automatically and with her usual precision. She still had her arms around him. It made him blush.

"Quite right. Forgive the rounding; it's the product of my natural exuberance." He disengaged her arms and turned in his chair. "Now, if you would let me get at that money…" He looked at her interrogatively to see whether she might be starting to shift on this point and see things his way.

She straightened up. "We need to know when the war's going to start," she said, evading the topic by returning to the subject of war. "If you hear of troops heading south, you'll know it's too late to get out of the army. Don't think for a minute you'll be allowed to disappear once war is imminent." Merobauda continued pressing the point with her usual relentless determination, though her tone was softer than usual.

Gaius was anxious too at the idea that it might even now be too late to leave the army. The more Merobauda talked about it, the more he began to appreciate the danger of war. It seemed foolish of him to rely on chance to get through it unharmed, which had been his earlier plan—if it could be called that. "I'll start casting about tomorrow and see who's interested in buying my commission. I should be able to find someone within the next month."

Merobauda looked doleful. "We may not have a month." She thought for moment and added, "Eighty. Even eighty solidi would do. The arithmetic works out."

He nodded. "We'll talk some more when I get back from the drill field." He looked at Faustinus. "Tell Archelaus to get Dulcina saddled. I'm leaving shortly."

* * *

Meanwhile, Scaevolus Volusianus and his three hired soldiers were stepping out of the barge onto the dock at Augusta Treverorum. "The camp is this way." He stumped off, leaning on a staff. He did not say anything further—he saw no use in talking to underlings; it led them to think too highly of themselves. An edge of the sun glinted out from a gap in the gray featureless clouds. He decided it was a sign: this was going to be a good day.

Gaius was settled on a campstool at the edge of the field. Dulcina browsed the grass near him and Arverno sat his horse out in the field drilling the men, watching their maneuvers and inspiring them with occasional jagged aspersions on their competence. Gaius turned his face up to the watery sun and closed his eyes, thinking wistfully of how it was probably a sunny day in Rome or back home in Narbonensis. Still, one took what one could. The thumping of the horses's hooves passed over him in comfortable waves; the ground trembled as the troop cantered past, circling in their exercises. It was soothing. He could just imagine the troopers wheeling about, sweating under their armor, wiping bits of turf from their faces. It was good just to imagine it all—that was enough; he didn't need to see. And then he felt Dulcina's slippery tongue as she licked the back of his head. He sat up suddenly to see her watching him with her lips drawn back from her great yellow teeth. She seemed to smile at him. Well, perhaps she was smiling—she hadn't bitten him in years. He straightened his cap and began to think things through.

So, it was to be war. Well, war brought opportunities—there was that to be said for it. Merobauda had always been adamant about leaving the money buried under the hearth of the tavern; her arguments about the danger of coming into sudden unexplained wealth had been pretty convincing up till now. But he'd have to sell his commission at a steep discount in order to do it quickly. Add to that the loss of his army pay and skim, and the money buried at the tavern ought to look a lot better to her. And with that money they could head south and set up a nice little estate somewhere where he could stay out of trouble. On the whole, things were looking pretty good.

He noticed four men approaching from across the drill field—three soldiers, to guess by their clothes, led by a small bent fellow who helped himself along with a staff. The four of them trudged across the muddy pocked field, heedless of the cantering troop, which had to veer around them. Gaius frowned. No one should do that. No one should interfere with army business. Unless perhaps they were officers. But they clearly weren't.

As they came on, Gaius watched them curiously. The little man in the lead seemed familiar, and the closer he got, the more so. He shifted uneasily on the camp stool and then, when he was certain of him, he put on a contemptuous expression.

"Well, well," Gaius said, in a vague greeting. Because he was sitting, he had to look up at Scaevolus Volusianus, even though the fellow seemed even smaller than he had been, bent by another five years of age. He didn't like looking up at the little bugger but, all the same, sitting showed his disdain. "Well, well," he said again, for want of anything better. The three soldiers stood around Volusianus, hands on their hilts, but clearly uneasy when they saw from Gaius's clothes that he was a high officer.

Volusianus leaned on his staff and squinted at him for a few long moments and then nodded, satisfied. "It is you." He turned to his men. "Go away." He pointed with this staff. "Go to the edge of the field until I call for you."

One of the men, who looked as though he enjoyed confrontation, made a play at staying. "But this man, Excellent Volusianus, he may be dangerous." Dulcina put up her head and snapped her great yellow teeth at him and stepped back, startled.

"His horse, maybe. But him? I'll take my chances. Now get going." He waited silently until the soldiers had trudged off out of earshot, then he turned to Gaius and regarded him with quiet malevolence.

"You seem to be regarding me with a certain malevolence," Gaius said.

"I am."

"But are you sure you're in a position to act upon your malevolence?" That was a good one. Gaius smiled to himself. He always liked to get in a good one.

"Quite sure, yes, quite sure."

"Oh? What about? You'll forgive me if I point out that your shabby appearance suggests you lack the position to do me any harm." He pointed at Volusianus's cloak. "Last year's? Or was it someone else's once? You've had it properly laundered, I suppose. One never knows what strangers are like."

Volusianus's faced hardened and he took a step forward. Then he took himself in hand. "I'm here to talk about something that happened a while ago."

"Really? You came all this way to reminisce?"

"Don't provoke me—I'm at the limit of my patience. I didn't expect to have to travel this far to find you."

"Ah. So you must have stopped at the fort and met the new tenants. They're Franks. A little rough around the edges, don't you think?"

"As I say, I'm here to talk about something that took place years ago."

"Oh, that little disturbance at the fort?" He flapped a hand at the mention of something so trivial.

The old man straightened himself up as far as he could while leaning on his staff. "I've undertaken a rather miserable journey up here to discuss something quite different." He came a step closer and leered down at Gaius. Because the old man lacked so many teeth, and his chin and nose were much too close together, his grimace was almost inhuman.

Gaius involuntarily pulled back from him. "I can't imagine what."

"Oh, Tribune Dolo, don't try to imagine. Instead, let me tell you." He rested the staff against his shoulder and rubbed his hands. "It concerns money. A great deal of money."

Gaius was flush with confidence. "Money? You won't get any from me. Your rank error was pointed out to you at the time." That ought to sting, Gaius thought. He stood up so that he could look down at Volusianus. "Now, would you like to leave the drill field, or would you prefer to give me the great pleasure of having you dragged away?"

Volusianus looked surprisingly complacent. "You mistake me. I'm not here to talk about that trickery. It was over a mere pittance." Gaius recalled his hours of dread in the darkness of the fort jail. It had not seemed a pittance then.

"A great deal of money," Volusianus watched Gaius's face carefully as he stated a figure. "Thirteen hundred solidi." He smiled inwardly when he saw the surprise on Gaius's face. Good. He was right: Dolo did know about the money, doubtless had it, or most of it. Let him deny it all he might, he had already betrayed himself. Volusianus took a deep breath to remain calm. This was only the beginning of his gambit, and he dared not fumble. "Thirteen hundred solidi." Volusianus repeated. "That's the figure."

Gaius watched him narrowly; that figure Volusianus gave was altogether too close to what he'd made off with during Gratian's defeat. That number—how had he come up with it?

"What thirteen hundred solidi?" Gaius tried to sound casual, but he couldn't quite pull it off. The money under the tavern hearth was only eight solidi short of the figure. Volusianus was talking about Gratian's money—he had to be.

"You have it." The old man pointed at Gaius with the staff for emphasis.

Gaius straightened—but slowly—to hide his unease. "I don't know what you're talking about." But it was a weak response and he knew it.

"Look, Dolo, I haven't come all this way to argue. I came all this way because I know to a certainty that you've got that money." Gaius opened his mouth but said nothing. It was hard to think fast enough when things like this came at you. Volusianus continued: "I saw you and your troop take off with Gratian's treasury under the walls of Lugdunum, just before he was killed. It took me a while to track you down, but now I have. The accounts of the late Emperor Gratian are, of course, open to me in my official capacity; the amount in round figures is not in doubt."

Gaius's mind raced as he tried unsuccessfully to come up with a plausible denial.

Volusianus continued: "And don't think you can threaten me. Don't think you can get out of this by killing me."

That happy solution hadn't occurred to Gaius, but it was certainly worth considering. In the distance Arverno was castigating the troop for a sloppy maneuver. His crudely inventive imprecations carried over faintly. "Well, now that is a strikingly attractive suggestion…" Gaius let his voice trail off as he considered it further. It had its appeal, he had to admit it. If he called the soldiers over and ordered them to do it, would they? On his authority alone? Probably—he was a popular commander. So, how? Maybe he should tell them to take Volusianus to the river and see to that he had an accident, the sort that would result in his remains washing up, if they ever did, several miles downriver. Or would it turn out that the little bastard could swim? It would be just like him to have some unexpected talent. And then what about the soldiers at the edge of the field? What would he do with them? They were a problem; still, there must be a solution. He was a Protector, after all. He could order them on some errand into the city while his soldier took Volusianus over to look at the river. But they were Valentinian's soldiers, so perhaps they wouldn't obey. His men outnumbered them though.

"Well?" Volusianus grasped his staff with both hands and leaned forward leering.

"I'm still thinking."

"About what?"

"Killing you, actually. It's the details—they take some working out. By the way, do you swim?" But he knew he wasn't convincing. He couldn't do murder; he just wasn't that sort of fellow. Volusianus just gave him a dry chuckle; he could tell that Gaius didn't have it in him to kill him. The crooked old man smiled his toothless ugly smile.

"You force me to choose between two courses. One: you give me the money and I go away. Two: I go to the Palace and inform His Serenity Maximus that you have the money. After the usual judicial process—that means torture, of course—you'll be very clear about where the money is, and I'll take the usual informer's cut. I'll be disappointed in not doing any better, but your confession will lead to your summary execution, and I'll take a good deal of satisfaction in that."

Gaius considered his choices, tried to harden himself entirely against the old man, tried to make himself call Arverno and the men over to get rid of Volusianus, but he just couldn't do it. He grimaced, sighed, and said, "There's a tavern in the village outside of the fort." He hoped that Merobauda was correct that they had enough to live on when he got out of the army.

XXXIII

GAIUS DECIDES THE TIME HAS COME TO LEAVE THE ARMY

* * *

"You couldn't put him off until tomorrow, so we might have had time to discuss this?" Merobauda's footsteps echoed off the bricks of the little courtyard behind the house. She folded her arms and paced about, not looking at Gaius, just thinking.

"It wasn't that simple, Carissima."

She looked at him as though to say, "Really it was, if you'd only thought about it." Or maybe it was just his imagination.

He put his hands out in a gesture of reasonableness. "I thought about killing him. It was tempting—even he mentioned it—but I just couldn't do it."

She surprised him with a short laugh. "Don't be absurd—of course you couldn't."

He smiled guardedly, relieved at her tacit approval. He ventured, "As for the money, well, you've always been uneasy about having it, and this takes it out of your hands." He braced himself for a sharp retort, but she only shrugged.

"Don't worry about the money," she said. Gaius was startled. She had been, at best, equivocal about keeping the money, true enough.

But from her tone he'd have said she seemed entirely indifferent to losing it. He was marveling over this when she interrupted his thoughts with a question.

"How many days have we got?"

Can a question be gnomic? This one seemed to be. "What do you mean?" he asked. "How many days have we got for what?"

"How many days before Volusianus gets to Ripae and shows my cousin the note you wrote about where the money's hidden?"

"Why does that matter?"

She stamped her foot, exasperated. "Just answer the question. It's important, Gaius. Really, it is."

"Oh, I'd say about five days. He's too old to walk. He'll have to take a barge, but it's upriver so, yes, about five days."

Merobauda folded her arms. "And then about three days to get back here, since he'll be going downstream."

Gaius was puzzled. "But he won't be coming back here." What was she thinking?

She sat down on a bench against the courtyard wall and put her chin in her hand. Gaius sat down next to her and wondered what she was pondering. Shutters squeaked open across the little courtyard and three young solemn faces looked out from a second-floor window: Una and her twin sisters—Gaius and Merobauda's children. They were turning out as serious as Una. He reflected that his world was dominated by serious women and by Faustinus, facetious and affectionate by turns.

"Keep your voice down," Merobauda patted his thigh.

"Why?" he asked, but he whispered. He smiled at the children and waved. They waved back.

Merobauda shifted on the bench so that she was sitting right up against him and murmured, "We've got to be away from Treverorum before eight days are up."

Gaius waved at the children until they left the window and then turned to Merobauda. She explained. "In eight days days or a little more, Volusianus will be knocking at the door of the Palace to inform on you."

"Why would he do that?" Gaius was puzzled. "He'll have the money. That'll keep him quiet. If he reports on me, he'll have to give up the money."

"When he gets to Ripae he won't find the money."

"Of course he'll find it. He can't miss the tavern. The place is tiny and it's right at the edge of the forum."

"He won't find the money at the tavern, and then he'll be back to inform against you."

"But why won't he find the money?" he asked. There was something Merobauda knew that he didn't. Typical.

"Because it isn't there."

"Did you let on about the money to your cousin who runs the tavern? Is that what you're telling me?" His heart began to sink. Losing the money had been bad enough, but facing prosecution for theft on such a grand scale? His mind shied away at what lay at the end of such a prosecution. But then was it really theft, under the circumstances? He hadn't spent the money, so could he still make that stale old argument that he was merely holding the money for the Emperor? But the money was gone, so that argument, stale or not, was utterly hopeless. His head swam for a moment.

"No, Gaius. I didn't tell anyone."

"So, then how is it that he won't find the money? How..." His voice trailed off. In view of his new circumstances, he'd lost interest in the question.

Merobauda looked him in the face with marked concern for his distress and said, "I put sand in the bags before I let you bury them."

Gaius thought about this interesting confession and in a moment was giddy with relief. "How did you get the sand in the bags without my knowing it?" He just had to know. He suspected Faustinus.

"Faustinus helped me," Merobauda confirmed.

Gaius reflected on this for a while; there were so many implications. Then Merobauda took his hands in both of hers. "I know. You think I don't trust you. Actually, I don't sometimes—you're careless. I love you, Gaius, but that doesn't change it."

"Where is the money?" If he could still get at the money, things might turn out well. Or not so badly anyway.

"Don't worry about the money right now. I keep telling you—we've got to get away from here."

"How can I not think about the money?"

"We've got just those eight days." She squeezed his hands for emphasis.

"But the money?" he persisted. "What happened to it?"

"Nothing happened to it."

"But where is it?"

"If I tell you, then you've got to do more than promise not to tell anyone."

"What do you mean 'do more'?"

"I mean, you actually have to not tell anyone."

"What do you think I'm going to do? Make an announcement?"

"No, I think you'd be more subtle." Merobauda threw a glance at the outbuilding at the end of the courtyard where her beer was brewed. She nodded at it. "It's in there."

"In there? The money's in there?" He started to get up, but she wouldn't let go of his hands. "Where? Under the floor?"

"In a beer barrel."

He was shocked. A beer barrel? It just wasn't the way to treat a fortune in gold coins—it didn't show the proper respect. Burying it, now that showed the proper regard for tradition, but a beer barrel?

"It's in the bottom half of one of the beer barrels. The rest of the barrel is filled with beer."

"It's been in a barrel for five years?" He just couldn't take it all in.

"Not the beer, just the gold. Nothing hurts gold—and it doesn't hurt anything else. I just draw the beer off now and again and put fresh in."

He shook his head dumbly.

"Shh. The point is, we need to get out of here before Volusianus gets back."

"We..." he trailed off. Things were moving too fast for him.

"Yes we: you and me. And the girls. And Faustinus and his wife and their boy. And there's Parvinus and Archelaus and Vilfrida. She's old, but I can't leave her behind—she raised me. That's eleven. We'll have to abandon the house I suppose."

"This is like a troop movement."

"So it should be easy for you."

"Easy?"

"Find Mus. He's in town—you said he was back from Lugdunum. Tell him to take us down the Little Saône and get us to the Rhone and down to the sea. He'll do it. He owes you his start and you can forgive him the rest of his debt.

"And then?" Gaius couldn't keep up.

"Italy. Italy is next." She got up, already throwing herself into the plan.

"Italy? Where in Italy?" He followed her.

"Wouldn't you like to see your brother?" She strode off to the house and turned back at him from the doorway. "And while we're getting ready to leave, I don't want to hear you've been poking around the beer barrels." She went into the house before he could reply.

XXXIV

GAIUS EXPERIENCES AN EXPENSIVE WELCOME

* * *

The journey south presented the usual difficulties and inconveniences but nothing worse than those. Gaius had sat up in the bows with a sword and a crossbow much of the time, feeling faintly ridiculous and wondering how well things would turn out if they met bandits along the way but, if there were any nearby, they kept away from the riverbanks, which were studded with little forts and towers sheltering handfuls of border soldiers and militia watching the crossings and ferries. A day into the journey, Gaius wished that he'd bought Mus a better barge, a newer one, one that wasn't patched like a beggar's quilt and eager to spring into flinders at the first touch of a submerged rock. He was certain that there must be rocks lurking along the whole course of the upper Saône, but Mus and his crewmen knew what they were doing and they didn't strike any.

It was spring, the rivers flowed fast, Merobauda insisted that they keep on even at night when they could, and they soon joined the speeding Rhone to find themselves at Arles in a week. From there they coasted on a little freighter from to Genoa without any of the sort of excitement Gaius had experienced on his trip to Britain. The journey from Genoa on the Via Postumia to Cremona and then down the Via Helvetica toward Milan was expensive. It cost a lot for eleven people to travel. The purchase of a wagon, a pair of oxen, a pair of horses and daily food and lodging had pretty much cleaned him out of his ready cash, but he smiled to himself, thinking of all that gold coin jostling gently in the bottom of the beer barrel in the wagon. The sunny southern weather cheered him too, and he had grown quite philosophical about the loss of the house up in Treverorum, and about his lost commission and its perks—it was easy for him to indulge in his natural optimism with all that money in the barrel. He would meet his brother on more than an even footing. He looked forward to seeing Arcadius's face when he learned of his fortune.

* * *

Aeliana came out of the peristyle into the formal garden where Arcadius was sitting on a bench in the spring sunlight, quietly fretting. She threw a shadow over his shoulder and he turned to frown up at her.

"Yes?"

"I'm sorry to interrupt you, dear."

He waved a piece of vellum at her. "This," he pointed to it, "is another damned request for money." He threw it away.

"From Silvanus?"

He nodded. "He says I've got to grease another palm or two now that Gaius has had the bloody case reinstated. And yet…" He mused silently for a few moments.

"And yet?" Aeliana sat down next to him on the bench.

"What's the point of it all?" He shook his head. It seemed to Aeliana that he was groping toward some larger question. "That little bastard of a brother of mine's been tormenting me for five years over the estate. Things go back and forth, back and forth, and every time I get ahead, there's a setback." Aeliana nodded at him sympathetically. He went on: "And now the Emperor Valentinian and his mother have run off to the East to Theodosius's realm and Maximus's army has broken through the Cottian Alps. His men approaching Milan now—everyone's talking about it. The army didn't have any faith in

Valentinian." He held up the note and laughed without any humor. "So, maybe there's no need to pay anything more. Now Maximus has added Italy to his domain, we're sure to lose the estate to Gaius!"

"He is your brother," Aeliana said, trying to soothe him. "I'm sure he he'll be reasonable."

"I don't see why he'd start now. As one of Maximus's Protectors, what's to stop him from just marching in and taking the whole estate!" He surged to his feet and paced, heedlessly trampling the grass between the graveled paths.

"Try not to excite yourself. After all, he only wanted half the rents before this all started. Maybe he'd be happy with that."

"Half the rents! He's got no reason to compromise now." He put his hand on the edge of a marble fountain and looked up the sky, as if for help. He shook his head. "Gaius a Protector! What was father thinking when he asked Syagrius to get him a commission?" He turned to his wife. "I suppose father thought Gaius's general ineptitude would keep him from rising to any position in which he'd pose a danger to anyone but himself." He shook his head ruefully. "Father fumbled terribly."

"Aren't you exaggerating a bit, dear?" She thought of going over to him in a show of sympathy but knew it would just agitate him.

Arcadius closed his eyes against an alarming future and then blinked and staggered away from the fountain. "If he turns us out, there's nowhere to go!" He put out his hands. "The Nebulosi have our old estate in Narbo." He hoped that Aeliana couldn't see him sweat.

"Well, my people, they…" Aeliana began.

"Yes, your people…" Even as his voice trailed off it held a slight trace of dismay. It wouldn't break Aeliana's heart if Arcadius and she had to depend on her people; she'd take it in stride with her usual irritating good nature, but he wasn't about to go to her family cap in hand. He thought what it might lead to: they'd have to travel back to Narbonensis where her father might make them tenants at that minor estate of theirs deep in the arse-end of nowhere. He considered this for a moment. And he might even have to work it, too—more than just bossing the bailiff and keeping the accounts. He rubbed his hands over his face. "These damned civil wars."

Aeliana said, "At least they leave us out of the fighting here in Italy."

He shook his head. It wasn't much comfort. "That won't matter when we're turned out from here!" He wrung his hands, and then put them behind him, so that he could wring them further without showing her, but it didn't matter, because Aeliana wasn't looking at him. She had turned to the steward, who had approached at the edge of the garden and was looking at her meaningfully. She went over and they talked quietly while Arcadius stared fixedly at a statue near the fountain, a slender nymph—more slender than Aeliana, anyway—and wondered if he should take it with him when they lost the property. Or would it just remind him of his bad luck? He turned when he heard Aeliana approach. "What is it?"

"Gaius—"

"What about him?" He turned back to the statue. He didn't want to talk about his brother any more.

"I'm going to ask you to control yourself, Arcadius. It's important."

"I am. I'm controlling myself perfectly. Just perfectly." Her maternal tone just made things worse.

"Of course you are." She patted his arm. "And you must keep on doing it so that we don't have a scene."

"We're not having a scene! If we were having a scene, it would be obvious and you wouldn't have to tell me." His voice was rising.

"Good, good." He wished she would stop patting his arm. He wasn't a child. "Because your brother's here and I've just invited him in."

"Gaius? Here? Now?" He was so stupefied by the idea of his brother's arrival that he couldn't come up with a full sentence about it.

"Yes, Gaius. He apparently arrived a short while ago—while we were talking."

"And you let him in? Aeliana! What were you thinking?" He scowled."Hello, Arcadius," Gaius said as he stepped out from the shadows of the peristyle. His tone was distressingly hearty and his expression altogether too cheery. "You're certainly looking fit these days!"

Arcadius stared as a handful of other people came to cluster around his brother: the supercilious Faustinus, a lanky blond woman in traveling clothes, and three blond girls—twins of about three and another girl of about ten. Next to and slightly behind Faustinus and gripping his arm stood a small woman with thick dark hair and blue eyes. Others huddled further back in the shadows of the peristyle. He didn't know how to take it in. Who were these other people? For a crazy moment he wondered if they were to be new tenants. The situation took on a sharp unreality, as in a dream where one knows, somehow, that one is in a familiar place—home, a familiar town, a market square—but nothing looks at all the way it ought, and still, somehow it is what it is.

He shook his head, violently like a horse, to clear it. Gaius must be here to take the property already. And yet, he wasn't wearing any military garb—no military belt, no little cap, no sword—and this consternated Arcadius even further; it showed an alarming confidence on Gaius's part that he would stroll up in dusty traveling clothes to give Arcadius news of his eviction.

As much as his soft face allowed, Arcadius scowled across the garden at his brother. Then he walked over to him, but slowly, so that he would have time to find the most fitting invective to use when he reached him. And maybe something piteous too, if that wouldn't be too demeaning—it was a delicate balance. If he was about to lose the property, he would get a good one in while he could.

"Listen, you troublesome little bastard. You can seize this property—you've got the soldiers; you're a Protector. Fine! Fine! Do your worst. Turn out your own brother and his family! Watch us trudge along the highways, homeless, destitute, victims of rain, hunger and banditry!" Arcadius knew that Gaius was rather vague about Aeliana's family, and he might take the remonstrances at face value. He paused a moment for emphasis and then went on. "Sit here in this gracious house and forget us as we fade, dwindling figures, receding like ghosts into the dark distance, never to trouble your thoughts again."

Faustinus said, "Master Arcadius's turns of phrase rather recall yours, Master Gaius. There's a certain ornate familial eloquence."

"Be quiet, you insolent bastard!" Arcadius said, before turning back to his brother. "Call your soldiers in. Get them to back you up. Menace us all you wish. You won't find us truckling and crawling to you to spare us."

"Yes, well. No truckling. That's a good start, Arcadius. We don't want any of that do we? No truckling, not on anyone's part." He flashed a smile at his brother. "No, let's deal with each other as equals. Yes, as equals." Merobauda was giving him the look she did when she wanted him to just stop talking. He went on. "The lawsuit?" Gaius waved it away. "Pfft! That was nothing."

Arcadius gaped.

"In fact, I forgive you entirely for trying to defend yourself against my claim."

Arcadius, staggered as he was at the prospect of losing his estate, could still be stunned by his brother's effrontery. He stood like a statue, but blinking. Aeliana drifted up. "You're not being at all clear, Gaius." She put her hand up to silence Arcadius, who looked as though he were ready for a second outburst but couldn't decide quite what it would be. "Just tell us why you're here and who these people are." She glanced at Merobauda and at the three girls standing all solemn in a line. Arcadius flinched at the question: he dreaded the reply. He preferred a painful delay over a terrible answer.

Gaius assessed Arcadius's expression for the first time and grasped that his brother was afraid of him. He couldn't make out the reason, but why not use a tool that came to hand? "We've come to live with you. We'll share the estate and bury the hatchet."

Arcadius scowled, confused. Half the estate? Was this some subtle trick? Surely he was about to use his position to seize the whole thing. He assumed his most stoic attitude. "Why palter with us? Just do what you will."

"That's awfully good of you, Arcadius. Really quite big of you, really in keeping with the noble character of the Obsequens family. It's just what father would have expected of you. I can imagine him smiling down at the two of us as we rub along here, that old twinkle in his eye."

Arcadius looked at Aeliana to see whether she'd heard what he had. The feeling of unreality was seeping back, like a stain at the base of a wall. And the twinkling eye, where did Gaius get that ludicrous phrase from? He opened his mouth but, before he could speak, Aeliana said, "What, exactly, do you want?"

Merobauda stepped up before he could answer. "Unfortunately, Gaius seems to be having a bit of difficulty getting to the point. You know how it is once he begins talking."

"And you are?" Aeliana asked, with a warm look.

"Cornelia Merobauda, Gaius's wife." The two women smiled at each other.

"Now, Carissima, let me handle this." Gaius put his hand on her arm, but she gracefully shook it off before going on: "We've come here to live with you," she said plainly. "Gaius and the children and I. And a few dependents, of course. You'd expect that." When Faustinus heard this, he bowed courteously to Aeliana.

Arcadius was still trying to make sense of the situation. He opened and closed his mouth a time or two, like a fish. Aeliana asked, "And why is that, exactly? Has there been some development that we're not aware of?" She smiled warmly at Merobauda's girls—they were so pretty and demure.

"Gaius has…" Merobauda hesitated a moment, "given up his position in the army. You wouldn't have had any way of knowing about that."

Gaius's beaming expression faded the instant Merobauda mentioned the end of his military career. Arcadius felt the first stirrings of opportunity. "Desertion?" He looked hopeful.

"I prefer to think of it a sort of peremptory retirement after several years of valuable—one might even say exemplary—service guarding the frontier." As he nattered on, Gaius regained his composure. "In the usual course of events, I'd have found a buyer for the commission and regularized by situation—you understand how these things work. But in the rush of recent developments—active civil war and so on—I simply skipped that formality and came down here for a while. I really think that it's a mischaracterization to consider it desertion.

In fact, the term invites misconstruction of what is, frankly, quite an innocent situation."

"So, you don't have any soldiers?" Arcadius stood unconsciously on his toes, just the littlest bit, and looked past Gaius and his family. He didn't see any lurking in the shadows of the peristyle.

"I'd guess they're all back in Treverorum." Gaius replied.

"Are we going to live here, Papa?" one of the twins asked.

Arcadius felt a stab of pity, but he was able to suppress it. Aeliana, however, went over and stroked the girl's head, which sent entirely the wrong message, in Arcadius's opinion.

"I'm no lawyer, but surely the punishment for desertion is rather hard," Arcadius mused out loud. "Something unpleasant? Involving death, I'd suppose, at least at some point." He watched Gaius closely for the effect of his words.

"Why talk about hypotheticals?" He stepped forward and ostentatiously regarded the garden, the fountain, the lawn. "I'd forgotten what a really nice place you have here."

"You don't recall the penalty? You, a former military man?" His tone was sneering.

Gaius shrugged. "I'm sure it's bad, but I imagine it's been a dead-letter for ages."

"You'd better hope so."

"Surely you're not threatening your own brother!" Aeliana was shocked. Frankly, Arcadius did want to threaten his own brother, though, upon reflection, not with death. That was a bit much. He rubbed his jaw as he thought and then took another approach. "We need to think what Gaius's situation means for us, Aeliana. There's doubtless some penalty for harboring a fugitive." He looked coldly at his brother. "One of such a high position. A Protector." He looked at Aeliana who had knelt and was cooing at the children as though she didn't have enough to do with her own. "Frankly, my dear, the risk is too great for us."

Gaius said, "If worse came to worst, you could just deny any knowledge of the, ah, irregularity behind my situation."

Gaius's glib response and smooth delivery brought back to

Arcadius many memories of their childhood in Narbo, so he said, "Shut up. Just shut up for a moment."

"Arcadius!" Aeliana protested.

"Don't think anything of it, Mistress Aeliana," Gaius said gallantly. "This just reminds me of our happy childhood in Narbo years ago: Arcadius and I passing golden hours sparring amiably under father's twinkling eye."

"We could get into trouble," Arcadius repeated, trying very hard to ignore the return of the twinkling eye.

Merobauda said. "We'll go on our way if you say so, Arcadius, but I think you may want to consider what we have to offer you in return for refuge."

Arcadius regarded her open honest face. Had Gaius said this, he'd have taken it for nothing—for a mere ploy, but there was something so guileless, so practical about this woman that he had no doubt she could offer them something.

"Please tell us, Cornelia Merobauda! I'm sure there's something we can do." Aeliana said. Arcadius glowered at her.

"I suppose I could deed over my half-interest in this estate." Gaius gave a broad smile. "In return for a year's lodging." He could well afford to do that, what with all of the money in the beer barrel. He could no longer pursue his lawsuit now that he was a deserter anyway. So, in return for taking them in, why not give Arcadius what he was going to get anyway? He was pleased at his craftiness.

"Don't try to trick me." He pointed a finger at his brother. "If you need to hide out, then you don't have any case."

"Oh, you see that," Gaius, abashed at being caught out.

"Hush, Gaius." Merobauda turned from him to Arcadius. "We can offer you twelve-hundred and ninety-two solidi."

Gaius and Arcadius looked at each other, and Aeliana looked at both of them. She couldn't tell who was the more shocked.

XXXV

GAIUS CONCOCTS A CANNY PLAN TO MAKE MONEY

***

Gaius, at loose ends, found Merobauda wrangling the twins in the peristyle, getting them to settle down around her for a lesson in reading. She sat on a bench with a wax tablet.

"You're not introducing those novel spellings of yours?"

She ignored him.

"I suppose it doesn't matter, really," he said generously. "They'll get the hang of it after they've read a bit. Properly spelled stuff, that is."

"Is this why you came out here? To talk about my spelling? I thought we were done with that years ago."

"I keep thinking about the money. I still can't believe you gave it all away."

"Then don't think about it."

"You've really put us in rather a precarious position, Carissima."

"That is an *F* ", she said to the girls, showing them the tablet. "It goes Fffff.""Ffffffffff!" the twins said in unison.

"How is it precarious?" She carefully drew an *O* on the tablet and showed it to the girls.

"You do know that *G* comes next?" he asked, disconcerted at her disregard of alphabetic convention. Not *O*?"

"Ohhhhh!" the twins said.

Merobauda shrugged. "Why do you say that *G* comes after *F*?"

"Well, it does. It's a convention."

"Oh, yes? What about *favola* or *frater*. There's no *G* after *F* in those words. There isn't any *G* in them at all."

"Carissima, that's not how to look at it—"

"In fact, Gaius, I don't think anyone can even pronounce *F* and *G* together. I can't. Can you?" She looked at him challengingly.

"About the money." He reverted to the earlier subject.

She dropped the tablet into her lap and looked up at him. "I didn't put us in a precarious position; I saved us from one. And I saved your brother from a precarious position."

"What? You saved him from a precarious position? I don't see what you mean at all. Now, I do admit that you saved my life up at the fort by fomenting the mutiny, but I don't see how giving the money to Arcadius does anything more than enrich him."

She put up her finger. "First, it's not our money, so I've gotten you out of that. That's a sin you're not committing." She put up another finger. "Second, by offering your brother the money, we saved him from the temptation of making a bad decision."

"What bad decision?"

"The decision to turn us out. That would have been extremely uncharitable of him."

"Weren't you just appealing to his greed? I defer to you on theology, but isn't greed a sin for you Christians?" He recalled that there were a number of sins—some of the apparently Deadly—though how many, and how they were ranked, he couldn't say. He thought he would slow her down with that question, but she continued on. "Arcadius doesn't dare ever turn you in. He'd have to surrender the money—and suffer for his cooperation in helping you desert, which must be a crime of some sort. You see? And the longer he keeps the money, the harder it will be for him to turn it back. So, he'll keep quiet and we can live here as long as we need to."

"So, as I just said, you're appealing to his greed." ***Let her get out*** *of that one,* he thought.

"It's a start. It may lead him to improve himself." The look on her face showed she had decided to the conversation was over. "Now, I have a lesson to give." She tapped the wax tablet with her stylus. "Why don't you go and do something useful?"

Gaius looked around vaguely. "Such as what? I'm a bit at loose ends here, as you might have noticed. One moment a Protector standing between Rome and the Barbarian—" Merobauda rolled her eyes at his bombast, so he started again. "Anyway, I've got a lot of time on my hands here now that my only goal is to stay hidden until we're sure the army's forgotten me. It's a damned nuisance that Maximus has seized Italy—now it may take years for the administration to lose track of me."

"Maybe you're not as important as you think," Merobauda said with her usual bland realism. "You know the country's full of rumors that the Emperor Theodosius is backing Valentinian. The rumors are that he'll go to war with Maximus. Just give it a year. Who knows what might happen after that? Now, go talk to your brother; he's over in the vineyard." She looked down and wrote *K* on the tablet. It was a clear dismissal. He wanted to stay, if only to be sure the girls learned the difference between *K* and *C*, but after a few moments of being ignored he drifted off. He could tell the girls about the vagaries of *C* later, when their mother wasn't around. It could be their little secret.

He ambled off to the vineyard, where Arcadius was inspecting some new grafts. He was stooped over, hands on his knees, squinting at them. As Gaius walked up, his brother straightened up, rubbed his hands together and actually smiled at him. He was out of practice smiling at his brother, and the expression came off as slightly crazed.

"You seem happy to see me, for some reason," Gaius said, disconcerted at Arcadius's welcoming rictus.

"Well, you know, the money really helps with that. It's made me reassess our relationship and look back on all of our—ah—misunderstandings in the past. It has inclined me to understand why you caused all of them. I've really developed a lot of perspective." He clapped his hand in a friendly way on Gaius's shoulder. Gaius glanced at the hand and tried to recall the last time his brother done it. Was the gesture worth all of the solidi? Was it in fact the costliest shoulder pat in history?

"I've just been talking to Merobauda about the money and why she gave it to you," Gaius said.

"You do look a bit down in the mouth," his brother replied. "But look at it this way: she appreciates what things cost. I'll give her that, even if I disagree with her sense of value." He looked meaningfully at his brother. "Let's see. What does that put your survival at? He looked up and calculated in his head. "You and your family are eleven people. We divide the money eleven ways—that comes to a little over a hundred and seventeen solidi apiece for each one of you. That seems reasonable—apart from you, perhaps."

"She isn't looking at it that way," Gaius said defensively. "She wanted to save you from some sort of sin."

"By giving me a lot of money?" Arcadius grinned. "I can't say I grasp the ethics of it, though you won't find me arguing."

"It has something to do with her religion."

"She's a Christian, then?"

"Yes."

"Well, good. So is Aeliana. It will give them something to talk about." He waved at him. "I'm going this way. I've got some grafts from Tuscany at the far end. Try to show some interest, will you? As long as you're living here." He walked off abruptly. Gaius sauntered after him looking off beyond the vineyard to the fields where wheat would be swaying in a few months. He thought about it in a vague way. An idea was forming at the back of his mind, an idea about money, about making some. He didn't have much anymore, but surely there must be a way to fix that.

* * *

The late spring sun glowed warmly on Gaius and Faustinus as they trundled down the road toward Milan in the back of an ox-wagon. They lounged on a dusty straw mat thrown over a load of wine jars and jounced about as they leaned back against the driver's seat and watched the country slowly pass alongside. Oxen pull slowly, but it was better than trudging into town. The two spoke quietly and in Gaulish so that the driver, who was Italian, couldn't follow them.

Faustinus said, "I suppose there's no point in reminding you that Merobauda forbade you to go to Milan? How did she put it?" He waited for Gaius to answer, to make him recall her injunction.

"Oh, something along the lines of 'Your asylum cost so much, you mustn't gamble with it.' Something like that. But it's just a suggestion, really. You put an absolute construction on her statement which, I think, is quite unwarranted."

Faustinus grabbed at the side rail as the wagon went over a bump. "You might want to reconsider the construction *you* put on the state-ment—it's an idea, Master."Gaius looked out over the fields to show how little he thought of the idea. "What could go wrong?" The wagon struck a rut and threw him against Faustinus. He resettled himself. "Who could even recognize me? His Serenity Maximus? Is that what you're thinking?" He laughed at Faustinus's concern. "We're not going to run into him on the street. Besides, he's got a thousand things to worry about now. Theodosius, for instance. He'll attack Maximus from the east next spring. You can bet on that."

Faustinus made a sour face. "You're taking a risk. I can feel it."

"You agree with Merobauda that we should sit things out until there's another usurpation or two, and then settle somewhere obscure where I can practice law."

"Yes, I do. By then the government will have lost track of you entirely."

"There's no need to wait. I understand the approach, really I do, but I reckon there's enough disorder right now. And you know what that means: it means opportunity. And I have to think of the future. All our futures." He looked meaningfully at Faustinus. Let him get out of that one.

"Would you care to divulge your plan, Master?"

"I would, actually. I have to say, I'm rather proud of it. Really, I am." He turned his face up to the spring sun and closed his eyes, just enjoying the warmth—and his cleverness.

Faustinus sat back silent, conceding nothing; he reckoned this scheme would be like Gaius's others: superficially clever, but freighted with some unforeseen danger.

"So, it's this way. You have to be the front man," Gaius told him.

When Faustinus still said nothing, Gaius took it for agreement. "You're going to make a couple of contracts for the purchase of grain. Wheat, barley, millet. We'll see what's on offer."

"Is there any particular reason why I'm going to do this? You do realize that my personal fortune comes to about three solidi?" He steadied himself as the wagon went over another bump. "And you do realize this year's wheat is still in the field."

"It doesn't matter that the wheat is still in the field—in fact, that's an essential part of the plan. You buy it anyway—or sort of." He smiled slyly at Faustinus, who took it as a bad sign. Gaius went on: "I can see from your expression that you're perplexed, but I understand that." Merobauda would have wiped the crafty smile from his face with a sharp word or two. Faustinus, who had even greater experience of Gaius, was more tolerant. He merely said, "Why do *I* have to buy this 'unready wheat' anyway?"

Gaius glanced around him at the peasants scattered across the fields as though to be sure they couldn't overhear. Faustinus took this for a bad sign too. Gaius said, "Because I don't want to be recognized."

"So, you concede that Merobauda was right in telling you not to go into Milan?"

"Leave her out of this. She always thinks she knows better." Faustinus nodded in agreement. Gaius, who went on: "There's only the smallest chance I'd be recognized, but I still mean to play it safe."

Faustinus gave him a sour look.

Gaius continued. "You used to be a slave and no one pays any attention to them. No one knows you at all. So, here's what you do: for this business you drop 'Obsequentianus' and just go by 'Aquitanius.' Faustinus Aquitanius, like back in Ripae."

"I had a bad feeling about this jaunt when you asked me to wear my best clothes." Faustinus brushed straw off of his tunic. "And I'll still need a third name if anyone's going to take me seriously."

Gaius shrugged indifferently. "Make up another, then."

"Furtivianus.[66] I think I'll take 'Furtivianus.' I'm sure it's consonant with whatever scheme you have in mind."

"This isn't a joke. Don't try to sound as if you're a senator. If you can't do better than that, I'll come up with another. I'll tell you what: just put 'Flavius' at the front like everyone else. Simple. Flavius Faustinus Aquitanius."

"So, I'm to enter into a contract to buy wheat that's still in the field, while pretending to be someone else."

"I'll do all the talking. I'll pretend to be your agent. So, you'll be the master and I'll be the servant. It will be just like Saturnalia, but in the spring."

"You might tell me what I'm supposed to do." He looked over his shoulder at the walls of Milan in the distance. "We'll be in the city in an hour."

"It's simple. You just let me do the talking and you nod in approval."

And he went on from there to explain the scheme—the beautiful scheme. It was like this: they'd go to grain merchants, most of whom had their offices in an area near the forum, and offer them contracts of a new sort that they hadn't seen before: contracts that would give Faustinus (but, of course, really Gaius) the right to buy a quantity of grain next summer for a price agreed upon today. In return for this right to buy at the agreed price next year, he would pay a small amount of money now. The figure at which Gaius proposed to buy the grain was what he guessed would be well under market value when Theodosius and Valentinian marched east and Maximus's army needed grain. The merchants, of course, should be willing to do this, because, if it came to war, grain prices would shoot up, but they would be compelled to sell their grain to the Imperial government in disregard of Gaius's contracts, so anything Faustinus (but, of course, really Gaius) paid them, was free money. But Gaius was more canny even than they. Oh, yes. Faustinus (but, of course, really Gaius) had no intention to ever exercise the contacts. Instead he would immediately sell them to an Imperial supply officer who could use his position in the government to buy the grain under the low contract price, sell it

---

[66] A clever nonce-adjective suggesting trickery. Faustinus knows Gaius very well.

to the Army at the high government price, and pocket the difference. Gaius summed up the situation: "A few documents get shuffled and, with luck, we'll end up with a couple of hundred solidi in return for an investment of twenty." He shook a purse at Faustinus. "Here are my last twenty solidi. But we'll come home a good bit richer today, and try again, on a larger scale, after the war is over. Maybe then I can even bring in Arcadius and share profits with him. Two-thirds, one-third in my favor of course."

"It seems as though you're buying and selling things that aren't there." Faustinus frowned. "Except the government corruption. That's certainly there."

"I don't see why government corruption can't be turned into a negotiable asset like anything else."

A cold shadow fell over them as they passed through the city gate and into Milan.

XXXVI

GAIUS FINDS HIMSELF
IN JAIL AGAIN

MEROBAUDA SPRINGS
INTO ACTION

* * *

In the late afternoon they approached a government building mid-way between the forum and the racetrack at the west side of Milan, where the supply officer's headquarters were located. Faustinus went ahead in his capacity as specious grain-speculator, Gaius following at a respectful distance like a clerk, with a satchel holding half a dozen contracts for the right purchase, in August of the next year, a thousand bushels of wheat well below the anticipated market price. The two were directed to the second floor and, when they had reached the head of the stairs and stood glancing about to see which way to go next, an old man sidled up to them and scanned Gaius's face as though he was really delighted to see it. His smile was a mere fold in his face, his chin and nose too close to each other. Gaius couldn't take any satisfaction in the man's poor dentition. The old man was Scaevolus Volusianus. "Welcome to Milan, Dolo." He shuffled to the stairhead and called down to the clerk for soldiers.

* * *

"You let him go into the city." Merobauda said to Faustinus with a tone like pane of ice over the water in a bucket on a cold morning.

"I couldn't stop him, Mistress." He put his hands out helplessly. "I'm free, but I'm still his client."

"But you could have told me." The chill in her voice was the one she used on Gaius from time to time, but it was more effective on Faustinus, who wasn't used to it, and he cared even less for the anxious look on her face. She went on: "And I could have kept him here." But her tone was softening. "Honestly, you shouldn't let him order you around like that." Merobauda circled the room, bent over slightly, her arms crossed. Her fear touched him, and he shifted uneasily from foot to foot. She stopped and turned to him. "You say he's already been charged?"

"Not with desertion. What with all the unrest, no one seems to know about that." He tried not to sound hopeless as he went on. "But Volusianus plans to see that he's charged for taking the gold at Lugdunum. He wants the informer's fee." He shook his head as he thought of it. "We might consider turning over the money…"

Merobauda looked at him incredulously. "Do you want to ask Arcadius for the money back? Or do you want to tell Volusianus he's got it and hope that Arcadius isn't charged along with him?" She put her head in her hands. "By the way, how did you manage to get back here?"

"I haven't been charged with anything."

"Yet."

Merobauda lapsed into a chair. "Gaius doesn't seem ever to realize when he's walking into danger." She shook her head. "And yet he's educated. What in the world do they teach in Rome?"

"They teach us how to express things well." Faustinus thought how inadequate this sounded. Merobauda looked up at him. "Get me a tablet. I've got to write something down."

"Yes, Mistress."

"You can help me express what I have to say." She sounded bitter, but not hopeless. "You can check the spelling."

"I wouldn't worry, Mistress. Gaius won't care about the spelling in the straits he's in."

"It's not for him." She took a deep breath. "I'm writing to Flavius Syagrius."

* * *

Gaius had found what he judged the driest area of the straw on the stone floor of the prison and sat there in the oppressive darkness. A handful of other prisoners sat or lay here and there against the walls, but he hadn't made their acquaintance; most were awaiting execution or examination under torture. And they smelled bad. Come to think of it, he probably did too, though it was hard to tell over the stink of urine and feces from the tub by the door. The door was heavy, which was a good thing because it half blocked the screams wafting in from the judicial wing of the building.

He was quite afraid, almost sick with fear. This prison was different from the jail in the fort—darker, filthier and more populated— and he had no friends within ten miles. Faustinus would have long since carried the news of his predicament to Merobauda and Arcadius, with his plea that they get him a good advocate and try to pay the judge, but his situation looked bad even to him, who usually took the best view of things. Would Arcadius part with a few hundred solidi to save him? Probably. But even so, would it be possible to successfully arrange things in the middle of the imperial transition, or would the brutal machinery of justice summarily deal with him before anyone could help?

He thought of his death and that, of course brought him to the edge of panic, though he tried to take a philosophical view. He'd had a good run. He'd have liked a longer span, but it had been a good run. Colorful, anyway, and amusing at times. But he feared for Merobauda and his family. It was bad enough to face execution, but he'd betrayed his family and dependents by larking off to the city to practice his cunning.

When he had been tossed into the cell up at the fort, only Faustinus was left behind to fend for himself. He should have considered

322

his fate more, but things had happened so fast back then, and Gaius's mind turned naturally to his own problems first. But now somehow, in a fit of his usual inattention, he'd collected a rather large family, and they all depended on him. Well, perhaps Merobauda could handle things. Actually, there was no doubt of that. Would his family miss him when he was gone? He hoped so. He wondered at the question, enjoying the thought of his death in a perverse way. But then one of his cell mates turned over in the straw and a particularly vile smell crept over him, a concoction of stink and fading hope. He wondered how much it would hurt before he died.

* * *

Milan simmered. The ambitions of Maximus's courtiers blended uneasily with the anxieties of Valentinian's former followers as they threaded their way through the twisted paths of the new, unfamiliar court. Syagrius sat apart from all of this confusion in his study, sparely furnished and white-walled. He stood at a window and gazed at the blue spring sky above and the red-tiled roofs of the imperial palace in the distance and at Maximus's troops strolling about, making the city their own. Valentinian's Palatine troops had declared for Maximus as a matter of course after the young emperor and his mother had fled, but they still kept themselves out of sight in their quarters, waiting for a chance to demonstrate their loyalty. Syagrius considered how he might demonstrate his loyalty too—or continue to do it. He had fed Maximus's troops from his estates as they had crossed southern Gaul and made for the Cottian Alps. Some might say it was disloyalty to Valentinian (no longer "His Serenity" but merely "The Tyrant"), but then to whom did Syagrius owe his loyalties?

What, really, was a true emperor? Any usurper who succeeded in keeping his throne, if history was a guide, and what other guide was there? Well, certainly, he owed his first loyalty to his clients in their estates and towns, great and small, scattered throughout southern Gaul and Italy. Such loyalty served him directly, but that hardly smutched his honor; it was just the way the world worked. He and the other great men looked after their own affairs, cooperated with each other, protected those under them, advanced friends and clients and tried to make their way in world that too often tossed up an obscure provincial soldier scrabbling for the throne. If a usurper failed, he died and his memory, like the last orange glow of an errant spark, winked out. If he succeeded, well then, he was transmuted into His Serenity The Emperor, his usurpation suddenly legitimate.

What loyalty could such an emperor command? What loyalty should he command? Such men were not aristocrats in any sense, not nobles at all: they were jumped-up soldiers, men born in the provincial camps who, until they saw Rome or Milan, judged a walled town a jewel of civilization. They goggled at three-story buildings. Still, Syagrius mused, such men were dangerous; they had armies behind them and must be properly handled. If he let himself stumble over some abstract principle of legitimacy, no good could come of it. And so, when Valentinian and Justina needed ships for their flight to the east, he had arranged and provisioned them. After all, he had some estates in Dalmatia, and Valentinian and his mother would always be grateful, and this would matter if the boy ever regained the throne. That was unlikely, of course, but still, it was good to have him in his debt. Maximus, though, if he learned of it, might take it badly, or keep it up his sleeve to use against him later. As he grew older, Syagrius found juggling with his head had grown tiresome.

He folded his arms and he looked up at the sky. He'd done what he had to in both cases. The trick was now to be seen to bend to the new Emperor, to be seen to be loyal before any suspicions to the contrary might arise. Chances to do so would come—they always did. He would just have to look for them as they flitted by in the whirlwind of political change. New bureaucrats, new generals, a new emperor, old bureaucrats, old military officers caught on the losing side. It could be handled and would be somehow. A crow floated effortlessly by the window on jet-black wings. Syagrius followed its progress until it swept up and perched on the very top of a cypress, swaying, but holding firm on the top. Well, perhaps Maximus could balance as well as the crow, but Syagrius—he would keep his feet on the ground. He would stay in Milan; he could hardly convince Maximus of his loyalty if he drifted into the country, and he was too prominent a man to hide. He imagined the scene in the palace: Valentinian's courtiers bending obsequiously to Maximus's officials, Valentinian's Palatine officers, staggered by their emperor's flight, reckoning their chances with the new regime. It would be a morass for a year, maybe more. But he could wade through it; there were always paths to be found.

He heard footsteps in the corridor but kept his eyes on the crow. "Enter." The crow shifted his position easily, expertly, keeping its position on the apex of the cypress as it shifted in a light breeze. Quite the little acrobat. "Yes?"

The attendant bowed low. "There is an insistent woman, Your Magnificence, who has forced her way into the audience hall with a letter."

Syagrius nodded mutely.

The attendant continued. "It is an odd message. No one can read it; it is clearly enciphered. She insists, however, that Your Magnificence has the key and will understand it." Syagrius put out his hand and received it. Upon unfolding it, he saw that it consisted of twenty meaningless words, each five letters long. "Show her in," He said and sat down to wait for her.

When she entered, he saw that she was a provincial. She wore fine Roman clothes, but her accent and the complex German work on the brooches of her dress made it clear that she came from one of the Gallic provinces. She was thin, on the tall side, a blonde, a half German of some kind—perhaps more—but her clothes were well made, and she held herself with a good deal of poise. "You introduce yourself with a remarkable note," he without preamble.

Did the woman bow? If so, she was subtle about it; it was no more than a slight bend of the knees and a bob of the head, and then she was down to business. "Please don't trouble yourself to work it out, Your Magnificence. I wrote it in that way to get an introduction to you."

He gave her an encouraging look; he found the encoded note intriguing and wondered if he might learn something useful from her. She glanced over at the servant, and Syagrius waved him out. "And now you are here. Well?"

"Your Magnificence, my name is Cornelia Merobauda Obsequentia."

"I know many people. I don't know you." But he studied her closely; forty years of high politics had ingrained the habit. She was anxious, he could sense that, but she was not frightened of him—or not unduly—which was unusual for someone of her station. That was mildly interesting.

"You know my husband—or of him, anyway, Excellence. He is your client." She searched his face, but it was impassive, like the face of an emperor in public.

"I have thousands of clients. Thousands upon thousands." He was matter-of-fact. His estate was so high that he was beyond arrogance.

"He's was a military tribune and then a Protector. Gaius Obsequens Dolo. Your Excellence got him his commission years ago when his father was ruined. His father was a client of yours in Narbo." She was bold—she dared put up a hand to forestall him. "You sent him to carry a message to His Serenity Magnus Maximus in Britain years ago. It was back when Maximus was a Count."

"Yes, I remember." And he did. "Why have you come to me?"

"Because, Your Excellence, my husband has been arrested." She hesitated and added, after a moment of searching for the right word, "improperly." She watched Syagrius's expressionless face. "And he's facing…well, the usual difficulties." She left them to Syagrius's imagination: torture, a likely guilty verdict and a death sentence. She kept herself from wringing her hands or otherwise showing emotion, but her pulse was growing faster and she felt hot. She had no fear of Syagrius himself, only that she would fail to convince him to help.

"The charge?" He asked. *Well,* she thought. *He's willing to listen, anyway.*

"They say he stole gold from the army." She left it at that.

They all do that one way or another, he thought. *There must be something more.*

"Wrongly accused, you say?" Syagrius watched her face closely.

"I did not wrongfully accused, Excellence. I said 'improperly.'"

Her candor was refreshing; she didn't claim outright that he was innocent. He cast his mind back to the last time he had seen the fellow—well-mannered and with a certain polish and suavity marred by a dollop of provincial naiveté and rhetorical excess. He recalled the message the tribune had brought, its text scrambled in just the same way as the one from this woman.

"Improper but not wrongful. A very fine distinction, Domina Cornelia." He addressed her with an honorific. Merobauda took this as a hopeful sign. He went on: "If you concede the charge, you will understand that my hands may be tied, however much my duty lies in the protection of a client." He was lying. His hands were seldom tied.

"I concede nothing, Excellence."

There was so little boldness in his orbit that it was refreshing to come across it. He smiled thinly and relaxed to the extent of leaning back in his chair. "Very well, Domina Cornelia. Now explain this difficulty." He wouldn't mind helping this little client who, after all, had been helpful to him.

Merobauda knew this was a great concession from such a powerful noble, one of the men who persisted when emperors came and went. She moderated her tone—no sense in risking putting him off. "I can only guess at the law."

Syagrius nodded. "Go on."

She told him a skeletal version of the events surrounding Gaius's seizure of the gold, and went on, "But it seems to me that seizing gold from the tyrant Gratian in the middle of a battle with His Serenity Magnus Maximus—acting as my husband did, in his capacity as your client and agent, wasn't any crime at all." She paused. "My husband says it was a canny blow he struck for the benefit and restoration of the State under His Serenity Maximus." She watched Syagrius's expressionless face and went on to put more words into Gaius's mouth. "He sees himself as your agent acting directly in your interest." She waited a moment and repeated. "Your interest, Your Magnificence."

Syagrius gave her the ghost of a smile. "He took a good deal upon himself." Did she catch the hint of amusement in his voice?

"Well, Your Excellence, he's just that way, always thinking of his duty." She hoped it sounded true. "It's an act that redounds to your glory, Excellent Syagrius. Furthermore, it adds further luster to the Great House of the Syagrii." This last was the sort of grandiose phrase Gaius himself would have concocted—she had known him long enough that she could turn out this sort of flummery as well has he could, though, unlike him, she knew when to do it. She knew when it was more serviceable than annoying.

Syagrius reflected quietly for several moments. It was not a bad argument, he had to grant that. He was seldom swayed by any argument that was not expedient, but perhaps this one was. Perhaps there was some advantage hidden away, like an opal at the bottom of a laundry basket. He mused in silence.

Merobauda forged on. "Of course my husband had to decide on the spot what to do, acting as he was in the middle of a campaign. In the middle of a battle, in fact."

"Quite." But his tone did not suggest a concession, at least not yet. Still his ghostly smile had encouraged her.

"My husband is scrupulously honest," Merobauda said. She would confess later to a priest somewhere; at the moment, there was Gaius's life to save. "But, under torture, who knows what he might say?" The willowy woman looked at him sharply, quite openly trying to gauge his reaction. He sensed an opportunity in what she said, and he tried to winkle it out, but before he could quite find it, she had pressed on with the temerity of one of his own circle. "Your agent"—she emphasized the word slightly—"your agent, the Tribune Dolo, helped in the fall of the tyrant Gratian." Syagrius hid his amusement at the boldness of the claim. The tribune's wife went on. "He did it by seizing the monies Gratian needed to retain his soldiers and pay for the defense of Lugdunum. It seems to me—if I may give my opinion—that he should be rewarded, not punished."

Merobauda looked modestly down at her shoes and peeped up after an instant, to see him smile thinly. So far, so good, if he did not trouble her for details. Gratian's position was already hopeless by the time the gold was seized—that would undermine the argument. But perhaps a man as powerful as Flavius Syagrius could successfully disregard this detail—if it ever came up.

Syagrius nodded at her to continue. She went on. "I would never dare to suggest to Your Magnificence what he might do, though it seems to me, a mere provincial woman, that if my husband makes a statement under torture, or even a threat of it…". She trailed off. Syagrius glanced out of the window for a second, though she could see that he was considering what she said.

"Because, who knows who will examine him? And though nothing he could say would harm so great a man as yourself, still, whatever he might say to your advantage might be lost." She took a deep breath and recapitulated the idea. "Whatever there might be to your advantage could be lost or twisted in a forced confession. As Your Magnificence readily grasps, an inquisitor might decide what he wants Gaius to say—and those things to your advantage would go by the wayside."

He turned back to her and asked in a flat tone. "And the gold?" His tone made it clear he was indifferent to the gold itself; he wanted only to know more about the situation.

"It came to twelve-hundred ninety-two solidi. But it's gone now, Your Excellence."

He put his hand up to stop her from saying any more. The money was utterly trifling to him; the cost of a moderate estate. It was nothing in itself to a man of the highest position, such as he, but it was a large enough of sum that Maximus might believe that, had it gotten into the right hands, it could—just—have bought Gratian sanctuary in Lugdunum until he was reinforced. Yes, this woman had given Syagrius rather a good opportunity to ingratiate himself further with the new Emperor. He would arrange the release of this little officer of hers, but it would be best to ask for his release from His Serenity Maximus himself. In this way he could indicate personally how his agent had done his part to help in the defeat of the tyrant Gratian. Yes, that was it: ask it as a favor of Maximus himself, a favor that would point up Syagrius's quiet and unwavering support of him. The gold? Unimportant, that. And, if it came to it, he could indemnify the Emperor himself. But what were the chances that, after five years, there would be any need? Maximus, exulting in his bloodless seizure of Italy, would not be in the least concerned.

"I will look into things, Domina Cornelia." He turned back to the window. The crow had flown off. He stood up; the audience was over.

XXXVII

GAIUS FINDS HIMSELF BACK IN THE ARMY AND PROMOTED

* * *

The prison door swung open with squeaking shudder and relieved the darkness of the cell the littlest bit. A draft of fresher air weakened the fecal stink. Gaius sat up in the straw he'd scrabbled together for his bed and squinted at the doorway as he strained to make out the two figures on the threshold. The jailer stood in the doorway, a coarse squat man, shaven-headed, tapping his truncheon against the door to get the prisoners' attention. The other man was taller, younger, and of a much better station: the jailer kept a respectful distance from him.

"Gaius Obsequens Dolo!" The young man called in a loud voice that echoed faintly from the brick walls of the cell. That way he did not have to enter the gloom and miasma of the cell. Some of the unfortunates stirred, and a few looked over at Gaius with faint curiosity. He rose and said, "Here!" with as much of an appearance of confidence as he could muster, but his effort was rather pitiful. The visitor who had called into the cell took a single step forward, put a handkerchief to his face against the stink, and waved to Gaius to follow. In the corridor with the door swung, the visitor took a deep breath and looked Gaius up and down. "Dolo?"

"He is," the jailer said, sliding the bolt shut on the door.

Even the weak lamplight glinting from the slimy walls of the corridor hurt Gaius's eyes after three days in the dark, so he blinked at his visitor, a clerk of the higher sort—he wore the military belt and a tunic with embroidery. He must be a fellow from the courts.

"It seems rather soon for my trial." Gaius tried to sound confident, but his voice was weak and he coughed. "Not that I mind a speedy disposition." He wondered whether they would use hot irons and whether they hurt right away. If he confessed to what they asked, could he avoid the irons entirely? Or would the interrogators use them anyway just to demonstrate their commitment to their profession? He couldn't keep the question out of his mind, so he volunteered: "I am prepared to make an immediate and full confession." The clerk looked at him quizically. Gaius went on. "Of course it will help if I'm told in detail what I'm asked to confess. It saves so much…ah…time."

The clerk sniffed the foul air with a sour expression and seemed suddenly impatient to be out of the dungeons. "Follow me. And brush that straw out of your clothes." He put the handkerchief back up to his face. "I'd tell you to stop stinking, too, if that would do it. Just keep your distance."

Gaius tried to fight the urge to ask what was next; he wanted to remain ignorant as long as possible but, in the end, he could not resist. "Where are we going?" He strode after the other fellow as he passed at a fast clip down the hall and up a flight of stairs. The man stopped halfway up the flight and turned, stuffing his handkerchief up a sleeve. "The charges have been dropped." He seemed uninterested in Gaius, as though he had other things to do, other people to meet.

"Dropped?" he said, stopping in his tracks. He wiped the sweat from his forehead with his sleeve and left a fetid streak above his eyebrows. Then he rushed up the stairs after the clerk.

"You've got a powerful friend somewhere." The clerk frowned at Gaius's forehead and then turned away and climbed another step. "Don't dawdle. I want to get away from here." Gaius raced after him, his step springier with each tread. As usual, things were working out for him. When they'd reached the ground level, the clerk set off down the corridor. "This way," he called over his shoulder. "You've got some documents to sign."

"Documents?" Gaius was frustrated at the idea of any formalities—he wanted to be out and nothing more.

"A few."

"What sort?" Gaius asked, coming alongside the other.

"You've got a better idea than I do."

"What do you mean?"

"These documents, they have to do with your new commission as a Tribune in the Protectors of His Serenity Magnus Maximus. Welcome back to the army."

* * *

Gaius sent one of his cavalrymen ahead with a message for Merobauda and the family. He himself arrived home the following day, all shaved, bathed, togged in military garb, and followed by a pair of troopers leading pack-horses with his equipment. Another change of luck: Fortuna might be lurking the bushes with her hand on the rudder, ready to trip other passers-by along the road of life, but Gaius had slipped by her again right enough. He rode jauntily on a fine piebald cob, and the bright afternoon sun picked out the colors on the flashes and patches embroidered on his red tunic. His little military cap was perched on the back of head with what he judged would be just the right touch of snap and dash. Merobauda would be not only relieved but proud. How to get out the army was a persistent problem, but his reinstatement as a Tribune of the Protectors—a nice promotion that!—certainly boded well, and in the short term, at least, it would give him a comfortable living. The army probably presented no further dangers for him, apart from those of combat. But he had avoided that for years, and the change in his luck doubtless portended further good fortune, likely in that very respect. How could it be otherwise? So, while war was certain, his involvement in combat was probably out of the question. In meantime, he'd make as good a living as he could and find some way back into private life. He was clever; something would turn up. The first thing was to rent a house in Milan and get established. Just a small place, a dozen rooms, a stable for his horses, perhaps a shed where Merobauda could keep herself busy brewing instead of looking into his affairs. It wouldn't be a bad start. He'd spend the afternoons drilling soldiers, or find an optio to do it.

Merobauda, the girls, Arcadius, Aeliana and Faustinus and his son were waiting for him in the garden at the edge of the villa. Gaius swaggered (he kept just this side of vulgarity) and stood smartly in front of everyone with his hands on his hips. The entire family stood silent and, just when Gaius felt a flash of disappointment that no one had demonstrated any great happiness at his arrival—or was it survival?—Merobauda rushed over and hugged him. She released him abruptly, flushed at showing emotion in front of everyone. It was that natural seemliness of hers. The girls surrounded him like satellites.

"That's better!" He smiled broadly and patted the blonde heads that bobbed around him.

His smile struck Arcadius as bordering on the idiotic, and he was annoyed to see Aeliana clap her hands with joy—after all, Gaius wasn't her husband. Arcadius found most everything Gaius did annoying. Not that he wanted his brother in prison and facing death—no, not that— but still, couldn't fate work out something more consonant with true desserts? Arcadius would be willing to give advice on the question.

"Apparently my patron Flavius Syagrius got wind of my situation and decided he ought to do the right thing. That was to be expected, of course. I think it's fair to say that I've acquitted myself rather well in his service."

Arcadius wondered exactly what Gaius could possibly have done for him. Surely Syagrius, former Consul and former Prefect of Gaul (and Italy), didn't rely on little men such as his brother? Or was his brother more capable than he seemed? That was an appalling thought, but odd things did happen from time to time. By focusing his mind on the gold he had been given, he managed a genuine moderate heartiness and said, "Let me commend you on your good fortune." He put on a broad smile that he hoped was less idiotic than his brother's. "I expect you'll be establishing yourself in Milan soon. You know, finding yourself a house and surrounding yourself with your beloved family." He liked the thought of that: the family would, of course, include the insufferable Faustinus. "I imagine your military duties are quite pressing, given your reinstatement. A new troop to familiarize yourself with and all that sort of thing." Aeliana frowned at her husband's undisguised enthusiasm for his brother's immediate departure.

"Not so fast, Arcadius!" Gaius put up a hand. "I plan to…well, billet here—that's army talk, as you know—for a few weeks, before heading back to the capital."

"I see. No doubt you've a reason of some sort?" His tone betrayed suspicion and disappointment.

"In fact I do." He gave Merobauda an affectionate squeeze across the shoulders. "A little recuperation after my harrowing experience—I'm sure you'd agree that's called for. And there's nothing happening on the military front these days. The army can spare me for a few weeks, and in the disorder of the new political transition, no one will miss me. And, of course, the army pays for my billeting." He put his hand up to forestall any comment from Arcadius. "You won't need the money, of course, given what we've already handed over to you for our upkeep, so you won't mind if I just pocket it."

"I suppose it can't come to that much," Arcadius said, hoping it was true.

"Of course, I have a couple of troopers as attendants, and there's the billeting money from them too. I won't offer to give you a cut of that, because that would imply that you're grasping, and I wouldn't think of insulting you."

"Then they'll sleep in the stables," Arcadius said.

Gaius turned back to the others. "Let's not concern ourselves with these trivialities. Instead, let me say how much it means to me to see the everyone assembled to greet me after my recent quite unmerited and unpleasant experience."

Merobauda, despite her obvious relief at his return, frowned at him. She said, on the edge of tears, "I can't leave you alone for an hour or you'll traipse off on some hare-brained scheme to make a a little money."

"More than a little, Carissima. And it was, if I may say so, an altogether novel scheme. Quite brilliant, apart from the arrest and imprisonment, which weren't part of the plan. But that might have happened to anyone."

"It happened to you." She stepped back from him and grimaced as though in pain. "And now you're back in the army!" She stood shaking her head in dismay. "We had everything we needed here…" her voice trailed off.

She'd forgive him, of course. He would take her aside and talk to her and promise to do better. And try hard to do better. Then he was distracted from these thoughts by Arcadius, who was muttering something at him.

"Five solidi," his brother said quietly, taking him by the arm and leading him aside. "Five if you leave in the next week and take your family."

"Ten," Gaius said, before he'd had a chance to think whether fifteen might have been the better number. "And we leave in two weeks."

"Seven. And two weeks."

"Eight. And two weeks," Gaius countered.

"Eight and ten days."

Gaius thought to himself. Added to his billeting money, eight was more than enough for a lease on a passable house in Milan. He nodded to Arcadius and took Merobauda by the hand. Together they walked off, into the garden. He began to tell her how he would do better in the future.

XXXVIII

MAGNUS MAXIMUS PREPARES FOR CIVIL WAR

GAIUS FINDS HIMSELF INVOLVED

* * *

Gaius leased a house just inside the walls of Milan, one wing passably refurbished, the other a touch shabby, but then that was for Faustinus and the rest of the staff. He foresaw no opportunity to work his way out of the army during the next several months. He was a Protector and *"Tribunus Vacans"*—that is, he was on the General Staff—sent here and there on the occasional errand for the Master of the Infantry or the Master of the Cavalry. Not a bad position, but without much opportunity for peculation, though the pay was good. Unfortunately, as a Tribune in the Protectors, he had to attend upon His Serenity Magnus Maximus from time to time, and never at a great enough distance for his taste. He took care in the Imperial Presence to lurk behind the other tribunes and, as far as possible, to efface himself behind the backs of the taller aristocracy. Of course there was no way he could merge entirely into the back wall of the throne room and join the figures in the decorative frescoes, so he just held still and tried to look as though he had.

In the early spring of the year after Gaius and his family had relocated to Milan, the suspicion of war with His Serenity Theodosius began to take on solidity. Ugly news drifted from the east: Theodosius had arrogantly appointed his own prefect over the diocese Illyricum—a western diocese and therefore one of Maximus's. This was not simply a provocation.

"This is the start of war," Maximus said. He sat stately in his throne and spoke deliberately to his court—Tribunes of the Palatine troops, Tribunes of the Protectors (Gaius, as usual, trying to fade into the back wall), and a handful of the Great Men whom he trusted—Flavius Afranius Syagrius among them. "Theodosius's action discloses his plan: to take control of the Illyrian provinces if possible or, at the very least, to loosen Our hold on them." The court murmured its polite outrage—a dignified susurration. Maximus went on, motionless as a statue. "This is a reasonable strategy, quite such a one as We might expect from Theodosius, a seasoned soldier. It reveals his intent to advance through those provinces. Once having unsettled them, he hopes to make his way through with little or no resistance."

"Your Serenity, he has erred. He ought to have rushed north and west with his troops," the Master of the Infantry said. "He could have fought his way to the Adriatic before we before we had the time to prepare as fully as we now will."

Maximus gave his answer to the court at large. "Theodosius has given up surprise for the chance of an easy passage. Is it a wise decision?" He looked around as though for an answer, and when no one spoke, he said, "Only the outcome of the war will whether it was sound." He spoke with the complete detachment of great confidence or of fatalism. Gaius didn't share either; he had just been charged with the command of a small cavalry troop and given orders to head to the north-east to join those of Maximus's forces moving out of Gaul. War implied a good deal more to him now than it had behind the walls at Castellinum Ripae. He was struck with sudden wistful memories of his life in the fort on the Rhine, rubbing shoulders (well, in a manner of speaking) with the garrison soldiers behind high stone walls. Yes, it had been rather gloomy much of the time, but as the commander of border troops he hadn't been called on to take much in the way of risks. His Serenity lifted his hand, and the cloud of courtiers and military officers bowed deeply and proceeded to back out of the room, Gaius among the very first of them.

* * *

Maximus's army advancing out of Italy was a thin snake twenty miles long, crawling on its way east. It left behind it a litter of trash, shattered wagon wheels, ruptured boots, broken strapping, horse dung and the merds of soldiers: a grimy mess marking the passage of ten thousand men and two thousand beasts. This snake gathered and stretched itself by turns along the Via Postumia across the flat lands of the Veneti toward Aquileia and the foothills of the Julian Alps. Once past them, the Italian troops were to meet up with Maximus's main army, which should then be out of Gaul. Once joined, they would head east to face Theodosius's army somewhere in Illyricum. The eastern forces were said to number forty-thousand, many of them Gothic allies. Gaius doubted there could be so many; the column of which he was a part, though much smaller, stripped the country bare of food and fodder a good five miles to either side of its way. As usual, the peasants had disappeared into the countryside with all the goods they could carry, driving as many of their flocks and herds as they could into woods or marshes beyond the ambit of foragers. Theodosius's army must face the same problems—even more so if their numbers were as great as reported. But their number, if it was at all close to what spies said, was unsettling.

The early July sun was remorseless, and the tread of the foot soldiers and hooves of the cavalry drove up clouds of dust followed them like a shadow. Gaius and his troop rode in the rear of the column, and they were charged, when they weren't foraging, with bulldozing stragglers and protecting the rear of the column and its part of the baggage train: a hundred oxcarts and a hundred or so mules. He was happy enough with that—unless the scouts were mistaken, there was no enemy for a hundred miles, so there was no chance of attack until they passed through the mountains into Illyricum.

As the column moved along the head of the Adriatic, Gaius had to make a side-jaunt to a small town to gather a requisition. The town stood on the edge of large lagoon in the Veneti, really just a shrine or two, a church, a forum with a small basilica and a dozen other buildings of various sizes that ran down to the edge of a long wharf. A ton of wheat had been requisitioned there from the local town councillors, but the councillors weren't there when Gaius and his troop arrived with a pair of wagons. In their place, his men rounded up a half-dozen townsmen—uneasy men who would not meet his eye and who glanced from time to time over the wide shallow bay beyond the wharf, where fishing boats and coasters passed in the distance, driven here and there by the breeze in their sharp triangular sails.

Gaius ordered the townsmen into the warehouse to show him the requisitioned grain. The interior was dark and cool, for which Gaius was grateful. Motes of dust shimmered in the shafts of light that shot through the small windows between the ceiling beams, and the rammed earth floor was empty apart from shards of broken amphorae and a dozen sacks of millet that no one had thought worth hiding. Gaius clucked his tongue as he guessed at their weight. Maybe two hundred and fifty pounds, maybe not. He looked about the place and noted that it had been not only emptied, but neatly swept, perhaps as a slap to the advancing army. He took off his straw hat, wiped his forehead on his scarf and sighed. Well, they were clever bastards, the local nobles. In a week or so, he reckoned, when the army was a hundred miles away, the warehouse would be full again. He turned to the townsmen, frightened men who glanced here and there as though for some way to escape. No hope of that, though—a dozen soldiers lounged just inside, staying out of the sun.

Gaius was unhappy at the situation. Supplies had been short all along the way—the supply officers had skimmed more from the army depots along the Via Postumia than they ought to have done, and they had been surprised by the war—the greedy bastards. Anyone should have seen it coming.

The soldiers were angry and shoved an old man back and forth between them. "Leave him alone," Gaius said sharply. He looked at the other townsmen. "Soldiers were sent ahead last week to tell your councillors how much his Serenity called for." He paused and looked at the old man and, oddly, he smiled at him. It was a gesture of reasonableness. "I can see that was a mistake. Your town council has rather more initiative than most. Now, I don't want to threaten you with rough stuff—I don't go in for it for myself, but the boys here are hungry." He continued to smile at the old man. "Or they will be soon enough, so you can see that it would be quite helpful all around if you'd tell me where the grain's been moved." It couldn't be that far, he thought. Ox-drawn wagons travel slowly and they leave tracks. If he were given the general direction, he should have no trouble running the requisition down.

The old man was too frightened to speak. He glanced over his shoulder at the other townsmen, but they said nothing either. After several long moments, a young man with a bold expression prompted him. "There's no harm in telling the Tribune."

"No harm!" the older man said.

"No," the young man said, talking to the old man as though Gaius and soldiers weren't there. "If these men—" he waved an arm toward Gaius and his troop, "if they could get the grain, we'd have to answer for it, maybe. But they can't." A soldier grabbed him by the front of his tunic but let go when Gaius shook his head.

"Explain yourself," he said.

The young man smiled fearlessly. "Let me show you something..."

"He's 'Your Excellence,'" a soldier said, in a menacing voice.

"Let me show you something, Your Excellence," the young man bowed perfunctorily. He strode to the far door of the warehouse, which opened on the dock, Gaius at his heels. When the soldiers had drawn the bar and swung it open, everyone looked out across the glittering bay. The young man pointed east across the water to a scatter of islands, some large, some tiny, that began a mile or so away and faded into the distance. The sea all about them swelled gently, the sun glinting and shifting about on the water in a lively dance of bright gold and dark green. Gaius squinted to make out the green of trees and of gardens on some of the nearer islands, the white or gray, a hint of houses and villas. They were inviting, sitting out there, out of reach.

So, Gaius thought, *the local nobles have their estates out there. The grain's been transferred out there, well out of reach of any passing army.* He thought about it for several moments. A soldier coughed politely behind him. Well, there was no time fuss over the matter; it was hopeless—he had to get back to the column.

"Do many people live out there?" Gaius asked the young man as he turned to leave.

"Yes, Your Excellence. Many of them—and all the nobles."

"Seems rather convenient in troubled times, living out there, I should think."

"They're a law unto themselves." The young man smiled with a touch of insolence. "I suppose you haven't brought any boats with you?"

Gaius kept the soldiers off of the young man with a wave of his hand. "I can't think of everything." He walked back through the shadows of the warehouse, back to his horse, the sun, the dust, the ride across country to the column, to the war.

What an interesting place this was. Off the beaten track, literally.

* * *

A week later, Gaius and his twenty horsemen had passed through the town of Forum Iulii perched at the top of a gorge through which the river Natisone runs between high rocky banks. Always at the rear of the column, they pressed on toward Pannonia and the river Sava to join the rest of Maximus's army. Upon arrival, Gaius, along with the other staff tribunes, was briefed on the composition of Maximus's army, the various units and their disposition in the camp. Thus Gaius learned that the Second Pannonian Horse had been privileged to join the campaign, and he learned where they had been posted in the camp. He just had to see Arverno and the boys before things got rough.

When Gaius found the Second Pannonians, Arverno was delighted to see him and started off, as though no time had passed since their last meeting, with one of his typical irrelevancies. "Here we are in Pannonia." He looked out over the turf rampart of the camp at the countryside. "That's what they call this part of Illyricum, Your Excellence," he told Gaius quite unnecessarily and with his usual enthusiasm for the obvious. It was just like old times. "It seems as if it might mean something, we being Pannonians and all. Except that none of us are Pannonians really. No one's been a Pannonian in the troop for..." he thought hard, "oh, a good fifty years, I suppose. Certainly no one back at Ripae could ever remember seeing one. It makes a man think." The old soldier talked just the same way as he always had, though now, somehow, Gaius didn't find it annoying; instead he was surprised at an upwelling of affection for the old fool as happens, for example, when someone long gone is recalled in a touching story. So he broke into Gaulish, bridging the distance between them with their shared language.

"I hear they're on the other side of the Sava." He inclined his head to the northeast. "Do you have any idea how many?"

Arverno sucked his teeth. "A lot," he said finally. "The scouts say a lot. The ones that come back." He smiled vaguely, quite evidently enjoying the feel of Gaulish on his tongue.

Gaius looked back at him. "Lost a few scouts, eh?" He tried to look unconcerned.

"A few. Captured or dead maybe. Or maybe just deserted." Arverno shrugged. "As happens when it's civil war."

"Anyone might be forgiven for wondering what he's fighting for in a civil war. One like this, anyway."

Arverno nodded. "I gave my first oath to the Old Valentinian—Gratian's father—and then to his son Gratian." He looked around vaguely. "But Maximus? Well, of course to him too, but..." He shook his head. "It's hard to know what to do sometimes but, in the end, a soldier shouldn't let his comrades down. There's always an emperor, but they come and go, and so who are they to us? Apart from being emperor? But your comrades, though..." Gaius couldn't follow Arverno's rambling train of thought, but he could guess what he meant: that emperors, were always with them, like the weather. They were sometimes good, sometimes bad, most often indifferent, and it was everyone's work to get on with life despite whatever the emperors got up to. Or something like that. It was as though Arverno, slow-witted as he was, had struck upon a truth too obvious for a thinking man to notice until it was pointed out. Gaius thought vaguely of his family, of Merobauda and the girls. Of Faustinus, even of Arcadius—all three hundred miles hundred away, safe south of the Alps. He felt suddenly alone and exposed, a paradox as he stood behind the ramparts of the camp surrounded by thousands of soldiers. He shook off the feeling and turned back to Arverno.

"The men in the troop—they're the same old fellows?"

"For the most part, Excellence. "We've picked up two or three new men during the last year."

Gaius nodded and moved on to his principal concern. "I just arrived this evening. There are rumors throughout the camp about a battle tomorrow. Any truth to them?" Arverno nodded. Gaius went on: "Are we to keep Theodosius on the farther bank of the Sava?"

"It's too late for that. His men forced a crossing this morning. There are a dozen units on this side of the river." Arverno seemed resigned. Gaius wondered how he had missed this unwelcome news as he approached the camp. So, not only would the river not protect them, Maximus had suffered a defeat. Minor, perhaps, but a bad sign all the same.

Arverno said, "I wouldn't worry about this little setback, Excellent Tribune. His Serenity Maximus will surely find a reply." Gaius could tell that he was forcing some brightness in his tone, like a workman gilding plaster. He was quite moved that Arverno would try to reassure him; he was an old friend afraid to give bad news.

Gaius was a staff officer and didn't yet know where he would be assigned during the battle. But an idea was coming to him. An odd one, perhaps. It was selfless, really, and that was part of its oddness. He felt an uprush of emotions, a swirling as when leaves mill in a whirlwind in the corner of a courtyard in autumn. One of them was fear; that was to be expected before a grand set-piece battle. He should repress that. After all, the world was a dangerous place, and he was paid to muck about in it taking risks. Anything might happen, even in peacetime, to the extent that there was much of it. Fine. But what was this whole enterprise about in the end? Maximus fighting for his life, now that he'd overreached himself by snatching Italy. Theodosius marching his army hundreds of miles to take back the West and give it to that boy Valentinian. Fine. But what, really, was anyone else's interest? What was his? Whose man was he? Maximus's? Syagrius's? Should he have been Valentinian's and thus Theodosius's? And, now that he thought of it, where did Syagrius stand, really? In one moment these and other thoughts came to him: that though he had tried over the years to make his own way, he had always been a thrall to the ambitions of the great men. He'd dodged where he could, survived, prospered in a modest way, but it could all be swept away in an afternoon as a pair of emperors tossed dice in a game between themselves. So, though he might die, Arverno and his little troop needn't die—certainly not so that Maximus and Theodosius could match themselves against each other and see who was the more skilled—or the more lucky. Gaius had the chance to protect the Pannonians, and he suddenly had the determination to do it, no matter the cost. His resolution had come in an instant. It was the right thing to do.

He waved a hand at the soldiers milling about, some cooking their dinners, some leading their horses to the paddock to be picketed. "You're in command?"

Arverno nodded. "In a way—I'll be there with the boys, though there's an officer over us." He scowled. "Probus Martialis. I thought we'd seen the last of him years ago, but he's been jumped up to command us tomorrow. It's funny how things go full circle sometimes."

Indeed it was, Gaius thought. But an experienced soldier might be given a command ad hoc, particularly when he'd led a unit—that very unit—before. Things got churned up in war; lines were blurred, procedures ignored. Maybe Martialis had managed to insinuate himself into this position in hope he could parlay it into a promotion. As he considered that possibility, Gaius's idea grew even more appealing to him.

"You're all here? All of the Second Pannonians?"

"That's quite right, Your Wonderment. All sixty-eight of us."

"Any orders yet from Martialis?"

"We're to be toward the right in the second line tomorrow, joined up with more cavalry, the Third Stablesiani. No more details than that. It's my guess we'll be called on to do a sweep or to stop one, but who knows?"

"I don't see the bastard about." Gaius turned his plan over in his mind, studying it. He liked it quite well.

"We're to be ready in the morning—by the third hour. We expect Martialis then."

"I see," Gaius said. "There's been a change of plans, so be ready at the second hour."

Arverno looked quizzical.

"The second hour. I'll see you then," Gaius repeated and walked off.

✕✕✕✕

TRIBUNE DOLO LEADS HIS MEN GALLANTLY THROUGH THE BATTLE OF THE SAVA

* * *

The next morning Gaius was with the Second Pannonians bright and early—in fact, even a little before the second hour. It seemed odd to the men that he came leading his own horse— no calo or attendant to do it for him. Arverno had the troop assembled and was giving orders in his simple, rudimentary way: stay together, pay attention, do what you're told, no one leaves the formation.

"Marvelously practical advice, Arverno!" Gaius told him.

"Good morning, your Commandingness." Arverno bowed and the men suddenly came to attention. "It always helps to remind the boys of the basics."

"Indeed it does!" Gaius rested his hand on his hilt and looked them over. He walked past the men and peered at them, stopping now and then to level trivial unjust criticisms of their appearance and deportment in order to impress them with his arbitrary power. It was his usual tactic when he had the deplorable luck to have to actually command soldiers personally in field—as hadn't happened, he reflected, since he had been on Gratian's last campaign. He found that his fussing seemed to inspire the men. Or perhaps it just inspired

346

him. Well, this was no time to work out which it was.

"As I suggested last evening, and you might suppose, there have been some recent changes in the dispositions and commands of the various units," he said to Arverno. "The usual adjustments in the closing hours before a major battle."

Arverno nodded.

"I will, for instance, be resuming command of the Pannonians today." "Very good, Your Excellence. I take it that we are to be joined with some other unit, you being a Tribune of the Protectors?" He was alluding, of course, to the small numbers of the Pannonians, too few to be commanded by a man of Gaius's station.

"Just you and the men, Arverno." He drew Arverno off to the side a few steps. "We have a special mission," he said very quietly. "We are entrusted with a special maneuver."

Arverno nodded and smiled with pride, and then his face fell. "But Martialis?"

"Forget him. As I said, there's been a change of plans. I will command you."

Arverno nodded happily.

Men from other units were passing by, some on foot, some mounted. Officers were bawling, and signal horns blared here and there like angry cattle. Dust was already rising into the sky to tell Theodosius that his enemy was moving out. Gaius straightened, settled his sword-belt, absently drew a hand over the iron scales of his armor as though to be sure they were there and then called on the mwn to mount up and move out.

Maximus's army—legions, cohorts, and auxilia—flowed out in streams from each of the camp's four gates. Three of the columns circled around the camp to join those headed out of the east gate. There was much shouting, shoving of men into blocks (more or less) as they made for the river in a slow jostling column a third of mile wide and mile long. A screen of scouts, light infantry and horsemen ranged ahead. Gaius led his troop with a great deal of snap and dash, confident that, in the complications of the advance, Martialis wouldn't find them until deployment—if even then.

As they neared the battlefield, Gaius kept an eye out as the units began to maneuver from the marching column into a horizontal front. Maximus's most trusted units moved off to left and right while the Palatine Infantry from Italy took the center. So placed, they would have to fight, or at least hold the center steady. As the front line was forming, the second line began to do the same thirty yards behind it. Gaius waited in the column for his chance to lead the Second Pannonians toward the right flank of the second line. It was the usual sort of place for them to be—and where he needed them to be.

Meanwhile he scanned the countryside, which flattened out as it approached the river across which Theodosius's troops advanced in their thousands over a pair of floating bridges improvised over barges. Dust from their advance rose in a curtain and floated in roils over the river. Gaius could smell it; it pricked his nose like pepper.

He looked about. The land hereabouts was a patchwork of meadows and peasants' fields, footpaths flanked by low scrub, and frequent stands of trees. During the advance, the legions and cohorts had moved in their blocks around these obstacles and halted as the officers on foot and horseback bossed the units into the semblance of a line before once again taking up the advance. Gaius followed along just behind, leading his little troop, staying as far back in the second line as he could without attracting attention. And he kept his eyes open. To his right, to the southeast a mile away, was a proper forest. Now, that looked inviting: a dozen shades of cool green pierced with welcoming black openings and channels between the pines and the boughs of oaks and chestnuts quivering in the early morning breeze. Once there, a man could disappear in moments; so could sixty-eight of them.

Maximus's front line was now formed up and moving forward, but there was a sense of hesitancy in its movement. To Gaius's now practiced eye—yes, he'd learned a few things about the army over the years—there seemed a tinge of reluctance. The blocks of men moved ahead, but some of them a bit too slowly to keep the front line properly dressed, so it undulated as it advanced, like a line of clouds on stagnant air. By contrast, here and there an eager block of men pressed forward, units from Maximus's British field army, but their enthusiasm only pointed up the dull advance of the others.

"Some don't want to fight, Your Excellence," Arverno said quietly. Gaius nodded without saying anything. Why should they be eager? An errant shaft of sunlight poked for a moment through the dust and struck him for an instant, sharp as a painful memory, and then as quickly faded. It seemed a sign, but of what? He wouldn't dwell on it; he had decided what he would do.

When the time came to move to the end of the second line, Probus Martialis cantered up with a pair of troopers from a gap in a line of bushes, gesticulating wildly, swearing at Arverno, execrating him for leaving camp before he'd taken command of them. "Get these men into position!" He cocked his head back where he'd come from. "Now! What they hell are you doing over here?" Martialis panted, speechless for several moments in fury, and then he added, "Move! Now! Or I'll have you flogged till the bones show through your back."

Arverno pulled up and sat his horse calmly, the rest of the troop halting around him. "We're just following orders, good soldiers that we are." He nodded toward Gaius. "Meet our commander here, a Tribune of the Protectors."

Martialis looked narrowly at Gaius, whose face was shadowed by his helmet, and then he suddenly grasped whom he was dealing with. Gaius gave Martialis one of his favorite looks, an artful blend of the smug and the supercilious. Martialis straightened in the saddle, momentarily at a loss.

"As you see, there's been a change of plans." Gaius stared at him pointedly. "Not the sort, apparently, that's been communicated far enough down the chain of command to reach such as you."

Martialis glowered at him and, recovering, said, "Change of plans?" He didn't hide his incredulity. "Horse shit! You're disobeying orders. And in battle! You'll finally get what's coming to you, you little bastard."

"These recurrent death threats of yours are tiresome. Really, their repetition betrays a serious paucity of invention." He leaned in the saddle toward Martialis. "And it's not wise to threaten superior officers." He glanced over at Arverno. "Not wise at all, is it?"

"No, Your Excellentness. Not wise at all."

"A serious offense, in fact."

Martialis tightened his hands on the reins in order to turn his horse about and, just at that moment, Gaius added, "You may go." He flapped his hand as though he were flicking away a fly, and he did it with perfect timing so that, to Martialis's troopers, it looked as though he were obeying a dismissal. Martialis turned his horse about in a tight circle again and pointed at Gaius. "Win or lose today, you'll die. Count on it!" And he cantered back the way he had come, the troopers after him. Gaius shrugged indifferently and led his men obliquely to the right, placing them twenty yards behind a large troop of cavalry set to protect the right flank. Their tribune turned to stare, wondering what they were doing there. No matter—things were in train, and it was too late for anyone to do anything about Gaius's aberrant maneuver. The other tribune turned away; he likely thought the Pannonians had been placed there as some sort of reinforcement to him.

Directly ahead, about a mile away, Theodosius's army was forming up. Once over the river, it had divided and flowed to either side to form a front a mile wide behind a screen of units that had crossed the river the day before. Each troop had its own gaudy shield, and the variegated appearance of the enemy legions, auxilia and cohorts seemed oddly festive. In the middle, not in neat blocks like soldiers of the Imperial Army but in a drab undifferentiated mass, were Theodosius's Gothic allied foot soldiers. Somewhere on the flanks, Gothic lancers were finding their places between blocks of Imperial cavalry.

Time passed, the heat of the summer morning exacerbated by Gaius's armor. He could stand the weight of it easily enough but, beneath it, he was soaked with sweat, and his jack and tunic clung to him uncomfortably. Stinging sweat ran into his eyes beneath the helmet, and he blinked at the world—much as he might have done had he come out of a dark place, like a jail, for instance, as seemed to happen to him from time to time. He shrugged his shoulders to settle his armor—there was a bothersome crease somewhere deep in the various layers below it, but discomfort was the order of the day, and since there was a battle in the offing, there seemed no point in complaining.

At midmorning, messengers on horseback trotted among the units to see that the lines were dressed. Shortly after that, trumpets sounded, and the first line moved ahead at a walk, the cavalry covering the flanks. Theodosius's ranks moved forward and the lines approached each other until they drew within a few yards of one another, when they stopped and faced off. Arrows dropped here and there among the lines, shot by archers from the back of the formations, and soldiers bent their heads as the arrows, for the most part, bounced off helmets or rattled away from armored shoulders. Although he couldn't hear their commands clearly at this distance, Gaius knew that centurions, praepositi and tribunes of both armies were bossing the men, working them up to make feints and approaches, urging them to move close enough to attack with leveled spears.

Gaius, with his men seventy yards back and just behind the second line, watched closely, judging the best time for his maneuver, waiting to see whether the first line would advance and seriously close in or be menaced into pulling back. He glanced to his left, but at this distance the middle of the first line was a mere blur of men fading from sight as it extended north. He leaned out of his saddle toward Arverno. "See those woods over there" he pointed to the right beyond the army's flank. "Spies tell us there's infantry hidden in them—an ambush when our line advances. We have to go there and divert them—keep them occupied before the rest of our line advances that far." Arverno turned to regard the woods and nodded, accepting Gaius's statement without question.

Meanwhile, here and there along the first line tight knots of men shuffled toward each other, menacing their opponents with spears, sometimes advancing closely enough to strike each other's shields before shying away back into the safety of their units. It was hard for Gaius and his men to await events, to sit their horses as this sporadic fighting took place at various points along the line. The horses were no more at ease than the men. They flattened their ears at the sound of the clashing, the shouts, the clapping now and again of shield on shield. They flared their nostrils at the dust and shook their heads. Some of them curveted and kicked; a few screamed uncannily.

Arverno and his optios rode about the troop to keep the formation from spreading out. Gaius patted the shoulders of his horse to calm her. She stamped and sidled a good deal but generally kept her place. Now and again an arrow bounced off a trooper or landed at an angle in the ground. At one point Gaius found one sticking out of his shield; he'd been too occupied to notice when it had struck.

Up ahead and to the left there had been a brief clash in the front line—he could hear the shouts, some rattling of spears against each other and the clatter when one struck against the edge of a shield. It had been a real clash, vicious, no mere demonstration; the line moved forward a dozen yards and Theodosius's men moved back but they kept good order. A pause followed, during which the lines ordered themselves again about ten yards apart from each other. This done, a pair of soldiers passed back out of their formation with a wounded comrade, whom they set on the ground. They hurried back, leaving the man to crawl slowly away from the fight. And so it went for a good two hours, so far as Gaius could gauge it by looking at the sun, red in the dusty sky. Sometimes Maximus's line advanced a dozen yards; sometimes it pulled back as far. Gaius's troop followed or pulled back accordingly. During the pauses in the infantry fighting, men at the very front of the line slipped back to the rear of the formation as fresh soldiers took their place. Gaius looked longingly to the southeast, to the dark cool of the forest.

About midday, the cavalry troop just ahead of them turned to the right and began to trot and then canter off, and Gaius realized they had moved to fend off a sweep from the enemy. As he watched them, a troop of Theodosius's cavalry passed through them at a canter. The horses moved instinctively to let the Theodosian troop pass neatly through, almost as though they hadn't been there at all. A half dozen men had managed to strike with lances as the troops passed through each other—Gaius could hear the thumps and scrapes as shields were hit, and three men were knocked from their saddles. Arverno called for the Pannonians to level their spears and countercharge, but Gaius countermanded the order—he had something quite different in mind. Theodosius's men swirled past Gaius's troop, pursued soon after by those they had just passed through. The two opposing troops veered off to the south in their private quarrel and disappeared. Meanwhile the men who'd fallen to the ground stumbled to their feet and stood looking for their mounts, but these had followed the other troopers and were long gone.

Gaius heard shouting from up ahead and saw standards moving forward to indicate a general advance of the right flank. Well, it was as good a time as any. He commanded the Pannonians to advance obliquely to the right, and he led them at a steady trot toward the wood. Within a few moments they had passed the infantry of the front line and the flank of the enemy too. As they left behind the clashing soldiers their shouts and screams dissolved into a vague rumor, indistinct but unsettling, like a fading nightmare half grasped as it leaches away.

Gaius's troop kept in reasonably good order as it crossed the field, veering here and there around stands of trees, splitting briefly into twos or threes to pass through breaks in low hedges or stone walls. Gaius could hear the snap of the standard, the drumming of the hooves as they moved at a trot. The air grew fresher, the sky bluer as they left the battlefield behind. The wood ahead rose up as they drew closer, its features growing clear: the brown and gray of the tree boles, the dozens of different shades of green, some rich, some dusty, some almost black. The crowns of the tallest trees gently brushed the sky, unconcerned with affairs playing out a mile away.

As Gaius and the Pannonians drew up in the tall grass at the edge of the wood, he turned his horse sharply about so that he could address the men. "All right, men! Keep a sharp eye out as we get into the trees—the enemy is in there; that we know. How many? That we don't know. How armed? That we don't know either, so be prepared for arrows or spears. Don't take any unnecessary chances—we just have to keep them occupied—no more than that. At the same time, I expect each man to conduct himself with the boldness, grit and fortitude of Roman Field Troops, a status to which you have had the good fortune to be promoted." He successfully fought a tendency to lapse into irony on this last point. In fact, he sounded so masterful (to himself at least) that he wished Merobauda could hear him. She might be less inclined to tell him what was what, if she could see him distinguishing himself in the field. "When you find the enemy, keep him worried, men. Keep him busy and guessing so he can't leave the woods and hit our infantry's flank when it pushes Theodosius back toward the river." He pointed to Arverno. "Get the men in a line Praepositus." Arverno nodded and barked the usual orders, and the men dismounted. Every fifth man took the reins of his horse and those of four others, the rest formed themselves into a loose line, half turned behind their shields, their spears leveled. Gaius glanced over them and, when he was satisfied, he stood among them and led the troop into the wood.

It was an old wood, the tall trees grown straight as pillars, the canopy of leaves thick and dark. The air was cool here and pure, dim after the sunlight of the open field, and, because the wood was so old, there were alleyways between the trunks and very little underbrush. *This is the forest primeval,* Gaius thought vaguely, as though the start of a poem were rattling about in his head. He saw at once that was enough a good deal of space between the trees, that he could see the contours of the land, where it dipped and rose, and its gradual descent to the Sava, which ran past it something more than half a mile away. It was rather a pleasant setting. There would be room to lead the troops' horses among the trees and, unless Gaius was dreadfully mistaken, there was nobody for them to fight. He sent a dozen men back to bring the horses along behind. He could tell from Arverno's face that he was alarmed at the danger of it, but Gaius just gave the old fellow one of his masterful smiles, and the troop, men and horses, pressed on through the trees.

It was quite a nice little sylvan excursion, much pleasanter than the grinding conflict a mile away, during which Maximus's army began to dissolve, first the cavalry wings driven from the field, then the rear units of the infantry, who, sensing a bad turn of events, came apart and fled while they had the chance. Finally the front ranks, lacking support, collapsed. Men dropped their shields and weapons and tossed aside their helmets as they hared off toward the camp; those units still amenable to the command of their officers formed tight knots, shields together and spears out in rings, and stood their ground as Theodosius's men swept past them, looking for easier targets. Here and there riderless horses cantered about in confusion. On the right flank, a handful of units managed to keep good order and retreat toward the camp, but the battle, which had lasted a good four hours, ended with shocking suddenness. The dust began to settle, and the sky to brighten over several hundred bodies lying here and there across the field, most of them with wounds in the back.

Meanwhile Gaius and his troopers moved deeper into the woods. The men were wary, of course, alert to find the illusory, and thus elusive, ambushers that Gaius had lied to them about. Even Gaius was cautious—after all, there might actually be some of Theodosius's soldiers hidden in the wood—it was just possible. Even though he had concocted the scheme, it might accidentally hold a grain of truth. But in the end, there was no truth in it at all, which was a great satisfaction to Gaius. What was the good of lying if the truth intervened to upset one's plans?

"Your Boldness," Arverno said, when the troop approached the far end of the woods, where they could hear the river murmuring close by. "May I say, if you don't mind my boldness to do it…" He stopped to consider the two boldnesses and was lost for a moment.

"Yes, Arverno?" Gaius sheathed his sword gratefully; it had grown heavy during the stroll through the woods. That done, he set his shield down and leaned casually on it.

"My point, if you follow me, Your Perspicuity…"

"It's difficult at times, Arverno." He took off his helmet and handed it to him. Much better, that. The woodland air felt wonderfully cool on his sweat-soaked head. "I think you have now concluded, Praepositus, as of course I did some time ago, that our spies have misinformed us, and that there are, in fact, no enemy soldiers here."

"Your Brevity puts it so succinctly."

"I didn't realize you knew that word."

"I learned it from you, Your Erudition. Years ago up on the river."

Gaius smiled at him. "I'm gratified to find that my earlier command of the Pannonians has improved you so much further even than I had supposed."

Arverno smiled warmly and asked, "And now?" A number of the men had clustered around clearly wondering the same thing.

"A good question." Gaius turned to the troopers. "We have done our duty—always something to be proud of—and we have done it, as always when men are under my command, without loss." He allowed a moment for the men to give him a cheer. He put his hand up. "Enough, men! Enough. It was no more than my obligation to you as your commander to see to your safety in this, perhaps the most perilous situation you may ever face." He rubbed the sweat from his face, which rather diminished the effect of his address, but he went on. "It may be that today you will hear braggarts tell of their feats, but remember that a man may claim any sort of glory, may weave any rags of experience into a sordid tapestry of prevarication..." He hesitated at the appallingly mixed metaphor, but then shrugged and pressed on with his usual half-merited confidence. "But remember that you plunged fearlessly into this daunting wood and pressed through Stygian darkness..."

"Stygian?" one of the soldiers asked involuntarily.

"Very dark," Gaius explained. Years ago he'd have resented the interruption, but today he just smiled.

"So, 'very dark darkness?'" Arverno needed more clarification.

"You pressed through deep darkness," Gaius simplified, surprised at his patience. The men had all come through unhurt and that was what mattered. He went on: "You were ready to face innumerable enemies of unreckoned ferocity. That they weren't here, well..." He shrugged his shoulders and waved a hand. "But this is the thing to never forget, so long as you live: you are alive." Even Arverno narrowed his eyes for a second at this, but Gaius forestalled further discussion by ordering a long rest before they left the wood to find out how the battle had come out. If Maximus had won, well, that might be the end of it for him. If Theodosius? Well, who could say?

XXXXI

GAIUS SAVES A LIFE—AND PAYS FOR IT

***

After what he reckoned a safe interval, Gaius led his men back through the wood, and this took rather a long while. He didn't dawdle—no; instead, he led them astray at one point so that they doubled back for quarter of a mile. But, eventually, of course, he had to let them leave the protection of the woods. This was the unsettling part—if Maximus had won the battle, then he couldn't see how he would explain his actions well enough even to save his life. Then again, life took many turns and despite—or perhaps because of—his many and varied experiences, Gaius took a positive view of things. Thus, even though he didn't know the outcome of the battle, he felt elated by what he had done. He expected Merobauda would be proud of him for taking this chance on behalf of others—she was a Christian and had strong convictions about charity, though they might be tempered if he were executed for desertion. But would he be? It was time to turn his mind to the outcome of the battle.

Arverno had the men count off, and when he was satisfied that no one had gotten lost in the woods, he ordered them to mount up. Meanwhile Gaius had settled himself in the saddle and was scanning the battlefield as well as he could from so far away. It seemed safe to head back—men were wandering the field here and there in scattered groups. Light infantry and troops of cavalry patrolled the edges of the battlefield and beyond, but the battle was clearly over. Theodosius's army still held the banks of the Sava, so it looked pretty certain that Maximus had lost. Gaius felt a wave of relief. Now the only thing to do was find someone to surrender to. He turned his horse about and looked at his troopers.

"Men, it doesn't look good for Maximus, not good at all." There was some half-hearted murmuring from the men, who felt an obligation to show some regret over the Emperor's loss. "I know how you feel, men," Gaius said with some truth, because he didn't feel much regret either. He ordered a leafy branch to be cut from a nearby sapling and tied to a lance in sign of surrender, and the troop set off using this as a standard. Things were looking good indeed; with Maximus defeated, his little unauthorized maneuver would never come into question. He had taken a dangerous chance on behalf of others, and there would not be any cost. After his surrender, this little episode would be forgotten. Maximus would hightail it to the west, but he was finished for Theodosius would stoop on him like a hawk and end the war soon. Had it gone otherwise, Gaius might have found some bitter-sweet satisfaction in his summary trial and execution for disobeying commands in order to spare his men, but now that he didn't face the ordeal, he found that he didn't miss the prospect of it in the least. It had been an emotional decision to protect his men by leading them out of the battle; he hadn't given due consideration to his own inter-ests. He had better make sure that didn't happen again. He looked around, searching the field for someone to surrender to.

The battlefield was the usual unsettling clutter: colorful shields scattered about, swathes of trampled grass or scuffed ground where men had advanced and retreated. Bodies lay here and there, often in grotesque attitudes; the injured called out here and there for help. Archers strode about the field pulling out arrows stuck in the ground at various angles, and calos went about gathering up scattered weap-ons and tossing them in piles to be taken away later. Shabby fig-ures began to slink onto the field—scavengers looking to strip the wounded and dead of valuables. Gaius pointed them out. "Scatter those vultures if they come near, but otherwise I don't want to see any weapons brandished."

He led his men toward the center of the battlefield; it seemed a likely place to find someone of at least moderate authority to surrender to. Before he could do so, though, he saw a cavalryman sitting on the ground, holding his arm. His shield lay next to him split in two and folded over, its halves held together only by its canvas facing. As Gaius and his men approached, the soldier looked over at them, undid the chin strap of his helmet clumsily with one hand and tossed it away. Gaius could see his face quite clearly now; the man was Probus Martialis.

"Help me!" he called and beckoned with his right hand. "My left arm's broken." He nodded at his shield. "Some bastard got me with a mace as he rode by." He looked vaguely about. "My horse has run off." He grimaced in pain and then gingerly touched his left arm.

Gaius took his time pulling off his own helmet and hanging it on his saddle. He rubbed his sweaty head and enjoyed the sensation of fresh air passing through his hair. Then he deigned to look down at Martialis. "You can appreciate my hesitation in view of your incessant death threats, Martialis. Some would think it extremely unwise to offer you any assistance whatsoever."

Martialis regarded him sullenly. "You bastard!" he said and winced.

Gaius circled his horse around Martialis. It was hard not to exult. His men had survived and Gaius wouldn't pay any penalty for leading his men away from the battle. And here was Martialis brought down another peg—maybe three or four. It was turning out a good day.

"What the hell are you staring at?" Martialis put his right hand to the ground and steadied himself as he staggered to his feet.

"You, Martialis. Just you."

"Why?"

"I'm trying my best to gloat, but I haven't succeeded as far as I'd like, and despite my experience of your character, I can't bring myself to just leave you out here. It's odd, when you come to think of it." And it was a bit odd. Looking after the men of his old command was one thing; looking after this bastard was quite another.

"Are you going to help me or not?" Martialis bent over and snatched up his helmet by the chin strap. He seemed about to fling it at Gaius but reconsidered.

"Just give me a moment more to savor your situation." A clever remark, but Gaius's heart wasn't really in it. He sensed that he had softened recently.

Arverno called out to him in Gaulish. "Leave him, Your Excellentness. Just leave him. He'd have let us starve years ago." He spat, something Gaius had never seen him do before. Martialis frowned; he didn't speak the language, but he fully appreciated Arverno's tone.

"If you don't get me off the field the scavengers will kill me for my money and equipment. Or Theodosius's men might do it. They might kill me to save the trouble of looking after me."

"I agree with you, Martialis. Those are both extremely likely possibilities."

Martialis took deep breaths, chuffing like horse, to settle his nerves. Gaius could see that he was very afraid—more afraid now than when Gaius had found him. Of course he was—he had briefly hoped to be rescued and then he discovered that he was simply facing a different enemy. He stared at Gaius for a moment and saw a flicker of sympathy in his expression. He said pleadingly, "I can't walk to the camp. I just can't." He dropped his helmet and held up his right hand to show a gaudy ring. "It's yours." He tried to slip it off with his teeth as his left arm hung limp at his side, but couldn't do it; he stopped, exhausted, and staggered.

"Keep it," Gaius said. The desperation in the man's voice had moved him, and he had decided to take him from the field. To accept the ring would cheapen his decision; the offer angered him, in fact, as though Martialis had slighted him. He ordered a trooper to take Martialis behind him, and the troop set off at a walk. There was what looked like a couple of auxilia, or perhaps it was a legion, still on the field about a half a mile away, probably from Theodosius's reserve or second line. They looked promising. He led the troop that way.

As they rode along, Arverno asked Martialis, "How was the battle lost?" He spoke to him directly and with no titles or honorifics.

"We were doing all right all along the line, but somehow—I don't know how—the left flank was turned and began to crowd the center. We turned—my troop—to meet the flankers, but they bowled past us and got behind the center of the first line." He shrugged and winced with the pain of it. "It all fell apart then." Gaius listened without comment as he led them toward Theodosius's foot soldiers.

Before they could reach them, Gaius's troop attracted the attention a Theodosian cavalry squadron, a good two hundred and fifty men, who rode up to them warily. The drew up twenty yards away with leveled lances, and their tribune rode out a little before them, covering himself carefully with his shield. He held his sword up, ready to reply to any surprise.

"Wave the bough," Gaius told the trooper. "Everyone stay calm. No sudden moves."

"Who are you?" the tribune asked. "I don't know your shields." He had a strong accent and spoke slowly, his Latin pronounced in a way Gaius hadn't heard since he had lived in Rome and had heard Greeks talk in the street.

Gaius swept his hand back. "These are the Second Pannonian Horse."

The tribune frowned at the name. "In whose service? Maximus's?"

"Yes, Tribune. We are lately in the service of Magnus Maximus. Perhaps you can tell me in whose service we are now?" That was a canny reply.

The officer smiled faintly. "If you give us no trouble and take the oath to Theodosius, you should all be sent home."

"Very good, Tribune."

"Your name?"

Probus Martialis spoke up from somewhere behind him. "His name is Gaius Obsequens Dolo, Your Excellence. He Excellence here is a Tribune of the Protectors in the service of the Usurper Magnus Maximus."

The tribune lowered his sword but looked quite interested.

Martialis continued. "Yes, Tribune of the Protectors. Rubbed shoulders with Maximus himself. In fact," he looked over at Gaius with a twisted smile, "he was himself responsible for some of today's tactical maneuvers. That should tell you how high he stands in the Usurper's service. Some might even say he's one of the Great Men at Maximus's court. Don't let his modest command fool you; he's a cunning fellow and set himself up so that he could pass as one of the lower officers if things went badly, as they did. Just ask yourself what a Tribune of the Protectors is doing at the head of this little troop. He was trying to make his escape back to his master's court."

The tribune looked closely at Gaius's shield, which was decorated sumptuously with a scarlet rim and a bright green laurel wreath circling the boss. It really lent a bit of snap and dash, but it differed entirely from the quartered red and black of the Second Pannonians.

Gaius was too startled by the allegation to reply handily; Martialis's sudden power of invention had left him quite flat-footed. The tribune called out to one of his optios. "You take half the men and lead these Pannonians to the camp and see that they take the oath." He turned to Gaius. "You come with me. Consider yourself arrested for high treason against their Serenities Theodosius and Valentinian." Gaius was taken aback, not only at Martialis's betrayal and at the tribune's charge but at his own response: a calm, even philosophical acceptance. He shrugged and waved at the Pannonians and said in Gaulish to Arverno: "Farewell and look after the boys for me." He turned to the tribune. "Very well. Let's go." He rode off alone, hemmed around by seventy-five of Theodosius's cavalry.

XXXXII

MEROBAUDA BARGAINS
WITH SYAGRIUS

* * *

At the time of the Battle of the Sava, Syagrius enjoyed the office of Prefect of Milan, an honor bestowed by Magnus Maximus. That emperor, once His Serenity, was now of course, reduced through the usual governmental hindsight to the status and style of a tyrant when he was discussed at all. Syagrius had expected a summons to the palace at the conclusion of the war, no matter how it turned out, and he had prepared things as well as he could to face any outcome. Things might have been better—safer for him in any case—if Maximus had won the war, but he was fairly confident that he would successfully slip through the nets of intrigue that formed as a result of the shifting structure of the palace administration and find himself in a good position. But he needed information in order to guide his actions to a successful conclusion.

He sent minions to the periphery of the palace with enough money and subtle threats to winkle out a good deal of information or, in the absence of it, to elicit reasonably informed speculation. Chief among the facts adduced were the names of high officials struggling under the suspicion of the victors, a handful of whom had already been arrested, among them, interestingly enough, his little client Gaius

Obsequens Dolo. The Tribune just couldn't seem to keep out trouble, but that was a good thing, really, because Dolo's misfortune might just be turned to Syagrius's advantage. It had certainly helped him when Maximus came to power to suggest that Dolo, as his agent, had undermined any last chance Gratian might have scrabbled together at the last moment by snatching his treasury below the walls of Lugdunum. It had not mattered in the least that Dolo's actions could not have had any bearing on the outcome. Only the illusion had mattered. Still less did it matter that Dolo had not even understood the situation. After all, great events were to be guided by Great Men, men such as the Petronii, the Anicii—and of course the Syagrii—— men who floated above the Imperial Court and, like the stars in the sky, exerted their invisible, irresistible influence. Little men such as the Tribune Dolo were mere counters on a game board, to be moved here and there by the players. What they knew or thought mattered only to the degree that it might determine precisely how they could be used.

Syagrius had a prodigious memory for names and positions, for relationships and personal histories, and so he recalled Dolo's wife too, who had come to get him out of trouble a few months before. Syagrius had not only had him freed, but had skipped him like a stone across a pond, and perhaps the fellow had risen high enough, gone far enough, to be useful before his fall? Perhaps.

Syagrius got up from his chair and slowly paced the room, his hands clasped behind his back. Now and then he stopped at the window and looked out across the city at the roofs of the Imperial Palace in the distance, which seemed to shift in the heat, as though they were part of some distant world not entirely in touch with this one. He asked himself a question: could much the same gambit he had used with Maximus be used with Theodosius and Justina? As for Valentinian, he did not matter; he decided nothing. Syagrius rang a silver bell and told an attendant to summon the Tribune of the Protectors Tribune Gaius Obsequens Dolo, who was, regrettably, being held in jail. He would see him in the mid-afternoon in the private audience chamber at the back of his palace. "Have an order prepared for me to sign in my capacity as Prefect of this city." There would be no trouble.

* * *

Gaius appeared Syagrius's palace right on time. This was no surprise; he was escorted by six of Theodosius's Palatine soldiers, who whisked him across the city, clearing townsfolk out of the way with shouts and truncheons. A servant of Syagrius showed these strangers the way, and behind them trailed the willowy Merobauda, keeping pace with long strides. She had been visiting Gaius at the jail when the soldiers had come and would not be separated from him. Her face showed anxiety, but then gave way to a slight relief as Gaius and his escorts approached Syagrius's palace. Given that destination, it did not seem likely to her that he was headed for trial and execution—at least not on this day. The soldiers tolerated her without comment; she was the wife of a man of high rank who, however great the odds against him, had not yet been judged guilty of anything. The ferment of Imperial politics could produce odd outcomes; it was best to be circumspect.

The accusations of Probus Martialis were just a murderous ploy to recover the position he had lost after the mutiny; that was obvious to her, but the ploy might work. What did he care if Gaius was burned at a stake, so long as he was settled back among the Protectors? And yet Syagrius wanted to see Gaius. Merobauda suspected that he had some need of him, though she could not imagine what it was. But that need might be something that could save him. As she trailed Gaius and his escort, she wondered how to get in to see Syagrius with Gaius, and what to say to him when she did. She feared that without her help Gaius might blunder his way into execution, might unwittingly say something to undermine whatever plan Syagrius had which, as a side effect, might result in Gaius's survival.

Gaius, meanwhile, was tormented by both fear of an unpleasant death and a desire to preen himself for saving his men at the Battle of the Sava. His vanity competed with his fear. Sometimes it was terror, actually, and then it faded into mere fear. And then there was this irritating aspect: Martialis's allegation that Gaius had been part of Maximus's inner circle was not merely false, it drew attention away from his actual moral decision to take his men away from a pointless battle, to spare them needless death and injury. Perhaps that shouldn't matter to him, but if he was going to die, he wanted it known that he had sacrificed himself for his men. He couldn't take a great deal of consolation in dying as a hero, but he could take a little, and that was something. Call it vanity—nobody was perfect. Quite obviously, Merobauda did not share in his righteous indignation. She crossed had her arms tightly in front of her and paced the cell, kicking up clods of moldy straw. She had obviously been trying to come up with some way to save him. He loved her for it, but he wished she'd pay a little more attention to his feelings. And, the next thing he knew, he was traipsing across the city under guard to Syagrius's palace, Merobauda following closely behind, her face a picture of grim determination.

At the palace gate, Theodosius's men surrendered Gaius to Syagrius's private soldiers. Merobauda passed the gate under the claim that she once again had valuable information for Syagrius. *Information* seemed to be a magic word in dealing with Syagrius, a key that would open the door to him. Now, the trick was to keep Gaius in hand.

Syagrius's met them in the same austere room in which he had spoken with Merobauda weeks before. He seemed much the same to Gaius as he had the last time he had seen him: old, but no older. His dress was much the same, sumptuous but quiet, on this occasion of dark blue. Syagrius nodded curtly at his soldiers, they faded from the room and silently closed the doors. Gaius and Merobauda were alone with the Great Man and waited to be addressed. Syagrius signaled them to approach. They stopped at a respectful distance, but he waved them to come closer.

"I'm quite busy, so attend closely to my questions and answer them directly. No wandering off the point." He spoke quietly but clearly, as though he didn't want them to miss anything that he said.

Gaius and Merobauda both nodded.

"I understand that you have been detained…"

"Arrested, actually, Your Excellence," Gaius interrupted. Merobauda stepped smartly on his instep. How could she do this so accurately without looking? She had many talents. Syagrius graciously ignored the interruption.

"You have been arrested on the grounds that you were among the Tyrant Maximus's inner circle and perhaps one of his chief advisors."

Gaius nodded and managed not to say anything. He could sense Merobauda watching him from the corner of her eye.

"Of course, anyone with a grasp of reality can see how absurd the accusation is."

Gaius nodded and again managed to keep his mouth shut. Merobauda bumped him gently with her shoulder, as if by accident, and that helped too. He began to wonder if there was some hope for him. If his great protector understood the ludicrousness of the charge, then a way might be opened for him to slip out of trouble.

"Still, the truth of the accusation hardly comes into play," Syagrius added.

Gaius cocked his head to the side, unable to decide if this was good or bad. But he still kept his mouth shut.

"The accusation may be useful to Their Serenities Theodosius and Valentinian and, if so, they may decide to treat it as true." He leaned back in his chair, his hands on the chair arms, and went on. "In such an unsettled time as we find ourselves, I suspect Their Serenities may choose to avail themselves of the accusation against you because it would encourage others to demonstrate a steadfast loyalty to them. Furthermore, there is no risk to them in prosecuting you, even though you are doubtless innocent. A miscarriage of justice in the case of a man of your station will not hurt them in the least. Your only consolation will be in knowing that your execution has helped, in some small way, to steady a tottering regime." Syagrius was silent a moment to let them take it in. His demeanor was so bland that it was impossible to tell whether he was being sardonic but, sardonic or not, what he said seemed true enough. Merobauda's knees weakened for an instant, but she mastered herself and opened her mouth to speak. Syagrius raised his hand to stop her. "Hush," he said, with a surprisingly avuncular tone. "It may not to come to the worst." He looked at Gaius. "Now tell me, Tribune, carefully and in detail, how you were involved in Maximus's campaign."

Gaius began. "As Your Excellence must know, the charges against me are utterly groundless. There are Protectors, and there are Protectors, by which I mean that, yes, the position may seem exalted. In fact, from the perspective of a border soldier, it is exalted, but only some of the Protectors are close to an Emperor."

Merobauda intervened after giving Gaius a sharp look. "Your Magnificence, my husband was on the fringe of things. He was given the occasional minor administrative task and, apart from that, he was kept busy looking after a troop of cavalry."

"That was an important task, Carissima." Gaius's look was defensive.

"Which he mostly left to an officer named Arverno, who had been his second in command on the Rhine frontier."

"But during this latest campaign?" Syagrius looked at Gaius. "And keep to the point." He had to winkle out any information that might help him stabilize his position at court, and if this fool couldn't give it to him, he needed to move on.

"I commanded some cavalry at the rear of the advancing column."

"Yes, yes." Syagrius began to let his impatience show.

"And we collected supplies, of course," Gaius added, as though it were an afterthought.

"And when all this was done? What about the battle?"

Gaius thought a moment. He thought of his position, standing before one of the Great Men, one who had casually placed him in the army, a man whose relationships with Maximus and Valentinian and Theodosius were ambiguous. What should he say?

"Well..." It wasn't much a beginning.

"Please move on from there. I'm to be received at the Imperial Palace at the ninth hour."

Gaius took the hint and told Syagrius the truth in plain terms—that he had not been part of Maximus's war-council at any time, still less before the Battle of the Sava; that, without warrant, he had assumed the command of a troop of horse; that he had led them off the battlefield on a wild a goose chase. Syagrius listened to him in silence, looking over Gaius's head in a disconcerting way. Gaius wondered, idly, if the old man was really paying attention. But of course he was. He hadn't flourished at the Imperial Court for forty years by doing otherwise.

"And I did this, Your Magnificence, for the men." Gaius took a wide stance and pushed out his chest like a hero in a stage-play. "They had served with me on the Rhine, and I simply was overcome by the desire to do what I could to protect them." He blushed at the grandiosity of his last clause.

Syagrius continued to gaze into middle distance for another moment or two, and then he rose from his chair and began a slow, graceful perambulation about the room, his heavy blue silk robes hissing like a snake as the folds slid together with each stride.

"It looks like it's going to be death for me, Your Magnificence," Gaius said, perspiring now that he made the penalty more immediate, more real, by speaking of it openly. "But one thing bothers me greatly." He looked down and scuffed a shoe on the mosaic floor like a bashful child. "What bothers me..."

Syagrius circled behind them in his pacing and ordered Gaius to be quiet.

"No!" Gaius said, surprising himself. He turned on his heel to face the old man. "I'll tell you what bothers me, and you'll listen." Merobauda gasped, grasped his arm and tugged it like ferry hawser to recall him to good sense, but he shook himself free. Syagrius said nothing, just watched him with raised eyebrows. Gaius straightened his dalmatic (Merobauda had brought him one, bless her heart, to cover his grimy jail clothes.) and tried to resume his earlier dignity. "I can't say that I don't care about dying. Don't believe anyone who tells you that—they're lying. I do care. But I'll accept it better if I'm convicted of what I did and not what I didn't. Call what I did mutiny or desertion or whatever you like, but I want it known that I did it for the men."

Now that he'd said his piece, he felt his confidence ebbing, he felt afraid, almost faint. Merobauda took his arm again, this time to steady him. She rested her head on his shoulder. "I don't know why it should matter to me, Your Magnificence. Perhaps it has something to do with power." He thought a moment and shook his head. "No. That's not it. It's the lack of power. It's powerlessness. I've never had much power, not really. Who does? A few. Men like you—you have power. But men like me? Still, here was something I could do, something I could choose and do, and it was a good thing to do. I took no money; I submitted to no threat; I got no advantage from it—far from it. It was simply a free act and a good one. That's what I want to be convicted for." Gaius felt a measure of peace as long as he talked, but now he was done and he felt once again very small and very afraid.

Syagrius continued to watch him inscrutably. After a moment he spoke completely off the point.

"How many men did you command on the day of the battle?"

Gaius shook his head as though Syagrius had struck him with a plank.

"Come now! How many? And what is the name of the troop?" He walked back to his regal chair and sat down.

"The Second Pannonian Horse. Sixty-eight men."

Syagrius gave himself away to the extent of nodding to himself very slightly. It was too small a gesture for Gaius, who was not particularly observant. Merobauda saw it, though, and narrowed her eyes.

Syagrius thought: *sixty-eight witnesses to Tribune Dolo's slipping away from the battlefield. More than enough—and men who come out of a battle without a scratch appreciate their commander. Better and better.* He knew just how to use what Gaius had told him in order to ensure that his own life remained safe and untroubled—and the Tribune would be saved too by the way, and that was a fine thing; protecting one's clients was a duty and a mark of honor, and this fellow had been quite helpful over the years. Quite helpful.

"Tribune Dolo," Syagrius said, with the merest hint of an encouraging smile. "I don't see any reason why you should die." Gaius and Merobauda glanced at each other and back at him. Syagrius let a moment or two pass for Gaius to take in what he had said. He could tell from Gaius's expression that the chance of escape from execution had won his complete cooperation. Syagrius went on: "You must be prepared to speak to His Serenity Theodosius about your part in the defeat of Maximus. You must be prepared to make clear how instrumental your maneuver was in the tyrant's defeat."

Gaius couldn't help himself; he had to talk. "But the battle was lost on Maximus's left. Our ramble through the woods—call it desertion or whatever you like—couldn't have had any effect on the outcome of the fight."

"Please be quiet, Gaius and let the Prefect save your life," Merobauda said.

Syagrius continued: "I am dealing with a political situation whose details do not concern you. Let me say only that the realities of the battle hardly matter." He looked Gaius meaningfully in the eyes and went on. "Here is what happened, Tribune. You, as my client and agent, were carefully placed as a Tribune of the Protectors at the court of the usurper Magnus Maximus. You were placed at its edge, but still at the court, waiting for opportunities to advance the cause of His Serenity Valentinian and his protector, His Serenity Theodosius, Emperor in the East. In your capacity as my client and agent, you were to carry out any instructions you were given. In the absence of instructions, you used your good sense to determine where Valentinian and Theodosius's interests lay, and then you decided what my instructions might have been and acted accordingly." Gaius frowned. This was putting it on a bit thick. He opened his mouth to speak but then remembered Merobauda's injunction.

Syagrius continued. "At the Battle of the Sava, you daringly took a troop of cavalry that was to be joined to another unit, and you headed off to the flank, thus cunningly disrupting that formation. Once the battle began you led the Second Pannonian Horse—a vital unit, by the way—off the field. They were no longer available to reinforce any places along the line that might fail under the pressure of Theodosius's troops. Your decision was a tactical masterpiece; it caused a small fissure in Maximus's second line. It was small, but it was just enough to cause a breach through which His Serenity's (by which we mean Theodosius's) troops could pour, dividing Maximus's line and rolling it up toward his left flank. All of this culminated in Maximus's flight to Aquileia and his subsequent execution."

"Umm," Gaius said.

"Can you remember all of that?"

"Well, yes." He was rather stunned by the false construction put on the battle, and he felt quite slighted by Syagrius's utter indifference to—and disregard of—his moral courage.

"That's good, because this story will save your life. Now, get yourself cleaned up. I will have clothes sent to you. And be ready to attend me at the ninth hour today. You will stay here and leave as part of my train." He took a delicate silver bell up from the ebony table by his chair. The audience was over. But before he could ring it Merobauda spoke up.

"Just a few moments more, please, Your Magnificence," she said. He set the bell down and looked at her closely. He reckoned he could listen to her for a short while—after all, she had been very helpful during her last visit—but he remained standing to hurry her along.

"It seems that Your Magnificence faces some danger these days. Forgive me my bluntness. I'm a provincial." Merobauda was thinking back to the message she had decoded, to the message Gaius had brought back. In broad outline she had guessed Syagrius's game months ago, though she refrained from making this clear to Syagrius. Vagueness would do. "You mean to save my husband's life, and for that offer we are immensely grateful, Your Magnificence. Not that the Tribune values his life overmuch. He's had a good run, left his mark and is quite willing to end his days in the knowledge that he has sacrificed himself for his men." Gaius goggled at her. She continued imperturbably, "It would be a good death."

Gaius thought furiously to figure out what Merobauda was doing. The receding threat of death came rolling back like a tide. He just wanted to shut her up, but he couldn't think how to do it. He thought of clapping a hand over her mouth, but that would be unseemly.

Syagrius smiled thinly. "Go on. Tell me your point."

"It is apparent, Your Excellence, that this version of the events of the recent battle is as important to you as it is to my husband the Tribune. For reasons that I can only guess—but I am a good guesser (she looked Syagrius in the eye)—those reasons are important and must bear on your exalted position—even, perhaps, on your life. Why else seek out my husband, question him, and rehearse this story?"

She's brilliant, Syagrius thought. *She's wasted on this officer.* He could see instantly that there was no use denying her point, no use in caviling with her—but no use in confirming it either. No. In delicate matters, the important things are better left unsaid, and so he said nothing but only raised his eyebrows, prompting her to continue.

"In view of my husband the Tribune's willingness to submit to trial and execution, perhaps even a desire for it now that he stands, as it were, on the crest of a wave of virtue…" Gaius shuddered at her cold-blooded willingness to discuss in front of him his death with a man whose inaction might secure it. And he flinched at her mixed metaphor.

Syagrius looked narrowly at Merobauda and smiled wryly. "In view of your husband's reluctance to set aside a noble end, perhaps something more might be offered the Tribune than merely his life."

Merobauda face brightened just as though she were surprised by Syagrius's vague offer. Gaius looked at Merobauda out of the corner of his eye. He finally saw where all of Merobauda's talk was leading. Syagrius said, "The Tribune's exoneration would, of course, result in a restoration of his position as Tribune of the Protectors, this time among the Protectors of His Serenity Valentinian. A command of one of the Palatine Legions would seem reasonable in the circumstances. Or perhaps the command of a pair of Palatine Auxilia. The details can be worked out later." He picked up the silver bell. "We must be going soon."

Gaius found his courage again. "No!" he said. He was as surprised as Syagrius, who frowned in irritation for the first time and retorted sharply, "Don't give me any more talk about making a sacrifice of yourself. You may wish to do it now, but when the time comes it will be an entirely different story."

"I'll tell the story to Their Serenities, Your Excellence. Really, I will. But no more military service."

"Ah. You've had enough of that. I don't wonder. But what will you do? What will you live on?" He cradled the bell in his hand to mute it. Gaius took a deep breath and said, "I want an estate."

"An estate," Syagrius repeated. It was little enough to ask, and he had land; he had it everywhere.

"Your Excellence, I ask for an estate on one of the many islands in the Lagoon of the Veneti."

Syagrius looked at him with curiosity. "Why there? It's nowhere."

"Precisely."

"All right." If he didn't already have an estate there, he would get one. He would call in his accountant after the audience with the Emperors.

"And the money to establish it properly." Gaius decided to press his luck.

"Some time ago your wife came to me about some difficulty arising from a large sum money." This was a vague way of introducing the price of Gaius's demand. Men of Syagrius's position didn't lower themselves to name figures.

"We spoke of twelve-hundred and ninety-two solidi," Merobauda said, not trusting Gaius to remember the exact figure.

Syagrius nodded. "You shall have that too." The figure, like the estate, was nothing to him.

Merobauda clasped her hands before her and glanced down at her feet for an instant just like a shy girl. She calculated that the gesture would soften the effect of what came next, and it did. The gesture reminded Syagrius for an instant of when he had first met his wife, dead now so many years. Merobauda said, "That was eight months ago."

"So?"

"As Your Excellence will know, the prices go up every year at about the rate of one twelfth, so a rise of one twelfth per year over eight months (which is three quarters of year) means that the twelve-hundred and ninety-two comes to something more than the original figure."

"Indeed," Syagrius said. He smiled at her boldness. "I will add a hundred solidi to the figure."

Merobauda, who could not help herself, said, "The difference is less, Excellence. It is only eighty and three quarters of one solidus. The total, then, comes to one thousand three hundred and seventy-two and three quarters of a solidus."

Syagrius looked at her, bemused. But, of course, he couldn't be outdone by a mere provincial woman, however remarkable. "We will make it fourteen hundred." He rang the silver bell before there could be any more talking. "Now we prepare to see the emperors. My notary will take your statement and produce a copy for presentation to Their Serenities." He looked to Merobauda. "Make sure the Tribune does not wander from the version of events that I have adduced from him." An attendant entered the hall, and Syagrius gestured them to follow him out.

A while later the two of them sat together in a small room near the entrance of Syagrius's palace, waiting for Gaius to be called to accompany the Great Man at his audience with the Emperor.

"How could you risk my life by haggling with Syagrius?" Gaius asked Merobauda. She smiled at him indulgently. "Don't be a fool. There was no risk. He's too astute not to see that he needs you alive. Surely you saw that." She took his arm and squeezed it. "And you did the same thing to win the estate."

"I did?" He looked at her, startled. "Well, of course. I see that."

"Of course you do," she said with a hint of dubiety. She squeezed his arm again. "Clever you!"

"Yes, it was rather an astute thing to do," he said, wondering how far Merobauda believed him. Well, no matter. They had an estate and money, too. And he was finally through with the army.

* * *

When he was once again alone, Syagrius thought, *This little story will do. It will be taken as evidence of a very deep and subtle game on behalf of the victors. But all of this intrigue—it's tiresome for a man of my age.* He walked to a window and stared west through the sky, imagining his home in Narbonensis hundreds of miles away. His eldest son lived there; he hadn't seen him in years. Really, he must find the time to visit once again. *All of these machinations,* he thought to himself. *I'll probably end up Prefect of Rome once more.*[67]

---

[67] And he did.

XXXXIII

394 AD: THE LAGOON OF THE VENETI

* * *

Merobauda and Gaius stood at a window on the second story of their villa and looked out over its walls, over their estate and over the great lagoon, now flecked with gold in the late summer afternoon. Here and there boats rode the mild evening breeze toward the town on the shore two miles away or went on long tacks to other islands, their sails orange triangles in the setting sun. Gaius rested his hands on the sill and looked out at a quiet world. Down in the courtyard below, the twins sat listening as Una read aloud to them. Gaius and Merobauda's little son stood nearby, scratching designs in the dust with a stick, but listening with half an ear to his sister's voice.

Merobauda asked. "Did your brother and Aeliana get off all right on their journey home?"

"Oh yes. It was rather a long week with them here, don't you think?"

"No," Merobauda said simply. "And was there any news from the town?"

Gaius tilted his head from side to side in a show of indifference. "A little." He was thinking of his day at the little basilica in town where he and Faustinus had argued a pair of small cases. "Things turned out pretty much as Faustinus had guessed they would."

"So, you won onc and you lost one."

Gaius waggled his head equivocally. "Faustinus won one and I lost

376

the other. But I had to take the losing case." Merobauda smiled wryly at the way he put it: that case was the loser, not him. He went on: "I took the case as a favor to Rufinianus." He nodded his head vaguely toward the other end of the island where the other man's estate lay. "I wish he'd defend his own clients." He mused, looking out at the lagoon. "He knew he'd lose, so he asked me do it instead. Still, I suppose he owes me a little something now." Gaius pointed across the water. "That ship out there with the patched sail. She reminds me of the one we took from Marseilles to Genoa years ago, and that makes me think of Mus."

She joined him at the window. "I'm sure he's doing well. He's the sort who knows how to make his way." She glanced at Gaius, who continued to watch the little ship.

"I don't really enjoy arguing cases, you know, Carissima."

"It's good for you to do it. It keeps your mind in trim." She adjusted a comb in her hair in which a few strands of gray were appearing. "And it's charitable. That's important."

"I suppose so." The two were silent a few moments. "It's rather a quiet life out here." He was thinking about his life in Rome years before, the theaters, the bustle in the forums, the chatter in the streets and in the taverns and food shops. He thought back to the crowds jostling each other as people made their way from one neighborhood to another. But then, Merobauda must miss her old home too. There was no going back; the Rhine had been handed over to the Franks.

"What about this new war?"

Gaius thought of it for a moment. In one way, the war had not been so far away, fought just over the Adriatic in Illyricum again. But it might as well have been in Africa for all it affected the provincial nobility settling on the islands hereabouts. Gaius thought back to the day he'd looked out of the warehouse across the lagoon to the islands so far out of reach. And now he lived safely on one of them. Neither the fighting nor the requisitions could touch this small community of islanders. The war had been, as usual, a civil war—Theodosius against another usurper. As usual, peasants had been stripped bare by passing armies and soldiers had died. When the fighting was done, who knew how many units in the western army would be reposted to defend the provinces, how many might simply have dissolved, how many more barbarians would be settled on the provincials and given their land in return for service?

"The word in town is that there was a big battle a few days ago. A ship came in today with the news. They say it lasted for two days but, in the end, Theodosius won."

Merobauda looked over the lagoon. "Well, these things don't concern us anymore. You know, Gaius, this reminds me that you've never told me what it was like when you and Syagrius met the Emperor Theodosius."

Gaius half turned and leaned against the sill. "I can't say that I met him, when you come down to it." He looked at her and smiled. "I saw him. That's about it."

"What was he like?"

Gaius thought back. "He was a little man with intense eyes—I could see them from the back of the hall. And he spoke with a Hispanic burr; I remember that—it reminded me of a tribune I knew years ago by the name of Terentianus."

"And what did you think of Theodosius?" Merobauda called him back.

"He's a remarkably competent soldier, you know. He's won battles all over the place, though he didn't look like a soldier when he was sitting on his throne in the imperial robes. They obscured his personality. I suppose that's what I mean. They're heavy, you know, like purple curtains, and he sat there motionless, all wrapped up in them. He held an orb in one hand and a scepter in the other. The only thing that moved was his head, and even that not much, so he seemed kind of fantastic, really. More like an effigy than a real man. I couldn't see much more than that—I had to kneel at the back with the lesser men, attendants and secretaries and such, and I had to crane my neck to see even as much as I did, but maybe there wasn't that much to see, really. Theodosius seemed more like a symbol than a man, as though the office of Emperor had transmuted him into something distant and uncanny."

"Something abstracted, removed from the world-as-it-is," Faustinus said, entering the room. Gaius and Merobauda turned to him.

"That's well put, Faustinus." Gaius thought a moment and then looked back over the lagoon. "A symbol, yes. A representative of something—the Empire, I suppose—as though he weren't entirely real. But then, what is this creaky old Empire?" He frowned, unable to join the ideas. He shrugged and went on: "Theodosius's guard stood just behind us in a half-circle and kept their eyes on us. They looked very fine in their white tunics and trousers. They wore gold torcs around their necks and shaggy hair like barbarians. The young Valentinian—he was still alive then—sat on a throne to Theodosius's left with his mother Justina. A handful of senators were allowed to actually stand in front of the Imperial family—quite an honor, I suppose. Of course, Syagrius was among them, and he spoke to the Emperor for a while, but they talked so quietly that I couldn't make out anything they said. It's funny, now I look back; their voices seemed faint, like the sound of those little waves that lap at the edge of the shingle when the wind blows."

"Evocative and vague," Faustinus said.

Gaius nodded. "Yes, like that."

"And what happened?" Merobauda asked.

"Something happened. Precisely what, I don't know. Syagrius must have told his tale, and the Emperor must have accepted it. I think each one was gulling the other: Syagrius misrepresenting the battle and Theodosius pretending to accept the misrepresentation. That must have been what was needed right then after the war."

"Not a misrepresentation. A fabrication." Years before, Merobauda would have said something more, something sharper, but she was less severe these days.

"Oh, Carissima, think about Theodosius's situation. He was a stranger in Milan. A strong man, certainly, but he needed to set things in order, and how could he do it without the Great Men? Only they have the experience, the knowledge, the money, the clients to keep order in the provinces. It would have been dangerous to reject Syagrius's account of the battle. There were other important men there, as well—two of the Petronii, one of the Symmachi, one of the Aureliani. You understand. If Syagrius were struck from his pedestal, well, the other Great Men might withhold their cooperation here and there. And these days, that might be enough to topple even an emperor.

"So you weren't even called on to corroborate Syagrius's version of events?"

Gaius shook his head. "It was only theater, and His Serenity decided to forego the second act."

Faustinus said, "Doubtless your mere presence served as sufficient corroboration." Gaius just smiled. The time had long since come for him to take Faustinus's sardonic comments in stride.

"Even though Syagrius had cooperated with both sides, he came out unscathed," Merobauda mused.

"I think he believed he had no choice." Gaius finished the story: "A month later we found ourselves here, the whole household, with a deed for the estate and a chest of money. When was that? Six years ago? We can turn our backs on emperors now."

Merobauda turned to Faustinus. "Have the boat ready tomorrow morning, the big one. Gaius and I are going to town to attend the installation of the new bishop." Faustinus nodded. Gaius turned to her as though about to protest, but she spoke before he could. "No shirking. You're a big fish in this pond, you know."

"It should be enough that you talked me into becoming a Christian. Not that I mind that."

"We can—we will—sit out their stupid wars and their thrashing around as things come apart. This is the start of a new..." She hesitated. "A new country, a different country, or era or something. A better one—it's obvious. And you're part of it. All the important men from around here will be there. You're one of them. Maybe they don't know it, but they're building a new, a new..." Merobauda searched for a word.

"A new *res publica*," Faustinus suggested. "A new republic."

"Well, well, Carissima," Gaius said, putting his arm around her shoulders, "I do believe

you're right." The three of them stood framed in the window and gazed at the lagoon, the sun's gold light shattered into a million flashes on the facets of the gentle waves, as the September evening darkened into a violet star-strewn sky.

—The End —

AFTERWORD ABOUT THE LATE ROMAN ARMY

* * *

By the middle of the fourth century, the Roman army had changed. Many new units, both of cavalry and infantry, were raised and called by different names: ***cuneus, vexillatio, numerus, milites,*** and so on. The officers of these units went by titles unheard of in earlier days. Meanwhile, the officers of the older units such as legions and cohorts retained their old ranks. The result is a confusing welter of different terms for infantry and cavalry units (and the titles of their commanders) that conceals many rough equivalents. It may help to know that the Late Roman Empire had professional generals, the highest of which was called the Master of the Infantry. Subordinate generals were called Masters of the Cavalry. Despite their names, both Masters both had command of infantry and cavalry.

The army was now broadly divided in three. The Border Army guarded the frontier, the Field Army was stationed in cities in the interior of provinces and called out for large campaigns, and the troops at the personal command of the Emperors (Palatine Legions and Palatine Auxilia) were stationed near the capitals and followed the Emperors on campaign. The status of a unit depended on whether it was part of the Palatine forces (the highest), the Field Army, or the Border Army (the lowest). Commanders of field troops held the office of Count (***comes***), those of border troops Duke (***dux***).

Over the centuries, legions had been divided into smaller units and posted where needed, often at great distances from each other. New legions were raised but probably numbered only about a thousand men and, in practice, probably even fewer. Other units, such as auxilia, cohortes, milites, numeri, vexillationes, equites, and cunei (these last three cavalry), seem to have numbered about five hundred men, though they were probably often smaller. In many cases units were divided up into even smaller troops.

Readers deeply interested in this topic should look at Volume II of A. H. M. Jones's *History of the Later Roman Empire*. To understand Gaius's story, the reader can do with much less detail.